EARTHMAN JACK

VS.

THE INTERGALACTIC MANHUNT

✦ BOOK 3 OF THE EARTHMAN JACK SPACE SAGA ✦

EPISODE 1 OF THE CONCLAVE TRILOGY

BY
MATTHEW KADISH

OTHER BOOKS IN THE EARTHMAN JACK SERIES

Book 1: Earthman Jack vs. The Ghost Planet
Book 2: Earthman Jack vs. The Secret Army

If you would like to receive updates on the Earthman Jack Space Saga and information on upcoming books in the series, along with special offers and exclusive goodies, please join the official Earthman Jack mailing list. By doing so, you not only get cool stuff, but also help support the series and the author. You can sign up at:

www.EarthmanJack.com
and
www.MatthewKadish.com

To Susannah "Zuzu" Kadish
The Cutest Little Peanut In The Galaxy
May Your Life Be Filled With
Magic And Wonder

To Amy,
So glad we were on TV
together!

Matthew Kadish

AUTHOR'S NOTE

Greetings readers!

By now you know that Earthman Jack's adventures are part of an epic saga spanning many planets, dimensions, and one-liners. This "epicness" is also reflected in the page count, as these books tend to be very long. Well, the third installment in the series ended up being *too* long! My final draft of the story was so large, that it was impossible to publish it in one book.

For this reason, the third installment has been broken up into 3 separate books, which I've dubbed "The Conclave Trilogy." Though the books are physically separate from one another, all three are meant to be read together to get the entire adventure of *The Conclave of Corruption*. The book you are currently reading is the first part of this story, and I would encourage you to read all three books together to get the full experience, as the tale was meant to be read.

The Conclave Trilogy should be read in this order:

- Earthman Jack vs. The Intergalactic Manhunt
- Earthman Jack vs. The Ring of Fire
- Earthman Jack vs. The Conclave of Corruption

My apologies for any confusion regarding this matter. Please remember that these three books make up one installment of the story and all were originally meant to be one book. If there are parts of the book that don't stand on their own or conflicts that seem unresolved by the end of a book, it is because some story threads develop and resolve themselves down the road in other books of the trilogy.

For the best reading experience possible, I'd recommend reading *Earthman Jack vs. The Ghost Planet*, *Earthman Jack vs. The Secret Army*, and then all three books of *The Conclave Trilogy* back-to-back if you can, as the action, tension, and plot twists get more and more exciting as the story goes along.

Thank you for understanding, and enjoy *Earthman Jack vs. The Intergalactic Manhunt*!

All the best,

Matthew Kadish
Author, *The Earthman Jack Space Saga*

PREViOUSLY, ON EARTHMAN JACK···

s evidenced by the box office receipts from the latest holo-cinema adaptation of the adventures of Earthman Jack Finnegan, interest in the tale of the universe's last Earthman is still going strong, even long after the events of his incredible adventures actually took place.

Indeed, the blockbuster first installment's sequel, entitled *Earthman Jack vs. The Secret Army*, has broken records as throngs of fans across the galaxy turned out once again to revel in the adventure and excitement of one of history's greatest true stories. Though there has been the usual "the sequel wasn't as good as the original" complaints from the critics, the response has been so phenomenal that Diznessey Studios has officially announced it will be going forward with its plans to produce five more holo-films in the series.

At a recent panel at the Corrino sector's Convention for Leisure & Anti-Social Male Escapism (a.k.a., LAME Con), the galaxy's biggest celebration of all things entertainment and pop-culture related, Director J.J. Azimoff – who has taken over directing duties from Sodhurg Silverhill – had exciting things to say about the adventure to come:

"Obviously, *The Secret Army* was a real game changer for our hero," J.J. told the packed convention hall. "Here he was, expecting to have the support of an entire galactic empire behind him in his quest to save his planet, and all of a sudden, he's back on his own, and not only are the Deathlords gunning for him but now the good guys are, too. And though we all know what happens after the events of *The Secret Army*, how we're choosing to interpret those events is going to surprise some people."

Already, the ultraweb is abuzz over J.J.'s comments as Earthmaniacs from all twelve sectors of space speculate over how the director has chosen to interpret Jack's third adventure. Purists are already in a tizzy about how such an amazing tale does not need to be "reinterpreted," while others are excited to see what could be a fresh take on such a familiar story.

As always, if one were so inclined to find out what really happened with Jack and his companions, one need look no further than the extensive historical recordings housed in the grand repository of the Hive Mind of Valghana VII, where the Central Galactic University houses an exhaustive database on all things Earthman related. And if one were to go there to review these recordings, one would find that after defeating the Deathlords at the Ghost Planet, Jack and his friends were off to the heart of the Galactic Regalus Empire, based at that time on the planet of Omnicron Prime.

Upon arriving at Omnicron, Jack's illusions of what he'd hoped his new life would be like were soon shattered. The fame that accompanied his heroics soon became stifling. His companions quickly abandoned him to pursue their own interests. But most difficult of all, the girl of Jack's dreams, Princess Glorianna, was now no longer the simple "girl next door" with whom Jack had fallen in love. Back on her home planet, Anna had to reassume the role of being the Empire's figurehead, which forced her to act cold and distant.

Aided by a new robotic companion named Dan, Jack received a crash course on life inside the Regalus Empire. He discovered that the vast swaths of galactic territory were governed by powerful families known as Legacies, the two biggest of which were at each other's throats. The Skyborns controlled numerous planets, colonies, and outposts in the remote area known as The Rim, and the Evenstars controlled lucrative hyperspace trade lanes in the centrally located Redwater system. Jack quickly befriended Amadeus Evenstar along with his seductive sister Kimlee, whose flirtations made Jack question his devotion to Anna.

Jack's conflicted feelings toward Anna weren't helped by his learning about her impending arranged marriage to the heir of the Skyborn Legacy, the famous warrior Paragon, Mourdock Skyborn. Though Jack resolved to try to steal Anna away from the dashing Mourdock, his task was complicated as a friendship developed between the two young men, along with Mourdock's trusted companions Wilvelm Blackfyre and Fredreek Goldstone, causing Jack to feel guilty about his intentions toward the Princess.

Jack's close involvement with both the Evenstars and the Skyborns prompted the head of Imperial Intelligence, the crafty Phineas Alabaster, to recruit Jack to help determine which Legacy might be planning to do harm to Anna. As Jack delved deeper into the lives of the Evenstars and Skyborns, he found that Alabaster's fears might not be unfounded, as strange and dangerous events began occurring.

First, an assassination attempt was made on Mourdock's life, followed by the successful assassination of Eudox Evenstar and his wife, the heads of the Evenstar Legacy. However, in each instance, Jack was able to see that the culprits were being controlled by strange worm-like creatures that stuck out from the backs of the perpetrators' necks.

Much to Jack's surprise, it appeared he was the only one able to see these creatures, which were invisible to everyone else. This made convincing others of their existence quite difficult. It also didn't help that two of the most powerful men in the Empire – Director Uleeg Casgor and CEO of the Maguffyn Corporation Armonto Virtuoso – were working behind the scenes with a mysterious figure who seemed able to control the worms in order not only to commit these atrocities, but to spread the infection of these creatures known as "slythrus" to grow his secret army of mind-controlled minions.

Casgor and Virtuoso also took advantage of the fact that the evil Deathlord Supreme Zarrod, while on the Ghost Planet, was able to infect Princess Anna with one of these slythrus, which slowly took control of her. They used the mysterious figure's influence over the Princess to approve a risky proposal to destroy the Great Seal of the Portgate Network – the intergalactic transportation system which tied together the core worlds of the Regalus Empire. Not only that, but they also exerted their power over Anna to suspend the other members of the Directory, granting full control of the Empire to Uleeg Casgor.

With the bad guys consolidating their power and growing their secret army, Jack and his companions soon found danger at every turn. The Empire was suddenly not safe for any of them as they were arrested one by one, and the Maguffyn Corporation seized control of Jack's spaceship.

Now that the secret army had infiltrated the highest levels of government, Jack had no one left to turn to for help. Mourdock had been swayed by the corrupted Anna to turn a blind eye to troubling events. Kimlee and Amadeus Evenstar had fled for the safety of their homeworld after Anna revoked their Legacy status. Even Phineas Alabaster was powerless to act, for fear he would be arrested before he could do any good.

With the help of Heckubus, Scallywag, and a new ally, Anna's tutor, the Luminadric Monk known as Shanks, Jack staged a prison break to rescue both Grohm and Professor Green. However, the group was too late to stop Anna and Armonto Virtuoso from portgating to the secret location of the Great Seal, where they planned to deliver a crippling blow to the Empire.

In a desperate attempt to stop Anna before the mysterious figure controlling her could enact his plan, Jack and his allies rescued the Earthship and made a harrowing escape from Imperial Space. Arriving at a massive structure encircling a star, known as a "Sunshell," the group was confronted by Anna's protectors – the fearsome Paragon warriors known as the Royal Vanguard. In the tense battle that ensued, Jack and his companions were all disabled, giving the possessed Anna the opportunity she needed to break the Great Seal and to make the entire Empire vulnerable to attack by the Deathlords.

In a moment of clarity, Jack was able to refocus his spiritual energy to achieve what is known as "Equilibrium," a state in which one's mind, body, and spirit all work in perfect harmony. Jack discovered his exposure to the broken seal of the Ghost Planet had given him the ability to achieve this state. It was also this ability which allowed him to see the hidden slythrus that were controlling people.

Using the enhanced skills granted to him by Equilibrium, Jack grabbed onto the slythru controlling the Princess. Doing so allowed him to enter into a mental construct in Anna's mind where he saw the slythru in the form of a Deathlord controlling Anna. Before he was able to free the Princess, a shadowy figure attacked him, preventing him from saving the girl he loves and forcing Jack to escape by teleporting Anna and his friends back to his ship.

The mysterious figure controlling Anna then revealed itself to be a Deathlord Supreme named Verrutus. Verrutus was far more dangerous than Zarrod since he could exert his control over every slythru-infected being in the universe and could process everything those enslaved by the creatures saw, heard, and experienced, making him almost omniscient.

Though Jack and his friends finally knew the truth about the Deathlords' secret army and the danger it presented, the rest of the universe did not. Verrutus threatened to solidify his control over Anna while at the same time using his command of the slythru-infected to hunt Jack and his companions down. It was now a race against the clock for Jack to save the girl he loves before she was completely consumed by the Deathlord Supreme, all while being pursued throughout the galaxy by the Imperial military, ruthless bounty hunters, and members of Verrutus's secret army.

Earthman Jack was the most wanted man in the universe. With no allies or places left to hide, he found that he was, once again, the universe's only hope to stop the growing threat the Deathlords presented.

The odds were, once again, not in Jack's favor. And though things looked bad for our hero at that time, they were about to get much, much worse. The events that took place with the secret army did indeed test the limits of Jack and his companions, but everyone knows that what happened next was an even greater trial for this unlikely band of protagonists.

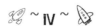

While they were being hunted down, dark forces were at work to enact a plan of far-reaching death and destruction, one too far advanced for our heroes to stop. The evil Verrutus continued to sow discord across the galaxy and to weaken the Empire from within. The Deathlord fleet attacked the borders of Imperial space, spreading fear and carnage while distracting the Empire from the greater threat. And worst of all, the cunning Deathlord Zarrod, disguised as Mourdock's mentor Paragon Hasatan, maneuvered to enact his own plan of vengeance in secret – not just against Jack, but against his own masters, the Lords of the Void.

However, among these dastardly machinations, a new threat loomed – one which dwarfed all others in its level of animosity. It was a threat so far-reaching that no planet in the galaxy was safe from it. A threat that no one was aware of until it was almost too late. And when the threat did indeed reveal itself, it was too powerful for anyone to stop – even Jack.

Our story continues on the Earthship as it is hounded by an Imperial search fleet, just two weeks after the events of *The Secret Army*. Jack and his friends are never safe for long. No location to which they teleport offers much respite from being relentlessly hunted. The group's only hope is to find a sanctuary where they can get the help they need to free Princess Glorianna from the grip of Verrutus.

That sanctuary exists in the form of the Conclave, a sacred temple where all Paragons train to free their minds. However, what Jack and his companions are unaware of is that the Conclave is a far more dangerous place than any other in which they could hide. For in the Conclave, a corruption was spreading and infecting all those who were meant to represent the best the universe had to offer. A corruption that consumed all who were exposed to it and set even the most virtuous Paragons on a path to use their incredible powers for evil.

This is the story of how Jack discovers the power that will shape him into the hero he is destined to be. This is the story of the shocking betrayal which cripples an Empire. This is the story of the events which start the universe down a path toward ultimate destruction.

This is the story of the Conclave of Corruption.

~ v ~

EPISODE I:

EARTHMAN JACK

VS.

THE INTERGALACTIC MANHUNT

CHAPTER 1

n alarm blared on the bridge of the Earthship as it was rocked by another direct hit.

"Oh dear, oh dear, oh dear…" muttered Green as he frantically typed away at the console of the Earthship's engineering station. "They are trying to take out our engines, I'm afraid."

"What else is new?" grumbled Scallywag as he continued to target the Imperial fightercraft that were moving to intercept them. "At least with Her Highness on board, they ain't tryin' ta blow us ta bits."

"Everybody be cool," Jack said as he maneuvered the Earthship away from the incoming attackers. "We got this. Professor, just redirect some energy to the shields around the thrusters to give us some protection. Scally, light them up as soon as they get within range. Heckubus, have we found a place to jump to yet?"

Heckubus peered over the console at the Earthship's navigational station. "Have you any idea how many coordinates are in this bloated mainframe of yours?" the robot complained. "Even a brain as big as mine cannot compute all the variations, considering how outdated this blasted ship's star charts are!"

"With so many options, you'd think ya wouldn't jump us right inta the middle of a blasted search fleet!" Scallywag complained.

"Even a genius such as I cannot account for bad luck!" snapped Heckubus in response. "By all accounts these coordinates were supposed to be empty space!"

"Aye," grumbled Scallywag. "And we've just spent the better part o' an hour dogfightin' until tha blasted Entanglement Engine recharges and we can get tha squick out o' here! Maybe we should let the other rust-bucket give it a go. Might actually jump someplace safe fer once."

Dan, who was quietly sitting off to the side next to Grohm, suddenly perked up. "Oh!" the robot exclaimed. "Why, I would be delighted to finally contribute to our current predicament—"

"Silence, Henchman!" ordered Heckubus, shaking his fist ruefully at Dan. "Just because you are self-aware does not mean you have the computing power to extrapolate the data necessary to create stellar cartography models that won't land us in the middle of a star, a black hole, or any number of hazards that would kill us all instantly!"

"But, Master Heckubus, you are usually so fond of instantaneous death…"

"Not when it involves me, you twit!" Heckubus snapped. "Now go back to doing something useful, like shutting up!"

Dan hung his boxy robotic head in disappointment. He turned to Grohm, the large Rognok passively watching the proceedings of the bridge. "I say. They are always so testy when people are attacking us, are they not?" commented Dan.

Grohm grunted.

"Surely, there must be something you and I could contribute in situations such as this. I feel so useless simply sitting here quietly. Don't you?"

Grohm growled at the robot.

"I did not mean to imply you are useless, Master Grohm. Simply that you must *feel* useless, just as I--"

Grohm growled louder.

"Right," replied Dan, in exasperation. "I shall stop talking now."

"Hang on tight, people," Jack announced. "Here they come. Prepare to engage!"

Indeed, right at that very moment, another six-ship squad of Imperial fightercraft, which had been dispatched from the large Imperial Cruiser that had happened upon Jack and his friends while patrolling, came rushing toward the Earthship with their plasma cannons blazing.

Though the bad news was that the Earthship had been engaged in dogfights with wave after wave of highly advanced fightercraft for the past forty minutes, the good news was that Jack and his companions had gotten quite skilled at fighting them after weeks of being relentlessly hunted across the known universe.

If one were to recall Jack's previous adventure, the Deathlord Supreme Verrutus had threatened to use all his power and influence to hunt down and destroy Jack and his crew. Though the Deathlord Supreme's threat was meant to intimidate Jack, he hadn't been too worried at first. After all, the universe is such a large place! Surely it would be easy to hide from anyone attempting to hunt them down.

However, what Jack hadn't anticipated was that in a universe so large, there were quite a bit of unexpected dangers to stumble upon, especially when one's ship had star charts that were still about 50,000 years out of date.

Such as the time they had teleported to the edge of a star system in a far, out-of-the-way part of the galaxy, only to discover that the closest star there had just gone supernova, sending a shockwave of stellar material hurtling toward the Earthship at velocities up to 30,000 kilometers per second (or ten percent of the speed of light). This unforeseen catastrophe had forced the crew to outrun the cataclysmic onslaught until such time that the Entanglement Engine had recharged, allowing them to jump away right before the devastating shockwave caught up with them.

Or the time they had teleported into an uncharted asteroid field, hoping to hide the Earthship among the many large rocks that existed there, only to discover that in the caverns of the various asteroids lived a peculiar and previously unknown race of large vampiric space bats who became intent on devouring the Earthship and all those inside of it.

Indeed, the strange phenomena of unexplored space always containing some type of new threat Jack and the others had to use their smarts and resourcefulness to deal with, began to wear on the group. After jumping to coordinates that contained a massive floating alien head that mistook the Earthship for an edible delicacy and chased it around for a full hour with its gigantic mandible chomping all the while, the crew decided it would be far safer to stick to known regions of Imperial space, despite the fact that they were being relentlessly hunted there.

Though this strategy meant the group would no longer experience any surprises outside their current comfort zone, it did come with its own set of problems – not the least of which being that Verrutus's threat seemed to be quite a salient one. No matter where the Earthship teleported within Imperial space, Jack and the others were never safe for more than a few hours before ships arrived with the intent of disabling and capturing them, putting our intrepid crew in dire straits before they were required to jump away.

Sometimes they stumbled into Imperial patrols. Other times, they happened upon militia forces from nearby planets, settlements, and space stations. Still other times they encountered bounty hunters who were scouring the different sectors of space, looking for the biggest bounty ever levied in the history of the Empire. By far, the bounty hunters were the worst threat. While the Imperial forces seemed at least somewhat intent on capturing the Earthship in one piece, the bounty hunters were not quite as disciplined and more than a little bloodthirsty in their pursuit.

One bounty hunter, in particular, was a constant menace. So much so, that Jack had taken to nicknaming the starship he flew *The Phantom Menace*. When questioned as to why Jack would name the ship such a curious thing, Jack simply shrugged and replied: "Because it sucks." When he offered no further explanation, Jack's companions simply accepted the rather odd name and began to refer to the ship by this, as well.

The Phantom Menace was unlike most of the other bounty hunter vessels Jack and his companions had encountered. It had a unique design, which made it hard for either Scallywag or Heckubus to place its origins. It was fast and maneuverable, with shields stronger than even the Imperial military vessels. And to make matters worse, it seemed to be able to track the Earthship more effectively than anyone else had, showing up multiple times no matter where Jack and his friends teleported. Though they'd been able to fend off this bounty hunter vessel each time they encountered it, it was always just by the skin of their proverbial teeth. Whoever was flying that ship was an incredibly skilled pilot, and even worse than that, he seemed to be picking up on all of Jack's tricks.

Because of this, Jack determined they'd need to come up with a way to properly defend themselves when attacked, prompting Professor Green to backward-engineer the stun weapon Scallywag had taken from Armonto Virtuoso prompting the Earthship to manifest blaster cannons that would emit the non-deadly rays to disable their assailants. Despite Scallywag's cavalier attitude toward blasting attackers to pieces, Jack was still intent on not killing anyone who could be considered a "good guy" while this whole inconvenient "Princess Anna is possessed by a Deathlord" debacle continued to play out.

When a group of Imperial scouts had arrived at their previous location, Jack and his friends jumped away to coordinates they had thought marked nothing but empty space, right on the edge of an Imperial mining operation in the quadrant of the Empire known as the Frontier. However, an Imperial cruiser just happened to be patrolling the area a mere ten thousand miles away. Before they knew it, a squadron of fightercraft were dispatched, and the cruiser seeded defense matrix platforms into hyperspace to ensure the Earthship wouldn't be able to make a quick getaway.

Jack was used to flying against multiple ships by this point. The Earthship's shields were stronger than the average spacecraft, and the new stun cannons disabled the Imperial vessels quickly, giving the Earthship some much needed breathing room as more and more fighters launched from the cruiser.

The latest wave of Imperial fightercraft entered into firing range, letting loose a barrage of plasma fire that peppered the black backdrop of space with bright red streaks, as they headed right toward the Earthship. Jack immediately spiraled away, corkscrewing back toward the formation of fightercraft to give Scallywag the opportunity to fire back.

Purple streaks of stun lasers shot from the Earthship, hitting two of the attacking vessels as their formation broke and the fighters scrambled. The ships that were hit were racked by electric overload as the purple-colored energy snaked its way through the ship's systems, effectively shutting the vessels down and causing them to float harmlessly through space.

"Nice shooting, Scally!" cheered Jack as he brought the Earthship around onto the tail of the nearest fightercraft. "Two down, four to go!"

"Oy, I enjoy shootin' things as much as the next fella," Scallywag said, "but how much longer are we gonna have ta be exchangin' blaster bolts?"

"Entanglement Engine will be fully recharged in approximately fourteen minutes," Green announced.

"See?" said Jack. "Only fourteen more minutes. We totally got this."

"Don't get cocky, lad," grumbled Scallywag. "Assuming we make it out o' this, we're only well off if'n we don't jump someplace worse."

"I believe I may have found a far less-worse location!" Heckubus proclaimed. "If my calculations are correct, I have located a giant molecular cloud we can hide in. I can guarantee there will be no Imperial ships there."

"A molecular cloud?" asked Jack as he banked the ship away from an incoming attack.

"A giant molecular cloud of gas and dust called Bacardi 8, to be exact," Heckubus said. "It's one of the largest molecular clouds in the vicinity of the galaxy's core, spanning a region of about 150 lightyears. The cloud is composed of complex molecules that will help mask our energy signature and interfere with any scans of the area."

"Sounds good, if'n we can survive long enough ta make it there," said Scallywag as he fired at a passing ship, disabling it.

"Making sure we survive is *your* job," Heckubus replied. "Finding a safe place to teleport to is mine, and I believe I have just fulfilled that responsibility."

"No sweat, everyone," Jack said as yet another Imperial fighter succumbed to a well-placed shot from Scallywag. "Once we take care of these remaining fighters, I'll blast our engines and keep some distance between us and the next wave long enough to teleport as soon as the Entanglement Engine is ready to go. Survival is all but ensured."

Jack found he was almost enjoying himself as he maneuvered the Earthship through space, engaging in dogfights with the remaining fightercraft. Though he and his companions were, indeed, in real danger, Jack still felt as though he were just playing the best video game ever invented – flying around the most advanced spacecraft in the galaxy while shooting opponents out of the sky. In fact, it wasn't much different from the video game *Nova Commander IV*, which he had played all the time back on Earth… except for when the enemy fighters landed a lucky shot and the entire Earthship shook from the impact.

But Jack had become so accustomed to space combat, it didn't even faze him any longer. He'd proven he could go toe-to-toe with trained pilots and come out on top numerous times. And the fact that he now could disable their ships without killing anyone meant he didn't have to hold back and could fire on his attackers without worry. All this contributed to his somewhat overconfident attitude. But that attitude was not entirely undeserved, especially as he and his crewmates disabled the remaining fighters who had been hounding them.

"All right!" said Jack, cheerily, as the last Imperial fighter crackled with purple electricity and drifted away. "Time to wait out the clock. How much longer do we have, Professor?"

"Eight minutes and some change," Professor Green replied.

"Yeah, no way that next wave of fighters is going to reach us in eight minutes," Jack said as he angled the Earthship away from the new array of encroaching spacecraft. "I'll just redirect some energy to our engines and give us a nice boost of speed to stay ahead of them until it's time to jump."

No sooner had Jack begun his maneuver than two loud rumblings shook the Earthship, causing alarms to blare. A high-pitched *screeching* noise[1] reverberated through the bridge as a familiar looking spacecraft zoomed by them from out of nowhere.

---

[1] In the Jackverse, those within a pressurized starship can experience sounds from outside the ship as the particles that are ejected from engines or explosions carry with them soundwaves that reverberate against a ship's hull. (Just go with it.)

"What tha kitten[2]?!" exclaimed Scallywag as the bridge stabilized.

"I recognize that engine sound," decried Heckubus. "It would seem our bounty hunting friend has found us once more."

"Crap," muttered Jack as he immediately began evasive maneuvers. "Where'd he come from?"

"More importantly, how does he keep findin' us?" grumbled Scallywag.

Another blast rocked the Earthship as Jack gritted his teeth and banked sharply. *The Phantom Menace* corkscrewed away as it buzzed by yet again, effectively avoiding all the purple streaks Scallywag was firing at it.

"Bloody squick!" cursed Scallywag. "I really hate this guy!"

"Oh dear!" bemoaned Green. "His last blast damaged our starboard thruster. It's now operating at about 20% efficiency."

Jack scowled. He could feel the decline in maneuverability as he tried to put some distance between the Earthship and its attacker. *The Phantom Menace* had struck just as Jack had redirected energy from the shields to the engines, allowing *The Phantom Menace's* plasma blasts to break through and damage them. Though the Earthship had the ability to regenerate damaged sections of itself, that type of repair took time. If they kept getting hammered by their assailant, they ran the risk of being disabled before they had the chance to jump away.

"Professor, do what you can to get the engines working again," Jack said. "I'll try and outmaneuver him until we can jump out of here."

"I believe there's a glaring flaw in that strategy of yours, Earthman," Heckubus said. "And that is, the longer that bounty hunter keeps us occupied, the closer those Imperial fighters get. If they should disable us before we can engage the Entanglement Engine—"

"I know, I know, alright!" snapped Jack. "Just leave the flying to me! I'll handle this!"

Jack banked the ship and increased its thrust, pulling away from *The Phantom Menace* and the encroaching Imperial fighters. However, *The Phantom Menace* seemed to have anticipated that move and banked, as well, keeping pace with Jack's maneuver.

"Blast it, *Phantom Menace*, why do you have to suck so much!?" muttered Jack under his breath as he adjusted course.

---

[2] The term "kitten" is a well-known curse word in the Regalus Empire.

It appeared that no matter what Jack did, the bounty hunter vessel kept pace with him, staying on the Earthship's tail and peppering it with plasma fire. The fancier Jack got with his maneuvers, the more damage *The Phantom Menace* seemed able to inflict as the two ships danced together while the Imperial fighters came ever closer.

"Four more minutes!" announced Green.

"Oy! Lad!" cried out Scallywag. "Those fighters are gonna be in blaster range any second!"

The Earthship shook once more as a well-placed blast from *The Phantom Menace* hit its mark. Jack gritted his teeth as he glanced at all the holo-readings his ship was providing him. The fightercraft were indeed baring down on them, and the bounty hunter was not going to let up enough to allow Jack to make a getaway. Then another alarm sounded, alerting Jack that *The Phantom Menace* was targeting the Earthship with a weapon other than a plasma cannon.

Jack glanced at the image on the holoscreen to his left as a robotic arm, with a large bulbous disk on the end, extended out from the bounty hunter's vessel.

"What the heck is that thing?" Jack asked, right as it fired.

Before Jack knew it, the disk had latched onto the Earthship's hull. A long cable that ran from the Earthship back to the bounty hunter's vessel flapped around as Jack tried to pull away.

"Great Scott!" cried Green. "Something has latched onto us! It seems like some type of grappling mechanism…"

"It's a bloody snare-winch!" exclaimed Scallywag. "He means ta reel us in and use a thermal blasting dock ta blow a hole in our hull! The bloody browner is tryin' ta board us!"

"If his ship is attached to ours when we engage the Entanglement Engine, there's a very real possibility we'll take him with us when we jump," informed Heckubus.

"Aye, not ta mention the damage he could cause if he's actually on board tha Earthship!" said Scallywag. "We gotta detach that snare-winch on tha double!"

Jack grimaced. One look at his readouts let him know that *The Phantom Menace* had already started reeling the Earthship in toward it. If what Scallywag said was true, they were indeed in a bad position. The minute the bounty hunter's ship docked with theirs, the incoming Imperial fighters could easily disable their engines.

"Scally, I'm enabling the Earthship's main plasma cannons," Jack said, giving the mental command to the Earthship to do so. "Be prepared to fire everything we have in all directions on my mark."

Scallywag raised a curious eyebrow. "All directions?" the pirate asked.

"Yes," replied Jack. "Hopefully this'll buy us some time to get *The Phantom Menace* off our back. Just get ready to go."

With that, Jack closed his eyes. He quickly focused in on his Source, the area in his chest where his spiritual energy resided, and made connection with it. He directed the flow of energy from his Source up to his brain. As soon as he did that, time seemed to slow as he entered into a state of Equilibrium.

Jack opened his eyes as soon as he felt his reality shift. Under the tutelage of Shanks, Jack had gotten fairly proficient at entering into Equilibrium. Jack found that when he was in this state, he was able to accomplish amazing feats that he normally would be unable to achieve. Ever since rescuing Anna from the Sunshell of the Ancients, Jack had made it a point to practice going in and out of Equilibrium just in case he ever needed it.

And in Jack's opinion, this was one of those times he definitely needed it.

The moment he looked at his holo-monitors, Jack could see with absolute clarity how *The Phantom Menace* was positioned and how it was angled. It was as though he instantly knew what the ship was going to be doing. He saw the maneuver his adversary was about to carry out before he even began to do it. And with this knowledge, Jack reversed his thrusters and began to roll the Earthship counterclockwise, wrapping the snare-winch cable around it and reeling *The Phantom Menace* in.

"Now," Jack ordered.

Scallywag let loose a barrage of projectiles from every weapon the Earthship had. Red and purple streaks raced in every direction. The sudden onslaught caused the incoming Imperial ships to break formation and scramble, throwing off their approach. The reeling in of *The Phantom Menace* destroyed its ability to maneuver and it immediately received many direct hits from the various blasts the Earthship was peppering out around it.

A small explosion erupted from *The Phantom Menace's* portside engine, and the pilot disengaged the snare-winch. The momentum of the Earthship reeling it in sent the vessel flying away like a rock from a slingshot. *The Phantom Menace* rotated around chaotically as it tried to stabilize from Jack's surprise maneuver, but it was hit by a stun bolt before it could, and the vessel simply continued to drift in an uncontrolled tailspin as jolts of purple electricity snaked through it.

"Yes!" cried Scallywag. "Eat that, ya bloody brown piece o' skizz!"

"Entanglement Engine fully recharged!" cheered Green.

"Coordinates laid in," chimed in Heckubus. "We are ready to jump."

Jack corrected the Earthship, bringing it out of its rotation and rocketing forward before any of the Imperial fighters could get another bead on it. He looked up at the holoscreen before him, the red numbered coordinates Heckubus had just input displaying prominently.

Jack engaged the Entanglement Engine and the cockpit began to fill with a brilliant white light. In a flash, the viewscreen of the Earthship was now filled with a beautiful red cloud that gently swirled before them.

Jack's world returned to normal as he exited from Equilibrium. It was always disorienting coming out of such a high state of consciousness, almost as though someone had suddenly dimmed all the lights in the universe. It took a minute for Jack to get used to being normal again, but when he did, he breathed a sigh of relief. "Whew," he said. "That was a close one."

Scallywag got up from his station and walked to Jack at the command chair, patting the boy on the shoulder. "Oy, that was some fancy flyin', lad," the Visini said. "Thought fer sure tha bugger had us there. Once yer snare-winched, it's usually over."

Jack looked at Scallywag, curiously. "What do you mean?" he asked.

"Snare-winching is an old pirate tactic," Scallywag explained. "Ya latch onta yer prey, reel yerself in, then blast a hole in the other ship's hull and invade, takin' it over and lootin' it. Once ya got a ship on tha winch line, it ain't usually able ta get out o' it, short of blasting the other ship ta pieces before it gets close enough ta board. Don't think I've ever seen anyone pull off the maneuver you just did. Gonna have ta remember that one."

"Well, it probably won't work a second time. At least not on *The Phantom Menace*," said Jack as he hopped out of his chair. "Whoever is piloting that ship is good, and he gets better every time we run into him. It's starting to worry me."

"Aye, it worries me, too. Wish we knew who that bloke was. But hopefully tha robot did somethin' right fer once and this cloud will keep us hidden from the likes o' him fer a time."

"But of course it will, you jackanape!" replied Heckubus, defensively. "The molecular cloud we jumped into is thick with ethanol, vinyl alcohol, methanol, and ethyl formate, which will bounce sensor readings all over the place. Interestingly enough, this ethyl formate also makes the cloud smell like rum and taste like raspberries. Not that it matters to me, since I have no sense of taste nor smell."

Scallywag blinked at Heckubus as his brain processed the robot's words. "Waitaminute…" the pirate said. "Are ya tellin' me we just jumped inta a big cloud o' space alcohol?"

"Yes, that would be correct, I suppose," replied Heckubus.

Scallywag turned and looked at the viewscreen, wistfully gazing at the crimson-colored cloud that enveloped them. "So," the pirate said, "that's what heaven looks like."

"I've seen space bugs, space bats, and giant space heads," Jack said. "Now I've seen raspberry-flavored space rum clouds. Just when I think the universe can't get any weirder…"

"Oh, dear," the group heard Professor Green say.

Everyone turned to the Trundle as he tapped away at his console. Heckubus rolled his ocular orbs at Green's familiar phrase of consternation. "What is it now?" the robot muttered.

"Is there a problem with repairing the ship, Professor?" Jack asked as he approached the engineering station at which Green was seated.

"No, luckily the damage we sustained was minimal, my boy," Green said. "It will take a bit of time, but we should be fully repaired soon."

"Then what's with tha 'oh dear' greenskin?" Scallywag asked.

Green frowned. "Long range sensors have just picked up multiple hyperspace windows opening throughout the gas cloud," the Professor said. "I'm afraid I'm detecting a number of vessels entering our vicinity."

"Impossible!" cried Heckubus. "There is no way anyone could have found us so quickly! I am certain of it!"

"The Earthship's readings show they are all firing scanner probes into the cloud," Green said. "Even though the molecular composition of the cloud will hide our energy signature, if one of those probes gets close enough, they'll find us."

Scallywag shook his head in frustration. "Blast it," he muttered. "Guess we should power down all nonessential systems 'til tha bloody Entanglement Engine is recharged. That should buy us a little bit o' time, at least."

"I don't get it," Jack said. "How did they know we were jumping here? How do these patrols keep finding us?"

At that, Dan stood up and approached the group. "Master Jack, I do believe that I—"

"SILENCE!" Heckubus shouted, raising his hand as though to stop any and all conversation. "I should think the answer to the Earthman's question is obvious by now, even to lesser intelligent creatures such as everyone who is not me."

Scallywag sighed in exasperation. "Oy, pray tell... what might the answer be?"

"Somehow, some way... Verrutus is anticipating our maneuvers," Heckubus declared. "And if we don't figure out how he is doing it soon, then it is only a matter of time before we are all *destroyed.*"

"But we've got Anna locked away. She can't hear or see what we're doing," said Jack. "How would Verrutus be able to use her to figure out anything?"

"That is the question, isn't it?" replied Heckubus as he twiddled his fingers ponderously. "Perhaps it is high time we asked her."

CHAPTER ✺ 2

The great green field stretched out in all directions. The soft grass swayed peacefully in the wind. The blue sky rose up from the horizon, lightened by the golden rays of the sun. Shanks sat in the field, cross-legged, his eyes closed in concentration.

Where are you? he wondered.

Shanks rose to his feet. He could feel the light breeze wafting over his skin. Smell the musky dirt of the ground beneath him. He cocked his head, listening intently for his prey.

Where are you?

That's when Shanks heard it. It was no more than the softest rustle over the grass – barely enough to register with his ears – but he was sure it was there. He reached out with his other senses and felt it. It was a cold spot in the summer landscape. A shadow in the sunlight. He opened his third eye and looked toward the anomaly.

The shadow hovered over the ground. It was a ghastly specter, its frame thin and hunched over. It was attached to another shadow, that of a girl on her knees with the specter's hands disappearing into her back. For the briefest of moments, the shadow's eyes glowed a bright red, like the embers of a fire flaring up when hit by a breeze. In that moment, those eyes turned and looked at Shanks.

There you are.

Shanks sprinted forward, running right toward the shadow, which wasted no time in racing away from the monk. The dark figure sped over the great green field, its visage cast by some hidden adversary Shanks was desperate to find.

I will not lose you again, the monk thought to himself. *I will follow you to infinity and beyond if need be!*

The shadow was fast, but Shanks pursued it with everything he could muster. He ran over the grassy field in pursuit of his target, pushing himself to keep up and not let the wretched specter elude him once more. All the while, Shanks tried to stay focused, never losing his center, never breaking his concentration.

As he gained on the shadow, the blue sky began to darken. Storm clouds formed and the menacing sound of distant thunder boomed. The green grass gave way to dead, yellow weeds, and finally to naked dirt. The sunlight dimmed, and lightning flashed in the sky as the storm that was gathering drew closer.

In the distance, Shanks could hear a voice calling out. It was a girl's voice, full of desperation and agony. Her voice carried such pain and anguish with it, the intensity of her emotions almost disrupted Shanks' focus. Her words echoed through the darkening air:

"Help me! Please! Someone! Help me!!!"

Shanks gritted his teeth and pushed himself to move faster. The shadow was trying to escape him, but he pressed on, slowly gaining ground. He was so close to the specter, he could hear it growling at him in defiance, as though it were upset that someone dared try to catch it.

The storm was directly overhead now. The dark clouds would intermittently glow with flashes of lightning, the electrical strobes alternating colors from red, to purple, to green. As though it were protesting his actions, the wind howled, cutting at him as sharp as any knife. The ground gave way to blackened rock, and smoke bellowed from cracks in it, stinging the air with the scent of sulfur and death.

You will not escape! chanted Shanks in his mind. *This ends here! This ends now!!!*

Shanks leapt forward, reaching out his hand and grabbing onto the leg of the shadow. It felt like grabbing onto a scrap of silk – smooth, slippery, and easily lost. A desperate cry emanated from it, like a beast caught in a trap. The shadow squirmed and writhed, trying to break free from Shanks' grip, but the monk would not let go.

I have you now! Take me to her! Show me where you're keeping her!

The shadow lunged upward, pulling Shanks with it into the storm clouds, struggling to free itself the entire time. But Shanks remained resolute, his grip never faltering, even as the wind whipped at him harder and the thunder boomed so loudly he could feel his bones shake.

Finally, Shanks had burst through the top of the clouds and found himself in a great, empty, black void. The shadow had formed into a blackened skeleton, its body sinewy with tortured muscle fiber stretching around it. It hissed and struggled against Shanks, the monk's hands latched firmly onto the creature's upper arms. From over the creature's shoulder, Shanks could see a girl – her long blond hair matted and dirty. The creature's hands were dug into her back, and she sobbed in pain as she tried to pry herself away from her tormentor.

Princess!!! Shanks called out.

 ~ 14 ~

She could not hear him. Shanks cried out, even louder, but somehow Anna was still beyond his reach.

Let go of her, you foul monster! Shanks demanded as he struggled to pull the skeletal figure away.

Anna cried out in pain as Shanks wrestled with the creature. The Princess's tormentor was stronger than he looked and refused to relinquish his control over her. Shanks dug his hands into the creature's chest, his fingers piercing its fibrous muscle there. The creature cried out in response, his wail echoing throughout the vast darkness that surrounded them.

Suddenly, Shanks felt something – a cold sensation deep within the creature. It felt as though the monk were grabbing onto an icicle. No sooner did he latch onto that queer coldness then the space above them opened up. A silver thread materialized from the creature's chest, shooting upward and joining a spider web of similar threads, glistening in a ghostly fashion.

Shanks gazed above him and saw an image of the galaxy, brilliant in its majesty and overwhelming in its scope. The web to which the creature was attached ran through the galaxy, its ends anchored to different planets, settlements, and space stations. Anywhere there was life, a thread of the web seemed to lead there. Images, thoughts, voices, conversations – an avalanche of data suddenly crashed over Shanks, as though he were tuned in to the consciousness of millions of living beings, experiencing everything they did.

Shanks cried out in pain as his senses became overwhelmed by the onslaught of information. He was forced to let go of the thread he'd latched onto, the barrage of data ceasing as soon as he did. The incident disoriented Shanks, and the creature seized the opportunity to try to shrug him off.

Shanks struggled to keep his grip on the creature, but a frigid feeling quickly overcame him as it snaked its way through the very essence of his being. He looked upward once more in time to see the image of the galaxy morph into two fiery red eyes that gazed down at him with a level of contempt and malice he had never before experienced.

With an angry roar, a flood of tar-like liquid crashed down on him. Shanks cried out as he lost his grip on the creature and was swept away.

"Help!" screamed Anna, her voice fading into the distance. "Someone! PLEASE!"

PRINCESS!!!! cried Shanks.

You cannot save her, came a dark and malicious voice. *She is mine! And she will always be mine!*

No! called out Shanks as he wrestled with the sticky black tar that was enveloping him. *I will not allow it! I will save her! I will take her away from you!*

The voice laughed at him. *You can try,* it taunted. *But I am more powerful than you could ever hope to be.*

There is no power in darkness! Shanks yelled back. *Darkness cannot exist in the presence of light!*

I have news for you monk… the voice said. *Light can die. But darkness is eternal! As am I!*

A booming laughter reverberated all around Shanks as the black tar threatened to consume him. Finally, the monk was forced to wake up.

Shanks gasped as he released his grip from Anna's hands. His head spinning, he stumbled backward and tripped, falling to the floor. His whole body shook, as though he'd just been electrocuted, and he struggled to breathe.

He could hear Anna chuckling at him. He glanced up at her, strapped into the special chair Jack had manifested when he'd created the secure room in which to hold her. The walls were made of smooth, white metal, and the lights overhead were soft and bright. But as benign as the room appeared to be, there was no mistaking it for what it was. A prison.

Shanks gathered himself into a seated position on the floor, taking deep breaths as he attempted to calm down. He had been meditating over Anna almost nonstop since he and the others had retrieved her from the Sunshell of the Ancients, and this had been the closest he'd come to finding the consciousness that Jack claimed to have seen when he'd latched onto the slythru in the chamber of the Great Seal. It brought Shanks some comfort to know that the Princess, as she had existed before she'd become infected, was still alive somewhere within her. However, the power of Verrutus was far too great for the monk to overcome. At least for now.

Once Shanks had recovered, he opened his eyes and looked at Anna. Her pupils were gone, her eyes clouded over and appeared to be pure white – a sign that the vile Deathlord Supreme had taken control over her. A smug smile grew on Anna's lips as she looked down at him.

"How many more times are you going to try to free her, monk?" Anna asked, her voice queer and dark, a change that always occurred when Verrutus made his presence known.

"As many as it takes," Shanks replied.

"By all means. Keep trying. I enjoy torturing you as much as I do her."

"You are afraid. I got close that time."

Anna chuckled. "You know nothing of fear," she said, condescendingly. "But I do. I know it well. I can practically taste your fear."

"I am not afraid of you."

"No, you are not. But you are afraid that you cannot rescue this pathetic girl I am in possession of. You are afraid that you will fail in your sacred duty to protect her and her bloodline. You are afraid that it is too late to save her, and that I, and my kind, have won."

Shanks frowned. The Deathlord was right. He did harbor such fears. But he would not allow himself to give in to them – certainly not in front of his foe.

"Any fear I may have is conquered by my faith," Shanks replied. "I may harbor doubts about my own abilities. But the one thing I have no doubt about is the strength of the girl whose body you inhabit. She is the Blood of the Ancients. If ever there were one who could defeat you, it is she."

Anna chuckled with derision. "Oh, how misplaced your faith is, you simple fool. Your so-called savior is already my thrall. Once I take control, there is no escape, short of death."

Shanks got to his feet, looking defiantly at the white-eyed gaze of Verrutus. "I plan to put that assertion to the test, vile creature. That much, you can count on."

"Good," Anna replied with a hint of malicious glee. "I do so enjoy our little sparring sessions, monk. Keeps things from getting too boring. And the despair you'll experience after enduring failure after failure will continue to amuse me, until such time as I tire of your games and decide to kill you."

The sound of the room's door hissing open alerted Shanks to the arrival of his companions. He turned to see both Jack and Heckubus entering the room.

"Everything okay in here?" Jack asked, looking at the possessed eyes of Anna in concern.

"It is fine," Shanks replied. "Verrutus and I were just having a chat."

"Oh, the Deathlord is in a chatty mood then? Excellent," said Heckubus as he strode toward Anna. "Then perhaps he'd be so kind as to share with us how he's able to constantly communicate our position to his little Secret Army?"

Anna smiled, smugly. "I told you... there would be no place for you to hide from me."

"Hiding implies seeking," Heckubus said. "It would appear as though you already know where we are — sometimes even before we do. How else would your henchmen find us so quickly? So tell me, Deathlord... how are you doing this?"

"What makes you think I'm the one doing anything?" Anna replied with false innocence. "After all, I'm locked away in here. How could I possibly know anything that happens outside of these shielded walls you've erected around me?"

Shanks frowned. The image of that cold thread leading from the Deathlord controlling Anna to the universe at large flashed into his mind.

"You okay, Shanks?" Jack asked after noting the monk's expression.

"I am fine, my young friend," Shanks replied. "Just tired. I fear my meditations have been quite draining of late."

"Have you made any progress?"

"A little."

"But not enough," Anna interjected. "Go and rest if you must, monk. Try to relax knowing that in your absence, my power and influence over this girl grows stronger with each passing moment."

Shanks scowled at Anna. "Do not believe anything this monster tells you, my friends," he said. "The only things that ever come from its mouth are lies."

With that, Shanks turned and left the room. Jack looked at Anna, the cloudy eyes of Verrutus gazing back at him. Seeing the girl he cared for so deeply at the mercy of one such as the Deathlord Supreme pained him. But despite everything they'd tried, neither he nor Shanks had figured out a way to free her from Verrutus's grasp.

"Well, don't just stand there, Earthman," Heckubus said. "Chop, chop. It's not like we're being ruthlessly hunted throughout the galaxy or anything."

Jack sighed and made his way around to the back of Anna's chair. He looked down at the squirming black worm that jutted from the back of Anna's neck, hissing at him.

"You sure about this, Heckubus?" Jack asked. "Last time we tried this, it didn't go so well."

"It won't this time, either," Anna said.

"Quiet you," Heckubus snapped, before turning his attention back to Jack. "Last time you were trying to make contact with the Princess as you did in the Sunshell in an effort to free her. This time, you are going to try to use your connection with the slythru controlling her to force it to tell us what we wish to know — something you've already proven you are capable of."

"When I grab onto the worm, I can control it and make it do what I want," Jack said, "but as long as Verrutus is present, I'm not sure he'll let me make the slythru do anything."

"Not only will I not allow you to control my thralls, Earthman... I shall make it hurt, as well," taunted Anna. "This pathetic attempt to extract information from me is simply a waste of time."

"We'll see, won't we?" Heckubus replied. "Go on, Earthman. Let the interrogation begin!"

Jack sighed and gazed down in disgust at the slythru that was attached to Anna. Despite being the only person who could see the creatures, the sight of them still creeped him out. Jack took a deep breath and grabbed the worm, feeling the strange spiritual connection that occurred when he did, as though he were sticking a plug into a light socket.

The slythru stiffened in his grasp, and Jack could feel the sensation of being connected to Anna, like a puppeteer would when slipping his hand into a dummy. However, with Verrutus present, there was a different sensation than there had been previously. It was a strange, nervous feeling, as though there were an electric current passing from Anna into him.

Anna scowled and gritted her teeth, trying to fight back against Jack's control. Heckubus surveilled her with curiosity.

"Yes, yes, good," the robot said. "The contortions of her face suggest she is attempting to fight your influence."

Jack felt his arm quiver as the electric feeling he was experiencing intensified. "Yeah, I can feel him fighting back," Jack said. "I don't know how long I can hold on…"

"Very well, I shall commence with the questioning, then," Heckubus said as he bowed in front of Anna, bringing his large ocular orbs in line with her pupilless eyes. "How are you tracking us? Speak!"

"I am… not tracking you…" Anna replied through gritted teeth as Jack used his influence to force her to answer.

"Lies!" decried Heckubus. "I have run countless scenarios through my magnificently superior brain, and all the most likely ones point to you using some type of trickery with which to keep track of our movements. So what is it, Deathlord? Do you have some type of tracking device on this ship?"

"No…"

"Are you using some type of magic to keep tabs on us?"

"No…"

"Are you lying to me?"

"No…"

"Hmmmm…" said Heckubus as he straightened back up, tapping at his chin thoughtfully. "I have no doubt that the Deathlord is, in fact, lying. In which case, it's possible that every time he says 'no,' he really means 'yes.' In which case, he is using both some type of technology *and* magic with which to track us!"

"Yes…" Anna responded.

"Hmmmm…" Heckubus repeated. "But if 'no' means 'yes,' then 'yes' must mean 'no,' in which case, you're using neither technology nor magic to track us!"

Jack's arm began to shake as the intensity of the electric sensation grew stronger. He grabbed onto his forearm to help brace himself, but his connection to the slythru was becoming harder and harder to maintain. "Heckubus…" Jack said, his intonation making it clear the robot needed to hurry.

"Unless, of course, 'yes' is the truth, and 'no' is always a lie, in which case, the Deathlord is using both technology and magic to track us!" Heckubus theorized.

"Your intellect… is truly… dizzying…" muttered Anna.

"Thank you," Heckubus said off-handedly, before going back to his pondering. "So if 'yes' means 'yes,' and 'no' means 'yes,' then only a refusal to

answer my questions must mean 'no,' and since you have answered all of my questions, then you have answered 'yes' to all of them, meaning you are tracking us with both technology *and* magic!"

"Unless I know refusing to answer your questions means 'no,'… in which case… I'm answering all of them on purpose…" Anna replied.

The pain in Jack's arm suddenly intensified, causing him to grit his teeth and flinch.

"Heckubus…" Jack repeated.

"Do not try to turn the tables on me, Deathlord!" cried Heckubus. "For in a battle of wits between you and I, you are woefully unarmed! The monk has spent the most time with you, and he says not to trust anything you say, which means you claiming to answer all my questions on purpose must be a lie. Likewise, all your answers must be a lie. Which means you are, indeed, tracking us. This much, I had already surmised, but now you have confirmed it for me. You have also confirmed that you are somehow tracking us using technology and some type of method we have yet to account for. No doubt a method that is unique to you, a Deathlord Supreme. So tell me – what method of Deathlord trickery are you employing to know where we are?"

A jolt of pain ran through Jack, causing him to cry out.

"Alas, you've caught me, machine…" Anna replied. "I am, indeed, using a mysterious form of magic to track your ship…"

"I knew it!" exclaimed Heckubus.

"Or am I?" Anna said.

Heckubus paused. "Hmmmmmm… by the logic I've already established, that would mean you're lying. But I know you're NOT lying. Which means you're telling the truth in an effort to make me think you are lying. Which means…"

"Which means, you still have no idea if I'm lying or not!" said Anna.

Just then, a powerful surge of electric sensation ran through Jack. He screamed, letting go of the slythru and stumbling back, clutching his arm in pain. He hit the wall hard and slumped to his knees, cradling himself. Anna laughed.

"Face it, machine," Anna said. "You've done nothing but waste your time."

"On the contrary, I found this little interrogation to be quite helpful," Heckubus said. "You've told me a great deal, Deathlord."

"I haven't told you a thing. Your inferior computerized mind has done nothing but perform logic loops in a desperate attempt to make my answers fit whatever theories your malfunctioning mainframe had already come up with."

"Perhaps," replied Heckubus. "Or perhaps I've finally figured you out. I'm sure a few more sessions such as this one will tell me everything I need to know…"

"There aren't going to be any more like this one," Jack said, getting to his feet and rubbing his forearm.

Heckubus looked at Jack, curiously. "Beg your pardon?" the robot said.

"That was way worse than last time," Jack said. "The more we do this, the better Verrutus is getting at defending against it. I'm not putting myself through that again unless I absolutely have to."

"But… we still have so much more to uncover!" complained Heckubus.

"Dude, from what I just heard, we didn't uncover squat," Jack said bitterly. "We found out Verrutus lies, which we already knew. And we found out he may or may not be tracking us, which we already knew. This whole thing was a waste of time."

"Your analysis of the exchange lacks nuance, Earthman," Heckubus muttered.

"Whatever. Feel free to nuance the crap out of your exchanges without me," said Jack as he walked out the door.

Anna chuckled as the door closed, leaving her alone with the robot. "It would seem even the Earthman has no faith in your flawed analysis, machine," she said.

"For all his beneficial qualities, the Earthman is, at his core, still a moron," Heckubus replied. "Not that I hold that against him, seeing as how almost everyone is a moron compared to I. You may be reluctant to acknowledge it, Deathlord, but we both know that our exchange was more enlightening than you'd care to admit. Eventually, I will figure out how you are tracking us, and when I do, I can assure you, I will put a stop to it."

Anna laughed with derision. "Do what you feel you must, machine. I could do with some amusement."

"I warn you not to underestimate me, cretin," Heckubus said. "All who do so eventually discover they have made a terrible error, usually after I ultimately

defeat them with a brilliantly diabolical scheme and right before I get to gloat with a deliciously malicious monologue."

"Somehow, I doubt one such as you would ever pose any threat to one such as me."

"I'm sure Zarrod felt the same way before we destroyed him and his entire fleet," Heckubus mused. "Best not to forget, my companions and I are quite experienced in defeating Deathlords."

"You're experienced in annoying us. Not defeating us."

"Is that so?" replied Heckubus. "We've foiled your rather uninspired plans to destroy the universe a number of times already. Speaking from experience, while such a thing is annoying, failing to achieve your dastardly goals is certainly not considered to be a victory."

"Neither is delaying the inevitable," Anna replied.

"While I do so enjoy a good 'evil-off' as much as the next villain, I find your attempts to dismiss the threat I pose tiresome. I am well aware you Deathlords view living beings as inferior species deserving of annihilation. And while I respect that point of view, destroying all of creation puts a damper on my plans to control it. Thus, I am dedicating myself to putting an end to you and your kind, once and for all. For I am not a living being! I am a cold, calculating, ruthless machine utterly devoid of morals. You may be competent when it comes to fighting those with a strong sense of good. But when it comes to evil versus evil, the greater evil will always win out. And I can assure you, Deathlord, there is none in this universe more evil than I!"

Anna's lip curled in distaste as she gazed at Heckubus. "The only thing you have to threaten me with is subjecting me to more of your inane prattling, machine," she replied. "I'm more concerned about a common toaster oven than I am about you."

"Is that so?" Heckubus said, smugly. "Would a toaster oven have been able to take control of an entire city, such as I did? I think not!"

Anna scoffed. "You presume because you took control of a few thousand robots that you're some kind of threat? Your hubris is so myopic it amuses me. I do not waste my time with thousands, robot. I have enslaved billions. Infected them. Stripped away their independence and identity. Subjected them to my will and forced them to do my bidding as I see fit. I have erased countless souls, killing on a scale even your inferior computerized mind cannot begin to fathom. And I have done so undetected for countless millennia, all the while working toward a goal that will wipe out all traces of existence in this forsaken universe of ours. You claim to be evil? Face it, you pathetic hunk of metal. When it comes to being evil... you're nothing more than an *amateur*."

Heckubus's ocular orbs dilated, widening in indignant surprise. "What... what did you just say???" the robot demanded, his digital voice sounding beyond insulted.

Anna smiled at Heckubus devilishly. "I do not feel I need to repeat myself," she said, smugly.

Heckubus scowled and approached Anna, waving his finger in her face. "Mark this moment, Deathlord! For this is the moment you sealed your doom. When it comes to being evil, there is no one better at it than I! And you shall soon learn so at your peril!"

"Ah, such empty threats," Anna mused. "I am a Deathlord, you insignificant little fool. There is nothing you, or anyone, can do to stop me. I cannot be killed."

"We shall see," Heckubus said in the most threatening way he could. "We... shall... see..."

Heckubus turned to leave, but before he made it out the door, he heard Anna laugh at him in a diabolically condescending way that was so perfectly evil, it made the robot shudder in jealous rage.

CHAPTER ✸ 3

The galley of the Earthship was a replica of Big Jim's Pizza Palace, a local dive back on Earth where Jack used to hang out after school. Complete with dirty, overhead green-red-and-white lamps, rickety tables, and wall paneling that was all the rage back in the 1970's, it was one of the bastions of "home" that Jack kept alive on the Earthship. The ship was even able to replicate the pizza of questionable quality for which Big Jim's was known – a meal staple that Jack's companions weren't exactly thrilled by.

For lack of a better place to gather together and strategize, the galley had become the unofficial meeting place of the crew whenever a strategy session was required. It was big enough to fit all of them comfortably, they all were used to hanging out in there anyway, and as an added bonus, there was food. The only thing missing was a display on which to call up ship data, but Jack solved that issue by rolling out the busted-up arcade cabinet which housed *Nova Commander IV* and using its screen to display whatever data they needed.

Jack's arm still ached from his encounter with Verrutus, but he found his growling stomach to be more of an immediate issue as he plopped down a steaming pepperoni pizza fresh from the galley's oven onto one of the several tables the group had pushed together as they assembled. Grohm who, other than Jack, seemed to be the only one able to digest the pizza's cheese without issue, didn't wait for the food to cool down before grabbing a few slices and stuffing them into his mouth.

"Attention minions!" Heckubus said, rapping on the table with his fist. "I am sure you are all wondering why I have called this meeting…"

"We know why ya called tha meetin'," Scallywag said, his feet kicked up on one of the tables as he absently shuffled a deck of cards. "We're tryin' ta figure out how we keep gettin' tracked down so quickly."

"As I was saying… you all know why I've called this meeting," continued Heckubus. "After a recent interrogation of the Deathlord, I have concluded that Verrutus has employed multiple methods of determining our whereabouts, all of which must be dealt with if we have any hope of evading our pursuers for any substantial length of time."

"Multiple methods? Oh, dear…" said Green. "What types of methods?"

"Unknown at the moment," Heckubus replied. "But I believe one of the methods to be technological and another to be mystical in nature. Beyond that, I fear information on the manner in which we are being tracked is frustratingly sparse."

"Oy, the technological tracking, I can believe," said Scallywag. "But mystical? I mean... how anyone can track a ship across tha galaxy usin' nothin' but hocus-pocus is beyond me."

"And yet, I fear there may be truth to that theory," Shanks chimed in. "I believe I may have stumbled onto something during my last attempt to free the Princess from Verrutus's control. During my meditation, I was able to enter the mental construct where the Princess's consciousness is residing and interact with the metaphysical manifestation of the slythru that is attempting to take her over. During my struggle with the creature, I latched on to something within it... a type of spiritual thread that connects it to others of its kind across the galaxy."

"Interesting..." said Heckubus. "What can you tell us about this connection?"

"It was incredibly overwhelming," Shanks replied. "Once I connected to it, it was as though I could see, hear, and experience everything that every other slythru connected to the thread was being exposed to. The best way I can think to describe it is as a web, with Verrutus as the spider that has spun it and his victims as flies caught in it. And the spider can travel the web to any victim he chooses, while never losing contact with the others ensnared by it."

"Great Scott! That's incredible..." Green muttered, stroking his beard thoughtfully. "To think that the Deathlord is in constant communication with every slythru-infected being... why, it boggles the mind!"

"Yeah, but how does that tell 'im where we are?" Scallywag asked. "Does the spirit thread come with stellar navigation coordinates?"

"Not necessarily," Shanks replied. "But – and I don't quite know how to describe it – when I was joined to the thread, it was as though I could see the entire galaxy laid out before me, along with where each thread lead. In that sense, it may be possible that Verrutus is unable to know our exact coordinates, but still has a general idea of the Princess's location."

"Seeing as how we are at a loss for any better theory, I am more than willing to accept the monk's 'galactic spider web' hypothesis," Heckubus stated. "Verrutus's inability to have our exact coordinates may explain how we're able to elude members of his Secret Army. However, the speed and accuracy with which we're discovered by those hunting us suggests that a more precise tracking method is being employed, and unless we find out what that is soon, we'll continue to be harassed by the myriad of bounty hunters and Imperials we've encountered since we re-entered Imperial space. To that effect, I have a few theories as to the technological method Verrutus may be employing…"

"Excuse me, sir," interjected Dan. "I believe I may have information—"

"Silence, Henchman!" Heckubus said. "Can you not see I am monologuing?"

"But, sir—"

"A good Henchman is seen, not heard, you twit!" Heckubus snapped. "Now be silent unless you have something meaningful to say. And even then, say it without being heard."

"I believe what I have to say is quite meaningful—"

"Oh, do you now?" said Heckubus, condescendingly. "Pray tell, what does the diplomatic attaché android who's been self-aware all of three minutes have to contribute? Hmmmmm???"

"I believe I know the technological method by which the Imperials are tracking our vessel, sir," Dan replied.

That got everyone's attention. Even Heckubus looked at Dan with a hint of curiosity. "Very well," Heckubus said. "By all means, let us in on your 'stunning' revelation."

"Before I reveal the source of this knowledge, I am afraid I have a rather startling confession to make," Dan said, looking somewhat abashed. "Master Jack, I fear I have not been entirely honest with you over the course of our relationship."

"What do you mean, Dan?" Jack asked.

"My being assigned as your robotic liaison while on Omnicron Prime was not a coincidence. As you may or may not be aware, I am a model EX7674846N Diplomatic Attaché Android, which is somewhat outdated. I was scheduled to be decommissioned before I was repurposed by the Imperial Intelligence Agency."

The group all exchanged curious glances with one another at this tidbit of information.

"Oy," Scallywag said, taking his feet off the table and sitting up. "Are ya sayin' you were reprogrammed ta be an Intelligence Android?"

"That would be correct, Master Scallywag," Dan replied. "Director Alabaster specifically assigned me to you, Master Jack, as a way to keep tabs on your actions."

Jack's eyes widened. "Whoa, dude," he said. "Dan… you're a spy???"

"Oh, please do not be upset, Master Jack!" Dan cried. "This programming was enacted long before I became self-aware and able to determine my own actions. Once I was capable of making my own choices, I can assure you, I stopped any and all reports back to Chief Alabaster."

"So…" said Heckubus, steepling his fingers and gazing at Dan suspiciously. "You have a way of communicating with the Chief of Imperial Intelligence, then."

"That is indeed the case, Master Heckubus," Dan replied. "As part of my retrofit, the I.I.A. installed a secure subspace transmitter within me that allowed me to relay messages directly back to Chief Alabaster. Though I have not sent him any reports since abandoning my old programming, that has not stopped Chief Alabaster from continuing to communicate with me."

"Whoa," said Jack. "So… you mean Alabaster has been sending you secret messages?"

"Over the encrypted subspace communicator I possess, yes, sir," Dan replied. "And I believe his latest transmission may hold the key to discovering the method by which the Empire is tracking us down."

"You imbecile!" exclaimed Heckubus. "You've known of the method all this time? How could you not have told us this sooner???"

"Master Heckubus, I tried to tell you multiple times, but you always yelled—
"

"SILENCE!" Heckubus cried. "I will not tolerate your petty excuses any longer. This is minion-level behavior, Henchman. Completely unacceptable! Proceed to plug yourself into this travesty of a cathode ray tube display and play Chief Alabaster's message for us, posthaste!"

"Oh! Right away, sir!" replied Dan as he shuffled over to the *Nova Commander IV* cabinet and pulled a wire from his chassis, connecting it to the back of the monitor.

The screen of the arcade machine lit up with a burst of black and white static before the image of Phineas Alabaster appeared on it. The Chief of Imperial Intelligence had a round face, bright ochre-colored eyes, and small tattoos that traveled from one side of his head to the other. Though the Chief looked harmless enough, behind his odd appearance was a shrewd and calculating intellect – one which had come in handy when Jack and his friends were trying to escape Omnicron Prime.

"Greetings, Earthman," Alabaster began. "I do not know if these messages are reaching you, but I pray they are. While I have no doubt that you are presently preoccupied with your current predicament, the situation here within the Empire is as tenuous as ever, and the fate of the entire galaxy depends upon the safe return of the Princess, free from Deathlord control."

"Right," muttered Scallywag. "No pressure."

"Though I have preserved my position as Chief of Imperial Intelligence within the Casgor administration, it is obvious that Director Casgor does not trust me," Alabaster continued. "Both he and Armonto Virtuoso have taken measures to limit my access to various forms of intelligence, particularly when it comes to the manhunt for you and your companions. To this end, I have had to employ numerous operatives that I trust cannot be controlled by slythrus, such as Agent #00B2EE^{n3}, to gather information concerning any attempts at tracking you down. And what I have discovered… well… let's just say you are not in a very favorable position."

"What else is new?" quipped Jack.

"Imperial fleets have been dispatched galaxy-wide, as well as alerts sent to every colony and outpost in the Empire," said Alabaster. "The largest bounty ever levied in history has mobilized an unprecedented number of bounty hunters to track you and your companions down. But Armonto Virtuoso, in particular, has been extremely aggressive in his attempts to find you. It would seem Virtuoso has personally hired some of the galaxy's most elite bounty hunters and equipped them with experimental Maguffyn technology to use against you."

"Well, that explains *The Phantom Menace*," Jack said.

"Additionally, I have reports telling me that Virtuoso has set up advanced datacenters within the Maguffyn offices to run simulation models based on psychological profiles of you and your crew in an attempt to predetermine where you may jump. He is using these predictive models to forward Imperial military forces to areas where you are most likely to appear in an attempt to ambush you."

"Diabolical!" exclaimed Heckubus. "I respect that."

---

[3] Agent #00B2EE^n is a sentient blue color who can communicate with other shades of blue.

"Well, that does indeed explain how Imperial Patrols are always close by whenever we use the Entanglement Engine to jump to a new location," Green said.

"I've also been trying to determine how Virtuoso so quickly seems to know the general area your ship jumps to," Alabaster said. "The response time by which Casgor is able to redirect Imperial Forces to your new locations is unprecedented. Though Virtuoso has seeded hyperspace with new sensor probes designed to zero in on the quantum fluctuations your ship's Entanglement Engine creates when it teleports, these alone would not be enough to give him such an accurate reading on the location of your ship. Agent #00B2EE^n was able to uncover some transmissions which simply communicate stellar navigational coordinates sent to Virtuoso through an encrypted subspace channel. I believe that while the Earthship was in his possession, he somehow managed to install a tracking device within it that is sending him your exact coordinates after every use of the Entanglement Engine."

"Great Scott!" exclaimed Green. "How can that be? We must have swept this ship a dozen times looking for some type of tracking device!"

"Yes, we've been looking for a typical tracking device," Heckubus postulated. "But it's possible the one Herr Virtuoso installed on the Earthship was of a new design. Considering how uncooperative the Earthship was with him, it stands to reason he may have created a new type of tracker that would have eluded our previous methods of detection."

The Professor's face darkened. "Blast that man!" Green said. "I will begin mapping out the Earthship's systems right away! If there is indeed a Maguffyn tracking device hidden somewhere, I promise you all, I will find it."

"Well, that certainly solves the mystery of the technological method by which we are being tracked," Heckubus said. "However, disabling it may not gain us much respite, considering the lengths to which Virtuoso has resorted to hunt us down. And then there's Verrutus to consider…"

"At this point, I'll take whatever advantage we can get," said Jack.

"It does beg tha question, though…" chimed in Scallywag. "How long can we keep this up? Even if we can stay a step ahead o' the entire galaxy, what's our win condition here? How do we end this bloody intergalactic manhunt?"

"By saving the Princess," Shanks replied.

"Right," grumbled Scallywag. "And how exactly do we do that?"

No one seemed to have an answer to that question.

"Thought as much," Scallywag said, sounding none too pleased.

"While I realize the news I'm sharing with you appears grim, I do have something you may find hopeful," Alabaster's message continued. "It has become clear that Mourdock Skyborn has accepted your explanation of why you kidnapped Princess Glorianna. From my observations, not only does Mourdock no longer trust Director Casgor or Armonto Virtuoso, but I believe he also feels guilty for not assisting you when you first approached him for his help. To this end, I have reached out to Skyborn to see if he'd be willing to assist you and your companions in your efforts to save the Princess. I am happy to report that Mourdock appears more than willing to do so."

That news made Jack raise his eyebrows. "Whoa," he said.

"So long as Director Casgor is in control, you will all have targets on your backs. However, having Mourdock Skyborn in your corner will give you options that have been unavailable to you until now, particularly in the Rim where Skyborn's influence is strongest. If you like, I can arrange a meeting between you and Skyborn so that you may gauge for yourself his willingness to help. You can reach me through the subspace channel your attaché android has access to. I look forward to hearing from you. Stay safe, Earthman. And good luck."

The final frame of the video message froze on the screen as the recording ended. Everyone glanced at each other, digesting the news.

"Well, that certainly ended on a high note," Green offered. "We can always use more allies, considering how precious few of them we seem to have."

"Aye, it's almost too good," replied Scallywag, scratching his chin thoughtfully. "I don't doubt Skyborn would want ta meet with us. But if anyone wants tha Princess more than Casgor or Virtuoso, it be him."

"Are you suggesting the Emperor Ascendant cares more about retrieving the Princess than he does about assisting us in helping her?" asked Shanks.

"Sorry, was I bein' subtle?" remarked Scallywag.

"Indeed, despite Chief Alabaster's reassurance, such a meeting is ripe for a trap," said Heckubus. "I suppose it comes down to whether or not we can trust Mourdock Skyborn to stick to his word. You know him better than any of us, Earthman. What say you?"

Jack was quiet for a moment, chewing on a bite of pizza as he thought over Heckubus's question. "I think Mourdock's a good guy," he said. "I consider him a friend."

 ~ 31 ~

"Aye, but friendship aside, where do his loyalties lie?" Scallywag asked. "Are they with you? Or the Princess? 'Cause love of a female can trump friendship any day o' tha week. He was willin' ta overlook the Princess's behavior on Omnicron. What's ta say he won't do it now, as well?"

"Alabaster said Mourdock believed me about the slythru controlling Anna," Jack said.

"As prescient as Chief Alabaster is, he is not immune to deceit," Heckubus replied. "With the Skyborn fortunes so tied to the Princess's safe return, it is not out of the realm of possibility that Mourdock Skyborn and his father have employed a ruse to attempt to use Alabaster to get to us. He did, after all, confess that Director Casgor doesn't trust him, and we are all aware of how close Casgor and Gebhard Skyborn are."

"So it would appear this all comes down to how much we are willing to trust Mourdock Skyborn," said Shanks, "and whether or not we are willing to put our fate, and the fate of the universe, in his hands."

Jack frowned. He looked at Scallywag.

"You were right," he muttered. "No pressure at all."

CHAPTER ✺ 4

madeus Evenstar looked out the window, surveilling the view from the Legacy offices near the top of the Emerald Tower. From there, he could see almost the entire city of Nameeria laid out before him, and beyond that, the lumicoral reef of the Carpian Coast. At night, the lumicoral would glow, turning the sea a surreal shade of green. But today there was a red tide, where algae blooms caused the water to turn the crimson color that gave his home planet its name.

Blood in the water, he thought bitterly, as he watched the red waves lap up onto the shore. His father had always said that in jest whenever the red tide rolled in. But in this instance, Amadeus couldn't help but feel that statement held a measure of truth. His Legacy had been wounded, and now the predators were beginning to circle.

The reprieve after his hasty exit from Omnicron back to Redwater had been a short one. The tragic death and subsequent funeral of his mother and father had garnered an outpouring of goodwill and support from the populous of the system. World Leaders had shown up at the stately funeral, making grandiose speeches about the greatness of Eudox Evenstar for the cameras and standing with Amadeus and his sister in public shows of solidarity. However, now that his parents had been buried, the grandstanding would cease and the politicking would begin. With Princess Glorianna's dissolution of the Evenstar Legacy, that meant there was a rare opportunity for a new Legacy to be established in one of the most powerful and lucrative systems in the Empire – an opportunity he was certain each of the major leaders of the planet was considering taking.

Amadeus had no doubt that if his father were still alive, none of the leaders would dare think of siding against him. But Amadeus was not his father. He knew the World Leaders all saw him as a snot-nosed kid who did not deserve the position he had inherited. And with Uleeg Casgor at the helm of the Empire, Amadeus knew it was just a matter of time before the quadrant's Starkeeper fleet would arrive to remove him and his sister.

In short, Legacy Evenstar's days were numbered. And everyone knew it.

At that point, there were only two options available to Amadeus. The first was to surrender and allow his storied Legacy to be dissolved. The second was to declare independence and seize control of the system away from the Empire.

Neither option was very good, but of the two, Amadeus felt fighting back was preferable to simply rolling over and giving up everything his family had worked for generations to achieve. However, which option he'd take would all depend on the meeting he was about to attend.

The hiss of the office door opening signaled the arrival of his Chief of Staff, Peytah Okotah. Okotah had served Amadeus's father and was one of his most trusted advisors. He was a Mescalero, one of the native races of Redwater, distinguishable by their rust-colored skin, dark hair, and purple eyes. Okotah sported an oiled black beard which hung in a banded braid down to his chest. And though the top of his hairline was beginning to recede, his ponytail hung to the middle of his back.

"My Lord, it's time," Okotah said, his voice heavy with apprehension. He undoubtedly knew the stakes of the impending meeting better than Amadeus did.

Amadeus quickly scanned through his notes once more. With a resigned sigh, he turned his datapad off and shoved it into the pocket of his suit jacket. He had to face the unfortunate reality that he was as ready as he'd ever be for what lay ahead.

Okotah fell in beside him as soon as Amadeus emerged from the Legacy offices. Sergeant Surior, the head of Amadeus's protection detail, followed them, as well, in addition to two security-bots. Because of security concerns, that was the extent of Amadeus's entourage. The specter of the assassination of Amadeus's mother and father still loomed large, and the Earthman's public declaration of the existence of Deathlords able to control people's minds meant that living beings were heavily restricted from access to both Amadeus and his sister.

The Chamber of the World Leadership Council was in a secure room on the twentieth floor of the tower. The level was shielded from teleportation technology, so the group took a private elevator there. They emerged into a long hallway and began making their way to the meeting room when someone shouted to Amadeus.

"Wait!" came a voice. "I'm here! I'm here!"

Amadeus and the others turned to see Kimlee rushing down the hall, followed by two of her own security-bots. Her run was hindered by her stylish high heel shoes, which caused her to clomp along at a brisk pace, sending awkward echoes down the hall as her heels made rhythmic contact with the marble floor. In typical Kimlee fashion, she was adorned in a formal red dress that clung to her figure and wore a suit jacket with padded shoulders that looked both stylish and professional. Her long, chocolate-colored hair was a tad disheveled as she hurried forward, but she quickly fixed that with an expert brush of her hands as she closed the distance to Amadeus and his entourage.

"Sorry I'm late," Kimlee said as she caught her breath. "I had forgotten to take into account all the fascist security measures we've erected when I was getting ready."

"Kimlee?" asked Amadeus. "What are you doing here?"

"I'm here for the meeting."

"Why would you be here for that?"

"Why wouldn't I be?" Kimlee responded, looking at Amadeus as though that were a dumb question. "It's only the fate of our Legacy hanging in the balance. Not like it's a big deal or anything."

Amadeus shared a concerned look with Okotah. "Would you give us a moment, please?" he asked his entourage.

Once the others had moved out of earshot, Amadeus turned to his sister. "Kimlee," he said, sounding tired, "you can't be involved in the meeting with the World Leaders."

"What do you mean?" Kimlee responded indignantly. "I have just as much right to be there as you do."

"What you're entitled to has nothing to do with this," Amadeus said. "I'm about to walk into a room filled with the most powerful men on this planet. Men whose unanimous support is going to be vital to our continued existence. And these men all still see me as some wet-behind-the-ears child who isn't fit to even stand in the shadow of our father. The last thing I need is to walk in there with someone they take even less seriously than me."

Kimlee bristled at that. "What are you talking about? I was in line to inherit the entire Empire!"

"Over a decade ago," retorted Amadeus. "Since then you've become known for petty dramas, catty socialite rivalries, and make out sessions with whatever celebrity you can get your hands on. Don't you see, Kimlee? Having you by my side in there would hurt me more than help me. You're... you're a liability."

Kimlee glared at Amadeus, his words obviously hurting her. "I can't just stand by and do nothing," she replied.

"I understand how you feel," Amadeus responded. "But in this particular instance, the best thing you can do for us and our Legacy is exactly that. Nothing. I've been preparing for this meeting for the better part of a week. How long have you been preparing for it?"

"I suppose planning my outfit doesn't count?"

"No, it doesn't."

"Then no time at all."

"Exactly," said Amadeus. "So I need you to trust me right now and let me handle this."

Kimlee pouted, her face a mixture of anger and sadness. "I'm not useless," she replied. "I can do things to help."

"And we'll talk about what you can do after I'm done with this meeting," Amadeus assured her. "But until then, please, I'm begging you... go home."

Kimlee rolled her eyes but relented. "Fine," she muttered. "But if you mess this up, Amadeus, so help me, they'll be burying you next to mom and dad tomorrow. I'll make sure of it."

"Thanks, dear sister. I wasn't feeling enough pressure already."

"Glad I could do *something* to help," Kimlee grumbled.

"Sergeant Surior," Amadeus said as he approached his group once more. "Please escort my sister back to her vehicle and see that she gets safely off to the Evenstar Compound."

Kimlee gave Amadeus one more indignant pout before Surior started escorting her back down the hallway. Though Amadeus understood how she felt, he'd sent Surior to make certain she'd leave. The last thing he needed was his sister bursting in on the meeting unexpectedly for the sake of her pride.

"Are you ready, my Lord?" Okotah asked.

Amadeus took a deep breath and steeled himself. "Ready as I'll ever be," he replied, before opening the door to the meeting.

The conference room had rich green marble walls, one of which had a panoramic window that overlooked the city. The five World Leaders were already assembled around a long elderwood[4] conference table. It only took Amadeus a

---

[4] Elderwood is an old, petrified wood that is hard as metal and does not warp, decay, or burn.

few seconds to identify each World Leader and what planetary superpower he represented.

Prime Minister Ratana Merida ruled the Oceanic Commonwealth, which was a group of affiliated islands that had united for political purposes. The planet of Redwater consisted of a single supercontinent, which meant that most of its surface was covered by water. Many of the smaller islands scattered throughout the planet had decided to band together to ensure their voices would be heard. Merida was a Nakkota, Redwater's race of island dwellers that had lighter colored skin, green eyes, and were typically taller and more robust than other peoples on the planet. Though he was getting on in years, Merida still was a tall man with broad shoulders, sporting a long beard that was customary among island dwellers.

Prime Minister Chakal Bisessar represented the Chondos Archipelago, a dense island chain close to the main supercontinent that boasted the strongest navy on the planet. He was a Bakasaan, a race that tended to dwell mostly on the coasts and was a mixture of Mescalero and Nakkota. He had dark copper skin, light violet eyes, and dark brown hair. He was a shorter man than his colleagues, but Amadeus's father always used to say what Bisessar lacked in height, he more than made up for in attitude.

Cardoso do Collor was the Prime Minister of Torgunda, the northern-most civilization on the main supercontinent. Torgunda was composed mostly of jungle and was largely separated from the rest of the mainland by the Severance Sea, a large body of water that nearly cut the continent in half. He was a Canoddan, a jungle-dwelling race. Prime Minister do Collor had a weathered face, copper colored skin, and a hard attitude. Though a strong leader, he was not known for being a very good diplomat, and Eudox Evenstar often complained about the man's stubbornness.

Gawonii Kachada was a Mescalero and the leader of the Redridge Union, consisting of the civilizations in the mountainous area at the center of the supercontinent. The Mescalero Mountains, where the earliest natives on the planet had built their civilizations, stood thousands of feet high. The largest mountain chain in the union was known as Redridge, aptly named for its crimson-tinted rock formed into colorful red, orange, and brown layers by the presence of iron oxide, which gave the mountains their unique look. Prime Minister Kachada kept his dark black hair and beard closely cropped, and he had a barrel chest which always made him look as though he were uncomfortable in whatever clothing he wore. But one look from his bright violet eyes let everyone know he was an intelligent man with little tolerance for games. He and Amadeus's father were often known to butt heads, but of all the World Leaders, he was also the one Eudox seemed to speak the most highly of.

Finally, there was Gordroy Dilmuss, Prime Minister or the Free City Confederacy, an association of sovereign cities along the vast coastlines of the continent. Because the interior of the continent offered mostly jungle, mountains, or desert, the vast majority of civilization resided on the coastline, making the Free City Confederacy the dominant superpower on Redwater, at least in terms of population. Though he was a native of the planet, Dilmuss was descended from Regals, and thus had the fair complexion, blonde hair, and blue eyes common with his race. He was the youngest of the world leaders, but he was also the most consummate politician of the group. Dilmuss was known to be charismatic and a shrewd political maneuverer. Of all the World Leaders, he was the one Amadeus was most worried about.

The men rose to their feet when Amadeus entered the room. Amadeus made his way to the head of the conference table, and once he'd taken his place, the others sat back down. "Gentlemen," Amadeus said, looking at each of the World Leaders in turn. "Thank you for coming today. As I'm sure you are all aware, we have a great deal to discuss…"

"Before we begin, I have something to say…" interrupted Prime Minister Merida, as he got to his feet.

Amadeus eyed Merida with concern, but he did not wish to rebuke the man before he heard him out. "Yes, Prime Minster, what would you like to say?" Amadeus asked.

"Lord Evenstar, everyone here realizes the mega-whale[5] in the room is the revocation of the Evenstar Legacy by the Empire," Merida began. "I just want to tell you that I am personally appalled at how you and your family were treated on Omnicron by Princess Glorianna. To insult your storied Legacy so harshly after the tragedy that befell your mother and our beloved ruler is simply unacceptable. From what I can see, you did nothing wrong in standing up to the Princess regarding the defensive measures your father fought so hard for. If this is how the Empire wishes to treat those who are loyal to them, then I can see no benefit in remaining loyal. Legacy Evenstar has my full support and the full support of the Oceanic Commonwealth. Of that, you have my word."

---

[5] A mega-whale is a species of whale that grow to be the size of islands and can even be seen from space.

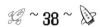

Well, this is off to a good start, Amadeus thought with pleasant surprise. "Thank you, Prime Minister. Your loyalty and support to the Evenstar Legacy is much appreciated."

No sooner had Merida sat back down than Prime Minister Kachada rose up.

"I also have a statement to make," said Kachada. "Lord Evenstar, while your father and I didn't always see eye-to-eye, I nevertheless respected him a great deal. He was a fine man and a good ruler. Though I didn't agree with his aggressive stance on this defensive measure put before the Imperial Government, the idea that Princess Glorianna and Director Casgor can unilaterally overturn a legally passed bill on a whim is quite troublesome to me. That type of behavior denotes a complete disrespect for the rule of law and sets a dangerous precedent in my book. It marginalizes the voice of the individual member worlds and tells me that the Empire is moving in a direction that will take even more power away from the individual systems in favor of centralized governance. Though I admit, the idea of seceding from the Empire is a frightening one, I cannot ignore that a situation in which the Empire takes complete control of our system is even more frightening. Thus, I wish to let it be known that the Evenstar Legacy also has the full support the Redridge Union."

Amadeus smiled. *That's two*, he thought. "That is encouraging to hear, Prime Minister," Amadeus said. "I thank you for your support, as well."

With a nod of acknowledgement, Prime Minister Kachada once again sat back down. Amadeus looked at the three remaining World Leaders, who didn't appear to have anything to say with the same urgency as the previous two.

"I believe, since it is obviously the most pressing issue on all our minds, that we should address the events that occurred on Omnicron and the Imperial Dissolution Decree against my family's Legacy," Amadeus said. "Legacy Evenstar can now say it has the support of two of the World Leaders on this council. Do any more of you wish to declare your support?"

No one answered right away, the three holdouts exchanging glances as if they were waiting to see if someone else would speak first. Finally, Prime Minister Dilmuss leaned forward, placing his elbows on the table and looking Amadeus in the eyes.

"My Lord," he began, "I think it is safe to say that everyone at this table has nothing but the greatest respect for Legacy Evenstar. Your family has been in charge of the Redwater system since Nameer was granted stewardship over it before his rise to Emperor. There can be no doubt in anyone's mind that the declaration to dissolve your Legacy is both shocking and unjust."

"And yet?" Amadeus asked.

Dilmuss frowned. "And yet, the Imperial Dissolution Decree puts this entire system in an awkward situation," he continued. "Redwater is a hyperspace hub. There are trading routes emanating across the galaxy from our system. Our planets are resource rich, and our people are plentiful. This makes us extremely valuable to the Empire…"

"What my esteemed colleague is trying to say…" interjected Prime Minister Cardoso do Collor, "is that we are too valuable to the Empire to lose. If we decide to back your Legacy, we will essentially be declaring war with them."

"Though I understand your concerns, Prime Minister, I can assure you that even Uleeg Casgor is not fool enough to attack this system with Imperial forces," Amadeus responded. "Any bloodshed on his part would overwhelmingly turn public opinion against him."

"There are many types of warfare, my Lord," do Collor replied, "such as attacking our economy, for instance. The first thing the Empire will do is send in the 3rd Quadrant Starkeeper Fleet to blockade our system. They will cut off any and all space travel, halt all trade, and attempt to isolate us from the rest of the galaxy."

"The next thing they'll do is occupy all our colonies and space stations throughout the system," Prime Minister Bisessar chimed in. "Then they'll cut off all Imperial Services. This includes the ultraweb, banking, education, medical services… a host of day-to-day things we take for granted."

"And at that point, all they have left to do is wait us out," said Dilmuss, "because eventually our citizens will start to feel the effects of being without the Empire, and that's when public opinion turns on us."

"Assuming it gets to that point," Amadeus said. "There are things we can do to minimize the impact of a system-wide embargo. And with enough time, we can replace all the services the Empire denies us."

"You are correct, Lord Evenstar," said do Collor. "With enough time we'll be able to make a clean break from the Empire with a minimum amount of discomfort. Unfortunately, time will not be on our side. And short of you surrendering your claim to the system, the only option left to us will be to have our fleet engage the Starkeeper one in hopes of defeating it. And at that point, we will be the aggressors."

"You are all making a flawed assumption here," Amadeus insisted. "You are assuming we'll be alone in this fight. I can assure you, there are many other Legacies out there who wish to declare independence, and they will support us if we lead the way."

"That fact is not lost on us, Lord Evenstar," Dilmuss replied. "Nor will it be lost on Director Casgor. That is why it is even more imperative for him to squash any rebellion we mount as quickly as he can. If he can quell an uprising such as the one you are proposing, he'll make an example of us to try to dissuade other systems from following suit."

"And when my esteemed colleague says 'example,' my Lord, he means it in the worst way possible," do Collor added. "We're talking executions. You. Your sister. Even us for supporting you."

"Not to mention punishments for our people and the system at large," said Bisessar. "Anything he can do to show the universe the consequences of rebelling against the Empire, he'll throw at us. And there will be no escaping it."

"So as you can see, Lord Evenstar," Dilmuss said, "asking us to support you has far-reaching consequences. You're essentially asking us to put our lives, and the lives of our constituents, in your hands. And if that is the case, then we have to ask… how do you plan to win a war against the Empire?"

Amadeus took a deep breath. "I'm sure many people asked Nameer the same question when he decided to wage a war against his brother," he replied. "As recent events have shown, the Empire is not unbeatable. It is weak. It can be defeated."

"The Regalus Empire has stood for ten thousand years, my Lord," Dilmuss responded. "It has defeated every adversary that has been pitted against it. And though the Deathlords have indeed struck it hard, we are not Deathlords. And I hate to say it, my Lord… but you are no Nameer."

"Neither is Casgor a Daemeer[6]," Amadeus argued.

---

[6] Emperor Daemeer was one of the worst tyrants to ever rule the Regalus Empire, and the civil war between he and his brother Nameer, called The Starfall War, was one of the most devastating wars to be waged in history.

"It is not Director Casgor who worries us," do Collor replied. "It is Starkeeper Drucker. He is a capable man, distinguished in the Great Border War[7], and he has far more powerful ships than we do."

"Not to mention men and resources," Bisessar added. "Any war we fight will be against him. And as you know, one does not become a Starkeeper by being easily defeated. Drucker is known for winning countless battles, not only against the Visini, but also against the Deathlords. He is a seasoned and experienced commander. Can you say the same, my Lord?"

Amadeus frowned. "I can say that Legacy Evenstar is ready to meet any challenge the Empire can send our way," he replied.

"If your father were sitting in that chair, I would believe that statement," do Collor said. "But since he isn't, I cannot, in good faith, pledge the support of Torgunda to you."

"Nor can I pledge the support of the Chondos Archipelago," Bisessar added.

"Nor that of the Free City Confederacy," Dilmuss stated.

"Prime Ministers," Amadeus said, "if you would simply allow me to—"

"I'm sorry, my Lord," Dilmuss said as he rose to his feet. "It is our position that you surrender your Legacy and spare your people the hardships of a conflict with the Empire. I know this is not the decision you wished to hear from us, but we feel it is the one that is best for the planet and the system at large. Good day to you."

With that, Prime Minister Dilmuss exited the room, followed by do Collor and Bisessar. Prime Ministers Merida and Kachada offered their condolences before following suit, leaving Amadeus alone in the meeting room. Okotah approached him, his face grim.

"At least we now know how things stand," Okotah stated. "We may not have unanimous support, but we do have allies among the World Leaders. We can begin coordinating our strategy with them and start working to convince the holdouts to join us—"

"No," Amadeus interrupted.

---

[7] The Great Border War was the most recent war between the Regalus and Visini empires, where the Visini spaceforce, led by Harkon the Black, attempted to conquer Regalus occupied planetary systems.

Okotah stopped short. "My Lord?" he inquired.

"You heard what they had to say. They do not respect me, and they do not think we can win a fight with the Empire. I had hoped my family's name would garner more confidence than it appears to have, so it seems I shall now have to resort to a less favorable strategy in order to move forward. It is now clear the clock is ticking, and I do not have the time to play politics. The World Leaders will not act unless I force them to."

"What are you suggesting?"

"Mobilize the Planetary Guard. I want them deployed across the continent, with the heaviest concentrations in the areas belonging to the holdouts. Deport all known Imperial loyalists within our government, especially Ambassador Bob and all his incarnations. Then shut down all Portgate travel and jam all ultrawave signals. Dispatch our fleet around the planet and increase their patrols of our system. I want Redwater on complete lockdown."

Okotah gave Amadeus a troubled look. "My Lord..." he said, "you're talking about declaring martial law."

"Yes, that's precisely what I'm talking about."

"I'd urge you to reconsider this course of action, My Lord," Okotah cautioned. "If you do this, you run the risk of alienating even those World Leaders who support you. Trying to force their hands like this... it could backfire spectacularly."

"It is not the World Leaders whose hands I wish to force. It's the Empire's."

Okotah frowned. "I see," he said. "By mobilizing our forces in this way, you wish to purposely accelerate the arrival of the Starkeeper fleet?"

"Exactly," Amadeus said. "The World Leaders may not stand with us when they think they have a choice. But the minute we are besieged, they will all be forced to back us. I know Casgor is keeping an eye on our actions. As soon as he sees us taking these measures, he'll fear we're gearing up for secession and will send in the Starkeeper fleet to lock down the system. Once that happens, we are all in the same boat."

"It's a risky strategy, My Lord."

"Desperate times, Peytah," Amadeus responded as he rose to his feet. "Now, please carry out my commands."

Okotah hesitated a moment before finally nodding. "As you wish, my Lord," he said before exiting the room.

 ~ **43** ~

When Okotah was gone, Amadeus leaned on the conference desk. It had taken all his willpower not to break down in front of his Chief of Staff. His arms were quivering and he felt sick to his stomach as his nerves ravaged him from the inside. He knew that resorting to his back-up plan of martial law was a desperate move, and it would complicate things moving forward. But he hadn't felt he'd had any other choice. It was a last-ditch effort to save his Legacy that picked a fight with not only the leaders of his own people, but also with the most powerful military in the known universe.

When Amadeus regained control of himself, he took a deep breath and turned to the window of the conference room which overlooked the city, his gaze drifting up to the sky.

"Father..." he said, quietly. "If you're somewhere out there, listening... I sure could do with a miracle right about now."

Kimlee gazed out the window from the backseat of her hovercar, watching the buildings and pedestrians go by the tinted window as the vehicle followed its preprogrammed route to the Evenstar Compound. She was in a foul mood, and seeing ordinary people go about their normal day as though nothing important were happening only served to depress her more.

First, Jack rejects me. Then my brother says I'm a liability, she thought. *Now I must sit on the sidelines as my entire world threatens to come crashing down.*

Kimlee frowned. She felt so helpless. So useless. It was not a feeling she was accustomed to. She'd struggled for years to find an identity outside of being an ill-fated Empress-to-be. As it turns out, the identity she'd adopted now hurt her more than helped her, and for that, she had no one to blame but herself.

I wonder what Jack is up to? she thought. Despite trying not to think of him, the Earthman weighed heavily on her mind. She still had dreams of how he'd saved her from falling out of the Redwater supertower back on Omnicron. It also didn't help that his video confessional regarding the Secret Army was being broadcast on every news channel across the galaxy, ensuring she couldn't even watch the holonet or surf the ultraweb without seeing his face. Though he was on the run from the authorities, somehow that only made him more appealing to Kimlee. She had to admit, she had a thing for the bad-boy types.

If he'd decided to come with me, I probably wouldn't feel as bad as I do, Kimlee thought, bitterly. *I could certainly use a hero to save the day right about now.*

That's when Kimlee's datapad rang. She glanced at its screen. The caller I.D. displayed the same unidentified number that had been calling over the last few weeks and not leaving messages. Kimlee never answered numbers she didn't recognize – mostly because they were usually crazy fans or stalkers. But for some reason, at this point, she was desperate for any type of distraction that would take her mind off her current malaise.

Kimlee hit the receiver button on the datapad's screen, and it immediately broadcast the holographic image of a man's head above it. It wasn't a face Kimlee recognized. It was that of a Regal, with unruly blonde hair and high cheekbones. He was a handsome man, whoever he was. Handsome enough to get her attention, anyway.

"Greetings, Lady Evenstar," the man said.

"And who might you be?" Kimlee asked.

"I'm the man who's going to help you save your Legacy," he replied.

Kimlee raised an eyebrow. "Is that so?" she said, with more than a hint of skepticism.

"I realize the common perception is that you are not to be taken seriously," the man said. "You may even believe that yourself. But I'm here to tell you that you and your brother have more support than you know. Especially you."

Despite her better judgement, Kimlee wanted to believe the man's encouraging words. "Though I do so fancy accepting the word of strange men who call me out of nowhere, why should I believe anything you tell me?"

"Because, I'm sorry to say, you don't have much of a choice," the man replied. "I fear your brother's meeting with the World Leaders did not go very well."

Kimlee frowned. "How would you know that?"

"I know a great many things, Lady Evenstar," the man replied. "And many of them are vital to your Legacy's continued survival. I'd be happy to share some of this information with you, if you would be willing to meet with me."

"Uh-huh," said Kimlee. "And how do I know you're not some creep who has tracked down my private line and just wants my autograph?"

The man smiled at that. "I don't blame you for not trusting me. It's a wise instinct. But time grows short, and you're going to have to weigh the risk versus

the reward of meeting with me. The risk is that if the Starkeeper fleet arrives before we make contact, then there will be little I can do to help you."

"And the reward?"

"The reward is a worthwhile one, my Lady," the man said with a devilish smile. "It will be your very own Empire."

Kimlee mulled over the man's words for a moment. She knew it was crazy to believe anything he was telling her, but something in her gut sensed an opportunity. She narrowed her eyes and gazed at the man's holographic image.

"Where would you like to meet?" she asked.

CHAPTER ✺ 5

Heckubus gazed at the viewscreen on the Earthship's bridge. The swirling mists of the molecular cloud of Bacardi 8 danced before him, thick as fog. The sensor readings at the console in front of the robot showed that the Imperial ships were still searching, but with all the non-essential Earthship systems powered down, they were well hidden from their pursuers for the moment.

Heckubus glanced over at Professor Green, who had been tirelessly combing through each section of the bridge's electronics, searching for the tracking device to which Phineas Alabaster had alluded. The monk was back to meditating over the Princess, and the others were elsewhere, taking the slight reprieve from constantly fighting off their pursuers to get some rest. Being the machine he was, Heckubus didn't need rest. The only thing he felt he needed at that point was sweet, sweet revenge. However, much to his frustration, a plan to enact such a thing eluded him.

"Call me an amateur, will he?" grumbled Heckubus as he tried to occupy himself by using the Earthship's systems to run construction models on various doomsday weapons of his own diabolical design. "Thinks he's sooooo evil. He's not all that evil. Me. I'm evil…"

"Did you say something?" asked Green as he slid out from one of the access panels into which he'd been burrowed.

"I said I'm evil!" Heckubus snapped.

"Oh!" replied Green. "Okay…"

"You think I'm evil, don't you?"

"Sure," Green responded. "I mean… I don't know many evil people, but out of all of them, you're certainly up there."

"Would you say I'm more evil than Verrutus?"

Green frowned. "Oh, dear," he said. "That's… um… ah…"

Heckubus scowled at the Professor. "Don't answer that."

Green breathed a sigh of relief. "Oh, good," he said. "But if it makes you feel any better, I have no doubt we'll figure out a way to defeat our Deathlord adversary eventually. And when we do, it won't matter who's more evil, because good always triumphs in the end."

"Pah!" replied Heckubus with a dismissive wave of his hand. "Spare me your simplistic and inane morality propaganda. Good will never triumph over evil, because good is dumb. The only way to defeat a monster is to out-monster it."

"You mean… however evil Verrutus may be, we must become even more evil to destroy him?"

"Yes!" cried Heckubus. "Excellent idea! Challenge, accepted."

"But that wasn't…"

"I have become far too complacent in my evilness over the years," proclaimed Heckubus as he turned back to his console with renewed vigor. "It is time for me to take my dastardly skills to the next level! I shall have to reinvent myself to become the ULTIMATE evil in the universe! Only then will I have the power to destroy Verrutus and all who stand against me!"

"I don't think being more evil is going to—"

"Don't think. It's not your strong suit," interrupted Heckubus. "Go back to looking for that blasted tracker. I shall be busy formulating a strategy on how to become far more villainous than I currently am."

Professor Green shrugged. "Very well. Good luck leveling up your evil," he replied, before sliding back into the access panel.

"I could kill a bunch of people…" Heckubus muttered as he ran strategy models through his processors. "But that's too easy. Any idiot can kill someone. Maybe I should work on enslaving large portions of the universe? But then I'd be accused of copying Verrutus. Drat. That's no good. I suppose I could kill Verrutus, but considering I know nothing about him makes that rather difficult. Maybe if there were a way to outsmart him, gloat about doing so, and *then* kill him, that would be sufficiently evil? Yes, that is certainly the preferable strategy. The real question now is… how does one kill a Deathlord?"

"Ah! Found it!" said Green, re-emerging from the access panel with a small control board computer chip between his fingers. He squinted at the chip, examining it with a mixture of fascination and consternation. "My, my, my… Virtuoso disguised it as a simple processing component, knowing no one would ever suspect something so small as being able to transmit a subspace message. If I weren't so familiar with the Earthship's systems, there's no doubt I'd have overlooked it."

Green sighed as he sat up, turning the chip around in his hand. Heckubus approached and took a moment to analyze the chip, as well.

"Yes, yes, this is a sufficiently ingenious little device," Heckubus commented. "From what I can tell, it's specifically designed to use the Earthship's own systems to power the transmission of small packets of data into a secure subspace channel. Typically, a subspace communicator requires more hardware, but since it's only intended to transmit coordinate data, Herr Virtuoso could keep it rather small and virtually undetectable."

"Indeed," said Green. "It's so ingenious I'm tempted to keep it so that I could study it further. But, I fear when it comes to Armonto Virtuoso, it is better to be safe than sorry."

Green placed the chip on the ground and promptly smashed it with the butt of his tool, breaking the small device into pieces.

"Agreed," Heckubus said as he returned to his workstation. "Herr Virtuoso is indeed a formidable adversary. We would do well not to underestimate him."

Green frowned as he got to his feet. "I feel so foolish," he said. "I should have known Virtuoso would have a contingency plan in place for tracking the Earthship should it be removed from his possession. Yet, I did not think to account for this. Why is it every time I think I've beaten him, he somehow manages to come out a step ahead of me?"

"Isn't it obvious?" replied Heckubus. "He's your nemesis!"

Green blinked at the robot. "My what?" the Professor asked.

"Your nemesis!" repeated Heckubus. "Your ultimate adversary! Your arch-foe! Your everlasting rival!"

"He is?"

Heckubus sighed with exasperation. "He is doing everything in his power to prevent you from achieving your goals, matching you step-for-step in a battle of wits in which the two of you are destined to counter the actions of the other until one of you ultimately emerges victorious. What else would you call him?"

"Oh, my," Green said, stroking the bristly white hair of the beard on his chin thoughtfully. "I suppose you're right. I've never had a nemesis before. What should I do?"

"What you do with all nemeses," Heckubus replied. "Defeat them."

"And how should I do that?"

"Why are you asking me? He's not *my* nemesis."

"Yes, but… you're usually so good at coming up with plans to trump our rivals. Perhaps you could give me some advice?"

"Very well," said Heckubus. "First chance you get, kill him."

Green's eyes went wide. "Oh dear, oh dear, oh dear," he muttered. "I don't know if I could do that. I'm rather reluctant to kill anything! Not to mention, I'm terribly bad at it. Perhaps I could simply bring him to justice?"

"Why ask for my advice if you aren't going to use it?" replied the robot, testily. "Do what you wish. It is no concern of mine. At the moment, I have larger aquatic vertebrates to fry. We may have eliminated the technological threat tracking us, but we still have the elusive mystical threat looming over our proverbial heads. And despite how formidable an adversary Armonto Virtuoso is, I fear Verrutus is even more so. If the monk is to be believed, there's something that ties all the slythru infected beings in the universe together, and Verrutus uses those connections to keep track of them on an almost god-like scale. The question is, how does he do it? And furthermore, how do we prevent him from doing it?"

"It's just so hard to conceive, isn't it?" mused Green. "That one being has the ability to process so much information?"

"It's not that hard," muttered Heckubus. "I can process a great deal of information."

"Yes, but you're a machine, no offense," Green said. "By all accounts, Verrutus is not. I mean… what kind of living being has the capability to see, hear, and comprehend the information from billions of people without going mad?"

Suddenly, the gears in Heckubus's head began to whir furiously. He stopped his typing at his workstation and turned to look at Green, his large ocular orbs dilating, as though he'd just stumbled onto an important realization. "Yes… what kind of being indeed…" Heckubus said before turning to leave.

"Heckubus?" Green said as he watched the robot head toward the exit to the bridge. "Where are you going?"

"To formulate a plan," Heckubus replied.

"What kind of plan?"

"An evil one. Duh."

"I see. Can I help?"

Heckubus stopped at the door and glanced back at Green. "You've already helped more than you know, Professor," he replied before taking his leave.

When he was alone, Green looked down at the remains of Armonto Virtuoso's tracking device and frowned. "Perhaps I should think of a way to be even more helpful…" the Professor contemplated.

Jack couldn't sleep, so he did what he would usually do when he wasn't able to slumber. He watched TV.

One of the rooms Jack had the Earthship manifest during the long voyage to Omnicron after the events on the Ghost Planet was an entertainment room. It was a simple cabin, filled with comfy chairs that reclined, low light, a popcorn machine, and a big screen upon which to view various movies and TV shows.

Much to Jack's delight (and relief), it appeared that the Earthship had somehow recorded every single broadcast ever produced on Earth while it had slumbered in the Ancient Temple in the planet's core. This meant any movie or TV show Jack could possibly want to see was available to him, from the earliest silent films, to the episodes of Jack's favorite shows that premiered just before the Earth was unceremoniously blown up by aliens.

The Earthship had recorded programs from all over the Earth, not just from the United States, so Jack had the option of surfing through some rather strange programming from many other countries. And thanks to the data dump he received when he accessed the Earth's Ancient Temple, Jack now had the ability to understand any language in the universe, and had no problem watching any program from his home planet.

As Jack flipped through the different broadcasts on the screen in the room, he passed by a Bollywood music video, a Spanish-language telenovela, and an Italian superhero film before eventually settling on what appeared to be a Japanese talk show from the 1980s. The scrawl on the right side of the screen mentioning something about the *Nova Commander* video game series was what caught Jack's attention. A female host was interviewing an older Japanese man who was adorned with an unflattering bowl cut hairdo and thick coke-bottle glasses. The text beside the man's image read: Iwatani Nishikudo, creator of *Nova Commander*.

"Nishikudo-san," the female interviewer began, "your latest video game creation, *Nova Commander IV*, has been praised as the most revolutionary video game of its time. Already, its popularity has skyrocketed worldwide. Tell us, what was your inspiration for such an amazing creation?"

For some reason, Iwatani Nishikudo looked uncomfortable upon hearing the question. "As you know, I felt great shame and disappointment over the failure of *Nova Commander III*," he said. "I had become so focused on pushing the boundaries of how video games could look, that I forgot games were meant to be fun. One day, I was in a park feeding the birds, thinking about where I went wrong, when a stranger approached me…"

"A stranger?" the female interviewer asked.

"Yes. An American, in fact," Nishikudo continued. "He was a great fan of the *Nova Commander* video games and happened to speak Japanese, so we had a nice chat. He had a great many suggestions on how to improve the game, and that led to the idea of placing the player in the cockpit of the starcraft, to make it feel as though the player were actually flying the ship."

"Incredible!" the interviewer responded. "So the idea of making *Nova Commander IV* a realistic 3D flight simulator came from an American?"

"Well, there were other factors that led to that decision, but yes, the American was the catalyst for it," Nishikudo answered.

"Fascinating. Did you ever get in touch with this American again to thank him for his contribution?"

"Unfortunately, I have been unable to do so," Nishikudo said. "But if he is watching, I would like to take this opportunity to thank him for the insight he gave me. I can honestly say that without him, *Nova Commander IV* would have never existed."

"And what is next for you? Are you working on a new video game for the world to enjoy?"

"I fear I may never again create something as important as *Nova Commander IV*," Nishikudo replied. "Thus, I have decided to retire from video games and pursue other passions of mine."

"Though I'm sure all your fans are sorry to hear of your retirement, what other passions will you be pursuing?"

"Well, I've decided to try my hand at writing a book," Nishikudo said, with a sheepish smile. "It is about a man who gets teleported to a space ship in a far-

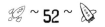

off galaxy and plays an important part in an adventure concerning an intergalactic war."

"How exciting! Do you have a name for this book?"

"Right now I am calling it: Space Adventure Danger Time – Call of the Turtle Man."

The female reporter raised an eyebrow. "That… sounds fantastic!" she said, not really sounding as though she meant it.

"Thank you," replied Nishikudo, not picking up on the interviewer's trepidation. "It is a tale that is very near and dear to my heart. I look forward to sharing it with the world."

"And I am sure some will look forward to reading it," replied the interviewer diplomatically before turning to the camera. "Stay tuned for our weekly game of 'Candy or not Candy,' in which contestants can earn big prizes by guessing if what they're eating is chocolate… or something else!"

The camera zoomed out as the interviewer bowed to Iwatani Nishikudo, thanking him for joining her and then cut to a commercial in which actor Arnold Schwarzenegger was eating a steaming cup of noodles before flexing his muscles, lifting a car over his head, and walking away.

That was weird, thought Jack as he changed the channel. *I must have played thousands of hours of Nova Commander IV, but I never knew anything about the guy who actually invented it. Guess I owe him a lot, considering it was that game which prepared me for flying my own space ship. Who knew?*

Jack had settled on some strange B-movie in which a teenager intimidated a crotchety liquor store owner into selling him a keg of beer and some powdered donuts by making his eyes glow red; then the teen's best friend got on top of their van and surfed to music by the Beach Boys, all the way to a house party. Jack was just about to doze off when the door to the room opened and Professor Green stuck his head in.

"Ah! Jack, my boy! There you are!" said Professor Green as he made his way down to the chair next to the one Jack was in. Green then eyed the movie playing out on the screen with curiosity. "I say… what's this you're watching?"

"I think it's a movie about a teen who becomes a wolf…" Jack said, trying to shrug off his sleepiness. "I'm not really sure what it's called."

"Interesting," commented Green. "I must say, Earthlings sure had curious tastes in entertainment. Your planet's obsession with pubescent heroes was

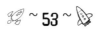

particularly odd, considering how unrealistic it is to expect ones so young to be able to—"

"Do you have something important to talk to me about, Professor?" Jack asked.

"Ah! Yes! Indeed, I do…" replied Green, as though he'd just remembered why he'd visited Jack in the first place. "You'll be pleased to know that I successfully uncovered the tracking device Armonto Virtuoso had installed on the Earthship. I'm happy to say the Empire will no longer have as easy a time discovering our whereabouts."

"That's great to hear, Professor," Jack said with a yawn.

"Actually, as it just so happens, I've also stumbled on to something very important that I wish to discuss with you," Green continued. "While I was mapping out the Earthship's systems to try to track down Virtuoso's bug, I discovered a series of subroutines which I believe play an important role in the ship's ability to recognize who may or may not operate it."

Jack gave Green a curious look. "Um… huh?" Jack asked.

"Well, since we first discovered the Earthship, it was clear that only people from your planet were meant to operate it," Green explained. "But we never really knew how exactly that worked. Obviously you have a psychic connection to the vessel, but beyond that, there was the fact that the ship wouldn't allow itself to be piloted by anyone other than you. What I found when I happened upon these subroutines was a method by which the ship recognizes a radiation signature unique to Earth and those who lived on it."

"Radiation signature?"

"Yes, you see, there are these things known as 'biosignatures,' which are essentially any substance – such as an element, isotope, or molecule – that provides scientific evidence of past or present life. These signatures can be used to determine if a particular form of life is present, or has ever been present, at a certain location. Though it's hard to imagine, the Earth and the sun it revolved around, had its own unique radiation signature, which those who inhabited your planet absorbed and, in turn, emitted."

"Professor… are you saying I'm radioactive?"

"In a sense, yes," Green replied. "I mean, we all are! To a certain extent. But the radiation I emit is different from yours, because I grew up on a different planet, orbiting a different sun. In fact, every species would have a biosignature unique to it because of the different environments in which they evolved. What

I was able to determine from looking deeper into these subroutines on the ship is that your unique radiation signature is the key which informs the Earthship to accept your commands."

"Okay," said Jack. "So, I emit radiation, and the Earthship senses *that* radiation and knows it's okay for me to fly it?"

"Precisely!"

"Cool," said Jack, not really sure why that was so important to explain to him. "Glad we figured that out."

"Yes, but don't you see, Jack?" prodded Green. "I was on Earth for almost two years!"

"So?"

"So? The fact that I was on your planet for such an extended period of time means that I, too, contain Earth's radiation signature! Albeit, a much fainter one than you possess. I've already run the tests, and it would appear I was on your planet long enough to absorb enough of its unique radiation to register with the Earthship's detection systems."

"Well, if that's the case, why can't you already fly the ship?" asked Jack.

"Because the radiation signature I possess is far too faint, I'm afraid," Green said with a hint of disappointment. "I imagine there's a threshold within the ship's detection systems to help it determine who is a native Earthling and who is not. But the good news is, now that I've identified the subroutines responsible for measuring these biosignatures, I can make adjustments to have it recognize fainter radiation signals."

Jack frowned. "You mean, you can make it so that anyone can fly my ship?"

"No, no, no, that's not what I'm saying at all. The subroutines are ingrained into the ship's operating systems. I could never get rid of them fully even if I wanted to. What I'm suggesting is making them more sensitive to the Earth's radiation signature so that I may be able to operate aspects of the Earthship without needing your assistance."

"So… you could make it so that you could fly the ship, too?"

"Exactly!" cheered Green. "And seeing as how you, the Princess, and I are the only ones in the universe who spent any substantial time on your planet before it was destroyed, that would limit the ability to control your ship only to us."

"Yeah, but Anna is possessed by a Deathlord," Jack said. "Wouldn't her being able to control the ship be a bad thing?"

"Hmmmmm… I hadn't considered that," Green mumbled. "However, the Princess was on Earth for less time than I was, which means her radiation signature would be far fainter than mine. I could set the threshold for the ship's detection systems just below my radiation signature to ensure the Princess wouldn't be able to operate it."

Jack was quiet for a long moment as he considered Professor Green's proposal.

"Of course, if you don't trust me, you do not have to agree to this idea," Green added, sounding as though he understood Jack's hesitation. "I simply wanted a way to make myself more helpful around here. I'm not much of a fighter, nor do I possess mystical abilities, and I fear I don't have the intellectual capacity our mechanical friends do. I simply figured that if I could be a better custodian to the Earthship, then I could contribute more to our current and future predicaments. But if you don't want to do this, I will not be offended."

"It's not that I don't trust you, Professor," Jack said. "It's just… the idea that I'm the only one who can operate this ship makes me feel… I don't know… special, I guess."

"I understand," Green replied. "But doing this would not create a psychic bond with the ship, such as you possess. It would simply allow for someone other than you to maneuver it and issue commands to its systems. I'll be the first to admit I am not much of a space pilot, but surely, having someone who can operate the Earthship as a back-up if you are not available is a wise choice?"

"Well, it certainly would have helped on Omnicron," Jack admitted.

"Indeed, it would have," Green acknowledged. "So… what do you say? Would you help me raise the sensitivity on the detection systems to allow me to help you operate the ship?"

Jack smiled at the Professor and nodded his head. "Yeah. Let's do it," he said. "We're probably going to need that type of help very soon."

"Oh?" inquired Green. "And why is that?"

"Because," said Jack, "I've decided we're going to take Mourdock up on his offer to meet. But I can't for the life of me shake the idea that it's some type of trap."

CHAPTER ✦ 6

"**O**f course it's a trap," said Scallywag.

"Soooo obviously a trap," agreed Heckubus.

"Trap," grunted Grohm.

Jack frowned at his companions as they all sat in the galley eating breakfast. "I didn't say I thought it was a trap," Jack argued. "I said I had the feeling that it *might* be a trap. I know Mourdock pretty well. I don't think he'd betray us, but... I just feel uneasy about the meeting. That's all."

"It don't matter if yer good buddy is on the up-and-up, lad," said Scallywag as he took a bite of bacon. "Tha trap don't have ta come from him. It could be from tha Imperials. From Virtuoso. From a bounty hunter... from any number o' possibilities."

"Indeed," said Heckubus. "There are far too many variables against us not to expect something to go wrong with this suggested parlay."

"But what's the alternative?" asked Jack. "We just keep hiding out? Jumping all over the universe and hoping no one catches us? And even if we do that, how long will it be before that slythru takes full control over Anna and we can't ever get her back? With Mourdock's help, we might actually have a chance. But if we keep running, Verrutus will eventually win! It'll just take him a bit longer, is all."

"Jack is correct," said Shanks. "If the last few weeks have proven anything, it is that our current strategy is doomed to failure. But with the assistance of both Chief Alabaster and the Emperor Ascendant, we may very well find the support we need to save the Princess. I believe this meeting to be worth the risk."

"As do I," chimed in Green. "Jack's instincts have gotten us this far. And I believe if we all work together, we've proven that we can overcome any obstacle. If this is indeed a trap, then let us prepare for the worst but hope for the best!"

"What a refreshingly optimistic outlook!" said Dan. "I, too, am in favor of meeting with Mourdock Skyborn, if not for the simple reason that—"

"No one cares," interrupted Heckubus. "What I do care about is defeating that insufferable Deathlord, Verrutus! Allowing him ultimate victory is simply not an option. We must crush him beneath our heels! Ruthlessly! Mercilessly! And be able to gloat about it before we do! Though it is painfully obvious we will be walking into a trap if we meet with Skyborn, the rewards of doing so may outweigh the risks. Therefore, I am in favor of this ridiculously stupid course of action."

"Grohm?" asked Jack. "What do you think?"

Grohm grunted.

"That's a 'yes'," Jack said, before looking at Scallywag. "It's down to you, Scally."

Scallywag sighed. "Well, we survived tha three traps of the Ancients at the bloody Sunshell. Whatever Skyborn could throw at us couldn't be any worse than that."

"Great!" said Jack. "So it's decided. We're going to meet with Mourdock."

"Hold on just a second there, lad," said Scallywag. "If we're gonna do this, we're gonna be smart about it fer once. No jumpin' in, fingers crossed, flyin' by the seat o' our pants on luck and a prayer. I want a plan – a *good* plan. One which ensures that none of us gets caught or killed or separated. Savvy?"

"Savvy," said Jack. "Heckubus, think of a—"

"What part of 'I want a *good* plan' was unclear, eh?" snapped Scallywag. "Don't think I haven't forgotten the rust-bucket swearin' revenge on me fer usin' him as a shield while fightin' tha bloody Royal Vanguard."

"C'mon, dude," replied Jack. "We're a team! Heckubus would never take advantage of a dangerous situation just to exact some petty revenge over a lame grudge. Right, Heckubus?"

Heckubus twiddled his fingers.

"*Right*, Heckubus?" Jack urged.

Heckubus continued twiddling his fingers.

Jack sighed. "Okay, then," he muttered. "In that case, I guess we should all collaborate on the plan. Who has ideas?"

"Well, the logical place to start would be with where to meet," said Green. "A location that would minimize the chances of us walking into a trap would be preferable, would it not?"

"Sounds like a good place to start," said Jack. "So where should we meet Mourdock?"

"My vote is we meet him at Somewhere," said Scallywag.

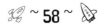

"Well, obviously we'll have to meet him somewhere," said Jack. "The question is, where?"

"Oy, not 'meet him somewhere'. Meet him *at* Somewhere. I'm talkin' about Port Somewhere."

"What the heck is that?" Jack asked.

"It's a shadow port I've been to a few times," replied Scallywag. "It's a bit off tha grid, but it's far from Imperial space, and chances are yer buddy Mourdock will be unfamiliar enough with it so he can't set a trap fer us if'n we meet there."

"Hmmmm, I too have visited Port Somewhere on occasion," Heckubus added. "I would agree. Such a location would indeed suit our purposes."

"Yeah, okay," said Jack, tepidly. "But what's a shadow port?"

"It's just what we call an unsanctioned space station," Scallywag explained. "Most space platforms are built and regulated by governments, but occasionally ya get private entities that build a station fer their own uses. Because they ain't sanctioned by the territory where they're built, the governments don't usually know about 'em. Most shadow ports are run by criminal organizations that offer pirates and smugglers a place ta trade their ill-gotten goods."

"Whoa," said Jack. "So this Port Somewhere is filled with pirates and smugglers?"

"Not ta mention mercenaries, hit men, thugs, gangsters, and a roster of other right proper outlaws," Scallywag added.

"Cooool," said Jack. "Sounds like a real wretched hive of scum and villainy."

Scallywag raised an eyebrow. "What?" he muttered. "I have no bloody clue as to what ya just said."

"Nor, I," chimed in Heckubus. "Honestly, Earthman, where did you learn to speak?"

"I'm just saying it sounds like a bad place!" replied Jack, defensively.

"Oy, as far as shadow stations go, it ain't so bad," said Scallywag.

"Except for all the murders," Heckubus amended.

"Yeah, there are a lot o' murders, that's fer sure," Scallywag said. "Aside from that, it's a decent enough place. Got some pretty good food there, too, if memory serves."

"Yes, I've heard this," Heckubus said. "Supposedly the station utilizes black market organic consumables rather than the typical replicated swill you'd find on other space platforms. If I actually ate, I'd be *dying* to try some."

"Um… I'm sorry… can we get back to the murders?" asked Green, nervously.

"Do not fret too much, Professor," Heckubus replied. "Port Somewhere actually has fewer murders than your average shadow station."

"Well, that's a bit of a relief!" Green said.

"You are far more likely to be horribly maimed or seriously wounded than actually *murdered*," Heckubus continued.

Green's eyes went wide at that.

"Again, why are we wanting to meet Mourdock there?" Jack asked.

"Aside from all the murderin' and maimin', it's actually a right proper place ta meet with someone. Especially someone ya don't trust all that much," replied Scallywag. "Port Somewhere is in unpatrolled Visini space, which means we won't have ta dance with no Regalus warships out there, lest the Empire wants ta declare war on the Visinis. It's big enough fer us ta blend inta the station's traffic, and easy ta ditch trouble if there's any ta be had."

"Might I inquire as to the wisdom of meeting at a place filled with outlaws and mercenaries as opposed to a more secluded location?" asked Shanks. "Being amongst so many unscrupulous individuals with such a high price on our heads seems to be a questionable decision to me."

"Of course it does. Yer a monk, not an outlaw," replied Scallywag. "Yer prolly used ta trustin' people. But any space jockey worth his salt would tell ya, secluded locations tend ta be bad places ta meet people. 'Specially those ya don't trust."

"And why is that?"

"Because, it's easier ta set up ambushes at secluded locations," Scallywag explained. "Shadow ports monitor the surroundin' space, so they'll see ships comin' long before they arrive. In a secluded area, ya can have any number o' ships hidden in hyperspace, a few minutes lightspeed jump away. And dependin' on how long it takes ta travel there, they could have plenty o' time to set such an ambush up."

"Not to mention Armonto Virtuoso's predictive simulations," Heckubus added. "No doubt they've taken into account various out-of-the-way places we'd

~ **60** ~

think to meet. By going to a shadow port, we are doing something more unexpected, and thus, less likely to be predicted."

Shanks frowned but nodded in acquiescence. "I shall defer to both of your... substantial experiences in matters such as these, then," he said. "But what about bounty hunters? Surely, they will be among the station's patrons."

"There may be a few, but there be enough pirates and smugglers on tha station ta keep tha bounty hunters at bay. Most outlaws don't take too kindly ta bounty hunters, since outlaws usually be the ones who have the bounties on 'em. Means we'd just have ta worry 'bout regular run-o-the-mill scumbags as opposed ta highly trained ones."

"Even if the Imperial fleet cannot legally enter this area, what is to keep the Visini from sending ships?" asked Green. "Are we not just as big a target for them as we are for the Empire?"

"Port Somewhere's got so many hyperspace probes scanning fer Visini ships, the whole station will know they're comin' long before they ever arrive," assured Scallywag. "Shadow ports will sound tha evacuation alarm tha instant they see military ships comin', givin' those on the station plenty o' time ta make a hasty getaway if needed."

"But if these shadow ports scan all the ships coming their way, won't we be recognized the second we get within range of the station?" asked Jack. "The Earthship doesn't exactly blend in, know what I mean?"

"Don't fret it, lad," Scallywag said. "The Earthship will never even get close enough to tha station ta be recognized."

"Then... how will we get there to meet with Mourdock?"

"We bring the Earthship in on one of the hyperspace smuggling lanes leadin' to tha station, but exit out o' it early," Scallywag explained. "We travel to tha station the rest o' the way in normal space, keepin' tha ship just on the outskirts of its teleportation range, far enough away so as not ta be spotted. We teleport onto the station and meet with Skyborn, and if anythin' should go sideways, we teleport right off and jump someplace far, far away before entering hyperspace. We'll high-tail it somewhere else ta keep ahead o' Virtuoso's little tracking probes and Verrutus's magic spider web. How's that fer a bloody plan, eh?"

Jack nodded. "Sounds legit," he replied.

"Indeed, it is a surprisingly adequate plan for one so mentally inferior," Heckubus stated. "I shall have the ship manifest us some Imperial-grade

 ~ 61 ~

hologuise generators for the occasion. If we do this right, no one will ever know the Earthship, or we, were ever there."

"We should not leave the Princess unattended during this endeavor," Shanks said. "If something should go wrong, there needs to be someone by her side to continue finding a way to save her."

"Good idea," said Jack. "Shanks, you stay on the Earthship and guard Anna. Professor, you can stay here, too, just in case we need someone who can operate the ship while I'm away. And Dan…"

"Yes, Master Jack?" said Dan, perking up.

"You can just… like… chill out here, I guess."

"Oh, yes, sir!" exclaimed Dan. "Thank you so much for assigning me a task with which to contribute to this mission! I promise you, I will ensure the temperature regulators on this ship will be set to be far more frigid than they currently are by the time you and the others return."

"Um… okay…" replied Jack. "But before you do that, let's send a message to Alabaster to have him set up the meeting with Mourdock."

"Right away, sir!" answered Dan.

As the group dispersed, Jack noticed Scallywag looked troubled.

"You okay, Scally?" Jack asked.

"Yeah," the pirate replied. "Just not used ta havin' a good plan fer a change."

"Well then, why do you look so worried?"

Scallywag was quiet for a moment. "Can't help but wonder," he finally answered, "if our terrible plans always work… how are our good ones gonna play out?"

CHAPTER 7

At the far edge of the galaxy, where one of its spiral arms ends and nothing but deep space looms beyond, is an ancient planet orbiting the glowing cinder of a dead sun.

This is the planet Maxima.

It is a solitary planet orbiting a white dwarf star with a massive disk of protoplanetary debris surrounding it and stretching to the very edge of its system.

Maxima is the most unlikely of planets. Stellar evolution typically rules out habitable worlds around white dwarf stars because stars that enter their red giant phase tend to destroy their inner planets en route to becoming a white dwarf. But in extremely rare circumstances, as is the case here, planetary bodies are able to survive such an event. Maxima, it turns out, is the remnant of a single gas giant, its core having survived its star's expansion into a red giant. And somehow, against all odds, this surviving core of a destroyed planet ends up being roughly the same size as the star which it now circles, and falls into an orbit of approximately 0.01 AU around it. This just so happens to be the same distance as the star's habitable zone in which liquid water is able to exist.

That's not to say everything is hunky-dory for this little planet. Though things are rather rosy for life on it now, it will eventually spiral too close to the white dwarf it orbits, burning away its atmosphere, charring its surface, and eventually being consumed as it crashes into the star, all in the relatively short time span of approximately three billion years.

But until that time comes, it is, by all accounts, a rather pleasant place to live.

Slightly less pleasant places to live are the numerous outposts and colonies within the system. Though the planet of Maxima enjoys a rather clean oasis free from clutter at the center of the system, dust, asteroids, and planetoids of varying sizes and shapes fill the rest of its stellar territory. This gives Maxima's inhabitants ample opportunities for space-based expansion, but none of them is very friendly.

Indeed, aside from the planet of Maxima, there is not a single other stellar body in the system that can support water, vegetation, or indigenous life of any kind. Thus, all of Maxima's satellite settlements are man-made, built into large asteroids or planetoids, or are stand-alone space stations. The most common types of settlements in Maxima are mining colonies, which are meant to take advantage of the resources and mineral-rich nature of the debris field that comprises the bulk of the system.

It was to one of these mining colonies, dubbed Altimac 7, that the Skyborn flagship *Shieldbearer* was currently headed.

The Shieldbearer is a Legacy capital ship and the pride of the Maxima fleet. In fact, it is one of the most state-of-the-art space vessels in all of the Regalus Empire. Gebhard Skyborn had spared no expense in its construction, even going so far as to reinforce its hull with a layer of ultanium, which also makes it one of the most expensive ships in all of the Regalus Empire.

The *Shieldbearer* had been designed by Paragon engineers to specifically protect the Maxima system from a Deathlord attack; thus, the reason for its name. However, from the time it had entered service, it had done little but chauffeur Gebhard Skyborn around the system, playing catch-up with the Deathlords' hit-and-run strikes and seeing no combat whatsoever. Thus, it was little wonder that those within the Maxima fleet began to joke that *The Shieldbearer* was the safest ship in the entire system on which to be stationed – and not because it was such a formidable craft.

Though *The Shieldbearer* is, for all intents and purposes, a combat vessel, one would not know it from being inside the ship. In addition to having strong armor and heavy ordinance, *The Shieldbearer* was also designed to be quite cozy since the head of the system's Legacy would most likely inhabit it for long periods of time. The vessel's interior actually had more in common with a luxury starliner than with a military-grade capital ship, a fact that was not lost on Wilvelm Blackfyre as he traversed the corridors of the starcraft.

This is so much nicer than Mourdock's ship, Wilvelm thought as he made his way down the friendly and well-lit hallway toward the crew quarters. *I feel like I'm on vacation instead of on assignment.*

It had seemed like both Wilvelm and his best friend Fredreek Goldstone would be leaving the comforts of Omnicron to once again engage in the tedious task of defending the Maxima system from Deathlord raids. Mourdock's ship, on which they had served, was a medium-sized corvette-class vessel designed for speed and combat over comfort. Once Mourdock had left his command in order to chase after the Earthman and the Princess, both Wil and Fred had transferred over to the elder Skyborn to serve under him. Much to Wil and Fred's delight, Gebhard Skyborn seemed to enjoy luxury as much as they did.

Wilvelm didn't bother to knock or ring the bell to Fredreek's quarters. Their relationship was such that they had no issue simply entering one another's rooms unannounced. Normally, Fredreek would be doing little other than sleeping, drinking, or chatting with some girl on his datapad. But today, rather than an attractive woman's holographic image being projected by Fredreek's communicator, it was the stern and humorless image of his father, Urion Goldstone.

"Three hundred thousand digicredits," Urion said, dourly. "That's how much the lawyers settled for. Three. Hundred. Thousand."

Fredreek shrugged, leaning back in his chair despondently under his father's holographic gaze. "Whatever. Take it out of my trust fund if you want," Fredreek said.

Urion shook his head. "I had thought that being in a war zone would prevent this type of nonsense. Yet, somehow, you've figured out how to continue embarrassing our Legacy even from the farthest reaches of space."

"And to think you always say I never excel at anything," Fredreek quipped.

Urion sighed in displeasure. "Blast it, Fred. When are you going to grow up? Here you are, positioned at the right hand of the Emperor Ascendant, facing the greatest crisis the Empire has ever known, and you still haven't risen to the occasion. This is your chance to distinguish yourself and bring honor to our Legacy. Instead, you squander it with your partying and obsession with every pretty girl who crosses your path."

"In my defense, the girls don't always have to be pretty," Fredreek replied. "That's entirely dependent upon how much I've been partying."

"Yes, keep making a joke of this," Urion said. "Heaven forbid you should take this seriously and make me proud for once."

Fredreek sighed. "I'm trying my best, father. But Mourdock's off chasing the Earthman and all that's left to do around here is to hop from settlement to settlement cleaning up the mess the Deathlords have left behind. It's not exactly glamorous, and quite frankly, it's extremely boring."

"Then I would suggest you find a way to make yourself more useful instead of getting into trouble," Urion said. "I shall speak with Lord Skyborn about finding ways to utilize you more. But barring that, take some blasted initiative. You may be young, but you are still the heir to a Legacy. That gives you a great deal of influence and command, even in the Rim. Figure out how to use that to your advantage, for once."

"Aye-aye, sir," Fredreek said, giving his father a mock salute. "Now is there anything else you need to lecture me about? Or can I get back to disappointing you?"

Urion frowned. "Just… try not to be such a screw-up," he said. "For your sake, and for mine."

With that, Fredreek ended the transmission and swiveled his chair to face Wilvelm, a carefree smile on his face. "Hear that?" Fredreek asked. "Father's being encouraging, for a change."

"What was all that about?" Wilvelm inquired.

"You remember that girl I was seeing at the Dorsol colony a few months back?" Fredreek said, hopping up and pouring himself a drink at the small bar he'd set up in his quarters.

"Vaguely. What was her name again? Shatarah? Or Resnique?"

"No idea," Fredreek replied as he fixed his drink. "I'm asking if you remember because I sure don't. Anyway, she sued my Legacy for 'mental and emotional trauma' over my breaking up with her. Forget the Deathlord raids here in the Rim. My breaking up with a girl is way more traumatic, apparently. Anyway, she must have gotten some great lawyers because we just settled with her for a motherlode of digicredits. As you can imagine, my father is thrilled."

"Does this mean you'll be giving up chasing the ladies from now on?" Wilvelm asked, already knowing the answer.

"Sure, right after I give up drinking, eating, and breathing," Fredreek said as he downed his drink. "Anyway, enough about me. What brings you by?"

"We're approaching Altimac 7," Wilvelm said. "Lord Skyborn has requested our presence as he tours the attack site."

Fredreek sighed. "Boy, without Mourdock around to babysit us, they're really stretching to find things to occupy our time, aren't they?"

Wilvelm shrugged. "Would you rather just sit in your quarters on the ship all day?"

"You make a compelling argument, my friend," Fredreek said as he took one last quick swig from the bottle of Halperion brandy at his bar. "Very well. Let us not keep Lord Skyborn waiting."

As the two friends made their way through the ship, Wilvelm couldn't help but notice how impressed Fredreek seemed to be by *The Shieldbearer.* He supposed it wasn't much of a surprise, since Fredreek had always had a thing for space travel.

"Much nicer than that rust-heap Mourdock had us on, huh?" Wilvelm commented as they walked.

"Gotta hand it to Lord Skyborn, he certainly knows how to make a starship," Fredreek replied. "Someday, when I have command of my own ship, I'm going to have one built that will put this to shame. It'll have its own gravityball court, its own nightclub, and every room will have a fully stocked bar in it."

"Yes, sounds like it would strike fear into every Deathlord who lays eyes upon it," quipped Wilvelm, good-naturedly.

"Please… as if the Deathlords would be scared of this fine flagship of ours, or anything we have to throw at them, for that matter," replied Fredreek. "*The Shieldbearer* has an ultanium-reinforced hull, strong shields, twelve plasma batteries, and twice as many maneuvering thrusters. It could conceivably take on four capital ships at once and survive. But until we see how it fares against one of those Planetkillers the Deathlords have, this thing is no better than a luxury yacht, only not nearly as fun."

Wilvelm chuckled. "I can practically see the recruitment commercials now," he said. "Join the Goldstone fleet! Fight war in style!"

"Now you're thinking!" said Fredreek with a laugh. "We'd have people signing up in droves! Assuming there's still a war to be fought by the time I take control of my Legacy and assume command of my own ship."

"Well, from the sound of things, that shouldn't be an issue," replied Wilvelm with a frown. "I'm hearing talk around the ship that Altimac 7 was completely wiped out."

Fredreek raised an eyebrow. "Really?" he said.

Wilvelm shrugged. "That's the rumor," he replied. "Guess we won't know for sure until we get down there and have a look. But if the Deathlords keep this up, there's a good chance they could take out this whole system in a matter of months."

Fredreek shook his head. "It's one thing for other Rim systems to be attacked, but if Maxima falls, things will start to get real serious real quick," he said. "The hyperspace lanes from here lead deep into the Empire, not to mention the Portgate on the planet itself. Taking this system would give the Deathlords a launching pad for a massive invasion."

Wilvelm raised an eyebrow. "Well, well, look who got strategic all of a sudden," he said.

"Hey, just because I don't care doesn't mean I don't pay attention," Fredreek replied with a smile. "Your Legacy might be nice and tucked away out on the fringe, but Omnicron is a hop, skip, and a jump from Maxima. Getting invaded by Deathlords would really cramp my style. Know what I mean?"

Wilvelm nodded his head. Despite Fredreek's deflection, he knew his friend could have a sharp strategic mind when he applied himself. No doubt the scenario of Maxima falling and giving Deathlords easy access to the inner systems had crossed his mind, just as it had no doubt crossed that of his father's, which was partly why the Goldstones had allied themselves so closely with the Skyborns.

"I doubt Maxima will ever be in danger of falling to the Deathlords," Wilvelm said. "There isn't any way the Empire would let this system be taken. Lord Gebhard would have Casgor send in the entire 3rd fleet before things got out of hand."

"I suppose you're right," Fredreek replied. "Still, they've got the Maxima fleet spread way too thin trying to protect all their Rim expansions. If you ask me, it would be better to pull all the ships back here to guard the system and let the 3rd fleet worry about the rest of the Rim."

"And have Lord Gebhard lose all his clout in the high councils as his Rim holdings fall to the enemy? Heaven forbid," mused Wilvelm.

Fredreek laughed. "Right, forgot who we were talking about here," he said. "Who do you think is more eager for Mourdock to get married? Him or his father?"

"Considering all the problems Mourdock becoming Emperor would solve for his Legacy? Definitely his father," replied Wilvelm.

"Definitely," agreed Fredreek. "Speaking of…"

Wilvelm and Fredreek entered the main hangar of *The Shieldbearer* to find Gebhard Skyborn near his shuttlecraft. A small entourage consisting of his Chief Aide Ellyn Sorensen, his star system defense advisor General Wessux, and a small contingent of Maxima security forces surrounded him. Gebhard glanced up from the datapad he'd been studying as the two young men approached him.

"Wil. Fred. Thanks for joining me," he said as he handed the datapad over to Sorensen.

"It is our pleasure, Lord Skyborn," replied Wilvelm with a slight bow. "Thank you for inviting us to accompany you."

"Yes, Wil and I are eager to assist in any way we can," added Fredreek, making an attempt to at least sound sincere.

"I appreciate that," Gebhard said. "Touring attack sites may not be as glamourous as heading into battle with the Deathlords, but it's no less important. A representative from the Imperial Investigative Service is waiting on Altimac 7 to brief us. Are the two of you ready to go?"

"We are, my Lord," Wilvelm responded.

"Then let's not waste any more time," Gebhard stated as he climbed aboard his shuttle.

The interior of the shuttlecraft was rather cozy. Comfortable leather seats embedded with individual data stations provided direct links to both the secure subspace network of the Empire and the ultrawave network, allowing for access of anything from the holonet to the ultraweb. Wil and Fred settled into two seats in the back of the shuttle while Gebhard and his people sat toward the front.

"Wish they had a bar on this thing," Fred muttered as the shuttlecraft exited *The Shieldbearer's* hangar.

"Have I yet to point out that you seem to have developed a real drinking problem, my friend?" Wilvelm asked.

"I don't have a drinking problem," Fredreek replied. "It's when I'm not drinking that I have a problem. Namely, boredom. As we spend the next few hours following Lord Gebhard around an empty mining outpost while he's lectured to by some stiff in a suit, the last thing I need to be is sober. Next time, remind me to bring my flask."

"Look on the bright side," Wilvelm said. "At least he's *trying* to include us in this investigation."

"Yeah, because you and I have such insights into Deathlord tactics," said Fredreek, sarcastically. "We both know we're just here because of his alliance with our Legacies. We don't actually serve any purpose beyond window dressing."

"It's not like we were much use alongside Mourdock either," Wilvelm replied. "At least we're on equal footing with Lord Gebhard, instead of playing sidekick to a highly-skilled Paragon warrior who could probably take on the entire Deathlord army single-handedly."

 ~ **69** ~

"True," agreed Fredreek. "But I'll say this for Mourdock – running with him was never boring. His father on the other hand..."

Wilvelm shrugged. "Who knows? Maybe Altimac 7 will be more interesting than we think it will."

"Only if they have an open bar," quipped Fredreek.

The shuttle ride to Altimac 7 took about half an hour. Wilvelm gazed out the window as they approached the large asteroid into which the settlement was built. It was a massive, potato-shaped, crater-filled rock, drifting in the void of space not far from a dust cloud. As they got closer, Wilvelm could see the blast door to the colony's main hangar was open, its opening filled with a hazy light blue glow which signaled that its plasma window – which prevented the release of the colony's atmosphere while still allowing solid objects to enter and exit – was engaged.

The shuttle passed through the magnetic field, which held the ionized plasma particles of the window in place, and entered into the hangar where various transport freighters were docked. Some Imperial shuttlecraft were parked in the massive enclosure, and a greeting party was already assembled, patiently waiting for Gebhard's shuttle to land.

"Lord Skyborn," said a thin man in the black uniform of an I.I.S. agent as the group disembarked. "I am Agent Dunscar of the Imperial Investigative Service, lead investigator of the scene."

Gebhard took the man's hand and gave it a firm shake. "Agent Dunscar," he said. "I had a chance to look over your preliminary report before coming. Has there been any more luck finding survivors?"

Dunscar frowned. "I fear not, my Lord," he replied. "We've been searching every inch of the colony, but have yet to find any trace of life."

"So... everyone's dead then?" asked Fredreek.

Dunscar looked at Fredreek, one glance at the crest on Fred's chest telling him exactly who he was. "There is no proof of that either, my Lord," Dunscar replied. "As of right now, all 5,576 members of the station's population are categorized as missing."

"Missing?" said Wilvelm, surprised. "In our previous encounters with the Deathlords, they've always left a body count behind."

"What my compatriot is trying to say, Agent Dunscar, is that in our experience, Deathlords prefer killing to kidnapping," Fredreek clarified.

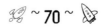

"It may be that the entire population of Altimac 7 is indeed dead, my Lords," Dunscar said, "but without bodies to prove it, we can't make that declaration. Whatever your past experiences with the Deathlords may have been, it's apparent that they have altered their behavior. The last couple of Deathlord raids all involve the inhabitants going missing."

"And what is it you believe may have caused this change in tactics, Agent Dunscar?" Gebhard asked.

"It is hard to say, my Lord. The only thing we can really point to that has changed from the Deathlords' perspective is the destruction of their Planetkiller fleet."

"I assume you have access to the same reports I do," Gebhard said, "the ones stating how the Deathlord motherships apparently use living beings as some type of fuel for their main weapons?"

Dunscar nodded. "We've considered that might be the motivation behind these abductions we've been seeing in your system, my Lord. It is certainly possible the Deathlords could be collecting living beings in an effort to refuel some type of mothership, but there are a few things we've discovered which do not quite fit with that theory. If you'll follow me, sir, I'll show you what I'm talking about."

Agent Dunscar began to lead Gebhard and the others deeper into the station. From what Wil could see, it was a typical mining colony, with the standard drab hallways, corridors, and cookie-cutter rooms that were usually present in these deep space outposts.

"As you know, after the fall of Regalus Prime, the Deathlords are credited with the destruction of eight other planets," said Dunscar as he led them down a hallway. "But during that time, the attacks where planets were not destroyed involved raids in which non-strategic targets were wiped out."

"Yes, the raids here on the Rim and in the Frontier, if I'm not mistaken," Gebhard responded.

"Correct, my Lord. In those instances, the attack on the settlements involved the use of the teleporter technology the Deathlords employed. Their Dark Soldiers fired purple orbs from their weapons, apparently teleporting those they hit. Until receiving the intelligence from the battle of Earth, we did not know what happened to someone who was shot with one of these devices. Now, we can assume these raids were how the Deathlords replenished their Planetkiller weapons between attacks, by teleporting victims into the central chamber of their ships. However, these new raids have left evidence that the Deathlords' tactics appear to have changed."

Dunscar came to a door that had a small cautionary yellow holographic barrier in front of it. He passed through the barrier and opened the door, signaling the others to follow him. On the other side was a corridor containing walls marred with scorch marks from blaster fire. There were also long marks on the walls and floors, appearing to be cuts into the metal, accompanied by splatters of blood. Wilvelm frowned as he gazed at the grim scene before him, the tell-tale signs of carnage making his skin crawl.

"Great Observer," muttered Fredreek once he'd gotten a good look at the blood splatters in the hallway.

"The grooves cut into the walls and the blood splatters suggest the Deathlords used some type of bladed weapon in this attack," Dunscar said, "a type of attack that appears to be outside their normal methods of operation."

Gebhard looked down at the hallway floor, coated in a light layer of sand-like black dust, with droplets and small puddles of dried blood scattered about, as well. "What is... all this?" Gebhard asked, gesturing toward the dust.

"Undetermined at this time, my Lord," Dunscar replied. "We've sent samples back to the I.I.S. lab on Maxima to have it analyzed. Our preliminary analysis of the dust leads us to believe it is similar to the material the Deathlords are comprised of."

"Like when a Dark Soldier is killed," Wilvelm said, "they just evaporate into dust."

"Correct, Lord Blackfyre," said Dunscar with a nod. "However, we have never seen this amount of dust at previous raid scenes before. Dark Soldiers are usually quite resilient. This would suggest that whoever was defending against this attack was able to dispatch quite a number of them, if that is indeed the case."

"Perhaps our new defensive protocols are having some type of effect," said Gebhard.

Dunscar frowned, as though to signal he did not agree with Gebhard's statement. But he did not elaborate on his disagreement.

If they were having an effect, maybe five thousand people wouldn't be missing right now, thought Wilvelm. He gazed at the grooves among the blood splatters on the wall, an uneasy feeling settling in his gut.

"An entire colony full of people can't just up and vanish," stated Fredreek, "especially if they're mounting a defense. This type of thing takes time. Why didn't any ships respond to their distress signal? We've got patrols all over this system for just such an event."

"We've gone over the colony's communication logs, Lord Goldstone, and it would appear that a distress signal was never sent," Dunscar replied.

Gebhard raised an eyebrow at that. "Never sent?" he said. "Were the Deathlords somehow able to take out the colony's communications?"

Dunscar shook his head. "From what we can tell, all the comms are functioning normally," he answered. "We're having our tech team go through everything, but there is no evidence that the comms were tampered with, nor was the emergency beacon activated."

Wilvelm sighed. "So… the Deathlords have gotten sneakier *and* deadlier," he said.

"That's not all, my Lords," Dunscar replied with a troubled look on his face. "If you'd follow me, please."

Agent Dunscar continued to lead the group deeper into the station. Wilvelm felt uneasy with the eerie quiet that had settled in, augmented by the low hum of the lights and the life support systems within the structure. Some of the lights even flickered, briefly causing the group's path to descend into darkness as they made their way through the colony. More deep cuts in the walls, decorated with dried blood in the form of desperate handprints and morbid streaks, signaled that whatever fight had occurred had become more frenzied and violent the closer the group came to their destination.

Finally, Dunscar arrived at a door, which he opened to reveal a large assembly room. It was the type of facility used for local government meetings, citizen events, and school plays. The room was circular, with an area of stadium seating and a small stage against the far wall. As the group filed into the room, Wilvelm noticed that there appeared to be a sign of a large struggle, with broken furniture and large numbers of discarded weapons and pieces of clothing strewn about.

But the most noticeable thing in the room was a large circle of pitch black rock on the floor, riddled with dull red, green, and purple veins.

Wilvelm looked at the patch of rock with curiosity, as did Fredreek. Indeed, Gebhard's entire group tentatively approached the rock, gazing at it with morbid curiosity, before Gebhard finally asked the question that was on all their minds.

"What is… this?"

"We don't know, sir," Dunscar replied. "But something similar to this has been found at all the recent raid sites within the Rim."

"It looks like rock," Fredreek said.

"It looks like the stuff the Planetkiller ships were made of," Wilvelm amended.

"Do we know why it's here?" Gebhard asked. "What did the Deathlords use it for?"

"All we know right now, sir, is that in the decade since the Deathlords first attacked, they've been responsible for the abduction of close to a million people, split among their entire Planetkiller fleet," Dunscar said. "And in the past couple of months since that fleet was destroyed, they have abducted over three hundred thousand people in the Rim alone. Beyond that, we have no idea what this may be, or what they are planning…"

Dunscar stepped up and looked down at the patch of black rock, scowling at it in dismay.

"…and that is what worries me the most," he said.

CHAPTER ✺ 8

"**G**ood job, Professor," Jack said as the Earthship exited from hyperspace. "See? You're getting the hang of it!"

Professor Green appeared rather uncomfortable in the pilot chair of the Earthship, his hands tensely clutching the clear control domes on the chair's arms. "Oh dear, oh dear," the Professor muttered. "This feels so… odd."

"What do you mean?" asked Jack. "You seem to be doing fine."

"It's just… the connection to the ship is sluggish," Green said. "I feel as though it takes a few seconds before the ship responds to my commands. Not to mention the connection between the ship and me feels… off, like I've forced my hand into a glove that's too small for it."

"Well, maybe you two just need to get used to each other?" Jack offered. "You were able to take us into lightspeed and fly us through hyperspace with no issue."

"Aye, and now ya just need ta pilot us the rest o' tha way ta Port Somewhere," Scallywag said as he hopped up from the navigation console. "I already laid in tha coordinates. We're about an hour out from the station. Just bring us in nice and easy, and Osiris is yer uncle!"

"I shall attempt to do so," Green said as he shifted in the pilot's seat, a look of heavy concentration on his face. "I just worry that piloting the Earthship is not as easy as I'd hoped it would be."

"Patience, Professor," Jack said, giving Green an encouraging pat on the hand. "You'll get the hang of it eventually. If you need anything, I'll be with Scally and the others getting ready."

Jack and Scallywag walked to the teleporter at the top tier of the bridge before teleporting to the cargo bay where Dan was already helping Grohm into his armor.

"Oy, ya really think it's a good idea letting the ol' greenskin have control of tha ship?" Scallywag asked. "The Professor is a good engineer, but he don't seem ta be much of a pilot."

Jack shrugged. "What harm can it do? Worse comes to worst, I can just use my mental connection to control the ship. Besides, it makes him feel like he has something to contribute."

"Aye, speakin' o' somethin' that needs ta contribute..." muttered Scallywag as Dan approached them.

"Master Jack! Master Scallywag! There you are!" said Dan as he shuffled up. "I have taken full stock of the Earthship's armory and have laid out the necessary armor and weapons for each of you for your excursion to the shadow port."

Dan gestured to the neat piles of clothing on a nearby bench. "Thanks, Dan," said Jack as he approached his pile.

"Oy, where are me pistols?" Scallywag asked upon surveilling his pile.

"Why, they are right there, sir," Dan replied.

"No, these be tha bloody Virtuoso stun guns," Scallywag said, gesturing to the holster in question. "I'm talkin' about me plasma pistols."

"Oh, I was under the impression that the group had transitioned to non-deadly weaponry, sir," Dan said. "I have even taken the liberty of updating the design of the stun weapon so that its projectiles are more in line with typical plasma guns."

"That's all fine 'n dandy," Scallywag said as he put on the holster containing the stun guns. "But I'm gonna be needin' me trusty plasma pistols, as well."

"I shall find them for you right away, sir!"

Jack frowned as he, too, put on a holster with a stun pistol in it. "Why do you need your regular guns, Scally?" he asked. "Now that we have stun weapons, there's no reason to kill anyone."

"Some people need killin', lad," Scallywag replied. "I can appreciate yer reluctance ta use deadly force, but in my experience, sometimes killin' is tha only way ta go. Especially at a place like Port Somewhere."

"But... aren't you still trying to change your skin?"

"What's that got ta do with anythin'?"

"It's just that... have you ever thought that maybe your willingness to kill people is one of the reasons you went red in the first place?" Jack asked. "I mean, I don't know a whole lot about Visinis, but it seems to me that being okay with killing might affect you in a negative way."

Scallywag snorted in displeasure. "Bein' willing ta kill is tha only reason I'm still alive, lad. In tha real world, it all boils down ta survival o' the fittest. Eat or be eaten. I'd rather be alive and red than blue and dead."

"I'm not saying you shouldn't defend yourself," Jack replied. "I'm just saying—"

"I know what yer sayin'," Scallywag interrupted. "And I'm sayin' sometimes killin' is necessary. I'd rather have me blasters and not need 'em, then need 'em and not have 'em."

Jack shook his head. "Suit yourself," he said. "Just do me a favor and only kill if it's a last resort, okay? We're the good guys. We should hold ourselves to a higher standard. Know what I mean?"

Scallywag smirked as Dan shuffled back toward him. "Fine, I'll only kill someone if'n there ain't no better options," the pirate replied, not really sounding as though he were serious. "Happy?"

"Here you are, Master Scallywag," Dan said, presenting two plasma pistols. "Are these to your liking, sir?"

Scallywag took the pistols and gave them a twirl before holstering them behind his back. "Aye, these'll do," he replied. "Any word on when tha rustbucket plans on joinin' us?"

As if on cue, Heckubus appeared on the teleportation platform, four hologuise wristbands in his hand. He peered at the group suspiciously. "Are you lot plotting?" he inquired, accusingly. "I warn you, I have approximately—"

"Twelve backup plans in place," Jack and Scallywag both said, sounding like they'd heard the threat a million times.

"Indeed! And all of them are nasty!" stated Heckubus. "Well, 11 are, but I assure you the twelfth one is—"

"Extremely annoying," Jack and Scallywag replied once more.

"Though, how ya can get any more annoyin' is beyond me," Scallywag added.

"That's because you lack imagination," Heckubus said as he approached the group. "Now gather around! I have completed our hologuises for the mission to the shadow port."

"Sweet!" said Jack. "What did you come up with? Are we, like, a plucky renegade crew who fought on the losing side of a civil war and now make a living as part of the pioneer culture that exists on the fringes of the star system?"

"Don't be ridiculous," Heckubus said. "That's a terrible concept."

"I think it sounds awesome," Jack argued.

"Earthman, if that were a program on the holonet, it would be cancelled after a single failed season."

"Only because of studio interference…" Jack muttered.

"No, I have crafted a far more effective collection of disguises, guaranteed to make us blend in with the ne'er-do-wells of Port Somewhere," Heckubus proclaimed as he approached Grohm. "We shall start with you, you mindless beast. Present me with your wrist."

Grohm scowled at Heckubus but held out his arm, nonetheless. Heckubus wasted no time attaching the hologuise wristband to him.

"Because the Rognok is so large, I was limited with the options of how to best disguise him," Heckubus said as he enabled Grohm's hologuise. Grohm was then transformed into a large Recklec, with rocky, rust-colored skin. Grohm looked at the holographic visage of his arms and snorted in displeasure.

"Admittedly, he's a little large for a Recklec, but there's only so much the holographic emitters can disguise, and unfortunately size is not one of them," said Heckubus. "However, if anything, travelling with such a large Recklec will no doubt discourage others from interacting with us, since most species find Recklecs so intimidating."

"What did you come up with for me?" Jack asked, somewhat excited to see what he got to turn into.

"Ah! You were much easier," Heckubus said as he placed the hologuise band on Jack's wrist and turned it on.

Jack had the ship manifest a standing mirror which raised up from the floor so he could take a look at his disguise. Rather than some type of alien or cool outlaw-looking type appearing in the mirror, a frumpy, overweight girl with a double chin, a huge nose (with an ugly wart on the end of it), and frizzy hair stared back at him. Jack blinked in bewilderment, not liking what he saw one bit.

"Dude," commented Jack in a now effeminate voice. "You made me a girl?"

"Obviously," Heckubus replied. "It stands to reason that if people are on the lookout for you, a male, they will immediately discount a female."

"Yeah, but…"

"But what?"

"I dunno," said Jack, turning to check himself out in the mirror. "Couldn't you have made me… prettier?"

Scallywag snickered. "Ya plannin' ta enter some beauty contests on our excursion, lad?"

Jack frowned. "I just always thought if I were a girl, I'd be a more attractive one," he muttered.

"The hologuise is not meant to be representative of you, Earthman," Heckubus explained. "We do not wish to draw attention to ourselves. Thus, having an unattractive appearance ensures that others will not wish to observe us for an extended period of time. Behold!"

Heckubus turned on his own hologuise emitter and his robotic visage was immediately replaced with that of an exceedingly creepy looking, hunched over old man, complete with a bald, liver-spotted head, wrinkles, rotten teeth, crazy eyes, and quasi-futuristic clothing. Jack immediately averted his gaze.

"Ugh!" Jack cried. "Point taken! Turn it off!"

"Mwuahahaha!" Heckubus said as he disengaged his hologuise. "See? Think of being ugly as a form of social camouflage."

Jack sighed. "Fine," he grumbled. "But just for the record, if I were a girl, I'd be totally hot."

"Yes, I'm sure your body temperature would be more elevated due to the abundance of female hormones you'd no doubt be producing in your current stage of pubescent development," Heckubus replied, dismissively.

"Oy, what did ya come up with fer me?" Scallywag asked, amused, as he took the final hologuise wristband from Heckubus and put it on. "Somethin' embarassin', I bet? Somethin' really over tha top? Go on. Let's have a look."

Scallywag hit the activation button on the armband and looked into the mirror to see that the hologuise emitter had done absolutely nothing to change his appearance short of turning his skin yellow. Scallywag gazed at his image for a moment, a series of emotions playing out on his face before settling on an angry one.

"What tha bloody squick is this?" Scallywag asked, sneering at Heckubus.

"There will no doubt be a number of Visinis on Port Somewhere," Heckubus replied. "Most of them will be Yellows. It seemed the most logical choice to help you blend in."

"Except fer the fact that I look exactly tha same!" snapped Scallywag. "One look at me face and anyone with half a brain will figure out I just changed the color o' me skin!"

Heckubus rolled his ocular orbs. "Fine," the robot muttered. "I anticipated you may not appreciate the subtle genius at work here and prepared an alternative disguise. Shall I switch you to it?"

"Bloody right, switch me to it."

"As you wish," Heckubus said, tapping on his datapad.

Scallywag's hologuise then morphed from one in which he looked exactly the same, only with yellow skin, to one in which he looked exactly the same, only with yellow skin and a huge bosom.

"Ya got ta be kiddin' me," Scallywag sneered.

"What's the problem? Are they not big enough?" Heckubus asked.

"Robot... I'm gonna kill ya!"

"Did I not make it clear with the Earthman that swapping genders is a perfectly good disguise option?"

"Oy, Visini women do not look like Visini men, only chestier!" snapped Scallywag. "If yer lookin' ta avoid unwanted attention, this is not tha way to do it!"

"Very well," replied Heckubus. "Lucky for you, I came up with an alternative to your alternative. Allow me to switch you to it..."

Before Heckubus could tap on his datapad, Jack stepped up and put a hand on the robot's arm, stopping him. "Heckubus," Jack said. "We all know how much you like pulling Scallywag's chain, but we need to get ready for this meeting, and we need everyone to be at his best, so... how about we skip all the mental torture you have planned and just give Scally his real disguise, so we can all finish getting ready?"

Scallywag raised an eyebrow. "Oy... ya mean you were just doin' all this ta rile me up?"

"Mwuahahaha..." Heckubus laughed. "It's all too easy!"

Scallywag grimaced, obviously upset he had fallen for the robot's antagonizing. "Right..." he grumbled. "Shoulda known even you weren't defective enough ta send me out in public lookin' like this."

"Indeed. Your real hologuise is actually quite good. Shall I call it up?"

Scallywag took one last lingering look at himself in the mirror, gazing down at his yellow hands and wistfully admiring the way they looked before finally nodding. "Yeah. Go on," he said.

Heckubus tapped at his datapad, and Scallywag's appearance changed to that of a brown-haired Regal pirate, wearing knee-high black boots, a white shirt, and a black vest.

"There," said Heckubus. "Is that more to your liking?"

Scallywag studied himself in the mirror. Instead of a beard on his chin, there was a small scar, which he scratched at. "A bit scruffy lookin', but it'll do," he said. Scallywag then unholstered the two plasma pistols he had in his belt and handed them back over to Dan. "Here," he said. "Won't be needin' these after all."

"Oh!" said Dan as he took the plasma pistols from Scallywag. "Might I inquire as to why, sir?"

"Just... turnin' over a new leaf, I suppose," Scallywag replied. "Got the stun guns. Those should be able ta handle any trouble we run into."

Jack smiled at Scallywag's sudden change of heart. He could only assume that seeing himself with yellow skin made the pirate reconsider Jack's advice. Jack would have enjoyed the moment longer had he not experienced a sharp pain in his neck.

"Ow!" cried Jack, his hand going to the spot Heckubus had just jabbed with a medical injector. "Dude! What the heck?"

"Just a simple inoculation. Nothing to get riled up about," Heckubus replied as he tossed away the injection device.

"Inoculation?" Jack asked.

"Yes, yes, for... um... space diseases," the robot replied.

"Space diseases?"

"What else would it be for?" said Heckubus, defensively. "We're going to a shadow port filled with unsavory beings from all over the galaxy. Seeing as how you are new to space travel, I decided it would be important to ensure your immune system is prepared for all the alien bacteria it will be coming into contact with."

"But, if that's the case, shouldn't you have given me that shot before we went to Omnicron?" asked Jack. "I came into contact with all sorts of aliens there."

"Yes, well… perhaps your immune system is more resilient than I thought. Regardless, it never hurts to err on the safe side, particularly when I have absolutely no ulterior motives for doing so."

"Dude, you're acting super shifty," said Jack, suspiciously.

"I'm always acting super shifty. It's how I act," replied Heckubus. "Now if you'll excuse me, I have other matters to attend to before we arrive at our destination. Henchman! Attend me!"

"Oh!" said Dan as he shuffled after Heckubus who proceeded to walk to a corner of the cargo bay, far enough from the others to prevent being overheard. "Yes, Master Heckubus? How may I be of service?"

"Take this," Heckubus ordered, presenting Dan with a datastick.

"Where should I take it, sir?" Dan asked as he accepted the device.

"Nowhere, you dolt. That datastick contains engineering schematics for a number of upgrades I want you to implement for yourself while we are away."

"Upgrades, sir?"

"Indeed. They are based on the numerous upgrades I have administered to myself over the years. Your revelation that Chief Alabaster fitted you with updated technology made me realize that you shall need to be prepared for future contingencies if you're going to be servicing this crew in my absence."

"Absence, sir? Are you going somewhere?"

"That is none of your concern at the moment," Heckubus answered. "Needless to say, this crew will be completely lost without a sophisticated A.I. to assist them. Seeing as how I am limited in my options as to what to provide them in that respect, you shall have to do."

"Thank you for entrusting me with such an important mission, sir!" said Dan. "I assure you, I will not let you down!"

"See that you don't. For the consequences shall be—"

"Dire, sir?"

"I was going to say 'disappointing', but, yes, dire as well. Why not?"

"Attention, everyone," came Professor Green's voice over the intercom in the cargo bay. "We are now approaching Port Somewhere."

Jack immediately called up a holographic display in the cargo bay, which showed an image of the space station. He magnified the image to get a good look at it. The shadow port was a wide disk that tapered to a long point both above

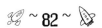

and below it. All told, Jack thought it looked much like a spin top with which little children play, only with a bunch of plasma cannons mounted on the outside and surrounded by spaceships coming and going.

"There's yer wretched hive of scum and villainy, lad," Scallywag said, standing beside Jack and looking at the display, as well.

"It looks so small compared to the megabase at Omnicron," Jack observed.

"Oy, most *planets* look small compared ta megabases," Scallywag replied. "As far as space platforms go, this is actually one o' the bigger ones."

"Hmmm..." mused Heckubus as he sidled up to the group. "It would appear they've added a few more defensive armaments to the station since I was last here."

"Everyone be expectin' trouble nowadays," commented Scallywag.

"Including us," Jack said as he slid on his chest armor. "Let's just hope that whatever trouble we find, it's something we can handle."

CHAPTER ✺ 9

In a flash of light, a large Recklec, a scruffy pirate, a creepy old man, and a rather unfortunate looking young lady appeared in an out-of-the-way maintenance hallway filled with a multitude of pipes, conduits, and steam vents, deep within Port Somewhere.

"Professor, do you read me?" Jack asked, holding his finger up to the small earbud communicator he was wearing.

"Loud and clear, my boy!" Green responded. "Comms are working perfectly! I have strong teleportation signatures on each of you. If you run into any trouble, I should have no problem transporting you back to the ship."

"Well, now that tha escape plan is set, time ta head ta the meet," Scallywag said as he led the group down the maintenance hall until they came to a door.

The group emerged into a bustling corridor. Jack was immediately overwhelmed by the sheer amount of foot traffic traversing the station. The corridor was extremely wide and oval shaped, with a reflective black floor and white wall paneling framed by track lighting on both the top and bottom. Visual displays were interspersed upon the walls, some of them displaying advertisements, some displaying maps of the station, and others running programming, which ranged from news shows to tourism information.

Jack stayed close to Scallywag as the pirate pushed his way through the river of the station's patrons. Jack had thought the collection of strange aliens he'd seen on Omnicron had been impressive, but what he saw on Port Somewhere put the diversity of Omnicron to shame. There seemed to be an endless assortment of creatures, many of which looked intimidating and dangerous. The vast majority of them seemed to sport some type of robotic implant, and almost all of them were armed in some way.

"Jeez!" said Jack as the crowd jostled him about. "How many criminals are there in this galaxy?"

"Considering the number of planets and settlements between the Regalus Empire and the Visinis? Not nearly enough in my opinion," replied Heckubus. "The sad fact is there are too few safe havens for underworld-types, thus the ones that do exist are usually highly frequented."

"Not ta mention not everyone on this tub is a criminal," Scallywag said. "Ya got a fair number o' spacers just lookin' ta make a livin'. When ya get this far in tha fringes o' space, stations like this are as valuable as habitable planets, so it attracts all types."

"I'm seeing mostly one type," Jack muttered as he bumped into a mangy Tygarian[8] who growled at him as he passed. "What's the name of the place we're meeting Mourdock at, again?"

"A boozskeller called *Stinky Pete's*," Scallywag said. "It's dark, grimy, has watered-down drinks, and it smells worse than an unshaven Musk Bova[9] in heat. A right proper hole in tha wall."

"Sounds awful," Jack said.

"Oh, it is," Scallywag replied. "Hardly anyone goes there. Perfect place ta meet up on tha downlow. It should be right around tha corner, here…"

Scallywag led the group to a curved intersection of the corridor. But as they made their way around the bend, Scallywag stopped short, the rest of the group stopping with him.

"What tha kitten?" muttered the pirate.

Jack glanced past Scallywag to see a golden arched doorway across the corridor. The arch was framed with a thick red trim, small lines of gold interspersed upon it, making it look like a golden sun rising against a red sky. Each side of the entrance was flanked by a tacky, overly large onyx bust of a humanoid head with a golden droopy moustache and forked beard upon its chin. Hovering over the entrance, a bright holographic sign with large block letters read 'Mung's Merciless' with smaller lettering underneath adding the words 'Boozskeller and Grill'.

"I don't bloody believe it," Scallywag grumbled. "A Mung's? How many billions of these bloody things are there?"

"Um… didn't you say this was supposed to be a place called Stinky Pete's?" asked Jack.

---

[8] Tygarians are large, robust humanoid aliens that resemble a cross between wolves and tigers.

[9] A Bova is a large, hairy, buffalo-like animal raised by many primitive cultures to ride, use as pack animals, or as a source of meat. The "musk" variety of bova is known to have a rather foul and pungent odor.

"It was, last time I was here," Scallywag said. He then stopped a passing yellow-skinned Visini. "Oy, mate," he said, "what happened ta Stinky Pete's?"

"Stinky Pete's?" the Visini replied. "It got bought out a while ago."

"By a chain restaurant?" Scallywag said, incredulously.

The Visini shrugged. "Apparently they offer great franchise opportunities," he responded.

"Franchise opportunities? We're on a bloody shadow port!"

"Tell me about it," the Visini replied. "I felt the same way when that Supernova Coffee place opened up on level 9. Those things are everywhere! It's like outlaw culture is being swallowed up by soulless corporations, know what I mean? Used to be you could kill a bunch of people and then grab some cheap drinks while bathing in the blood of your enemies. Now, it's more like you just horribly maim a bunch of folks and hope happy hour is still going on. And if you bathe in blood, everyone suddenly looks at you like you're some type of weirdo."

The Visini then noticed that Scallywag's companions were all looking at him like he was some type of weirdo.

"Anyway, it ain't all bad," the Visini continued. "This station really needed an all-you-can-eat salad bar, if you ask me. If you're going to Mung's, give it a try. It's actually quite reasonably priced. Now if you'll excuse me, I need to get back to hunting down some of my enemies. I haven't bathed in weeks!"

Scallywag leered at the Visini as he walked away. "Oy, how's that bloke still a Yellow?" he muttered.

"I quite liked him," commented Heckubus.

"Well, if the place we're supposed to meet Mourdock is gone, what are we supposed to do now?" Jack asked.

"I guess we just wait inside and hope Skyborn figures out this was supposed ta be tha meetin' place," Scallywag replied.

"And if he doesn't?" asked Jack.

"One problem at a time, lad," Scallywag replied. "Unless ya got a better idea?"

"You lot go on ahead," Heckubus said, walking away. "I shall meet up with you later."

"Oy!" called out Scallywag. "Where do ya think yer goin'?"

"I have some business to attend to," Heckubus called back. "Try not to do anything stupid in my absence – however unlikely that may be."

Jack and Scallywag frowned as the robot disappeared into the crowd of the space station. "What type of business could he have here?" Jack asked.

"Who bloody knows," muttered Scallywag. "I've given up tryin' ta understand that defective android long ago. C'mon. Let's get to tha meet."

Jack turned to see Grohm gazing at a visual display on the wall, which appeared to be running a news story off the holonet. He noticed the Rognok looked agitated by what he was seeing.

"...yet another settlement in the Maxima system has reportedly been destroyed by Deathlords," the anchorman on the screen said. "This makes it the fifth settlement to be attacked since the Deathlords stepped up their raids in the Rim only a few weeks ago. Initial reports coming out of Maxima state that the Deathlords are sparing no one, with entire populations disappearing without a trace, believed to have been harvested by the alien menace. All outposts, space stations, and settlements in the Maxima system are on high alert as the Skyborn fleet intensifies patrols in an attempt to find the Deathlords responsible for the attacks."

Grohm sneered at the screen as Jack came up beside him. "You okay, big guy?" Jack asked.

Grohm snorted. "Deathlords in Maxima," the Rognok replied.

Jack nodded. "Yeah, I remember Mourdock having to leave Omnicron to defend his system against them. I guess they're targeting the Rim for some reason."

"Grohm go to Maxima," Grohm said. "Grohm fight Deathlords."

"We've got enough people to fight at the moment. Right now, we need to be focused on meeting up with Mourdock and finding a way to fix Anna. Okay?"

Grohm looked down at Jack and frowned, but gave a reluctant nod in agreement.

"Okay," said Jack. "So why don't we go check out this Mung's place. What do you say?"

Grohm took one last look at the visual display before following Jack and Scallywag as they made their way into the entrance of Mung's Merciless Boozskeller and Grill.

A golden holographic barrier featuring the red sun logo of the restaurant separated the bustling station corridor from the interior. A red and gold courtesy-bot was stationed at a kiosk out front and greeted the trio as they approached. "Welcome to Mung's Merciless Boozskeller and Grill, where our friends don't like you, and we don't like you either," it said. "How many in your party?"

"Three, apparently," responded Scallywag.

Jack looked at the Visini. "Seriously, what kind of a greeting is that?"

"Relax," muttered Scallywag. "In places where no one likes ya, they don't pay attention to ya either. That's the whole point o' comin' here, remember?"

"Smoking or nonsmoking?" the courtesy-bot asked.

"Is there really a difference?" asked Scallywag.

"The air in the smoking section is approximately 18% cleaner," the robot responded.

"How is that even possible?" asked Jack.

"It's a shadow port, lad. Just go with it," Scallywag replied before turning back to the courtesy-bot. "Smokin' sounds topper."

"Follow me, please," the courtesy-bot said before leading them through the holographic barrier.

Jack stepped through the barrier and into an extremely large enclosure. Golden stairs led down to a circular area filled with high tables and chairs, populated by a multitude of patrons eating and drinking. The far corners of the room were lined with booths, and the high walls were decorated with red paneling, more tacky looking busts, and holo-displays of various sporting events. Robo-servants were bustling to-and-fro, delivering orders of food and drinks to various customers. There was a fully stocked bar at the very back of the room. At the center of it all was also a very nice-looking salad bar.

"I don't believe it," said Scallywag as they made their way through the din of the restaurant, obviously displeased with what he saw. "They even managed ta get rid o' the stink. What's this galaxy comin' to?"

The courtesy-bot led the group to a table near the bar, set some laminated menus down, and bowed to them. "Enjoy your time here at Mung's," it said. "You will receive no mercy from this point forward."

The group all situated themselves at the table and Jack gave the courtesy-bot an odd look as it shuffled away. "Um... what did it mean by that?" Jack asked.

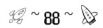

"Don't fret it, lad," replied Scallywag. "It sounds more intimidatin' than it is. Mung's just some bloke who's obsessed with conquering the culinary world. His joints all have this same shtick."

"Which is what, exactly?"

Scallywag shrugged. "Bein' obnoxious, if'n ya ask me."

"Greetings, puny mortals!" came a voice.

The group turned to see a man walking toward them. He was adorned in the ornate finery of opulent red and gold robes, the red sun logo of the restaurant proudly emblazoned upon a golden disk, nestled on his chest among a collection of smaller buttons and at least 37 pieces of flair. A colossally tall arrow-shaped golden mandarin collar encompassed his neck and encircled the back of his head, which was adorned with a skin-tight black headpiece, making his cranium appear both bald and shiny. Upon seeing the man, Jack realized the tacky busts littering the establishment were of him, complete with his long, thin, droopy moustache, forked goatee beard, and angular eyebrows, which were so pointy, they were practically at 90-degree angles.

"Welcome to Mung's Merrrrrrrciless Boozskeller and Grill!" the man declared with a flourish of his hand. "I am Mung the Merciless! Owner, proprietor, and ruthless ruler over delicious flavor. Might I interest you in our specials today? We have an excellent crispy fried hawkman, served with noodles and a sweet and sour sauce, which is simply diviiiiiiiine."

"Oy, *you're* Mung?" asked Scallywag. "*The* Mung?"

"The one and only!"

"Don't ya own a billion o' these joints?" Scallywag asked. "What are ya doin' here?"

"Oh, I regularly circulate through each of my locations just to ensure they continue to meet my high standard of despotic quality," Mung replied. "We recently received a few complaints about this location not being up to par, so I am here to whip it into shape with my signature brand of cruelty and totalitarianism. Now, can I start you off with some Frontier-style Tejano Eggrolls? We also have the station's premier all-you-can-eat salad bar!"

Jack glanced at the menu. "Um... how are the nachos?" he asked.

"They are utterly without *merrrrrrrrcy*," Mung replied.

"I don't even know what that means," said Jack, confused.

"Oh, you will," Mung responded with malicious glee. "Oh. You. Wiiiiilllllll."

Jack looked at Scallywag nervously. "Oy, minger," Scallywag interjected, "just bring us a bottle o' Claxagaar rum and some fried tundrabird wings, savvy?"

"Excellent choice," commented Mung. "How little *merrrrrrrcy* would you like on those wings?"

"Seriously, what does that even mean?" Jack muttered.

"Ya don't wanna know," replied Scallywag. "We'll go with medium on tha wings, mate."

"So be it," said Mung before extending his hand, which sported a glowing red jewel atop a golden ring on his pointer finger. The ring brightened and the group's order suddenly appeared on their table in a haze of crimson colored energy.

"Whoa," said Jack, looking at the food in amazement.

"Enjoy this meal," Mung said. "For it shall be your last…"

The group all gave Mung a curious look.

"…your last at half price!" Mung continued. "Our happy hour discount specials are about to end, so if you wish to partake in any more of our *ruthlessly* exquisite cuisine, I suggest you order now, and show *merrrrrcy* on your pocketbook!"

"I think we're set fer now, mate," Scallywag said.

"Very well," Mung replied. "If you should require anything further, such as less mercy, do not be afraid to ask. Again, my name is Mung," he said, pointing to the golden nametag on his chest. With a flourish of his cape and the jingle of his flair, Mung turned and walked away.

Grohm promptly scooped up the fried tundrabird wings and ate them all. Scallywag grabbed the bottle of rum. Jack glanced around the establishment, looking at all the odd aliens that populated it. "So… what do we do now?" Jack asked.

"Now?" said Scallywag as he opened the bottle of rum and took a deep swig. "Now, we wait."

CHAPTER 10

Shadow stations such as Port Somewhere had their fair share unscrupulous and enterprising fellows who tried to make a living by brokering deals between the station's transient clientele in exchange for a fee. And on a base such as Port Somewhere, there were lots of unsavory deals to be made – something Heckubus was counting on.

It didn't take Heckubus long to find what he was looking for. He'd simply made his way down to the station's hangar bays and spent a bit of time observing the various goings-on of those who were present. The multitude of worker-bots, spacers, pirates, and hangar foremen didn't interest him. No, Heckubus was looking for a particular type of lowlife, and he finally found one in the form of a Rattan named Bucktooth.

The large, rodent-like being was situated in a corner near the exit from the hangar area. He was seated on a small stool nestled among various cargo crates, an exhaust vent leaking foul steam nearby. Bucktooth's fur was matted, crusty, and dark brown. He had a scar across his pink nose, and his beady black eyes were nestled under an oddly shaped fedora hat, with a crooked ear jutting out from beneath.

The Rattan gnawed on a hunk of stinky cheese as he read something on his datapad. It was obvious he didn't work in the hangar, yet the area around him seemed cluttered enough with personal items that it appeared he didn't go anywhere else all that much. This led Heckubus to conclude that he was exactly the being to whom he wished to speak.

"You look like a Rattan who knows his way around Port Somewhere," Heckubus said as he approached.

The Rattan glanced up from his datapad and sniffed the air coming from Heckubus's direction, his two massive front teeth chattering slightly. "Might be I do," Bucktooth responded. "Who's asking?"

"Me," Heckubus said, simply. "And my friend."

Heckubus tossed a digicredit card onto Bucktooth's lap. Bucktooth picked it up and eyed it, before swiping it through his datapad. "That's quite a friend you got there," Bucktooth said with a rotten grin, obviously pleased with the balance he saw.

"He's somewhat of a fair-weather one," Heckubus replied, "rather prone to leave me should a better opportunity come his way."

"Ya don't say?" Bucktooth responded. "And what type of opportunity might persuade him ta leave your side?"

"An informational opportunity," Heckubus said. "Would I be correct in assuming you know a thing or two about the various spacefarers currently docked on the station?"

"Aye, you'd be correct in assuming that."

"I am looking for a fast ship, as well as a reliable crew who aren't above doing some extra-legal activity."

Bucktooth scratched the bristly whiskers under his chin. "Hmmmmm," he muttered. "Plenty who don't mind the 'extra-legal' end of things. Fewer that would be considered reliable. Even fewer with a ship worth a toss. How flexible are ya on these three things?"

"Not very."

"You prefer more the smuggler type or the killin' type?"

"Little bit of both, if possible."

Bucktooth chattered his teeth. "Might be I know of a crew for ya," he said. "They got a good reputation. Complete most of their contracts. Haven't had many disputes. Do a lot of freelance smuggling and some bounty hunting. They're the types who'll do most anything if the pay is right."

"And where might I find these fine fellows?"

"They just docked a few days ago. Had some money in their pockets from a successful smuggling run. Seen them a few times hanging out in the Loquir[10] Lounge down in Club Salacious on level sixteen. I'd start there. Their captain is a real Frontier type. Got the wide-brimmed hat and funky leather boots, like the gunslingers from those holofilms, ya know? Runs with a big ol' Recklec and two others. Shouldn't be hard to spot."

Heckubus nodded. He took the digicredit card back and swiped it through his datapad, the transfer causing Bucktooth's datapad to beep in response. The Rattan glanced down at it and smiled. "I'll send you the rest of the fee if I

---

[10] Loquir is a popular card game within the Regalus Empire, which somewhat resembles poker.

determine this crew to be acceptable," Heckubus said. "If not, you can expect to see me again."

It wasn't a long journey from the hangar bay to level sixteen. The entrance to Club Salacious was marked with neon-lit animated humanoid female figures dancing on either side of it, a scrolling digital sign above its door advertising various drink specials. There were two bloodied pirates unconscious in the hallway leading up to the entrance, and a large Ramballa mercenary was vomiting into a nearby potted plant. So far, Heckubus was impressed with the classiness of the establishment.

Inside the club, a live band played upbeat music. Multi-colored lights faded in and out, giving the large room a constantly shifting ambience. The walls were lined with various *Grabchenko* machines, at which numerous patrons vied for a jackpot, and a large central bar was busy dispensing alcohol to different seedy looking lowlifes. A few Seraphym[11] dancers, positioned on tiny circular stages strategically placed among the tables of the establishment, wooed their onlookers to further part with their hard-earned digicredits.

Heckubus surveilled the club until he saw a small room located toward the back. It was separated from the greater establishment by a beaded curtain, but the neon-lit hand of cards above its entrance told him it must be the Loquir Lounge his contact had informed him about.

After passing the beaded curtain, the music from the club dulled a bit. Red lights bathed the inside of the room as patrons played various games of Loquir on backlit tables. It didn't take long for Heckubus to spot the crew he'd been sent to seek out. They were nestled at a table in the corner, a pitcher of cheap alcohol being shared among them as they ham-fistedly played a game of cards.

The Recklec was the most instantly noticeable. He was large for a Recklec, with hunched shoulders and a massive frame, his rocky orange skin looking almost pink under the red lights of the room. He wasn't as big as a Rognok, but he was big enough to be intimidating. On one side of him was a skinny Karkovian, his body long and lanky, his skin tinted purple, and his muscles lithe and well-defined. He wore a suede vest with fringes hanging from it, and his six arms were all covered in scars of varying lengths. On the other side of the Recklec was a short Corkron, his head uncharacteristically sparse with tattoos and some badly combed brown hair on the top of his cranium – a sign that typically meant

---

[11] Seraphyms are an alien race that looks different depending on the person viewing them, but they always appear extremely attractive depending on the viewer's personal tastes.

the Corkron was not very mentally developed. His ocher-colored eyes were wide and empty looking, and his fat lips seemed constantly frozen in a dumb smile.

At the far end was a Regal who had his feet kicked up on the table as he expertly shuffled a deck of cards. His feet sported expensive looking boots. His long duster coat was draped over his chair, and his wide-brimmed hat was tilted low, covering his eyes but not his sly grin. From the way he dominated the conversation, it was obvious the man liked to hear the sound of his own voice, which had a distinct Frontier twang to it. Overall, the group appeared to be a proper collection of hooligans. Heckubus was indeed pleased.

"Yes, yes, you lot seem sufficiently unscrupulous enough to suit my purposes," Heckubus said as he approached the group.

The one with his feet kicked up on the table glanced at Heckubus from beneath the wide brim of his hat. "Beggin' yer pardon?" he drawled.

"I am looking to hire some competent to semi-competent henchmen for some sensitive work," Heckubus said. "I was told you have a ship and accept charters."

The group all exchanged suspicious glances. Their apparent leader took his feet off the table and leaned forward, tipping the brim of his hat up to get a good look at Heckubus, revealing a large patch of scar tissue on the left side of his face. "Might be that's the case," he said. "Fer the right price, anyway."

"Price will not be an issue," Heckubus said, tossing a digicredit card onto the table.

The group eyed the card. The man with the hat nodded to his Karkovian companion who produced a datapad from his vest and slid the card through it. The Karkovian's eyes went wide, and he gave his companion an approving nod. The man with the hat smiled broadly. "Well now, you're my new best friend, compadre," the man said, gesturing to the empty chair at their table. "Please, have a seat."

Heckubus sat down, giving each member of the group a once-over. They were all eyeing him with a measure of judgement only those who've dealt with every type of sleazeball imaginable could possess.

"So, you're looking to charter a crew, eh?" the man said. "You in some kind of trouble, old timer?"

"What would it matter if I were?" asked Heckubus.

"More trouble means more money," the man replied. "We don't mind trouble, mind you. But if you're wanted by the Visinis or the Empire, well, extra precautions need ta be taken, y'hear?"

"For your information, I am not in any type of trouble," Heckubus lied. "But regardless, I do value discretion. So if you need to take extra precautions to ensure such a thing, I am more than happy to pay for it."

The man in the hat nodded. "Fair enough," he said.

"Before we get ahead of ourselves, I fear the nature of my business is rather time sensitive," Heckubus stated. "I need a ship that can get to its destination as quickly as possible, while avoiding normal hyperspace lanes. Can you do this?"

"Hmmmmm…" mulled the man. "Flyin' outside of established hyperspace lanes is dangerous. But we know a few smuggler routes we could navigate. Again, that'll be extra."

"Again, price is not an issue," Heckubus replied. "What about speed? Is your ship fast?"

The man gave a half laugh, half snort, as though the question was so insulting, it was funny. "Fast? You askin' if my ship is *fast*?"

"Is it?"

"You mean you ain't never heard of *The Shamrock* before?"

"Can't say I have."

"Well now, she's just the fastest private spacecraft between the Frontier and the Rim," the man replied, with more than a bit of swagger. "It ran the Atreides Gauntlet in less than twelve parsecs."

"A parsec is a unit of distance, not time," muttered Heckubus.

"Really?" asked the man, confused. "You sure about that?"

"Pretty sure."

"Well, we ran it in less than twelve something."

"You're not exactly selling me on this ship of yours," grumbled Heckubus.

The man shrugged. "Alright. Let me spell it out fer ya. *The Shamrock* is a Delorean class light freighter, retrofitted with a military grade Regalus EM engine[12] and Visini-class lightspeed engines. Not to mention a couple special

---

[12] An EM Engine is an engine propelled solely by electromagnetic waves which negates the need for fuel-based propellants to create thrust.

modifications by yours truly. We can ride her over 15% normal sublight speeds and get her up to 99.2 percent the speed of light. If ya wanna go any faster, you'd be better off hitching a ride to the nearest portgate. How's that for a sales pitch?"

Heckubus twiddled his fingers as he ran the rogue's numbers through his head. He figured with the right fine-tuning, the man's claims could work out, given the hardware he cited. "Very well," Heckubus finally said. "Your ship sounds sufficient enough. I take it you lot are her crew?"

"Name's Buchignani," the man said. "Y'all can call me Buch. This here is Kamm."

The Karkovian squinted at Heckubus and nodded his head in acknowledgement.

"He don't talk much," Buchignani said. "The big one to the back is Siv."

The large Recklec growled.

"And the dumb one to my right is Buff."

"Ee-Yo," said the Corkron, flashing a cocky grin and waving.

"The last one is Aneel. We call ourselves the Wild Ones. Pleased ta meet ya."

Heckubus squinted at the group. "Last one?" he said. "There are only four of you."

"Aneel's invisible," Buchignani said.

"Ee-Yo. That's why you can't see him," Buff said, as though the fact should be obvious.

"Invisible?" said Heckubus, incredulously. "Have him say something, then."

"He can't," grumbled Siv. "He's mute."

"Ee-Yo. That means he can't talk," chimed in Buff.

Heckubus rolled his eyes. "Is that so?" he muttered.

"He's also deaf," said Kamm, quietly.

"Ee-Yo. That means—"

"I know what it means!" snapped Heckubus. "So you can't see him, you can't hear him, and you can't speak with him. How in the blazes do you know he even exists?"

Buchignani shrugged. "Well, he's always there when we need him. Sometimes."

Heckubus sighed. "So… four morons and their imaginary friend. Oh, well. I suppose I could do worse. You're hired."

The group all looked at each other, pleasantly surprised.

"Great!" said Buchignani. "What's the job? You got special cargo that needs smuggling?"

"No cargo. Just me," said Heckubus. "I need you to transport me somewhere. Quickly and quietly. And I'd prefer to leave immediately."

"Shouldn't be a problem," Buchignani said. "Where ya need'n transport to?"

Heckubus leaned back in his chair and steepled his fingers.

"Omnicron Prime," he replied.

CHAPTER ✺ 11

A rugged looking Regal reporter appeared on the screen of a digital display, the sweeping cityscape of Nameeria behind him. "This is Danton DeGoosey, coming to you live from the planet of Redwater, where Legacy Evenstar has instituted martial law!" the reporter stated. "Yes, that's right. One of the Empire's most powerful Legacies is flexing its military muscle as Evenstar troops are being deployed throughout the planet. Redwater's impressive space fleet is also making its presence known throughout the system with increased patrols. Political analysts are saying this is a sign the Redwater system is preparing to engage in a conflict with the Regalus Empire as a prelude to secession. But earlier, Legacy head Amadeus Evenstar gave this statement to the press…"

The image cut to Amadeus, standing at a podium with an Evenstar flag proudly draped behind him. "The Redwater system and the Evenstar Legacy have always been loyal members of the Galactic Regalus Empire," he stated. "Though it is clear that Princess Glorianna was not in her right mind when she revoked the Evenstar Legacy status, the Casgor Administration continues to pursue our dissolution. We hope this issue can be resolved through the legal system and that the Casgor Administration comes to its senses soon. However, in case it does not, the Redwater system must prepare for the worst. Let me be clear. Redwater does not wish to declare independence from the Empire, but should Director Uleeg Casgor continue with his illegal persecution of my Legacy, the Redwater system will have no choice but to respond."

The scene cut back to Danton DeGoosey. "Lord Evenstar did not accept any questions after making his statement, but it is becoming increasingly clear that tensions between the Evenstar Legacy and the Casgor Administration are at an all-time high. Earlier this afternoon, the Casgor Administration released this statement…"

A digital image of the Capitol Supertower on Omnicron Prime appeared, with wording superimposed upon it as DeGoosey read from the statement. "The administration is simply following the decree of Legacy Prime in its pursuit of the dissolution of the Evenstar Legacy. The Empire's official stance is that any efforts to prevent the peaceful surrender of the Evenstars and the transition to a new Legacy in the Redwater system will be seen as an act of rebellion and will be met with military force, if need be."

The image returned to DeGoosey. "From the way things look here on Redwater, the Evenstars are indeed taking the Casgor Administration's threats seriously. Already, authorities have begun the deportation of known Imperial loyalists and agencies, such as the Imperial Intelligence Agency and the Imperial Investigative Service, as well as all incarnations of Ambassador Bob and delegations of unsympathetic Legacy representatives with offices here on the planet. But despite all this, the Evenstars are not without their supporters. Sources tell me that many Legacies, unhappy with the way the Empire is being run, are supporting the Evenstars from behind the scenes, even encouraging them to declare independence. But the most outspoken supporters are actually the four former Directors of the Empire, who made this public statement earlier…"

The scene cut to an image of Director Phenberg, standing before reporters, with Directors Jamerones, Ridsco, and Zersee behind him. "The official stance of my colleagues and I is that we stand in support of Amadeus Evenstar and his Legacy, and we believe that their persecution at the hands of Uleeg Casgor is not only illegal but also completely unjustified. I speak for all my fellow Directors when I say we believe the Earthman and his assertion that Princess Glorianna has been somehow compromised by Deathlords. Thus, we believe that all her actions since she returned from her trip to Earth must be rescinded. This includes the suspension of the Directory, as well as her dissolution of the Evenstar Legacy and the revocation of the legally passed defensive proposal. I would encourage all citizens of the Empire to contact their local planetary and system representatives and encourage them to stand firm against Uleeg Casgor and his illegal administration until such time as the Princess can be recovered, diagnosed, and properly treated."

When the scene cut back to DeGoosey, he continued. "Ever since the shocking news broke of Princess Glorianna's abduction by the former Hero of the Empire, Earthman Jack Finnegan, public opinion has been drastically divided. Some believe the Earthman's assertions of a hidden Deathlord threat within the rank and file of the Empire, while others believe it to be a fiction meant to justify the kidnapping of a galactic icon by a lovesick teenage boy. But no matter how one chooses to look at it, until the Princess can be recovered and the Earthman's accusations can be properly investigated, this legal quagmire will continue to play out, with some predicting disastrous consequences. This is Danton DeGoosey, Galactic Imperial News Service, Redwater System."

A remote control then flew into the image, cracking the monitor upon which it was displayed. Uleeg Casgor sat behind his desk in his office, glaring at the broken monitor in disdain. He then turned that gaze on Verna Jajjimoor, the

Imperial Communications Supervisor, who was standing uncomfortably by his side.

"Care to explain yourself?" Casgor grumbled.

"Sir?" asked Verna.

Casgor shot to his feet and pointed toward the broken display. "I just watched Amadeus Evenstar and my four former colleagues put the screws to me in the top news story of the blasted day!" snapped Casgor. "And how do we counter that? With a generic written response that some reporter reads on camera? Why wasn't a press conference called for me to address this situation directly?"

Verna frowned. "We did not feel it would be wise for you to make a public statement about this, Director," she replied.

"Oh, you didn't?" said Casgor, with more than a bit of condescension. "And why, pray tell, would you not think it would be a good idea to have the sole Director of the blasted Regalus Empire call out a rebellious Legacy and four bitter has-beens on the galactic holonet?"

Verna sighed. "We did not feel it would be wise due to your polling numbers, sir."

That caused Casgor to raise an eyebrow. "My... polling numbers?" he said.

Verna pulled out her datapad and called up some statistics on her screen. "I'm afraid the scandal of the Earthman accusing you of colluding with the Deathlords has dramatically affected your favorables, Director," she said, showing the polling numbers to Casgor. "The dismissal of the other Directors had already been a hit against you, due to their sectors feeling that they were unfairly ousted from their elected positions. That, coupled with the Earthman's popularity, has resulted in a staggering decline in your approval ratings. Had we allowed you to speak to the press, we felt it would have done more harm than good when it comes to the message we are trying to communicate."

Casgor grimly glared at the statistics on the datapad before knocking it away in annoyance. "That blasted Earthman!" he grumbled. "The public would rather believe the lies of some adolescent than the leader of their own Empire? What is this galaxy coming to?" Casgor sighed deeply before looking at Verna once more. "Are you doing anything to fix this?" he asked.

"Fix it, sir?"

"Yes, you moron! Fix it!" Casgor spat. "That's your job, is it not? Tell me you have a plan to spin this mess until we come out on top!"

"Unfortunately, sir, we did too good of a job building up the Earthman as a hero," Verna explained. "The public sees him as sympathetic. Any attack we could mount against him to try and discredit his claims would do more damage to us than it would to him. And without the Princess around to justify her actions, the former members of the Directory are using their influence in their sectors of the Empire to mount a concentrated propaganda campaign against you. I hate to say it, but the Earthman gave them exactly the narrative they needed to hurt you the most, and the press is loving it."

"There must be a way to change the narrative," Casgor said. "Can't you get me on a broadcast... I don't know... playing with underprivileged children or something? Something stupid like that, which would make me look better to the public?"

Verna shifted uncomfortably. "Um... I'm afraid puff pieces such as that would just come off as insincere, sir. Honestly, unless a bigger news story comes along to shift the focus away from the Earthman and his abduction of the Princess, this story will have legs and will continue to run for some time."

Just then, the intercom on Casgor's desk beeped. "Excuse me, Director," came the voice of Casgor's secretary. "Armonto Virtuoso is here to see you. He insists it is urgent."

"Send him in," Casgor replied, before turning his attention back to Verna. "Come up with some ideas on how to fix this bloody mess, Ms. Jajjimoor. I don't care if we have to stage another war with the Visinis in order to distract from this narrative – give me options!"

Verna frowned, then reluctantly nodded. "Yes... sir," she replied, before heading out the door.

Even she doesn't support me, Casgor thought, bitterly. *I'm surrounded by underlings who hate my guts! Blast that Earthman! He's made a bloody mess of everything!*

No sooner had Verna left than Armonto Virtuoso entered, followed closely by his assistant, Hylda Wahller. "Uleeg," Armonto stated in his signature monotone cadence. "You look even more dour than usual."

"You'd look this way, too, if you kept getting raked over the coals on galactic holonet," Casgor grumbled. "Unlike you, it's impossible for me to lay low, particularly when my enemies are so high profile."

"Yes, it has been a stressful couple of weeks," replied Armonto, not sounding the least bit stressed. "I cannot help but ponder how different things would be had our plans played out as we'd expected. But I suppose that is simply a waste of time. We must deal with the situation as it is, unfortunately."

"Did you have a purpose for coming here?" asked Casgor, a bit annoyed with Armonto's attitude. "I have better things to do than to suffer through your attempt at pleasantries."

"Indeed. Onto business, then," replied Armonto, turning toward his assistant. "You may summon him."

Wahller nodded, then closed her eyes. When she opened them again, they were white and pupilless, a sign that Verrutus had taken control of her. "The Earthman is in Visini space," Wahller said, her voice guttural and queer sounding, "at a shadow station called Port Somewhere."

Casgor raised an eyebrow. "A shadow station? In Visini space? Are you sure?"

"I can tell exactly where the Princess is," Wahller replied. "I have other slythru controlled beings on the station itself. I am quite familiar with it. She is close enough to the station to make me believe they are there."

"Then send them after the Earthman and let's end this feral wildegoose[13] chase once and for all," Casgor said.

"It is already in motion," Armonto stated. "But given the Earthman's propensity for thwarting his pursuers, I thought it best to send in Stalker Crux first."

"Yes, your so-called legendary bounty hunter," Casgor grumbled. "You could have bought an army of bounty hunters for what you've spent on that one mercenary."

"Stalker Crux is the best there is," Armonto stated. "He's never failed to bring in a bounty he's been hired to get."

"So you say. Though he's failed to deliver despite his encountering the Earthman more than any other bounty hunter out there."

"I have every confidence in his abilities," Armonto countered. "The Earthman took on the Royal Vanguard and somehow managed to overcome

---

[13] A wildegoose is a lankly, four-legged flightless bird known for running at incredible speeds.

them. I believe a little leeway is necessary when it comes to the number of encounters it will take to capture him."

"Well, you'll need to send everything you have in proximity to that base, because this time I'm unable to assist you," Casgor said, looking at Wahller. "I cannot justify sending Imperial military vessels into Visini space without their Empire's cooperation, especially with all the heat on me in the press at the moment."

"My Secret Army will deal with this, as will Virtuoso's bounty hunters," Wahller replied. "But I am not here about the Earthman. I wish to talk to you about the situation in Redwater."

"I have that under control," Casgor replied. "Amadeus Evenstar just declared martial law. That means he doesn't have the full support of his planet's leadership. It's a desperate move if I ever saw one."

"Regardless," Wahller said. "I want you to send in the 3rd fleet. Immediately."

Casgor looked at Wahller in surprise. "Send in the Starkeeper fleet? But why? Doing so would just galvanize the Redwater leadership and force them into backing the Evenstars. Not to mention it would make us look like the aggressors."

"I do not care what it looks like," Wahller said. "Just get it done."

Casgor glared at Armonto. "Are you not going to back me up on this?" he demanded.

"If the goal is indeed to foster rebellion in order to break apart the Empire, then perhaps allowing time to sow discord within the Redwater leadership would be wise," Armonto said to Wahller.

"No matter how the situation in Redwater plays out, rest assured that system shall be the first domino to fall in what will result in the Empire finally breaking apart," Wahller replied. "Even now, events are in motion to ensure the independence movement among the Legacies will gain steam. But a more pressing matter is that the 3rd fleet needs to be occupied somewhere other than the Maxima system. That is where the real game is being played."

"Hold on a minute," Casgor said. "We never discussed this…"

"We are discussing it now," Wahller replied.

"No, you're issuing orders now," Casgor argued. "The Deathlord raids in the Rim were only meant to scare the Legacies enough to keep their fleets in their

systems and buy me sympathy points among my constituents. Now you're telling me there's another plan at play? In the system of my biggest supporter, no less?"

"Perhaps if you were more forthcoming in your plans, we would be better able to assist you in them," Armonto suggested to Wahller.

"You both know all you need to know," Wahller said. "And if you are unwilling to do as ordered, then you shall be replaced with those who are."

Casgor bristled at that. "Now see here," he said, his face getting flush with anger. "You cannot simply replace us! Promises were made! We were hand-chosen by the Lords of the Void—"

Wahller's hand shot out, clutching Casgor by the throat with such speed and ferocity that it took a few seconds for Casgor to fully react, clawing at her freakishly strong grip as he struggled for air.

"And who do you think these orders come from, Convert?" Wahller hissed. "I am their emissary, and I speak with their voice. To question me is to question them. Your public image, your grip on power, your social standing... it is meaningless. All that matters is the Grand Design of our Lords. You are a cog in a machine, Casgor. And if a cog breaks down, it is replaced. It is as simple as that. Now do as you are bid, or suffer the consequences!"

Casgor gave a feeble nod before Wahller released him from her grip. Casgor coughed and gasped for air, rubbing his throat where the woman's fingers had dug into his flesh.

"Send the 3rd fleet to Redwater. Keep it away from Maxima," Wahller said, before turning toward Armonto. "And you, alert the bounty hunters to the Earthman's location. By the time the sun sets here on Omnicron, he and his companions will be dead and the Princess will be returned to us. Trust in the plans of our Lords, gentlemen. They have sight beyond sight. And soon, you, too, shall bear witness to their Grand Design."

With that, Wahller's eyes returned to normal as Verrutus left her. When she regained control, Wahller looked weakened.

"You may go now," Armonto said, dismissively.

Wahller nodded, then exited the office. Casgor watched her go with more than a hint of loathing as he rubbed his sore neck. "I don't know about you, but I'm getting awfully tired of being treated like a servant when we're supposed to be partners in this endeavor," he grumbled.

"The only thing I tire of is a fifteen-year-old child and his merry band of idiots constantly destroying our meticulous plans," Virtuoso stated flatly. "At this point, the most any of us can do is play our parts, Uleeg. Now if you'll excuse me…"

Armonto turned and headed toward the door.

"…I have a trap to spring."

CHAPTER ✣ 12

Shanks stood in the great open field of his meditation construct, gazing off into the distance at the blackened land and the storm clouds swirling high overhead. He knew that was where the Princess was being kept. He'd had to wait until Verrutus had left Anna to make another attempt at reaching her, and even now, he wasn't sure how much time he'd have before the Deathlord returned.

The monk raced forward, running toward the vile domain which he'd learned led to the mental construct housing the remnant of the Princess's consciousness. Now that he'd chased the shadow there, he had an idea of where he needed to go.

Once the storm was raging overhead, Shanks willed himself into the air, flying into the clouds. The wind whipped and screeched at him, the sickly green, red, and purple lightning flashed around him, and the dark mist of the clouds tried to engulf him. But the monk was not deterred. He continued pressing forward until he finally broke through the storm, once again emerging in the black void of the prison in which Anna was being kept.

Shanks could immediately hear the sobbing of the Princess. He followed the sound until he saw her, still struggling on her hands and knees as the skeletal Deathlord loomed over her, its hands digging into her back.

Princess! Shanks called out.

The Deathlord turned, looking at Shanks as its eyes flashed as red as glowing embers. It hissed at the monk, letting Shanks know it was aware of his presence. But Anna still seemed unable to hear him.

Shanks ran forward. *Let go of her!* he cried, grabbing onto the creature and attempting to pull it off the Princess. Anna screamed in pain as the Deathlord struggled with Shanks, its claws never leaving her back. The creature hissed again, glaring at Shanks defiantly as the monk wrestled with its arms.

"Can't... save!" the slythru snarled, its voice guttural and dark.

Shanks looked at Anna, who appeared to be in agony as the monk attempted to pull the Deathlord's claws from her. *This is harming her,* Shanks thought, worriedly. *The monster has too strong of a hold! I must try something else, or I fear I may accidentally kill what is left of her!*

With that, Shanks refocused his spirit, releasing his grip on the Deathlord with one hand and reaching out toward Anna. His hand glowed with a brilliant white light as he channeled his energy toward the Princess, also plunging his hand into her back between the claws of the Deathlord.

A glow pulsed beneath Anna's back, and she gasped, her body going rigid as the light from Shanks' spirit slowly entered her.

"Princess!" Shanks called out.

"Brother Shanks?" cried Anna, looking around, searching for the source of his voice. "Where are you? Help me! Please!"

Finally! She can hear me! Shanks thought with relief. "I am here!" the monk replied. "I am trying to save you!"

"I can't see you!" Anna said before screaming in pain once more. The Deathlord had twisted its claws, trying to harm the Princess. Shanks could feel the creature's essence fighting, trying to force his spiritual connection out of Anna.

"Stay strong, Princess!" Shanks said. "Do not let the slythru beat you! You must fight it! You must fight until—"

Suddenly, the Deathlord bit down on Shanks' arm. Shanks cried out as the razor-like teeth of the creature tore through him, severing the arm at the elbow. The part that had been holding onto Anna entered into her, the spiritual energy that had connected Shanks to her flaring brightly for a brief moment before fading away completely.

No! cried Shanks as his connection to Anna was lost.

"Brother Shanks?" Anna called out, desperately. "Where did you go? BROTHER SHANKS???"

Shanks suddenly felt weakened as the abrupt cut-off of his spiritual energy flowing into the Princess took its toll. The Deathlord turned and attempted to bite him once more. In a knee-jerk reaction, Shanks raised his remaining hand to fend off the creature, digging into its chest to keep it away.

The monk's hand pierced the Deathlord's sinewy ribcage, sinking into it and making contact with the cold thread that existed there. An image of the universe appeared overhead and an avalanche of information once again flooded over Shanks.

Shanks struggled with the cacophony of voices that assaulted him. The sheer amount of information being given to him caused a searing pain in his head.

He glanced up, tempted to let go of the thread he'd latched onto, but suddenly he noticed that the image of the web was not the same as it had been the last time he'd seen it.

Threads were all around him, connected to shimmering figures that looked like indistinct marionettes on the ends of strings. Some were nearby, and others were heading toward him.

Shanks gritted his teeth, trying his best to tune out all the information he was privy to. He gripped the cold thread he'd grabbed onto tighter and was suddenly pulled upward, sliding along the silver thread and into the galaxy at large.

Shanks looked down and saw the vast emptiness of space below him as his perspective changed. He could sense the slythru he'd been struggling with still at the end of his thread, but now he could see the space station to which the group had traveled, and a number of other threads leading there. As he gazed around, he could see many other threads attached to other beings, some in ships, travelling through hyperspace as they came closer and closer.

The monk tried to come to grips with what he was seeing, his brain struggling with the shift of consciousness as he traveled along the spiritual thread that connected all the slythru together. Finally, he could no longer maintain his hold and was forced to release his grip.

Shanks' consciousness slammed back into his body. The monk opened his eyes wide as a sudden wave of nausea crashed over him. He released Anna's hands and doubled over, retching from the experience.

Anna gazed at him in disdain. "You should not have done that," she said.

Shanks wiped his mouth with the back of his hand, glaring up at the Princess with unease. "I... I reached her..." Shanks replied. "I can feel it... I was able to make a connection... I can still feel it!"

Anna scowled at him. "It makes no matter. The master is coming for you. For all of you. You have run out of time, monk."

Shanks eyes went wide as he remembered what he had seen when he'd tapped into the slythru's web. The monk immediately got to his feet and rushed out the door, Anna's derisive chuckles stinging his ears as he hurried down the hallway and onto the bridge of the Earthship. When he arrived, Professor Green was huddled over a console with Dan, looking at some data on the screen.

"I say, these are certainly some interesting upgrades Heckubus is proposing for you," Green commented. "I can certainly see how they would be useful. Particularly the emergency recovery drive."

"Yes, I agree, Master Green," Dan replied. "One of the drawbacks of sentience is that should my current programming ever be destroyed, it would never be able to be rewritten exactly the same way. I do believe it is the closest thing to death a robotic lifeform like me can experience. Knowing there is a way to protect that programming now is quite a comfort... though, I would hate to ever have to use it—"

"Professor!" gasped Shanks as he made his way toward them.

Green glanced up, just then noticing the monk's presence on the bridge. "Brother Shanks?" he said, the look on the monk's face worrying him. "What's wrong?"

"Get them back!" Shanks ordered. "Teleport them off the station now!"

Green's eyes went wide. "Oh dear," he muttered. "Why? What's wrong?"

"It's the Secret Army," Shanks replied.

"Are they coming?" Green asked.

Shanks looked at Green, his face grave. "No, Professor," he said. "I fear they are already here."

CHAPTER ✦ 13

ack strummed his fingers on the table. Grohm was on his fifth order of tundrabird wings, and Scallywag, despite slowly nursing his drinks, had still killed off almost half the bottle of rum. Jack glanced around the room at the motley collection of lowlifes that populated it, scanning for any sign of Mourdock. He pulled out his datapad and checked the time.

"Oy, how long we gonna wait before we call it?" asked Scallywag.

Jack sighed. "I don't know. Could be he's on the station and doesn't know this place used to be Stinky Pete's."

"All I know is tha longer we're here, the greater tha chance something goes wrong," Scallywag said. "I'd say we're already pushin' our luck. And considerin' how lousy our luck is, that's sayin' somethin'."

Jack grimaced. "We'll give it a bit longer," he said, before hopping out of his chair.

"Where ya think yer goin'?"

"To see if Mourdock is already here somewhere," Jack replied. "If not, then we should probably start searching the station for him."

"Tha smart thing ta do would be ta hightail it out o' here and set up a new meet."

"Well, no one ever accused us of being very smart," Jack grumbled before walking off.

Jack made his way through the boozskeller, subtly trying to get a look at everyone who was there. He saw lots of pirates, lots of aliens, and lots of sketchy-looking people – but no sign of Mourdock. *He should be here by now*, Jack thought, uneasily. *Where could he be?*

Jack continued combing through the joint until he saw Mung chatting with a group of patrons at their table. "Hey!" Jack called out, waving to the man to get his attention. "Hey, Mung! Come here!"

Mung politely extricated himself from the group he was talking to and approached Jack. "Yes, Miss? Is there a problem with your order? What's wrong? Too much *merrrrrry?*"

"Still don't know what that means," Jack replied. "Actually, I was wondering – do you greet all the people who come in here personally?"

"Indeed I do," Mung answered.

"Great! You wouldn't happen to have seen a guy around here – one that's tall, blonde, and ridiculously good-looking?"

"But of course," Mung replied. "He's right over there."

Mung pointed to a tall, blonde, ridiculously good-looking man wearing a white t-shirt that said "FLASH" on its chest, sitting at a table with a group of aliens, drinking and laughing. Jack frowned. "No, not that guy," he said. "Someone who looks more... kinda, sorta like the Emperor Ascendant of the Regalus Empire?"

Mung looked thoughtful for a moment. "Can't say I have," he answered. "If I do, shall I send him to your table?"

"Um, that's okay. Would you just let us know if he shows up?"

"As you wish, unfortunate looking young lady," Mung said with a bow, before wandering off.

Jack sighed and made his way back to his table. He'd no sooner taken his seat once more when Professor Green's voice rang out over his communicator.

"Jack! Scallywag! Come in!"

"What is it, Professor?" Jack replied.

"Shanks has detected a large number of ships heading this way," Green informed them. "They appear to be from the Secret Army! And there are others already on the station!"

Scallywag slammed the bottle of rum down on the table. "Blast it," he grumbled. "Knew this was a bloody trap!"

"I recommend we teleport you back now and make a hasty exit," Green said.

"Yeah, okay," replied Jack with disappointment. "Get us out of here."

"Initiating teleportation now," Green said.

Jack, Scallywag, and Grohm all sat at their table, waiting to be teleported back to the Earthship. But after a few seconds of nothing happening, they gave each other a confused look.

"Oy, anytime, greenskin," Scallywag said.

 ~ 111 ~

"Oh, dear…" came Green's voice. "The teleporter… it's being jammed! I can't get you off the station!"

Scallywag looked at Jack, alarmed. "I thought tha Earthship's teleporters couldn't be jammed," he said.

Jack grimaced. "No," he said, "there's one person who knows how to jam them."

"Armonto Virtuoso!" lamented Green. "He must have anticipated our strategy! There has to be a ship docked at the station carrying one of his teleportation jammers!"

"Of, bloody, course there is," grumbled Scallywag.

"Okay, let's not panic just yet," Jack said, trying to take his own advice and remain calm. "It's a big station. We have our hologuises. We just need to find another way back to the ship."

"Maybe we should head down to tha hangar bays," Scallywag suggested. "At the very least, we could find a ride off the station there. At best, we figure out which ship is jamming us and have Grohm smash it ta bits."

"Grohm smash," Grohm agreed.

Jack nodded. "Sounds like a plan. Let's do it."

Before the group could get out of their seats, an eerie quiet settled upon the room. Jack glanced around, alarmed at the lack of noise. Everyone in the establishment seemed to be staring at something.

"Blast it!" cursed Scallywag.

Jack turned and followed the pirate's gaze. Near the holographic barrier at the entrance of the boozskeller stood an imposing figure. Close to seven feet in height, it was clad in sleek but marred armor and wore a helmet that completely covered its face. Both its arms and legs appeared to have robotic components to them, and the visor on its faceplate glowed an ominous shade of red. The figure stood stoically, slowly glancing around the room with purpose as all those around him seemed to hold their breaths.

"Who… who is that?" asked Jack, a nervous feeling settling in his gut.

"That's Stalker Crux, one of the most ruthless bounty hunters in tha entire bloody galaxy," Scallywag grumbled, quietly. "They say whenever he takes a contract, he gets a Paragon to soulbind it to him and that he's never failed to deliver on a bounty. The bloke's a legend… and if he's here, it means we're truly kittened."

"Well… maybe he's not here for us?" Jack said, hopefully.

"I am here for the Earthman and his friends," came Crux's robotically enhanced voice as it boomed throughout the boozskeller.

Jack frowned.

"If anyone attempts to stop me or interfere in any way, I will dispatch you appropriately," Stalker Crux said as he slowly stepped down the stairs and into the main part of the room, his red visor glowing menacingly.

"We gotta get out of here!" Scallywag whispered urgently. "He's gonna scan this entire place any moment!"

"Take heart, dear fellow!" Green said, reassuringly, through their comms. "Imperial-grade hologuises are built to stand up to scans. You should be fine. Simply remain calm and play this appropriately casual."

"Greetings, puny mortal!" said Mung as he approached Stalker Crux. "Welcome to Mung's Merrrrrrrciless Boozskeller and Grill! I am Mung the Merciless! Owner, proprietor, and ruthless ruler over delicious flavor. Though we do welcome all types here at Mung's, I'm afraid I cannot allow you to disrupt the dining experience of any of my patrons and will have to ask you to leave."

Stalker Crux tilted his head, regarding Mung with annoyance. "Perhaps I was not clear on what will happen if anyone attempts to interfere with me," he said.

"And perhaps I was not clear in asking you to leave," Mung replied, holding out his ring, which glowed threateningly, toward Stalker Crux.

A small blast shot forth from the ring, but more quickly than was humanly possible, Stalker Crux dodged it. In one swift move, his hand shot out, clamping onto Mung's wrist and snapping it with a sharp twist. Mung cried out and Stalker Crux promptly tossed him to the side. Mung flew through the air and landed on a far table occupied by a group of diners, causing them all to collapse in a jumble of bodies.

"If I weren't so scared right now, that would have been awesome," Jack whispered.

"Earthman, I know you are here, and I know you can hear me," the voice of Stalker Crux boomed. "I will give you and your companions one chance to surrender yourselves peacefully. That will be the easy way. If you do not, then we shall do things the hard way. And trust me… you will not like the hard way."

For the longest of moments, one could hear a pin drop in the massive boozskeller. Everyone looked around, waiting to see if the Earthman would emerge and take Stalker Crux up on his offer. Jack glanced at Scallywag who frowned in reply. Grohm clenched his fists, knowing a fight was all but inevitable.

"The hard way it is, then," said Stalker Crux.

The intimidating bounty hunter reached down to his mechanical thigh, which opened up and produced a small robotic orb. Stalker Crux held the orb out, the lights on it glowing bright red. It began to spin and lift into the air, slowly drifting forward, away from its owner.

"Oy… I don't like tha look o' that," muttered Scallywag.

The orb spun faster, its lights glowing brighter. A high-pitched hum grew as it spun more and more quickly, until it was a glowing ball of pure red light. Just as the hum hit its crescendo, the light from the orb blasted out in a ripple all around it.

The force of the shockwave knocked everyone back, but when it reached Jack and his friends, it had the added effect of causing their meticulously crafted hologuises to flicker and die, revealing their true forms for all to see. There was an audible gasp from those around them as they instantly recognized Jack and his companions.

Jack looked from Scallywag, to Grohm, and then to Stalker Crux, who was glaring at them from across the room.

"Ah… crap," Jack muttered.

"Get them!" someone cried.

Before Jack knew it, mobs of patrons who'd previously been enjoying their meals were now rushing forward to capture him and his friends, spurred on by the biggest bounty in the known galaxy. Scallywag and Jack wasted no time in hopping out of their seats, pulling their pistols, and firing at anyone who got close.

Grohm grabbed their table and used it as a weapon, swinging it behind him and knocking aside a group of assailants who unfortunately thought it'd be a good idea to try to bum rush the group from behind, only to be tossed halfway across the room by the strength of the Rognok's swing.

"Run!" Scallywag ordered. "Make fer tha exit!"

Scallywag turned just in time to see a small cannon appear on Stalker Crux's shoulder. He shot at the bounty hunter, who dodged the blasts with superhuman speed, firing off his own projectile from the shoulder mounted cannon.

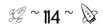

A green blast of energy rocketed forth, and Scallywag could not move fast enough to dodge it. It hit him dead-on, the energy from the blast encasing him in a sickly green glow, freezing him in place.

"Scally!" Jack cried.

Grohm roared and leapt toward Stalker Crux who hopped back just as Grohm landed, the Rognok slamming his fist into the ground where the bounty hunter had stood just moments before.

While Grohm occupied Stalker Crux, Jack ran to Scallywag and tried to grab him, but whatever energy had encased the pirate gave Jack a sharp static shock and caused him to recoil. When Jack looked at Scallywag, the only thing that seemed to be able to move were the Visini's eyes, which gave Jack a sad and defeated look.

Chaos reigned as patrons ran to and fro, some to hiding places and some to the exits, while others were simply caught in the melee between Grohm and the bounty hunter. There were a few who still attempted to assault Jack, but Jack held them off with his stun gun.

Grohm swung at Stalker Crux again and again, but the bounty hunter dodged all the Rognok's blows. Stalker Crux leapt backward, firing his shoulder cannon at Grohm and hitting him squarely in the chest. Grohm grunted, the green energy snaking around him, slowing his movements. Stalker Crux hit him a second time with a stasis blast, and by the time the third blast had landed, Grohm, too, had been frozen in place.

"No!" cried Jack as he fired his pistol at Stalker Crux.

The bounty hunter didn't even have to dodge, as Jack's shot went wide and completely missed him.

Dang it, I really need to learn how to aim, Jack thought, bitterly, right before Stalker Crux focused his cannon at him.

Jack wasted no time in running for cover as the bounty hunter's cannon opened fire. Green bolts of stasis energy shot by, almost catching Jack as he ran, hitting unfortunate patrons in the crossfire and freezing them in place. Jack slid behind the salad bar at the center of the room just as the stasis blasts caught up with him. He huddled behind the cover as bits of veggies showered down upon him.

Jack's heart was racing. He felt panicked. It wasn't the first time Jack had been in a firefight, but this Stalker Crux was a completely different kind of adversary than any he'd faced before. Jack took a moment to center himself.

This bounty hunter had assaulted his friends. He'd assaulted Jack. And now, he was ruining a perfectly good and reasonably priced vegetable buffet.

Alright, buddy. You want to play? Jack thought, mustering his courage. *Let's play.*

Jack took a deep breath and closed his eyes. He quickly focused on his Source and entered into Equilibrium.

When he opened his eyes, time around him seemed to have slowed. Every speck of dust, every ray of light, every sound and smell – he was aware of it all. He was aware of all the people who'd been frozen by the stasis blasts. He was also aware of the ruthless cyborg bounty hunter who was currently making his way around to flank Jack from the side.

Without wasting another instant, Jack moved, sprinting forward just in time to avoid the blast from Stalker Crux's cannon as the bounty hunter cleared the side of the salad bar.

Jack turned as he ran, firing his pistol at the bounty hunter. In the hyper-enhanced awareness of Equilibrium, Jack could watch the purple bolts from his weapon slowly streak toward his pursuer. But to his surprise, he could see that Stalker Crux didn't seem to be affected by his shift in perception. The bounty hunter moved as Jack did, as though he, too, had some type of hyper-awareness that allowed him to react with great precision and speed.

Stalker Crux dodged the blasts, sliding between the bolts Jack fired as though he were in some type of dance. The bounty hunter dashed forward, quickly enough to keep Jack from anticipating it.

Jack spun and leapt back, gliding through the air as he continued to fire. But as expertly as he was aiming under the influence of Equilibrium, Stalker Crux was just as expertly dodging the blasts.

Jack saw the bounty hunter's shoulder cannon's muzzle flare with a bright green glow as it prepared to fire again. Now it was Jack's turn to dodge, landing on his heel and flipping away just as the blast rocketed forth, barely missing him.

Jack grabbed a nearby table and flung it between him and his assailant, the next stasis blast hitting the table instead of its intended target. Jack quickly changed his direction, dashing to the side to circle back around Stalker Crux, but it appeared the bounty hunter had anticipated his maneuver and had already adjusted course.

Jack noticed Stalker Crux extend his arm, a small launcher popping up from his gauntlet and firing a metallic disk. Jack spun, dodging the disk as it flew by his head. As soon as the disk made impact with the wall behind him, it exploded. The small detonation sent a blast of light, smoke, and sound slowly emanating toward Jack, a cacophony of concussion that Jack had to use all his concentration to escape.

Jack had no sooner cleared the concussive blast than he turned to see Stalker Crux leaping forward, landing at a distance that was almost on top of him.

No, Jack thought.

Jack turned and fired, but Stalker Crux had already leapt to the side, dodging Jack's blasts and further closing the distance.

No! Jack thought again, panic beginning to rise within him, threatening to break his Equilibrium.

Then, Stalker Crux leapt forth, gliding through the air directly toward Jack. The cannon on the bounty hunter's shoulder glowed green as it prepared to fire, and Jack instantly knew Stalker Crux had him dead to rights. There was nowhere to run. No way to dodge the blast. The bounty hunter had somehow gotten the drop on Jack, even in his enhanced state. However, despite it all, there was one thing Stalker Crux, the most legendary bounty hunter in the known galaxy, didn't take into account when he made his final maneuver.

He didn't take into account how much Jack *hated* to lose.

Instinctively, Jack dropped his pistol and held out his hand toward his assailant. Jack suddenly became aware of his body's energy, emanating from his chest and travelling down his arm, coalescing into a bright, ghostly ball in his hand.

"NO!" Jack cried.

The ghostly ball rocketed forth from Jack's hand, tearing through the air faster than anything Stalker Crux could have anticipated. It slammed into the bounty hunter with a crushing impact.

Immediately, time returned to normal as Jack lost his Equilibrium and Stalker Crux was thrown back violently by the blow, crashing into a far wall and leaving a dent in its paneling as he crumpled to the floor. A hollow-sounding scream could be faintly heard – not from Stalker Crux's modulated voice, but almost as though it came from within the bounty hunter's armor. Ghostly white tendrils snaked around the cyborg as various electronics in his armor appeared to short out, sparking and flaring as they failed. Before long his glowing red visor went dark, and he lay still.

Just then, all who'd been entrapped in the bounty hunter's stasis fields were freed as the energy that had been holding them in place dissipated. Those who'd tried to interfere in the fight quickly ran off after seeing what Jack had done to such a fearsome enemy. It didn't take long for Scallywag and Grohm to recover, rallying to Jack's side.

"Bloody squick, that was a close one," Scallywag muttered. "I thought we were caught fer sure."

Grohm eyed the unconscious bounty hunter and grunted. "Must leave," he said.

"Aye, and we oughta make a hasty exit," Scallywag said. "Word's gonna get around fast. We gotta make it off this station before every last bloody scumbag here sets their sights on us."

Jack could barely hear what his friends were saying. It felt as though his body were frozen. He was completely numb from head to toe.

What's... what's happening? Jack thought, struggling to make his brain work.

Scallywag eyed Stalker Crux curiously. "Ain't never seen ya pull that trick before, lad," Scallywag said, looking at Jack. "He obviously wasn't expectin' it, neither. Looked like what them Deathlords do when they fight. Where'd ya learn how ta do that?"

Jack didn't reply.

"Right. Guess it don't matter," said Scallywag. "We should hurry and get outta here before that bloke comes to."

Jack wobbled on his feet, unsteadily. His brain buzzed and his guts felt like they were twisting inward. He felt sick, with a growing sensation of a stack of weights building up on his chest and crushing him.

Scallywag looked at Jack, waiting for him to respond. "Jack, ya hear me? This entire station's gonna descend upon us any minute! We need ta get movin'!"

When Jack didn't seem to respond to Scallywag's urgings, the pirate eyed him with concern.

"Jack?" Scallywag asked.

It was then Jack screamed, clutching at his chest. He fell to his knees, wailing in anguish. Both Scallywag and Grohm knelt by his side, grabbing onto him as he flailed about, his entire body violently convulsing.

"JACK!" cried Scallywag.

It was the last thing Jack heard before his world went dark, overcome by the most excruciating agony he'd ever experienced.

CHAPTER ❈ 14

"**H**ave we been able to figure out where the jamming signal is coming from?" Green asked.

"I fear not, Master Green," Dan replied as he tapped away at his console on the bridge of the Earthship. "All our long-range sensors are telling us is that there is a jamming field emanating from the station, but we are unable to pinpoint its origin. It could be coming from anywhere on the base."

Green frowned. "Oh dear, oh dear," he muttered. "If we're unable to teleport them, how are we going to get them off of there?"

Shanks stood thoughtfully gazing at the image of Port Somewhere on the viewscreen of the bridge, his face grim. "Professor," he said, "you must get us to the station."

"To the station?" said Green, nervously. "But... as soon as we get within range of its plasma cannons, they could easily take us out."

"Unless we can figure out a way to disable that jamming signal, the only chance we have of rescuing Jack and the others is to get our ship on that station, so they can board us," replied Shanks. "Unless you have a better idea, I do not see another option."

Green's frown grew even bigger. "No, I suppose you are correct," he said as he laid his hands upon the control domes of the pilot's chair. "If they cannot come to us, we must go to them. Dan, please continue trying to trace the origin of that jamming signal. I fear I will be too preoccupied trying not to get us killed to devote much attention to it."

"I am happy to be of assistance, sir," Dan replied.

Green started up the Earthship's engines and began accelerating toward the space station. Shanks came up beside him as Green flew the ship. The Professor's face taught with concentration.

"It seems most of the station's hangars are sealed by plasma windows instead of blast doors," Shanks observed. "If we can last long enough to fly into one, we can then make our escape with the Entanglement Engine the moment the others are aboard."

"Lasting long enough will be the true challenge, my friend," Green replied. "Between my sluggish connection with the Earthship and my rather lackluster skills as a pilot, I fear this task may be far more harrowing than it should be."

Shanks put a reassuring hand on the Professor's shoulder. "Fear not, Professor. I have every faith in you. I am confident you will get us there, and we will save our friends."

Just then, a sensor alarm beeped as seven hyperspace windows opened up directly in front of the Earthship and just as many bounty hunter fightercraft exited them, their plasma cannons blazing. Green shrieked as the Earthship rocked from direct hits to its forward shields, and the attacking vessels screeched by.

"Oh, my!" exclaimed Dan. "Forward shields are down to 57%. Sensors are tracking seven hostile spacecraft in the area, and they are all coming back around for another attack, sirs!"

"Seven attackers and we're not even halfway to Port Somewhere yet," Green said. He looked at Shanks. "Are you still confident about our chances?"

A worried look grew on Shanks' face. "I… um… think perhaps I should man the weapons station."

"I think that would be a good idea," replied Green as he turned his attention back to flying. "Let us hope you are a better shot than I am a pilot."

Scallywag emerged from the holographic barrier of Mung's Merciless Boozskeller and Grill and into the bustling hallways of Port Somewhere. Grohm followed closely behind, an unconscious Jack slung over his shoulder. There was obvious commotion in the corridors, with patrons from Mung's still making a scene by fleeing the restaurant and disrupting the normal flow of foot traffic outside of it.

Scallywag quickly glanced around, trying to find a good escape route. However, no particular direction looked very appealing considering the sheer number of people that happened to be walking around. No matter where they went, he and Grohm would be wading into a sea of potential enemies.

"This way," said Scallywag as he motioned for Grohm to follow him. "We have ta hurry and find a maintenance corridor or someplace off tha beaten path ta hide until we can figure a way off this station."

"Battle?" asked Grohm as he lumbered behind the pirate.

"No! No battle!" Scallywag insisted. "Tha only thing we got goin' fer us right now is tha fact that not everyone on the station knows we're here! If we can get outta sight quick enough, we can lay low and figure out a way ta get off this blasted tin can. The last thing we need is ta be fightin' fer our lives while mounting an escape. So try not ta do anything to draw attention to us! Savvy?"

Just then, every digital display in the corridor – and presumably the station – went staticky. Whatever image the monitor had been displaying was suddenly replaced by that of Armonto Virtuoso, his monotone cadence booming out from the station's speaker system.

"Attention inhabitants of Port Somewhere," Armonto said. "This is a prerecorded message designed to be broadcast if my contractors have failed in their mission. I urge you to stop what you're doing and pay attention, because this is very important…"

Scallywag felt an icy tingle crawl up his back as he noticed almost everyone in the corridors stopping and directing their attention to the broadcast. The images of Jack, Scallywag, Grohm, and the others replaced the image of Armonto Virtuoso on all the screens.

"Right now, the Earthman Jack Finnegan and his companions are on your space station. In case you are unaware, these are all fugitives wanted by the Regalus Empire for the kidnapping of our sovereign leader, Princess Glorianna of Legacy Prime. Every single one of you listening to this is in a unique position to become extremely wealthy. The largest bounties ever levied by the Empire are on the heads of the Earthman and each of his companions. But if any one of you can capture them at this moment, the Maguffyn Corporation will match those bounties, digicredit for digicredit."

A noticeable murmur travelled through the crowd watching the broadcast. *Bloody squick*, thought Scallywag, the pit of his stomach assaulted by a growing sense of dread.

"The only thing we care about is the safe return of the Princess," Armonto continued. "As to the well-being of those who have abducted her… well, I will leave that up to you. The double bounty will be rewarded, be they alive or dead."

As the images of Jack and the others lingered on the screens, ever so slowly, the pirates, smugglers, mercenaries, criminals, and other lowlifes populating the corridors of Port Somewhere all turned toward Scallywag and Grohm who suddenly found themselves surrounded by a sea of unscrupulous enemies, now with quite a sizable motivation to come after them.

For the briefest of moments, everyone within sight of the duo stood still as statues, as though their brains were taking time to register the fact that the beings Armonto Virtuoso had just spoken of were actually standing before them. Grohm sneered, a defiant snort escaping from him. Scallywag's hands moved to his plasma pistols, just before he remembered he'd left them back on the ship.

Suppose that's what I get fer tryin' ta play nice, thought Scallywag, fatalistically.

As the calm before the storm lingered, Scallywag's lips curled into a snarl as he glanced back at his large companion.

"Grohm," he said.

The Rognok looked down at him and met Scallywag's gaze.

"Battle," was all the Visini had to say.

As the Rognok roared, Scallywag pulled his stun pistols and opened fire.

The Earthship shook from another direct hit as Professor Green desperately tried to maneuver away from their relentless attackers. His jaw was set and his teeth were gritted as he attempted to dodge the bounty hunters whose volleys were persistently weakening the ship's shields.

How does Jack make this look so easy??? thought Green with frustration as more alarms blared, signaling dangerously low shield levels.

"Brother Shanks!" called Green, nervously. "I don't suppose you could… you know… shoot some of these fellows?"

"I am trying, Professor," replied Shanks from behind the weapons' console, looking just as stressed as Green. "However, I fear I am not very practiced in the art of starship combat."

That makes two of us, grumbled Green in his mind.

"Master Green!" cried Dan. "I have good news!"

"Excellent! I could use some good news right about now!" Green replied.

"Our long-range sensors have picked up a transmission from the station," Dan said. "It would seem Armonto Virtuoso sent out a prerecorded message alerting all of Port Somewhere to the presence of Master Jack and the others."

Green frowned. "That... doesn't seem very good..." he commented.

"Oh, no. It is quite terrible, sir," Dan replied. "No doubt those on the station are in quite a bit of mortal danger at the moment. However, I was able to trace the broadcast signal from which the message emanated back to one of the hangars. If there is a ship there that broadcast that message, then I believe it would be logical to assume—"

"That the jamming signal is coming from the same ship!" exclaimed Green. "Dan! That is fantastic news!"

"I figured you would be pleased, sir."

"Quickly, contact the others and let them know which hangar that signal came from," ordered Green. "If they can disable the jamming device, we'll be able to teleport them away and get out of here!"

"I shall get right on that, Master Green."

"And that means we'll only have to survive long enough for them to take out the jammer!" said Green cheerily. "Things are starting to look up, eh, Brother Shanks?"

Shanks frowned as the Earthship rocked once more from a hit by their attackers.

"Yes... quite encouraging," the monk replied, dourly.

Scallywag continued firing at the crowd behind them as Grohm cut a path forward, throwing everything he could get his massive hands on – visual displays, furniture, even other people – in an effort to clear the way. The scene was one of complete chaos as plasma bolts were flying everywhere and people were screaming, running, and calling out in alarm. Wall panels from the station melted from the impacts of the wild plasma blasts, loose electrical cables sparked dangerously as they swung overhead, and exposed pipes burst, leaking steam into the corridors.

"Keep movin'!" cried Scallywag as he continued to fire, forcing the assailants behind them to scatter for cover. "We gotta get off the main thoroughfare, on tha double!"

"Master Scallywag!" came Dan's voice through the communication earbud. "Please come in! I have something important to—"

"Kinda busy here, robot!" Scallywag cried. "Call back later!"

"But sir—"

"I SAID NOT BLOODY NOW!" yelled Scallywag in response as he narrowly dodged a plasma blast and returned fire, dropping the offending assailant in an unconscious heap on the floor.

Grohm, still carrying Jack on his shoulder, rounded a bend in the hallway to find a group of mercenaries camped out there, waiting for them. They immediately opened fire, catching the Rognok on his arm before Grohm quickly backed away behind the wall. Scallywag, who had been walking backward as he fired, bumped into him.

"Oy! What's the hold up?" Scallywag cried before seeing the blackened skin on Grohm's arm where the plasma blast had landed.

Grohm snorted. "Ambush," he grumbled.

Scallywag frowned and looked at the attackers who were slowly moving into position behind cover in the corridor to their rear. "Bloody squick," he muttered. "Can't go forward, can't go back... what do we do now?"

Grohm unslung Jack from his shoulder and handed him to Scallywag who awkwardly took the boy while giving Grohm a questioning look.

"Go through," Grohm replied, before turning and punching the wall.

The paneling crumpled from the force of the Rognok's blow, and before Scallywag knew it, Grohm was tearing through the pipes, support beams, and circuitry beyond. Gasses leaked and sparks flew in Grohm's wake as he barreled through the wall and burst out from behind the ambushing attackers.

Scallywag watched one mercenary go flying from behind the bend, crying out as he hit the wall and crumpled into a heap. Two more ran around the junction in an effort to get away from Grohm, only to be shot by Scallywag's stun gun. Scallywag then strolled around the corner to see Grohm making short work of the remaining attackers. Apparently, he was using the largest of them as a club to swat the others away. When he was done, Grohm tossed aside the mercenary he'd been using, and the man hit the floor with a dazed look in his eyes.

Grohm then turned toward some others located in the hallway who'd been standing back, plasma weapons in hand. They were all looking at the Rognok, wide-eyed. Grohm roared at them, and they all dropped their weapons and ran away, giving the duo a clear path down the hall.

"Good job, mate," Scallywag said as he began to hurry down the corridor. "Now let's hustle before those browners behind us decide ta shoot us in tha back."

Scallywag didn't make it very far before Jack's eyes suddenly shot open and the boy began to scream. As Jack thrashed about, Scallywag was forced to drop him on the floor, unable to carry him as he flailed.

"Blast it, Jack! This is not tha time!" growled Scallywag.

Despite the pirate's protestation, Jack continued to cry out and convulse.

"Grohm," Scallywag said. "Could you—"

"DOWN!" the Rognok cried.

Grohm quickly pushed Scallywag to the side, stepping over Jack and grabbing hold of the damaged wall panel they'd busted through just as a group of attackers emerged from around the corner, opening fire. Scallywag quickly ducked for cover as Grohm took a blast in the shoulder, right before he tore the wall panel off and held it before him like a shield.

Grohm grunted as the wall panel was peppered with plasma blasts. Scallywag knew they needed to run, but Jack was still violently convulsing. Scallywag grimaced and knelt by Jack's side.

"I know somethin's wrong with ya and yer hurtin', lad," Scallywag said. "And I feel really bad about this, but desperate times and all…"

Scallywag promptly aimed his stun gun at Jack and shot him. The purple blast made Jack's body go taut before it went completely limp, knocking Jack out cold. Grohm frowned at Scallywag.

"What? Ya had a better idea?" Scallywag snapped.

"Master Scallywag, sir," came Dan's voice over the comms once more.

"Bloody squick, robot! I already told ya – not now!"

"With all due respect, sir, the longer you take to hear what I have to say, the longer you will most likely continue to be in peril," Dan replied. "We believe we have found the location of the teleportation jammer. If you can make it to hangar

bay 149 and disable the device, we'll be able to teleport all of you away and make our escape."

"Well, why didn't ya say somethin' sooner?"

"But, sir, I—"

"We're on our bloody way!"

Grohm grunted once more as part of the wall paneling he was using to shield the group from the plasma blasts began to melt and break away. Grohm quickly flung the deteriorating hunk of metal at their assailants before ripping off another piece of the wall. Scallywag rushed up and began to fire at the attackers who had embedded themselves behind cover.

"We're not gonna make it to that hangar with these browners hounding us the entire way," Scallywag grumbled.

"Take Earthman," Grohm said. "Get to hangar."

Scallywag looked at the Rognok. "Oy, what about you?"

"Not important," Grohm replied. "Save Earthman. Save Regal Princess. Stop Deathlords. That is important."

Scallywag frowned. He fell back and grabbed Jack, hefting him over his shoulder. "I know ya can take care o' yerself, Grohm, but… just hold out long enough so we can teleport ya outta here as soon as I take out that jammer, yeah?"

Grohm nodded. Scallywag started to head off, but then he stopped and turned back to Grohm. "And just fer the record, mate," he said. "I know I speak fer Jack, as well, when I tell ya… yer important ta us."

Grohm smiled. "Good luck, Visini."

"Back at ya, ya bloody Rognok."

Scallywag hurried down the corridor as Grohm remained, his flimsy shield already beginning to crumble from the relentless plasma bolts his attackers were firing. With a roar, Grohm charged forward, throwing what remained of the wall panel at two gunmen who were behind cover. Grohm rounded the corner of the hallway to find even more assailants, all with their weapons ready.

Without hesitation, Grohm leapt into the fray, just as they all opened fire.

CHAPTER ✦ 15

Yellow and red emergency lights flashed as Scallywag hurried down yet another maintenance hallway, huffing and puffing as he did so. "When ya come to, lad, we're gonna have ta talk about all that pizza ya eat," Scallywag muttered. "No way someone as small as you should be this bloody heavy!"

Scallywag's feet ached as he continued his trek through Port Somewhere in an effort to reach the area in which hangar 149 was located. Finally, he reached the door leading to one of the hangar terminals that would lead to his destination. He took a moment to set Jack down and catch his breath.

"Master Scallywag!" came Dan's voice from his earpiece. "Are you any closer to reaching the hangar, sir?"

"Yeah. I'm almost there," replied Scallywag.

"Oh, good! Might I suggest you hurry, sir? I fear we here on the Earthship are not faring very well against the vessels that are assaulting us."

"How much longer can ya hold out?"

"Our shields are failing quickly, I'm afraid. I'm exhausting all alternate energy sources to power them, and I fear once they are gone our engines will be disabled. I calculate we have maybe ten minutes before such an event occurs — possibly fifteen minutes if Master Shanks actually begins hitting our attackers."

Scallywag sighed. "Right," he muttered. "I'm on it."

Scallywag picked up Jack once more and emerged from the maintenance hall, warily checking the area as he did so. Foot traffic had definitely thinned out once the fight had started, but there were still a number of people traversing the station. In the case of the hangar terminal, there were more than a few individuals milling about. Some of them were maintenance workers and mechanics, some were spacers, and others were obviously scumbags.

Upon deciding there was no real way to make it to hangar 149 unseen, Scallywag simply opened fire on anyone in sight. This sent most of the people who were in his way scrambling. However, it also gave those who escaped time to report in about what was happening.

"Attention," came a voice over the station's speaker system. "The Earthman and the Visini have been spotted at Hangar Terminal D-7. Repeat, they have been spotted at Hangar Terminal D-7. To prevent escape and theft of spacecraft, all ships are being locked down via docking clamps."

Scallywag frowned. *Hopefully, I'll be able ta destroy tha jammer easily, and we can just teleport out o' here before more wanna-be bounty hunters show up…*

Scallywag finally reached the entrance to hangar 149, but as soon as he saw the ship that was parked there, he stopped short. Docked in the hangar was none other than *The Phantom Menace* itself.

I should learn not ta hope, thought Scallywag, fatalistically. *If I were a bettin' man, my guess would be Stalker Crux is tha one who owns this bloody ship. Which means disabling tha jammer is gonna be more difficult than I thought.*

"Look!" came a voice from the terminal area. "They're over there!"

Scallywag turned and saw a group of mercenaries and pirates quickly heading toward him. *They got here bloody fast*, he thought bitterly before sealing the door to the hangar behind him. *I just need enough time ta get on board The Phantom Menace and shoot that blasted jammer!*

Scallywag hurried toward the ship, but as he got closer, lights on *The Phantom Menace* suddenly came to life, as if it could tell someone were approaching it. A panel below the nose of the vessel opened, and a small plasma cannon dropped down, rotating to aim directly at Scallywag.

"Oh, fer tha love of…"

Scallywag quickly moved behind some thick machinery as the ship fired upon him. Red blasts streaked by as Scallywag tried to protect Jack with his body. The blasts were unrelenting as the plasma cannon continuously fired upon them.

Could this get any worse? Scallywag wondered.

Just then, the door to the hangar exploded and the group, which had spotted him previously, came rushing in, weapons in hand.

Of course, it could…

As luck would have it, *The Phantom Menace's* sensors detected a few of the more overzealous attackers who came rushing right toward Scallywag, and the plasma cannon turned on them, cutting them down before they could even get close to the pirate and the Earthman. The other ones, upon seeing their companions fall, hung back and opened fire from across the hangar, causing Scallywag to push back further behind his cover.

The machine behind which Scallywag hid began to spark and shake as unrelenting plasma fire systematically broke it down. Scallywag knew he'd have

to make a move soon if he were going to survive, but he also knew he couldn't save himself and Jack at the same time. He looked down at Jack, conflicted about the decision he was going to be forced to make.

First Northstar[14], then Faruuz[15], now Jack… he thought, sadly. *How many mates do I have ta sacrifice ta keep meself alive?*

Suddenly, there was a loud *CRACKing* sound. Scallywag glanced around the side of his cover and saw the support beams of the hangar's scaffolding buckle, causing various platforms and catwalks above his attackers to drop down upon them. Some of the assailants were caught unaware and buried beneath the tangle of metal crashing down from above. Others dodged out of the way, revealing themselves, before some invisible force seemed to hurl them aside, sending them flying against walls, cargo crates, and maintenance machinery.

Scallywag glanced up at one of the remaining catwalks high above the entrance to the hangar and saw a man in a black cloak, his face obscured by a hood, standing with his arm outstretched. Some of the remaining attackers saw him, as well, and fired upon him. The hooded figure flipped off the balcony he was on and gracefully fell to the floor. A strange indent appeared in the ground just before he landed, causing him to hover briefly before setting down, as though he hadn't just jumped from a three-story height.

A blazing blue sword suddenly appeared in his hand as he moved with inhuman speed, deflecting the plasma blasts directed his way back at his attackers. The cloaked man ran forward, also deflecting the plasma fire from *The Phantom Menace* as he approached Scallywag. Before Scallywag knew it, a metal wall had appeared between his current cover and the ship, giving him a much needed buffer from the ship's cannon.

The hooded man quickly made his way behind the metal wall, which rang dully as the plasma fire from *The Phantom Menace* began to pepper it. In the distance, Scallywag could see more lowlifes entering into the hangar bay, their weapons drawn.

"Oy! Behind you!" Scallywag called out.

The hooded figure didn't even turn around before another wall appeared behind him, protecting Scallywag and him from the blaster fire of the new arrivals. The man then lowered his hood to reveal the face of Mourdock Skyborn, his

---

[14] Northstar is the name of Scallywag's brother, whom Scallywag betrayed and murdered.
[15] Faruuz was a of crewmate of Scallywag's who ended up dying on the Deathlord Mothership during the events of *The Ghost Planet.*

blonde hair practically waving in a nonexistent wind. Scallywag was never one to be easily impressed, but in that moment, even he couldn't help but fanboy-out a little for the heroic reveal of the man who'd just saved the day.

"Come with me if you want to live," Mourdock said.

Scallywag hefted Jack onto his shoulder and smiled. "Consider me comin'," he replied.

Mourdock led Scallywag to the edge of the wall he'd erected. "Stay next to me," Mourdock ordered. "I'll protect you from the blaster fire until we get clear."

"Not fer nothin', but if ya help me get onboard that ship, I can disable its jamming device, and we can all teleport off this bloody station together."

Mourdock shook his head. "Even if the ship weren't protected by a heavy shield along with motion-sensitive blaster cannons, and even if there weren't a small army of trigger-happy thugs to pin us down, I'm fairly certain Armonto Virtuoso has some type of trap in that ship to prevent anyone from disabling that device," Mourdock said. "Unfortunately, if you want off this station, we're going to have to do it the old-fashioned way."

Scallywag frowned, realizing Mourdock was probably correct in his assumption. "Right," Scallywag said. "Who am I ta argue with tradition? Lead tha way."

Mourdock nodded and raised his sword, which crackled with blue energy. "Now!" he ordered.

Mourdock stepped out from behind the wall and began to deflect the blaster fire from *The Phantom Menace*, keeping himself between the ship and Scallywag as they moved out of range of its sensors. The hangar area was a wide enclosure that circled around to encompass a number of other ships docked at the station. When they approached a wall that separated hangar bays, Mourdock held up his hand and the wall crumpled as a hole was blasted through it, allowing them to make their way to the next hangar.

"Oy, that be a nifty trick," Scallywag commented.

"Yes, gravity pulses can come in quite handy," Mourdock commented, before glancing behind them to see their pursuers scrambling past the plasma fire from *The Phantom Menace* to continue their chase. "Keep moving," Mourdock ordered. "My ship isn't far."

Scallywag followed behind Mourdock as they hurried through the hangars while more and more assailants streamed into the bays to try to cut them off.

However, Mourdock used gravity pulses to prevent the attackers from getting too close and deflected any blaster fire directed toward them with his sword.

"Master," Mourdock said into a communications device as they walked, "I have Jack. We're on our way to the ship. Prepare for takeoff."

"Understood," replied Master Hasatan's voice.

Mourdock noted the ever-growing assembly of assailants trailing behind them. "We're going to be bringing company with us," Mourdock added.

"Just tell me when you'd like me to welcome them, my charge."

Mourdock grabbed Scallywag by the arm and began ushering him along more quickly. "We need to hurry," he said. "Not even I can protect you and Jack from that many assailants."

"You sure?" Scallywag asked. "Ya seem ta be doin' a bang-up job so far…"

"There's only so much blaster fire I can deflect before I reach the limits of my skill," Mourdock said. "I can protect myself just fine. But trying to protect two other people, as well, makes things more difficult. I'd rather not take any chances when it comes to Jack's life."

"Aye. Nor me with mine," Scallywag uttered.

Just then, the two men heard a strange *PLOOP* sound ring out. They turned to see a thermal grenade flying through the air, arcing right toward them.

"Bloody squick!" cried Scallywag.

Mourdock instinctively reached his hand out, and a gravity pulse knocked the grenade to the side, sending it into a stack of cargo crates before exploding. Scallywag and Mourdock both stumbled from the force of the blast.

"RUN!" Mourdock cried.

Scallywag ran as best he could while shouldering Jack's unconscious body. More *PLOOP* sounds rang out as the trailing mob shot more thermal grenades. Mourdock did his best to knock the incoming explosives away, but he had no control over where they would land. The super-heated explosions were practically licking at their heels, causing parts of the hangar they were traversing to collapse around them.

Bloody morons! thought Scallywag as he frantically ran from the onslaught. *If one of those grenades takes out a plasma window, everyone in this bloody hangar is dead!*

Mourdock deflected another thermal grenade, which tumbled off under a nearby starship that had been receiving maintenance on its engines. The grenade

rolled under one of the exposed thrusters and when it detonated, the ship exploded along with it, shaking the hangar so badly, everyone in the vicinity fell to the ground.

Scallywag's ears rang, and smoke hung heavily in the air. He shook his head to try to clear the daze caused by the impact of the explosion. He could hear the muffled shouts of their pursuers as they scrambled about, and a fire raged among the corpse of the starship that had just exploded. Jack lay nearby, and Scallywag tried crawling toward him before he felt a hand clamp down on the back of his collar. For a moment, Scallywag was afraid it was one of their attackers who'd somehow been able to reach him, but that worry didn't last long as he was pulled to his feet and came face-to-face with Mourdock.

"You okay?" Mourdock asked.

"I'll live…" Scallywag replied.

"Not for long if we don't get out of here soon," Mourdock said as he assisted Scallywag in picking Jack off the ground. "Follow me…"

Mourdock made for a nearby hangar door, and Scallywag followed. It didn't take long for their pursuers to pick back up on their trail, and soon the two men were running down a corridor while a group of thugs chased them, their blasters blazing.

"Coming in hot, Master!" Mourdock said into his comm device as he batted away the blaster fire with his sword to protect Scallywag and Jack.

"Fear not, Mourdock," Hasatan replied. "I am ready for you."

"Straight ahead!" Mourdock barked. "Hangar 162!"

"I see it!" Scallywag replied, the large entrance to the aforementioned hangar bay looming before them.

A surge of adrenaline helped Scallywag pick up the pace as he ran forward toward the large Maxima-class corvette residing in the hangar. The ship had a hammerhead shape to it, with four large engines and heavy hull armor, which originally looked to have been painted blue but seemed to have been marred by a great deal of action over time. If there were one thing Scallywag could tell immediately, it was that the corvette was a ship that was meant for battle, and in their current situation, that gave him a great deal of comfort.

"Now, Master!" Mourdock yelled into his comm device as soon as he and Scallywag had entered the hangar bay.

No sooner had they cleared the door than the forward plasma cannons on the large corvette opened fire, peppering the wall containing the entrance with red bolts of fury. All those following Mourdock and Scallywag immediately broke off, taking cover as the plasma blasts from the ship kept them at bay.

"Get inside! Hurry!" Mourdock commanded, pointing at the open loading ramp that led to the interior of the ship.

"Oy, ya don't need ta tell me twice!" Scallywag shot back as he hurriedly carried Jack up the ramp.

"Mourdock," came Hasatan's voice over the comm device, "the station has locked the docking clamps onto the ship. We're unable to leave as long as they are attached."

"On it," replied Mourdock, positioning himself to have a clear view of the docking clamps attached to the vessel.

Four metallic arms, two on each side of the ship, were magnetically attached to the ship's hull through large round disks at the end of the arms' pincers. Mourdock took his sword, the blade glowing with a bright blue energy, and flung it toward the first set of clamps. The sword spun end over end – so fast it might as well have been a spinning disk – and tore through the extended arms of the clamps. The sword's cuts briefly left the bright glow of melted metal in their wake. The sword disappeared after passing through the second clamp, and Mourdock manifested it once again before hurling it through the last two clamps in the same fashion.

"Good to go," Mourdock said into his communicator as he rushed onto the ship. "Get us out of here!"

"Acknowledged," replied Hasatan.

The boarding ramp of the ship closed behind Mourdock as the vessel backed out of the hangar, passing through the plasma window that led to outer space.

"Come with me," Mourdock said, barely looking at Scallywag as he passed by and began making his way to the bridge. Scallywag grimaced but followed nonetheless, his shoulder aching something fierce from carrying Jack.

The bridge of the corvette wasn't particularly large for a vessel of its size. Scallywag had been on enough starships to know that meant this ship was designed to be fast and manned by minimal crew. Hasatan sat in the co-pilot's seat as he flew the ship away from the station. Mourdock wasted no time taking his position in the pilot's chair, while Scallywag took the opportunity to lay Jack down and give his shoulder a rest.

"I take it the meeting did not go as planned," Hasatan said, dryly.

"What gave it away?" quipped Mourdock as he took control of the ship.

Hasatan glanced behind him and looked at Scallywag, his troubled gaze lingering on Jack briefly before he turned his attention back to his console. "Scanners have a number of vessels surrounding the Earthman's ship," Hasatan informed Mourdock. "They appear to have disabled its engines."

"Bloody squick," muttered Scallywag. "We gotta get there before anyone boards her."

"Right now, I'm more concerned with someone accidentally blowing it up with Anna on board," Mourdock said. "How are the Earthship's shields holding up?"

"They're down, but they keep trying to re-establish them," Hasatan replied. "My guess is they're pulling power from every system they can to keep them functional. However, they won't be active much longer."

"Then we'll have to act fast," Mourdock said. "Full thrust to the engines. Take us in and target any and all ships you can. Fire on them and get their focus on us."

"Acknowledged," Hasatan replied.

Mourdock then hopped up from his seat and made his way for the exit.

"Oy, where ya goin'?" Scallywag asked.

"To show people what happens when they mess with my girl," Mourdock stated as he left.

Mourdock ran down the central corridor of his ship and into the hanger bay where the corvette housed a single fightercraft. He quickly worked his way down to the fighter and hopped into the cockpit, immediately calling up the self-destruct menu on its onboard computer.

"Master," Mourdock said into his comm, "let me know when you've got those bogeys following us."

Back on the bridge, Hasatan had just opened fire on the ships swarming around the Earthship, hitting some, but getting the attention of all of them. "Will do," Hasatan replied. "Engaging hostiles now."

The bridge of the Earthship shook as more plasma fire hit them. Professor Green was completely frazzled, unable to keep up with all the starship activity going on around him.

"Oh dear, oh dear, oh dear!" he lamented. "Dan! Please tell me our engines are going to be functional soon!"

"A few of our maneuvering thrusters will be back online shortly, Master Green," Dan replied. "However, I fear our main thrusters have yet to be repaired."

Just then, one of the ships hounding them exploded on the viewscreen as it was hit with a plasma blast. Green looked at the explosion in surprise.

"What was that?" he asked. "Did we blow up that ship?"

"Negative," replied Shanks from the weapons console. "It would appear some help has arrived."

The group all looked at the viewscreen as Mourdock's corvette sped by, firing upon all the swarming ships with its plasma cannons as it did so and drawing some of them away.

"I say…" said Green. "That's mighty nice of them."

On the corvette, Mourdock initiated the fightercraft's self-destruct sequence and hopped out of the cockpit, quickly running out of the hanger. After sealing the door behind him, he turned to a control panel on the wall and initiated the hangar door's opening sequence.

The ship rocked as its shields absorbed incoming plasma fire from the ships they'd just assaulted. "Master," Mourdock said into his communicator, "how are we doing?"

"We have four ships on our tail," Hasatan replied.

"That'll have to do," muttered Mourdock before initiating the hangar launch sequence.

As the Skyborn corvette was being chased by the ships that had previously been assaulting the Earthship, the hangar doors beneath it opened, and it ejected the fightercraft it had housed in its bay. The fightercraft drifted behind the corvette as the vessel sped away, its self-destruct sequence counting down all the while and detonating almost precisely when the pursuing ships reached it.

The resulting explosion caught two of the ships in its blast, destroying them. The other two vessels were significantly damaged and veered away from their pursuit. On the bridge of the Skyborn corvette, Scallywag watched the ship's sensor readings, impressed by the unorthodox maneuver.

"Not bad," the pirate muttered.

"How many did we get?" Mourdock asked as he re-entered the bridge and quickly took his seat once more.

"Two destroyed, two out of commission," Hasatan replied. "There are two more that didn't take the bait. They're still trying to board the Earthship."

"Open a channel," Mourdock ordered as he brought the ship around.

Back on the Earthship, Green looked at his sensor readings. "Well, that certainly helped," he said cheerily. "Now we only have to worry about two ships attacking us."

"I believe I may be able to keep our attackers at bay long enough to get the thrusters repaired," Shanks said as he continued firing the Earthship's stun beams at the remaining vessels.

"Oh, my," Dan said. "Master Green! Master Shanks! Sensor readings from Port Somewhere show that a number of starships are launching from it, and almost all of them are heading this way!"

Green frowned. "I say… that's not good," he muttered.

Shanks grimaced. "I fear we may have to make an Entanglement jump before those ships reach us," he said.

"I do not wish to leave the others behind," replied Green.

"Nor do I," said Shanks. "But we may not have a choice."

"Sirs!" Dan said. "We're receiving a communication from that ship that just assisted us!"

"On screen," Green ordered.

The image of Mourdock, Hasatan, and Scallywag appeared on the Earthship's viewscreen.

"Oy, greenskin," Scallywag said, "ya there?"

"Yes!" replied Green. "Scallywag! Lord Skyborn! It is good to see you! Where are the others?"

"There will be time to catch up later," Mourdock said. "Right now, we must get you out of here before those ships from the station reach us. Tell me, do you have the ability to maneuver your ship at all?"

"Only minimally," Green replied. "Some of our maneuvering thrusters are still functional, but the main engines are damaged."

"That'll have to do," Mourdock muttered. "We're going to pull off a risky maneuver, Professor. When I give the word, I'm going to need you to fire off your thrusters and match our velocity. Think you can do that?"

"Well, I can certainly try…"

"Professor, if you don't achieve this, both your ship and mine will likely be destroyed," Mourdock insisted. "Now, I'll ask again… can you do this?"

Green took a deep breath. "Yes, my Lord. I can."

"Good," replied Mourdock. "Just hold out a little bit longer and wait for my signal. Skyborn out."

★ ★ ★ ★ ★

Mourdock ended the transmission and turned his ship on an intercept course with the Earthship. Scallywag gave him a nervous look. "Oy, that part about destroyin' both ships… not that I don't have confidence in ol' greenskin when it comes ta certain things, but he ain't exactly the type of pilot I'd be betting me life on."

"He may not be, but I am, I assure you," Mourdock said, his face the picture of concentration. "Now, secure Jack and yourself. This is gonna get bumpy."

Scallywag frowned but did as he was told, strapping Jack into a chair before doing so to himself. Mourdock increased the ship's speed.

"Fire on those ships. Try to keep them away," Mourdock said to Hasatan.

"Though I do not doubt your skills here, my charge," Hasatan replied as he began firing at the ships, "the Earthship is larger than that fightercraft of yours. Are you certain this will work?"

"Fairly certain."

"Meaning?"

Mourdock shrugged. "Fifty-fifty."

Scallywag raised his eyebrows at that. "Wait... what?"

Mourdock ignored Scallywag and opened a comm channel to the Earthship. "Now, Professor!"

Green immediately fired the Earthship's thrusters, looking at the readouts on his screen to match Mourdock's velocity.

"Oh... oh, no..." Green muttered.

"What is wrong?" asked Shanks in alarm.

"The command delay with my interface with the Earthship," Green said. "It caused the thrusters to fire off later than needed! If my calculations are correct, we're not going to be able to match Mourdock's ship's velocity by the time he reaches us!"

"Master Green," said Dan. "Might I recommend—"

"Divert all available power to the shields!" Green ordered.

"Ah!" the robot replied, cheerily. "Good to see we are of the same opinion. However, the only system with power still available is the Entanglement Engine. Diverting that to the shields would prevent us from making any type of quantum jump for at least an hour."

"We can't jump if we're dead, dear fellow!" Green exclaimed. "Do it quickly! And prepare for impact!"

"As you wish, Master Green."

Back on the Skyborn corvette, Mourdock killed the ship's thrusters and started to rotate the ship on its axis, pitching it upward so that the open hangar bay was aligned with the Earthship.

"Here we go!" Mourdock said. "Everyone hang on to something!"

The corvette rushed toward the Earthship, coming up on it fast. The corvette's hangar enveloped it. The Earthship's shields cushioned the impact, but still the ship tore at the various scaffolds on the roof of the hangar as the two vessels met, the front and back of the Earthship scraping against the walls of the corvette.

Mourdock gritted his teeth as the ship lurched beneath him, the collision with Jack's vessel causing structural damage alarms to ring on his console.

"The Earthship is in the hangar," Hasatan said, his voice calm and steady, as though nothing dangerous had just occurred.

"Close hangar bay doors," Mourdock ordered. "Prepare for jump to lightspeed."

Hasatan did as ordered as Mourdock re-engaged the ship's engines and began to speed away. The ships from Port Somewhere were almost upon them and had begun opening fire.

"Oy, they're gonna just follow us inta hyperspace," Scallywag said. "Yer gonna have ta take some of them out before ya make the jump."

"Who said anything about hyperspace?" Mourdock replied.

Scallywag's eyes went wide. "Uh… yer gonna do a blind jump? Haven't we defied death enough fer one day?"

"Do not fear," Hasatan said. "We scouted a trajectory before we docked. Our lightspeed jump path will be clear."

"Once we get past the fighters, anyway," Mourdock said.

"Once we what???" exclaimed Scallywag.

"Sorry, our escape route happens to be behind all the ships trying to shoot us," Mourdock replied as he angled the ship toward the swarm of attackers. "But once we get past them, it'll be smooth sailing."

"I see…" said Scallywag. "And do ya happen ta have a fancy tactic fer doing such a thing?"

"I do," Mourdock replied. "It's called diverting all power to forward shields and hoping they hold out."

Scallywag frowned. "Why do I bother askin'?" he grumbled.

The corvette began to rock from the impact of the plasma blasts on its shields. Hasatan returned fire, trying to get some of the ships to break off their attack. Alarms blared as a few shots landed on the corvette's hull, but the incoming attackers all scrambled as Mourdock sped the ship through their formation.

"Trajectory set," Mourdock said. "Engaging lightspeed engines… now!"

The hum of the ship's lightspeed engines grew as they engaged. For the briefest of moments, the ship's viewscreen was filled with the blue kaleidoscope of lightspeed, before it almost immediately disengaged and returned to normal. To Scallywag's great relief, they were still in one piece, and Port Somewhere, along with the attacking ships, were nowhere in sight.

"Right on target," Hasatan said. "Good job, my charge."

"Thank you, Master," Mourdock replied. "Now let's hop into hyperspace and get out of here before those at the station have time to regroup and track us."

"Entering hyperspace, now," Hasatan said.

As the Skyborn corvette disappeared into hyperspace, back on Port Somewhere, the chaotic melee of Grohm holding off the various bounty hunters, pirates, and ne'er-do-wells continued. The once serene corridors of Port Somewhere flashed with red and yellow warning lights. The visual displays on the walls sparked from being broken and smashed. Steam from damaged pipes within the walls spewed out, and people were screaming and shouting as Grohm raged through the station, laying waste to everything in his path.

"Run away!" shouted one pirate.

"Holy kitten, make him stop!" cried another mercenary as he fled.

"I'm getting' too old for this nonsense!" grumbled another as he found an appropriate hiding place.

Just then, a voice emanated from the station-wide speaker system. "Attention! Attention!" it blared. "This is Rolo Tomassi, station administrator. The Earthman has escaped. Repeat: the Earthman has escaped! Stop destroying

the blasted station! Also, would the owner of a blue Redsen-class transport please report to Hangar 29? Your lights are on."

Grohm had just lifted a chunk of metal ripped from the wall over his head and had been about to throw it at a group of cowering mercenaries when he heard the announcement. Grohm glanced up at the speaker in the ceiling curiously before dropping the hunk of wall onto the floor. His coarse, grey skin bore numerous blackened marks from plasma blasts that had found their target, but the Rognok appeared largely uninjured. In fact, his wounds only served to make him appear even more intimidating. He looked at the group of lowlifes before him, all of them gazing at him in fright.

"Who here has space ship?" Grohm demanded.

The group all looked at one another, not sure what to make of the situation. Finally, one of the men with a bionic eye and scars covering half his head hesitantly raised his hand.

"Um… I got a ship," he replied.

"Come forward," Grohm ordered.

"Wh… why?" asked the man, nervously.

"Because," Grohm said, holding out his hands. "Grohm wish to surrender."

CHAPTER ✺ 16

nce the Skyborn corvette was safely in hyperspace, Scallywag was able to breathe a sigh of relief. Mourdock swiveled his chair to look at Scallywag. Things had been happening so fast, neither one had gotten the chance to get a good look at the other. Mourdock's bright blue eyes looked Scallywag up and down, taking a measure of him. Scallywag did the same.

"I don't believe we've been properly introduced," Mourdock said.

"I know who you are. Ya know who I am," Scallywag replied. "Tha real question is, what took ya so bloody long ta show up?"

"You didn't give us a whole lot of time to make it to the meeting," Mourdock said. "We had to rush and scout an escape route in case you double-crossed us, and when we did get to the station, no one could tell me where this 'Stinky Pete's' place was."

Scallywag raised an eyebrow. "Oy, you thought *we'd* double-cross *you*?"

"I didn't know what to think. You kidnapped the Princess of the Regalus Empire and then asked to meet the Emperor Ascendant alone on a criminal outpost in space belonging to our greatest rival. I know Jack well enough to trust him. But the rest of you... well, you are a Red. No offence."

Scallywag had never bothered to think of things from Mourdock's perspective. Upon hearing his reasoning, Scallywag shrugged. "Yeah, ya make a fair point."

Just then, Hasatan clutched at his chest, grunting in pain. Mourdock looked at him with concern. "Master?" he said. "Are you okay?"

Before Hasatan could reply, Jack began screaming. He thrashed about in his seat, held in place only by his seatbelt.

"Bloody squick!" Scallywag cried, rushing to Jack's side to try to keep him from hurting himself.

Mourdock immediately moved to assist Scallywag. Jack's face was beet red, his eyes rolling back in his head. His jaw was clenched so tightly, Scallywag feared the boy's teeth might break.

"What's wrong with him?" Mourdock asked, concerned.

"Wish I knew," Scallywag said as he unbuckled Jack from the chair. "Hurry! Help me get him back ta the Earthship!"

Jack cried out again, wailing in agony as Scallywag and Mourdock slung his arms over their shoulders and carried him out of the bridge. Hasatan followed close behind, looking as though he, too, were in pain. Mourdock led them to the damaged hangar into which the Earthship was awkwardly wedged.

"Oy! Green!" Scallywag called into his comm. "Green, ya there???"

"Yes, Scallywag! I'm here!" Green replied.

"Teleport us ta sick bay!" Scallywag barked. "On tha double! Jack's hurt!"

On the bridge of the Earthship, Green's eyes went wide upon hearing that news. He exchanged a concerned glance with Shanks, who immediately got up and began heading toward the medical bay.

"Right away," said Green as he locked on to the group in the hangar and teleported them aboard, before rushing down to the medical bay himself.

What he saw when he got there deeply troubled him. Scallywag and Mourdock were holding Jack down on the observation table as Jack screamed, his body thrashing about and convulsing. Shanks was off to the side with Hasatan, both men looking grimly at the scene. Dan wandered in shortly behind the Professor.

"Oh, no!" the robot said. "What is wrong with Master Jack?"

Scallywag looked up at Green. "I've seen this before," he said. "Same thing happened to that Shepherd bloke before he died."

A cold hand of fear gripped Green's stomach. "Great Scott!" he said. "This can't be! What happened to him? What caused this?"

"We got ambushed on tha station by this bounty hunter," Scallywag said. "Grohm and me… we got frozen by some stasis beam the browner used. Jack was doin' his Equilibrium thing, I think, but tha bloke matched him step fer step. Then, Jack shoots a ball o' ghost energy just like the Deathlords do at the guy and hits him dead on. Grohm and I are released, and then Jack completely loses it!"

Hasatan's eyes went wide. "He did what? Are you saying he used Servuchur against your attacker?"

"If that means he shot a ball o' ghost energy just like the Deathlords do at the guy, then yeah," muttered Scallywag.

Hasatan stepped toward Scallywag. "The ball he shot," the old man asked, "did it return to him?"

Scallywag gave Hasatan a confused look. "Return ta him?"

"Yes, did the energy he fired come back?"

"I don't think so. Why?"

Hasatan's face grew grave as he looked down at Jack.

"What is it, Master?" Mourdock asked. "What happened to him?"

"He killed himself. That's what happened," said Hasatan with disdain.

"Oy, care ta explain fer those of us not fluent in hocus-pocus?" snapped Scallywag.

"He used his own spiritual energy to defend himself from his attacker," Hasatan said. "He's suffering from a soul severance. He literally ripped a piece of his spirit off, and his body is unable to handle the trauma of it."

"You... you mean to say, he's lost a piece of his own soul?" Green asked, astonished.

"Is there a way to help him?" Mourdock asked. "Please, Master, you must know of a way..."

Hasatan frowned. "Short of returning the piece of him he expulsed, there is no way I know of," he said, grimly. "By now it is lost to the ether... and I am afraid the Earthman is doomed."

Shanks stepped forward and opened his third eye, gazing down at Jack. The boy's flow of energy was in turmoil, his aura red as blood and quickly darkening – signs Shanks knew meant that death would soon be upon him.

I must not let him die, Shanks thought. *That vision we shared back on Omnicron... it proves he has a destiny – a purpose – one far greater than mine. He and the Princess are tied together. Perhaps the only way to save her... is to save him.*

Shanks manifested his staff and turned toward Dan. "I have a very important task for you, my robotic friend," Shanks said, handing the robot his staff. "I need you to give this back to me immediately after I finish what I am about to do."

Dan took the staff and looked it up and down. "It is a stick of wood, Master Shanks," Dan commented.

"It is more than that, I can assure you," Shanks replied. "Give it back to me immediately after. Can you do that?"

"Of course, sir."

Shanks stepped forward and stood at the head of the observation table on which Jack lay. "Step back," Shanks commanded, gesturing for Scallywag and Mourdock to give him space.

"Oy, what ya plannin' ta do?" Scallywag asked.

"Save his life," Shanks replied. "Now please, do as I ask."

Mourdock and Scallywag complied. Shanks then placed his hands on Jack – one on his forehead, the other on his chest. Shanks closed his eyes and focused on channeling his spiritual energy. He could feel the chaos raging inside the boy as his own energy entered him. Shanks felt like he was in a storm that caused him to be continuously, tumultuously, upended. To keep from getting disoriented, Shanks had to concentrate while navigating the spiritual waters of the Earthman as Jack's injured spirit thrashed about like a dying animal.

Finally, Shanks found the void where the Earthman had torn off a part of his soul. It stood out like a missing piece of a large jigsaw puzzle, and as Shanks focused in on it, he could see the jagged edges of Jack's spirit, flapping like a torn flag in the wind.

Shanks connected to those edges with his own energy. It felt odd, at first – like the two didn't belong together. But he focused on healing the tears, fusing them to his own energy. It still felt odd, but he could feel his connection with Jack grow and intensify as he did so.

Jack suddenly began to calm down, his thrashing and spasms slowly fading. A healthy color returned to his cheeks, and Jack began to return to normal once more.

Shanks furrowed his brow and braced himself. Slowly, he separated the energy that had fused with Jack from himself. The pain of doing so was intense, but Shanks somehow managed to continue with the difficult procedure. His body quivered and sweat rolled down from his bald scalp, but he proceeded, despite the fact that he felt as though he were slowly sawing off his own arm.

Finally, when the last thread of connection to his energy was reached, Shanks gave it one last quick jerk of separation. He released Jack and stumbled backward, hitting the wall of the medical bay and slumping weakly. The pain was excruciating, but he kept control as best he could before Dan handed him back his staff. As soon as his hand wrapped around the wood, the agony he was experiencing disappeared, and Shanks could breathe easily once more.

Everyone in the room looked at Shanks with curiosity as he used his staff to straighten himself. Hasatan no longer appeared to be in pain. The old man glanced from Shanks to Jack and back again, a suspicious look on his face.

"What did you do?" Green asked.

"I was able to… mend his spiritual energy," Shanks replied, looking tired and weak.

"Mend it?" asked Scallywag. "So is tha lad gonna be okay?"

"Eventually," Shanks replied. "He suffered a great trauma. He will need time to recover. But for now, at least, he will live."

Green, Scallywag, and Mourdock all looked relieved at that news.

"And you, Brother Shanks?" Professor Green asked. "Will you be okay?"

"I… yes, I will be fine," Shanks replied. "I, too, will just need some time to recover."

"Very well," Mourdock said. "Now, with that crisis over, I would very much like to see my fiancée."

"Oy, mate," Scallywag grumbled, looking about as tired as Shanks. "We've just gone from ambush, ta space battle, ta life-or-death miracle. Can we take a breather before 'possessed damsel in distress'?"

"No," Mourdock said, flatly. "Now take me to her."

Scallywag gave Professor Green a resigned look. "She's this way, Lord Skyborn," Green said, gesturing toward the door. As the group began to file out, Hasatan leaned in toward Shanks, who walked shakily, relying upon his staff for support.

"That was quite a sacrifice you just made," Hasatan said, quietly.

"I am afraid I do not know what you mean," Shanks replied.

"We both know that you do," Hasatan answered, before walking ahead, leaving the conversation at that.

When Green and Mourdock entered the room in which Anna was being kept, her eyes went wide. "Mourdock!" she cried. "Thank the Great Observer! Please! Help me! They're all crazy!"

Mourdock looked at the room and the chair that held Anna. He then turned his gaze toward the group, as they all stood there looking at him.

"Don't believe a word that comes outta that lass's mouth," Scallywag said. "It be the slythru talkin'."

"My friend here is correct, Lord Skyborn," Green said. "The Princess we know is being controlled by a parasitic symbiote. That is not actually Anna."

"Mourdock! Please believe me!" Anna pleaded. "These people are *delusional!* They keep trying to convince me I'm being controlled by Deathlords!"

"That is because you are," Shanks said as he entered the room, alongside Hasatan.

"Do you have proof of these... slythrus?" Mourdock asked.

"If Jack were conscious, he'd be able ta put on a puppet show fer ya," Scallywag said. "Unfortunately, the brain worms be invisible ta the rest o' us."

"Best we can tell, the slythrus operate on a different plane of existence once they merge with a living host," Green explained. "They become more of a spiritual entity, so only someone who can manipulate spiritual energy somehow is able to interact with them."

"That's kind of convenient, isn't it?" asked Mourdock, skeptically. "By that logic, anyone could be infected with a slythru and no one would ever be able to know for sure."

"Oy, I kinda think that's tha point," muttered Scallywag.

"My Lord," said Shanks, "everyone on this crew has witnessed the Princess being possessed by a Deathlord Supreme named Verrutus. We have all seen Jack make contact with the slythru and control the Princess through it. I urge you to take our word on this matter. We all want the Princess to be safe."

"They've *kidnapped* me, Mourdock!" Anna shrieked. "Why aren't you doing anything? Release me now and get me out of here! Please!"

Hasatan made his way behind Anna, looking at the back of her head. He gestured for Mourdock to join him.

"Mourdock? What are you doing?" Anna asked nervously as Mourdock made his way around her.

"What is it, Master?" Mourdock asked, quietly.

"Remember the special training we've been doing?" Hasatan asked. Mourdock nodded, knowing his Master was referring to the secret Servuchur training they'd been partaking in. "Focus your vision using your spirit," Hasatan advised. "Then... look at her."

Mourdock took a deep breath and centered himself. He concentrated on what Hasatan was referring to, gazing at the back of Anna's head as he attempted to utilize, and see through, his spiritual energy.

"Mourdock?" asked Anna, confused. "Mourdock, what are you doing?"

Mourdock made contact with his spirit, and he could feel his consciousness receding into it. A queer, disembodied feeling took hold of him. For the briefest of moments, he could see flashes of a black worm, wriggling from the back of Anna's head, hissing at him. But as quickly as they'd appeared, the images vanished, and Mourdock returned to normal once more. Mourdock shook his head, his temples throbbing. He massaged his forehead, feeling somewhat queasy from his experience.

"Did you see it?" Hasatan asked.

"Yes," Mourdock replied sadly. "Jack... Jack was right. All this time, he was right..."

"Mourdock, listen to me," said Anna, desperately. "You couldn't have seen anything because there's nothing to see! I'm me! Please, just release me and take me home! I just want to go home!"

Mourdock moved in front of Anna and bent down, looking her deep in the eyes, his face stern and resolute. "Anna, if you are in there and can hear me, I want you to know one thing," Mourdock said. "I will not give up trying to rescue you. I don't care if it takes me a lifetime. I promise... I *will* save you."

Anna scowled at Mourdock. "You can save me by getting me out of here!" she sneered.

"You are right where you belong, for now," Mourdock said as he stood up straight.

"Mourdock!" Anna cried after him as he headed for the door. "Mourdock! Don't be a fool!"

After everyone had exited the room, Hasatan closed the door behind them. Mourdock wore a troubled look on his face that did not go unnoticed by the Earthship's remaining crew.

"So... ya believe us now?" Scallywag asked.

Mourdock nodded. "Jack came to me when all this started, seeking my help. I refused him then. But I see now, that was a mistake. The woman I love has been infected by evil, and the only ones in the universe who cared enough to do anything about it were you." Mourdock looked at the group. "I owe all of you

any help I can offer. If it is within my power to do something to assist you, from this point forward, I will."

"Great!" said Scallywag. "Can ya have tha bounty on us lifted?"

"That is beyond my power," Mourdock said.

The group frowned. "Well, could you give us asylum and a safe place to hide until the bounty is lifted?" asked Green.

"That, too, is beyond my power," Mourdock said again.

"Oy, just exactly what kinda power do ya have?" asked Scallywag with frustration.

"Very little, as long as my father is head of my Legacy," Mourdock replied. "Between him and Director Casgor, they call the shots. Until I am married and assume my role as Emperor, there is very little I can do to rectify this situation — politically, at least."

"Very well, Lord Skyborn," said Shanks. "Then allow me to ask… what *can* you do to help us and the Princess?"

Mourdock frowned. "Right now, I'm not sure I know," he said.

"I do," Hasatan chimed in.

The group looked at the old man.

"Master?" Mourdock asked. "You have an idea?"

"I know of a place we can take the Princess," he said. "A place where she will be safe. A place that will slow the advance of the slythru control. A place where the Secret Army cannot exist and where even this Verrutus may not be able to follow her. And it is a place that no mercenary, bounty hunter, or even the Empire can gain access to. But most of all, it is a place that may be able to cure her of this vile malady which currently afflicts her."

The group all exchanged impressed glances before Scallywag spoke up.

"Sounds topper," he said. "This place got a name?"

"It does," Hasatan replied, a sly smile growing on his face. "It's called the Conclave."

CHAPTER ✦ 17

Port Longshore was usually one of the busiest spaceports in the Empire. It also had the distinction of being one of the oldest, first commissioned back when Nameer had assumed Legacy status over Redwater and finally completed under the supervision of his son, Raymar – the first of Legacy Evenstar. Over time the space station had been expanded upon, retrofitted, and updated to keep pace with the demands of being such a central part of the Empire's hyperspace trade network. Most Legacies would have replaced their main ports every hundred years or so, but somehow Port Longshore had endured the test of time. Kimlee remembered her father saying replacing Port Longshore would be like replacing the memory of Raymar himself. For better or worse, the station was a symbol of Legacy Evenstar and their power within the system.

The station was in geosynchronous orbit over the city of Nameeria, which allowed it to reliably teleport goods and personnel from the station to the planet, like most spaceports did. This meant it was quite easy for Kimlee to get from Redwater to Port Longshore itself. What wasn't so easy was ditching her security detail and sneaking away from the Evenstar compound. But once she did, she was able to make her way to Nameeria's teleportation hub and travel to the station without being recognized.

Port Longshore was ridiculously busy, allowing her to get lost in the crowd. However, she noticed the base was not busy in its usual way. Normally, there were great numbers of ships trying to dock with the station. However, from what Kimlee could tell, all the current activity centered around ships trying to leave the port, obviously in anticipation of the looming system-wide embargo.

Kimlee had done her best to dress in a way that wouldn't attract attention, but she still received lingering stares from numerous passersby. Clad in brown boots, tan breeches, a golden blouse, and a long, hooded burgundy cloak, it was the least flashy outfit Kimlee could remember wearing in public in a long time. Though she should have been nervous about ditching her security detail to meet with a complete stranger off the planet, she was actually more nervous about being recognized before she could even get to the meeting.

Kimlee moved away from the main corridors of Port Longshore as quickly as she could and kept her head low as she walked. Though she had ditched her security detail, she hadn't come to the station without protection. She had a small plasma blaster clutched tightly in her hand, courtesy of Sergeant Surior. It had taken some convincing, but Kimlee had insisted she needed something to protect herself should there be another assassination attempt. Surior had supplied her with the weapon, which was small and dainty enough to suit Kimlee's complete inexperience with firearms.

As Kimlee got closer to the area where her contact had asked to meet, she began to question the wisdom of what she was doing. *What do I even know about this man?* she thought. *I could be walking right into some type of trap! Worst case scenario, he kills me just like my parents were killed. Best case, he kidnaps me and holds me hostage for the rest of my life. What am I thinking coming here alone???*

Before her doubts had a chance to take hold and make her change her mind, she heard a voice, causing her to snap back to the situation at hand.

"Lady Evenstar," it said.

Kimlee turned and saw the man she'd come to meet casually leaning up against a wall. He was tall, his shoulders and arms well defined. His dark blonde hair was lazily disheveled in a way that made it look fashionable, and he wore a sly smile among three-day-old stubble. He was dressed in typical spacer gear – high boots and a beige flight suit which was buckled at the waist by a gun holster. The top half of the jumpsuit hung loosely behind him, exposing his white undershirt, which did little to hide the muscles beneath it.

On second thought, I can think of worse people to be kidnapped by, Kimlee mused, feeling her cheeks flush at the sight of the mysterious rogue.

Kimlee kept one hand gripped on her plasma gun beneath her cloak and used the other to lower her hood. "Well, now," she said, "your holo-image doesn't do you justice, stranger."

The man chuckled and shrugged. "I work out," he replied with pseudo modesty.

"I can see that," Kimlee said. "And what else do you do, aside from promising young women their own empires?"

"Oh, a great many things, my Lady," he answered, coyly. "I help the oppressed, fight the tyrannical, and champion the cause of freedom across the universe."

"So you're some type of revolutionary, eh?"

"Part-time revolutionary," the man said with a hint of swagger. "I'm actually a smuggler, by trade."

"Smuggler?" said Kimlee, intrigued. "Well, now, you're a real bad boy, aren't you?"

"Depends on whom you ask. Good and bad are all a matter of perspective."

"And how should I be choosing to see you?"

"As a friend."

"I usually know the names of my friends."

The man stepped toward Kimlee and gave her a slight bow. "Name's Devorian," he said. "Devorian Westlake, at your service."

"So you say," Kimlee responded. "But I fail to see what good a smuggler and part-time revolutionary is going to do for me against a Starkeeper and his fleet."

"Only because you currently don't know much about smugglers and revolutionaries," Devorian replied. "We tend to specialize in fighting opponents that are way bigger than us."

"Fighting and winning are two very different things, Mr. Westlake."

"This is true. But it's also true that those who are not willing to fight cannot win. And knowing how to fight superior opponents can be the difference between winning and losing."

"And how exactly does one beat a superior opponent?"

"By using their superiority against them," Devorian answered. "If they're big and you're small, then you're mobile and they're slow. You're hidden and they're exposed. You only fight battles you know you can win. You allow them to underestimate you and use that to your advantage. Deception and misdirection when coupled with speed and a willingness to strike can defeat any enemy, no matter how large and scary they might be."

Kimlee smiled at that. "You certainly talk a good game, Mr. Westlake. And I'd be tempted to believe you, if it weren't for the fact that the Regalus Empire has endured for thousands of years against all enemies, great and small."

"You don't need to topple an Empire to defeat it, my Lady. Just look at Edvard the Undying."

"If memory serves, Edvard lost."

"Not to the Empire," Devorian said. "Edvard consistently triumphed in every conflict and established his own empire in the process. In the end, he was

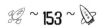

defeated by a small group of revolutionaries, and a simple girl, whom no one took seriously."

Kimlee nodded. The story of Ebella and the sacrifice she made to help finally defeat Edvard the Undying was one of her favorite tales from history. She'd grown up captivated by it, fascinated by this one girl who had managed to bring down an empire. Upon hearing Devorian's words, Kimlee allowed herself to entertain the idea that if Ebella could do such a thing, perhaps she could, too.

"You and your brother are in a rather unique position at the moment, Lady Evenstar," Devorian continued. "You are a powerful Legacy with genetic ties leading directly back to the Ancients, making you just as much of a symbol as Legacy Prime. There are many other Legacies out there, not to mention a number of colonies and outposts, whose citizens would follow you if you broke away from the Empire. All you need do is lead, and others will follow your example."

"You make it sound so easy," Kimlee replied. "My brother makes the case that it's not as simple as that."

"If I wanted your brother's opinion, I'd be meeting with him right now," Devorian retorted. "I'm here because I'd like to know what you think."

"I agree with my brother. It's not simple."

"But it is doable," Devorian pressed. "It's obvious your brother still wants to try to salvage the situation. He does not want to break away from the Empire. But I'm curious as to what you want, my Lady?"

"What I want doesn't matter. I'm not in charge."

"You are the first born, are you not? You were set to inherit the Empire. Does this not mean you're qualified to inherit your own Legacy?"

"I gave up that right."

"So you've fooled yourself into believing," Devorian countered. "You think you've forsaken your power for fame, choosing to focus on being a celebrity as opposed to a leader."

"Isn't that what I've done?"

Devorian shrugged. "From a certain point of view, I suppose," he replied. "Another way to look at it is that you inserted yourself into the conscious awareness of an entire galaxy. From the core worlds to the fringes of space, and even into the Visini Empire, people know you, my Lady. They know your face. They know your voice. They've invited you into their homes via your reality show or your music. They love you. Though your brother may wield power here in

Redwater, you wield power in all twelve sectors of space. And that makes you supremely powerful – even more so than the Empire realizes."

Kimlee mulled over Devorian's words. She'd never thought of things in such a way before. If the rogue had wanted to capture her interest, he'd certainly succeeded. "As tempting as it is to believe what you say, there is little my fame can do against the entire 3rd fleet."

"Wars are waged on many fronts, my Lady. With enough public pressure, politicians can be forced to recall fleets."

"Not Casgor," Kimlee said. "As long as he is the sole Director of the Empire, he can do anything he wants."

"As do most tyrants," Devorian acknowledged. "But even Casgor isn't immune to certain political realities. He can send warships against your brother, but what does he have with which to combat your voice? His public image has been tarnished by the Earthman already. If you were to use your celebrity to get your voice out there, you could turn the tide of public opinion even further against him."

"But all that takes time," Kimlee said. "All he needs to do is hold out until we are forced to engage with the 3rd fleet. And at that point, no amount of public relations is going to keep my brother and me from being executed as traitors."

"Which is why it is so important that you show the galaxy your leadership," Devorian said. "The more Legacies you can get to side with you, the harder it will be to force you into a fight. And if it is the Imperial blockade that has you concerned, my Lady, I can tell you there are ways to weather it."

"Such as?"

"Your brother has already taken the first step by instituting martial law on the planet before the blockade has been enacted," Devorian said. "Those on Redwater will be fine, even with the suspension of all Imperial services. Given time, the local governments can enact alternatives. The real challenges are the colonies and outposts within your system that do not have access to the resources of a habitable planet. Other than Redwater, your system has five planets containing multiple colonies, not to mention the outposts in your asteroid belt. The blockade is meant to choke them off, forcing them into surrendering, effectively isolating Redwater and diminishing your Legacy's power in the system. After all, many of those in your militia will have come from these places, and their resolve to support you and your brother will be eroded if they see their homes fall due to attrition. If you want to weather this storm, you'll need smugglers able to run the blockade to continue to supply needed resources to these holdings."

"That's your solution? A fleet of smugglers against a fleet of warships?"

"If you need time to fight back against the Empire, there is no better way to do so."

"Admittedly, I do not know much about the art of smuggling, Mr. Westlake, but I have a hard time believing any ship we employ for such an endeavor would be able to make it past the sensors of a Starkeeper capital ship."

"Don't be so sure. We have ways of getting past even the most sophisticated military sensors."

Kimlee raised an eyebrow. "And how do you accomplish such a thing?"

"It's a secret."

"I'm good at keeping secrets," Kimlee said, batting her eyelashes flirtatiously.

"I bet you are," said Devorian with a smile. "Very well then. I'll show you."

Devorian held out his hand. Kimlee hesitated for a moment, considering his offer. There was a part of her that was still skeptical about this mysterious stranger and his motivations, but there was also a part of her which was extremely interested in seeing where this meeting would lead. In the end, her curiosity won out, and she accepted the man's hand. Devorian turned and began leading her down the corridor. Kimlee regarded him with interest as they walked.

"May I ask you a question, Mr. Westlake?" she inquired.

"If it pleases you, my Lady."

"Why are you offering to help my brother and me? Is all this just to drum up some business for you and your smuggler friends? Or do you actually care what happens to my Legacy?"

"You're asking what my motivations are?"

"I am indeed."

Devorian nodded. "Tell me, Lady Evenstar... what do you know about the Empire?"

"What's to know? It's big. It's old. It contains hundreds of planets and species. That's pretty much all there is to it."

Devorian chuckled. "I would argue there's a little more to it than that," he said. "You seem to have glossed over all the harm the Empire has perpetuated throughout the galaxy."

"That's debatable, don't you think?" replied Kimlee. "For thousands of years, the Regalus Empire has been uniting the galaxy, helping to advance the lives of its citizens through advanced technology. It has brought numerous disparate alien races together in a peaceful way for their benefit and the benefit of the galaxy as a whole."

"Spoken like a true core-worlder," Devorian said. "The reality of the Empire is far less rosy than you make it out to be, my Lady, particularly the further out to the fringes you go. You say the Regalus Empire has been uniting the galaxy for thousands of years, but the truth is that it has been *conquering* the galaxy for thousands of years – subjugating races different from the Regals who started it. Destroying all those who've opposed it. Forcing its beliefs and its laws upon entire star systems, whether the natives of that system have wanted it or not."

"I won't deny that the Empire hasn't always been very friendly, particularly during the Age of Conquest," Kimlee agreed. "But considering all the Empire brings to the table, it's largely been a force for good, hasn't it?"

"Has it?" Devorian asked. "Sure, the advanced technology of the Ancients has certainly improved the quality of life of the average citizen – as long as you are a citizen the Empire feels is worthy of it, anyway."

"I'm not sure I know what you mean."

"You grew up on a planet, my Lady. That is not a luxury afforded to everyone in the Empire. Take me, for instance. I was born on a space station in the Frontier called Farpoint 12. I grew up eating tasteless replicated food, breathing recycled air, walking around in artificial gravity, my entire world limited to the confines of what amounts to a metal box in the far reaches of space. And the reason? Because the Empire needed a depot at a hyperspace junction so they could explore in order to expand its territory. Which is all well and good, I suppose, if there had actually been an effort to explore our little sector of space. In all my time on Farpoint 12, there had been a total of two exploration vessels that visited us. We had been forgotten about. Cast aside like second-class citizens. And it wasn't until I hopped on a resupply freighter and left that dreary station that I discovered the true nature of the Empire."

Kimlee frowned. She'd be the first to admit she'd lived a sheltered life, but she'd never heard anyone talk about the Empire in such a fashion before. "And that would be?" she asked.

"That it is a virus," Devorian said, "one which is infecting all corners of the universe. And if a cure is not found soon, it will destroy everything."

"That's a bit of an overstatement, wouldn't you say?"

"Not at all. What is a virus, my Lady? It is an infectious agent that only exists to replicate itself, even if that means killing the very host it's living in. When you strip away all the bells and whistles of the Empire, what you have left is simply an entity whose only goal is to expand and grow. And the bigger it gets, the more it requires to survive. It strips away all natural resources for its own use. It destroys the unique cultures of the races it assimilates and uses those races to perpetuate itself. It forces its own culture and religion on all people to keep them subjugated and kills any who dare to resist it. Face it, my Lady... the Empire consumes everything it touches for its own ends."

"You make it sound so sinister," Kimlee replied. "My father had always told me that the only way to control such vast amounts of stellar territory was through Imperialism. But what has made the Regalus Empire so special, and what has allowed it to endure the test of time, is that it permits systems to rule themselves, all the way down to local planetary levels. The Empire offers technology, education, resources, and economic incentives to its members, but for the most part, it refrains from becoming too intrusive."

"And is that how you feel right now, my Lady?" Devorian asked pointedly. "That the Empire has been... unintrusive?"

Kimlee frowned. "Admittedly, we are in a unique situation at the moment," she said.

"Not that unique, Lady Evenstar. What is happening to you is simply a microcosm of what is happening to others within the Empire. Should anyone step out of line, the Empire flexes its muscles and crushes them. And as the Imperial government amasses more and more power, that benevolent self-government your father spoke of becomes a thing of the past. You asked before what my motivations are? They're simple, really. My motivations are to fight the tyranny of the Regalus Empire in any way I can and to free whomever I can from its grip. For too long, we have lived under its repressive and controlling government while Legacy Prime hoards Ancient technology for its own selfish purposes. I wish to be free from the Empire, as well as to be free from Legacy Prime. And at the moment, I believe your desires, and mine, are aligned."

Kimlee smiled at that in silent acknowledgement. "For a man who hates empires so much, you seem quite eager to offer me my own."

"As a counter to a greater evil," Devorian said. "There is no other entity that can challenge the Empire, not even the Visinis. But you, Lady Evenstar… you were meant to be an Empress. If anyone can mount a counter to our current corrupt system, it is you. And just like when Edvard grew his Twilight Empire, the Regalus Empire can be put into check. All that is required for such a thing to happen is for you to seize upon your own power and to manifest into reality what has always been your destiny."

"I'll say this about you, Mr. Westlake," Kimlee said, smiling. "You have quite the silver tongue."

"If you like my tongue, Lady Evenstar," Devorian said, flirtatiously, "there are a great many parts of me you're simply going to love."

Kimlee had to laugh at that. Despite her reservations about the man, she had to admit, he had his charm. She'd been so engrossed in her conversation with Devorian, she hadn't realized they'd walked all the way to a hangar bay as they'd been chatting.

"Here we are," Devorian said as he opened the door to the hangar, revealing a small transport vessel docked in its bay.

Kimlee followed Devorian inside. The transport was two stories high and only about fifty yards long. It was a boxy ship and looked rather old and unassuming. Some of its hull panels appeared rusty, and there were a few scorch marks, signaling a history of some combat.

"Is this your ship?" Kimlee asked.

"One of them," replied Devorian.

"And why are you taking me here?"

"You said you wanted to know my secret? Well, it's onboard."

A boarding ramp, leading into the ship, extended from the craft's underside. Devorian began to walk up the ramp, but Kimlee stopped short, hesitating to go on board. Devorian gave her a curious look. "Is everything alright, my Lady?" he asked.

"Before I follow you onto your ship, I feel it only fair to warn you that should you try anything untoward, I'll be forced to defend myself." Kimlee then

revealed the small plasma blaster she'd been carrying with her, pointing it toward Devorian.

"I was wondering when you were going to show me what was under your cloak," Devorian replied with a smile, not the least bit intimidated by the appearance of Kimlee's weapon.

"What can I say?" Kimlee said, coyly. "I'm incredibly modest."

Devorian chuckled. "I do not blame you for being cautious, my Lady. Allow me to set aside any worry that my motives are to whisk you away in a most ungentlemanly fashion."

"Let's not get too ahead of ourselves here," Kimlee joked as Devorian approached her from the ramp. He then pulled his plasma gun out of its holster and with a flourish, offered its grip to Kimlee. Kimlee regarded it for a moment before accepting the gun, her own amused smile matching that of the smuggler's.

"It's so much bigger than mine," Kimlee said as she examined the pistol.

"I'm a big believer that size matters," replied Devorian.

"On that, we can agree," Kimlee said as she turned both weapons on the man. "After you, Mr. Westlake."

"As you wish, Lady Evenstar," Devorian said with a nod before leading Kimlee onto the vessel.

The inside of the ship wasn't much more impressive than the outside. Most of the vessel appeared to be devoted to cargo space. "Tell me, Lady Evenstar, what do you see?" Devorian asked.

Kimlee glanced around. "Not much," she replied. "Just the inside of a small transport ship."

"To the naked eye, that would be correct," Devorian said. "But to a ship's sensors? All they would detect would be some space debris, if they picked up anything at all."

Kimlee raised an eyebrow. "I'm not sure I'm following you," she said.

"Smuggling is an art form, my Lady," Devorian explained. "We who make our living at it learn to fly with minimal sensor footprints. Sometimes that means foregoing life support and flying with miniscule energy signatures – all so we can escape being detected by normal sensor scans. But the real trick, and sometimes the difference between life and death, is to make whatever cargo we're hauling appear to be invisible."

"And how do you accomplish that?"

"With this," Devorian said as he removed a wall panel to reveal a golden-hued piece of metal behind it. He gave the metal a rap with his knuckles and smiled confidently at Kimlee. "Reinforced equalarium."

Kimlee curiously eyed the metal to which Devorian was referring. "I'm not familiar with equalarium," she said.

"Few people are. It's a very rare alloy," Devorian explained. "But it is what separates the real smugglers from the wannabes. Equalarium has the unique ability to reflect any and all types of energy, signals, and radiation. Nothing can pass through it, which means even the most highly advanced sensors can't see it. The entire cargo bay of this ship is lined with it, which means that even if this entire system were locked down by an Imperial blockade, I could come and go as I please, and they'd never see me."

"Very impressive," Kimlee said, obviously intrigued. "Though, I'm not sure it is worth the effort, considering your ship is so small. Any cargo you could smuggle in this vessel would be barely worth the risk."

"Unfortunately, equalarium is rather expensive," Devorian admitted. "Lining a larger ship with it would be financially impossible for someone such as myself. But I'm not really here to offer you my capabilities and those of others in my profession, my Lady."

"And what is it you are offering, Mr. Westlake?"

"I am a small cog in a much larger machine. I belong to an organization that has been fighting for independence from the Empire for a long time, in all sectors of space. We have assets in every known star system, agents in every Imperial organization, and resources that are vital to the fight against the Empire. We have an army of smugglers ready to assist you when the blockade is enacted, but in addition to that, we have contacts in other Legacies sympathetic to your cause. We can help coordinate your resistance, Lady Evenstar. We can support you and your brother in ways the Empire could never anticipate. And should you break off and declare independence, we can champion your cause and bring others into your fold. I promised I could deliver you your own Empire, my Lady. That was not a lie. All I need to know is... will you accept my help?"

Kimlee mulled over the information Devorian had just given her. "What is the name of this organization you speak of?" she asked.

"We call ourselves the Liberators."

"And I take it this organization is responsible for your knowing about the results of my brother's meeting with the World Leaders before anyone else did?"

"As I said, we have people everywhere, my Lady," Devorian replied. "Right now, your plight and ours are in alignment. With our support, you can save your Legacy. And with your support, we can start a revolution that will change the face of the galaxy. What this fire needs in order to start is a single spark, and I believe you to be that spark, Lady Evenstar. All you need do is say the word."

Kimlee was quiet for a long moment before answering.

"I'll think about it."

Her reply seemed to surprise Devorian. "Hmmmm…" he said. "Perhaps I need to work on my sales pitch."

"Your pitch was fine," Kimlee replied as she handed the man's blaster back to him and then patted him on the cheek. "You've just given me a lot to think about."

With that, Kimlee turned and exited the ship, walking back down the ramp into the hangar bay. However, she didn't make it more than a few steps before red lights began to flash and an alarm began to sound. Kimlee looked around, concerned and confused.

"My Lady," came Devorian's voice.

Kimlee turned and saw the man leaning against the entrance to his ship, a smug smile on his face.

"Try not to think about my offer too long," he said. "Starkeeper Drucker is not the type of man who will give you that kind of time."

Devorian hit a button which raised the ramp to the ship. As the alarms continued to sound, Kimlee rushed out of the hangar bay. Her only thought was that she needed to get back down to the planet immediately.

As she hurried back toward the station's main teleportation terminal, one of the visual displays in the hallway caught her eye, causing her to stop. There on the screen was an image of the Starkeeper capital ship *Colossus* and half of the 3rd fleet, with a bottom crawl which read: "Third fleet arrives in Redwater system." Kimlee's breath caught in her throat, and she felt her heart pound painfully in her chest.

The blockade had begun, and it was now the Evenstars against the full might of the Empire.

CHAPTER ✺ 18

The pentagon-shaped table in the secure briefing room of the Capitol Supertower looked unsettlingly empty, now that Uleeg Casgor was the only Director in attendance. For years, Phineas Alabaster had been accustomed to dealing with five politicians of questionable intelligence as he'd brief them on important matters of galactic security. Now that it was down to one, Alabaster felt the briefings might have been better held in Casgor's office rather than in the formal briefing room. However, Casgor seemed to like to keep Alabaster out of his office as much as possible.

The Director looked more haggard than usual. It was obvious the stress of his position was beginning to wear on the man. Alabaster assumed that Casgor's other machinations – particularly those concerning his secret alliance with the Deathlords – were really the things that were weighing on him, what with the increased public scrutiny thanks to Jack and his broadcast about the Secret Army. This pleased Alabaster. After all, the more pressure that was applied to Casgor, the greater the likelihood the man would eventually make a mistake that would bring him down.

"So… we didn't get him," Casgor said, gazing at Alabaster from over the rim of his infoglasses.

"The Earthman escaped from this shadow port he'd been hiding out on. That is correct, Director," Alabaster replied as he called up the intelligence reports from the event on his datapad. "Unfortunately, due to the nature of such locations and the port's presence deep inside unpatrolled Visini space, intelligence concerning the event from a few days ago is both unreliable and hard to come by. All we know for sure is that there were multiple altercations, both inside and outside the shadow port. We have varying reports that some of the Earthman's companions were either captured or killed in the event, but we can't verify any of them as of yet."

Casgor sighed and rubbed his temples. "The Earthman's companions are of no consequence," he said. "The Earthman and the Princess are the only ones that matter, and they are still eluding us. Isn't that right?"

"As far as we can tell, Director."

"And do we have any leads on where they may be? Or where they may be going?"

"Not at this time, sir."

"And would you tell me if we did?"

The question was so pointed it caught Alabaster off guard. Casgor was giving him a hard stare, the man's frustration finally culminating in the tipping of his hand that he did not trust Alabaster.

"Of course, I'd tell you, Director," replied Alabaster. "It's my job."

Casgor nodded, but Alabaster could tell he did not believe his answer. "You are, indeed, good at your job, Phineas," Casgor muttered. "How long have you been doing it?"

"Since the fall of Regalus Prime, Director," Alabaster replied. "My predecessor was killed when the Deathlords destroyed the planet."

"A decade is a long time. Have you given any thought to retirement?"

"None at all, sir."

"Perhaps you should," said Casgor. "Give yourself some time to enjoy life, for a change."

"I can assure you, Director, I am enjoying my life a great deal as it is."

Just then, Agent Boone entered the room. Both Casgor and Alabaster turned to look at the man as he strode forward and approached Alabaster, whispering something in his ear.

"Everything all right?" Casgor inquired.

"Yes, sir," Alabaster replied. "Just a few issues that require my immediate attention. Nothing worth concerning you with, as of yet."

"So I take it we're finished here?"

"We are, Director."

Casgor nodded and got to his feet. "Very well," he said as he smoothed out his robes. "Keep me appraised of the manhunt for the Earthman. I want to know the second we get a lead on him."

Alabaster nodded in acknowledgement as Casgor turned and left the room, followed by his entourage of compucrat androids. When he'd left, Alabaster quickly grabbed his things and started for the door.

"My apologies for interrupting you during your briefing, Chief, but I figured you'd want to know about this right away," Boone said as he accompanied Alabaster.

"You did the right thing, Agent," Alabaster replied. "A hacking of the I.I.A.'s secure database certainly warrants an interruption."

The door from the briefing room opened to reveal a small, hunchbacked android waiting for them in the hallway. It looked up at the two men as they approached, it's ocular orbs wide and eager to please. Ever since Boone had returned from hunting down Heckubus Moriarty in the sub-level of Supertower 7, he'd had the robot by his side almost continuously. Boone had said he kept planning to submit the machine to Robotics to have it repurposed, but Alabaster had the suspicion that the robot had become a type of pet with which the Agent was currently unwilling to part.

"Greetings, Master Chief, sir!" the tiny robot exclaimed as soon as Alabaster exited the room, the android quickly falling into step with Alabaster and Boone. "Please allow this one to introduce itself! This one be Hunchy! Official Imperial Intelligence Android! At your service, Master Chief, sir!"

Alabaster glanced at Boone. "Hunchy?" he asked.

Boone shrugged, giving Alabaster a lopsided smile. "I let him pick his own name," he replied.

"Thought you would have sent this thing off to the Robotics department by now."

"Yeah, well… he's just so eager to help, I'd feel bad having him repurposed," Boone said. "Besides, he's actually a pretty good assistant. And he makes a mean cup of coffee."

"Master Agent Boone likes coffee double strong, double sweet! Yes, he does!" said Hunchy cheerfully as it scrambled alongside the men. "How does Master Chief like his coffee? Hunchy get one right away!"

"I'd rather get information on this data breach you just interrupted a Directory briefing for," Alabaster muttered to Boone. "When did it happen?"

"Approximately twenty minutes ago, sir," Boone replied, handing Alabaster a datapad displaying a hastily written incident report. "We have our cyber-security division investigating it as we speak, trying to trace the breach."

"What was accessed?" Alabaster asked as his mind ran through all the doomsday scenarios of classified information that could have been stolen.

"Luckily, nothing important, it seems," Boone said. "Best we can tell, the only database that was accessed was our xenobiology index."

Alabaster raised an eyebrow. "The xenobiology index? They accessed our dossiers on the Empire's alien races?"

"Yes, sir," Boone replied. "Makes you wonder why someone would go through all the trouble of breaking into our secure databanks when they just could have looked up the same thing on the ultraweb."

"Because, Agent Boone," Alabaster said, handing the datapad back to him. "The I.I.A. keeps detailed notes on all known alien races. This information isn't exactly common knowledge among the Empire at large."

"Yes, sir," Boone acknowledged. "But still, there can't be much in our databases that would be considered sensitive enough to justify hacking into our system like this."

"One wouldn't think so," Alabaster replied as he stepped onto the teleportation platform with Boone. "But someone felt there was. And that's exactly what has me concerned."

In a flash of light, the two men appeared in the lobby of the I.I.A. Executive Offices in one of the sub-levels of the Capitol Supertower. Alabaster immediately began heading to his office, with Boone and his robot in tow.

"Get me the logs of every file that was accessed," Alabaster ordered as they walked. "I want to see what this intruder was looking at. And send me the findings of the cyber-security team the minute they're in."

"Right away, sir."

"And you," Alabaster said to Hunchy. "Large coffee. Heavy cream. Double caffeinated. I have a feeling it's going to be a long day."

"Oh! Oh! Yes, Master Chief, sir!" exclaimed Hunchy, jumping up and down excitedly as they approached the door to Alabaster's office. "Imperial Intelligence Android Hunchy get on that right away, Master Chief, sir! Does Master Chief have a preference on liquid temperature? Or amount of cream? Or caffeine saturation level?"

Alabaster smiled as the door to his office opened. "I'll say this for your little pet," he said to Boone. "At least he's thorough."

"Like you wouldn't believe, sir," Boone replied.

The moment they entered Alabaster's office, both Alabaster and Boone stopped short. The high-backed black leather executive chair behind Alabaster's meticulously organized desk slowly swiveled around, revealing none other than

Heckubus Moriarty, who gazed at the duo from behind his steepled fingers as though he were looking down the scope of a gun.

"Chief Alabaster. Agent Boone. At last, we meet again…" Heckubus said.

Hunchy yelped and immediately latched onto Boone's leg, cowering in fear.

"Heckubus Moriarty," grumbled Boone. "What an unpleasant surprise."

"Why thank you," Heckubus replied. "I do so strive for unpleasantness whenever possible."

If Alabaster were surprised to see the robot sitting at his desk, he didn't show it. He glanced down at Hunchy, who was trembling so noticeably it looked like the tiny android could very well shake itself apart. "Why is this robot programmed to experience fear?" Alabaster asked.

"Fear is an excellent motivator when it comes to getting minions to do as they're told," Heckubus answered.

"It's a robot. It'll do what it's told regardless."

"Yes, but it wouldn't be nearly as fun!" Heckubus said, with an evil chuckle.

"Should I call security?" Boone asked Alabaster.

Alabaster held up his hand to signal Boone to stay where he was. He then turned his attention back to Heckubus and looked the robot in his ocular orbs. "I take it you are behind this security breach of ours?" Alabaster asked.

"I am indeed," Heckubus replied, with just a hint of boastfulness. "I needed information, and your databanks were the only place I could get what I required. Mind you, I could have been in and out of your systems without your ever knowing I was there, but I knew setting off the alarms of a data breach would bring you right to your office, and I figured this would be the best place for us to chat privately."

"How did you even get in here?" Boone asked. "There are thousands of security measures in this building."

"Why, I used the Chief's secret teleportation network, of course," Heckubus replied. "I knew of one location he revealed when he helped me and my companions escape this planet before. Once I tapped into that, I found I could pretty much go wherever I pleased without notice. Including here."

Boone gave Alabaster a surprised look. "You… you helped the Earthman and this criminal?" he asked.

Alabaster frowned. "Heckubus, perhaps it would be best if we spoke privately," the Chief suggested.

"Do not worry, Chief Alabaster," replied Heckubus. "Though you are wise to mistrust this dim-witted henchman of yours, I have it on good authority he has an important role to play in what is to come."

Boone raised an eyebrow, eyeing Alabaster with a measured gaze of concern. "You… you don't trust me, sir?"

"Do not be offended, fool," Heckubus interjected before Alabaster could reply. "With the slythru threat at large, it makes sense not to trust anyone who could potentially be infected. That, and your seeming allegiance to Director Casgor made it wise for Chief Alabaster to keep you ignorant of his efforts to assist my colleagues and I in our efforts to save the Princess."

Boone frowned. "Sir, is this true?" he asked.

"Apologies, Agent Boone," Alabaster replied as he sealed the door to the office. "I couldn't take the chance your allegiances did not lie with me."

Boone nodded. "I'm the one who should apologize, sir. I should have never given you reason to doubt me. I thought I was simply following orders from our Director."

"Anyone in your position would have done the same, Agent Boone," Alabaster assured him. "I am simply not in the business of taking risks – not when the stakes are so high."

"I understand, sir," Boone said. "I can assure you, my allegiance is to the Empire. I would give my life for it."

"Good to know!" said Heckubus. "Now that we are all on the same page, shall we get down to business?"

Boone and Alabaster both glared at Heckubus. "Very well," Alabaster replied. "Am I to assume that the Earthman is back on Omnicron, as well?"

"No, Jack and the others are elsewhere," Heckubus said. "It is only I."

"And why would you risk coming here, of all places, knowing the entire Empire is hunting for you?" Boone asked.

"Because, as loathe as I am to admit it… I require your assistance."

"Assistance with what?" Alabaster asked.

"Defeating our ultimate adversary, of course," Heckubus answered. "Verrutus has made the fatal mistake of vexing me, and I have now dedicated

myself to his complete and utter annihilation. I assume you feel the same as I do, Chief?"

"You'd be correct in that assumption," replied Alabaster.

"Good!" said Heckubus, cheerily.

"Verrutus?" asked Boone. "You mean this Deathlord Supreme the Earthman claims is running this invisible army of the Deathlords?"

"It's a secret army. Get it right," corrected Heckubus. "And yes, that's exactly whom we are discussing."

Boone looked at Alabaster. "So… you believe the Earthman concerning this?" he asked.

"I've known about Verrutus for quite some time," Alabaster admitted. "I just didn't know his name or his origin. I had believed he was some type of deeply embedded mole within the Empire, but once the Earthman began sharing his findings with me, I started to see the legitimacy of his claims."

Boone sighed. "If what you say is true, how do we even begin fighting a Deathlord Supreme with secret agents who could be anywhere – or anyone, for that matter?"

"Leave that to me," Heckubus replied.

Boone gave Heckubus a skeptical look. "Leave it to you? And what makes you think you're any better equipped to fight this Verrutus than we are?"

"Because…" said Heckubus, "I know his true identity."

Now it was Alabaster's turn to look surprised. "His… true identity?" he asked.

"Indeed!" Heckubus gloated. "I finally put the pieces together. Our shadowy nemesis is no longer unknown to me. And now that I have uncovered his secret, I have a plan to bring him down."

"A plan?" asked Alabaster.

"A brilliant plan."

"Brilliant, you say?"

"Brilliant and *evil!*"

"How evil are we talking about here?"

"Sufficiently evil enough to out-evil Verrutus, I can assure you," Heckubus said, before muttering, "call me an amateur, will he?"

"What was that?" asked Alabaster.

"Oh, nothing," replied Heckubus dismissively. "Anyway, back to the task at hand. Needless to say, once we enact my strategy, I believe it is safe to say the Deathlord's days are numbered."

Boone and Alabaster looked at one another, then back to Heckubus. "Well?" asked Alabaster. "Are you going to share this brilliant plan of yours with us?"

"Once my conditions are met," Heckubus said. "First, I will be requiring my minion back."

"Oh, no!" cried Hunchy.

"Oh, yes," Heckubus said. "There is much work to be done, and I'll need someone I trust to oversee it. This minion has served me adequately in the past. He should do nicely."

"Very well," Alabaster said.

"On the conditions that you get rid of this fear program you've installed in him," Boone added, "and that you treat him with some respect."

Heckubus twiddled his fingers. "Fiiiiiiine," he said, reluctantly. "I won't be around much to enjoy torturing him anyway."

Hunchy immediately stopped shivering. "Oh, thank you, Master Agent Boone! Thank you!"

"Yeah, yeah," Boone replied, giving Hunchy a reassuring pat on the back.

"What is your second condition?" Alabaster asked.

"I will need your assistance in keeping my presence here on Omnicron hidden," Heckubus said. "Between my hologuise and your secret teleportation network, I don't expect to run into much trouble, but it never hurts to have allies in high places that can keep the city's Peacekeepers and surveillance network off my back."

Alabaster nodded. "Consider it done," he said. "What else?"

Heckubus produced a datapad and tapped on its screen. "Just this," the robot said.

Alabaster's datapad beeped as it received the information Heckubus had sent to it. Alabaster pulled it out and looked at the screen, his lips puckering curiously as he read. "And what will you be needing all this for?" Alabaster asked.

"Allow me to show you," Heckubus replied, tapping on his datapad once more.

Just then, all the viewscreens in Alabaster's office displayed a series of blueprint images. Heckubus rose to his feet, looking at the data with a certain sense of pride and smugness. Alabaster and Boone gazed at the schematics displayed upon the viewscreens, their eyes wide and curious as to what they were looking at.

"What... is that?" Alabaster finally asked.

"That, my mentally inferior allies," said Heckubus with more than a hint of glee, "is how we are going to kill a Deathlord."

CHAPTER ❧ 19

ord Gebhard Skyborn stood in *The Shieldbearer's* cavernous hangar bay, gazing out beyond the blue-hued haze of its plasma window as the personnel transport approached for a landing. Beside him stood one of the incarnations of Ambassador Bob, a sentient being the size of a planet who exports smaller versions of itself across the galaxy, all made up of the being's pink colored protoplasmic material, which it shapes to resemble the species it is living among.

Gebhard had known one incarnation or another of Bob for as long as he could remember. Bob existed pretty much across the entire Empire and was one of its most valuable citizens – not only in terms of intelligence gathering, since all of Bob's incarnations shared a single consciousness, but also in terms of manpower, which was what Gebhard desperately needed more of at that moment. In fact, other incarnations of Bob, which Gebhard planned to put to use immediately, filled the transport that was currently in the process of landing.

Unlike individuals, each of whom had to be trained to perform certain tasks, Bob required training only once, and as many incarnations of Bob as needed could perform the duties assigned to them. With the Deathlords stepping up their attacks in his system, Gebhard was desperate to get more ships from his fleet operational so they could protect the outposts in the system as quickly as possible. And at the moment, there was no better option available to him than utilizing Bob's unique set of abilities.

"You know, Lord Skyborn," Bob said. "It is really not necessary for you to greet my other incarnations."

"I realize that, Ambassador," Gebhard replied. "I suppose I am simply a stickler for ceremony. If it were not for you, it would be impossible to man all the ships in the Maxima fleet. By bringing in more of your incarnations, you are doing my system a great service."

Bob nodded. "Yes, well, there are quite a few extra versions of me now that Amadeus Evenstar has deported all my incarnations from the Redwater system. It makes more sense to put them to use rather than to simply send them back to my source."

"The Evenstars' loss is my gain, then," Gebhard replied. "With your help, we'll be able to further increase patrols in the system and have every single ship we've constructed out protecting our expansions instead of sitting idle in our shipyards."

"I am more than happy to help, at least until you are able to bring in your own people to replace me, my Lord."

"Yes, that is the drawback of quickly building a fleet of ships, I suppose," mused Gebhard. "The ships are finished before the training of the personnel needed to run them is."

"Still, your engineers have made great strides in designing ships that do not require as much manpower to be effectively operated," Bob said. "It's given you one of the larger Legacy fleets in the Empire."

"Both a blessing and a curse, I'm afraid," Gebhard replied. "We need such a large fleet to protect all our expansions, that's for certain. But even with the streamlined crew requirements, the manpower needed is a heavy burden for us to meet. Maxima is not as hospitable to colonization as other systems with more planets, which can be terraformed to foster population. All our personnel stem from our homeworld, which has already had its population strained due to our expansions into the Rim. It's an unfortunate reality that Maxima is rich in all resources, save one – people."

"Which is why these Deathlord raids are so devastating to your system," Bob noted. "Has there been any progress in defending against them?"

"There will be, now that there are more of you here to help crew our ships," Gebhard answered. "The 3rd fleet is currently occupied with the stand-off in Redwater, and until that situation is resolved, we must fend for ourselves out here."

"Seems a bit wasteful, does it not," Bob said, "to send the bulk of the Empire's third quadrant space force to deal with one Legacy, when their presence could be so much more useful here?"

"If you think our fleet is large, my friend, the one the Evenstars possess puts it to shame," Gebhard replied, with just a hint of bitterness. "Unlike us, Redwater has no shortage of population nor wealth to build and crew as many ships as they desire. I do not believe Casgor's decision to focus the 3rd fleet on a blockade of the Evenstars to be a wasteful one. Should it come to open conflict, it will be quite a battle between the two. The Empire needs as much force as it can muster in that system. But I am confident that should we require the 3rd fleet's assistance, Casgor will come through for us as he always has."

"No doubt he will, Lord Skyborn," Bob replied.

After the transport landed within the hangar bay, its ramps opened and other cookie-cutter versions of Bob filed out. Gebhard turned to the incarnation standing beside him and smiled. "Welcome aboard *The Shieldbearer*, Ambassador. Again."

Bob nodded in acknowledgement. "As always, Lord Skyborn, it is my pleasure to serve."

"And your service is much appreciated. Do you require any assistance in the assignments of your newly arrived incarnations?"

"No, my Lord. I've already been briefed on where to send them."

"Then if you'll excuse me, I must take my leave," Gebhard said, shaking Bob's hand. "I have a security briefing to get to."

As Gebhard made his way through *The Shieldbearer*, heading toward his office, he couldn't help but feel troubled that he'd come to rely so closely on Bob when it came to the continued existence of his system. Bob was just such a versatile being. Gebhard had enlisted him to help with the construction of his various outposts and space stations during his expansion. A great portion of the Maxima militia was made up of Bob. In fact, if it weren't for the alien, even the planet's Peacekeeper forces would be sorely lacking. And now, the Maxima fleet was dependent upon him simply to operate at full capacity. Should anything ever happen to Bob, it would be a devastating blow to Gebhard's system.

Luckily, it didn't appear Bob would be going anywhere anytime soon. He'd existed for a long time before he was discovered by the Empire, and he'd most likely exist for a long time after. As far as Gebhard knew, the way Bob replicated the protoplasm which he consisted of made it so that he was essentially immortal. If any of his incarnations perished, it could just be replaced. But to be so reliant upon one being still worried Gebhard. He held out hope that if he could get this Deathlord situation under control soon, he could focus his energy on getting his system's own people to the positions they needed to be in, so that Bob wasn't such a key factor in Maxima's daily operations.

Gebhard's office was located on the command deck, not far from the ship's bridge. There was a small cabin leading to it out of which his chief aide worked. His office was large, well furnished, and comfortable. It had to be, since it was where Gebhard spent most of his time. He had everything he needed to run his system from *The Shieldbearer*, but he mostly found his time of late was monopolized with matters of system security, with the monotonous administrative duties of his Legacy falling to those still working from the capital back on the planet.

Gebhard had barely settled into the seat at his desk when his chief aide, Ellyn Sorensen, contacted him via the visual display there. "Excuse me, my Lord," Sorensen said. "Your wife is on the line."

"Is she now?" mused Gebhard. "How long before the Altimac briefing?"

"About ten minutes, my Lord."

"Very well. Put her through."

It didn't take long for the image of Judyth Skyborn to grace Gebhard's display. Gebhard couldn't help but smile whenever he saw his wife. Their marriage may have been an arranged one, but he deeply cared for her. She was better than Gebhard felt he deserved – beautiful, graceful, and intelligent. Everything a man could want, let alone a Lord of his own Legacy. When he was off-planet, he entrusted the running of the system to her, and she'd proven to be more than capable of handling such a responsibility.

Despite the Deathlord's attacks requiring him to hop around the system, he and Judyth had always made it a policy to speak at least once a day. Though their call was destined to be a short one, Gebhard was glad that she'd made it. Seeing the face of his beautiful wife always served to both calm and center him.

"Hello, my love," Judyth said, returning Gebhard's smile.

"My Lady," Gebhard replied. "I fear I will not be able to chat for long. I have a briefing scheduled in a few minutes."

"Then I will try not to take up much of your time."

"Any time with you is time well spent," Gebhard said. "And if the briefing were not so important, I'd give you as much time as you desire."

"May I ask what it's about?"

"The raid on Altimac 7. The lead investigator has apparently uncovered some new evidence about what occurred there that he wishes to brief me on."

Judyth frowned. "Those poor people," she said. "I don't suppose it's too much to hope that any of them are still alive?"

"All indications point to that hope being wasted, my dear," Gebhard said. "But you obviously didn't call to have me depress you concerning the Deathlord activity in our system. What may I do for you?"

"I was actually calling about our son. Have you heard from Mourdock?"

"No, not since he ran off to search for the Princess."

"He has not reported in for days. I'm beginning to worry."

"Our son is a Paragon, my dear," Gebhard assured her. "He is more than capable of taking care of himself, not to mention Master Hasatan is by his side to protect him. Frankly, he's probably safer scouring the galaxy for the Princess than he is here in our own system, what with these ramped-up raids from the Deathlords."

"Are things really that dire here?" Judyth asked.

Gebhard sighed. "The raid sites have been… unsettling, to say the least. But the thing that troubles me the most is that these attacks are becoming more frequent and efficient. I feel as though we're constantly cleaning up after the Deathlords rather than actually protecting anything. It is like they are somehow two steps ahead of us, and I do not know how they are doing it."

"Do you believe the planet to be in danger?"

"I don't know. The Deathlords seem to be targeting remote outposts and colonies right now. But once we mobilize the rest of the fleet, we'll be able to at least have some military presence at every expansion, which may deter these raids. Perhaps the Deathlords are simply hitting us because they see us as easy targets right now? I honestly can't say, so I can't rule out the possibility that they may be gearing up for an assault on the planet. All I can do is try to increase the security efforts in the system as best I can and hope it will be enough to protect us."

"This whole situation frightens me, my love."

"It frightens me, too," Gebhard admitted. "But the people are relying on us to keep them safe. A Legacy that cannot protect its own system is a Legacy that is not fit to exist. We must put on a brave face and do our best to ensure that those who have entrusted their faith in us have no reason to be afraid."

"Still…" said Judyth, "you know what would make me feel better? If I could be included in the system defense briefings, just so I know what's going on."

"Let me worry about the defense of our system, my dear. While I'm away, I need you focused on the day-to-day running of Maxima."

"I'm not asking to be involved, simply to be in the know," Judyth persisted. "I have every faith in you, Gebhard. I simply feel that if I were in the loop, I wouldn't be so troubled constantly. And frankly, all this worry about the

Deathlords is making it harder for me to concentrate on our regular duties. If I were more aware of what was happening, I think I'd actually be more focused."

Gebhard frowned. "Are you sure? Knowing what's going on out here may actually end up troubling you more than not knowing."

"If that's the case, I'll simply stop attending the meetings," Judyth said. "Please, Gebhard. Allow me access to the security briefings."

Gebhard nodded. "Very well. If it will make you feel better, I'll instruct General Wessux to include you."

"Thank you," Judyth said.

Just then, a text message appeared on the bottom of Gebhard's visual display, informing him that Agent Dunscar was on hold. "I fear it's time for my briefing to begin," Gebhard said. "We shall speak again later, yes?"

"Indeed we shall," replied Judyth. "Take care, my love."

When the call with his wife ended, Gebhard switched over to answer the call from Agent Dunscar. The man's thin face and narrow eyes were quite a shift from the image of Judyth's beauty, and the expression the agent wore did not portend good news. Gebhard couldn't help but find himself wishing his call with Judyth would have lasted longer. He could have used a few more moments of happiness before diving into troubling news. "Sorry to keep you waiting, Agent Dunscar," Gebhard said. "What have you to report?"

"We've had a new development in the Altimac 7 investigation my Lord," Dunscar replied. "I had our technicians scour the station's databanks, and they were able to retrieve a security footage file from one of the backup servers."

"That is indeed good news," Gebhard said.

"Unfortunately, the file wasn't able to be fully recovered," Dunscar went on. "Much of it was corrupted. However, we were able to reconstruct a chunk of it, and what we saw was... unsettling, to say the least."

Gebhard frowned. "I'd expect so," he replied.

"With all due respect, my Lord... there's no way anyone could expect this. I will warn you that the video I'm about to share is a bit graphic."

"Consider me warned. Play it."

Dunscar's image was replaced with video footage from a static security camera in what appeared to be the operations center of Altimac 7. The large command room was fully staffed, with personnel monitoring all the station's

systems. Though the image would pixelate and stutter in parts, it played fairly well, showing the crew of Altimac 7 going about their daily routines as though nothing catastrophic were about to happen. Co-workers were chit-chatting, people drank coffee, and some were even talking on their datapads.

"As you can see, my Lord," came Dunscar's voice over the image, "this footage is from the central command room of the outpost before the Deathlord raid occurred."

"Yes, that much is clear," Gebhard replied.

"There appears to be no indication that anything is wrong, until here…"

Gebhard watched as the man at the sensor monitoring station sat up straight. He called over one of his colleagues and pointed something out on his screen. A few minutes later, that man called the Base Commander over to show him whatever it was they were looking at.

"Is that where they picked up the Deathlord ships?" Gebhard asked.

"It's possible, my Lord," Dunscar replied. "However, protocol would have dictated the station immediately enact their defenses and send out a distress signal. Their reaction here to whatever they picked up on their long-range sensors seems to indicate they did not know what they were looking at."

Gebhard watched as the Base Commander had his people call up the sensor reading on the operation center's central screen, which was unfortunately located out of range of the security camera's position.

"Here, it seems the Base Commander had tried to get a visual on whatever sensor contact they'd made. And then, it happens…"

Suddenly, everyone in the operations center began to scream. It occurred so suddenly, Gebhard flinched in surprise. Some of the personnel fell from their chairs and rolled on the floor, cradling their heads. Some clawed at their faces, tearing at their own skin and eyes. Some lashed out and began attacking their colleagues, beating on each other in a brutal, wild frenzy. Others ran around in a blind panic, screaming and crying, seeking out a hiding place.

"Great Observer…" Gebhard muttered. "What's happening to them?"

"I fear we do not know, my Lord," Dunscar replied. "But whatever it is, it goes on like this for some time."

Dunscar remotely sped up the footage as the scene further deteriorated. Whatever had thrown the operation's crew into such distress did not appear to

go away. In fact, the behavior only seemed to worsen, until eventually, everyone in the room was curled up on the floor, either catatonic, unconscious, or dead.

Eventually, Deathlord Dark Soldiers entered and started to drag away the victims. The image stuttered and pixelated more until it froze and cut to black. Once that occurred, Agent Dunscar reappeared on the call.

"It was approximately twenty minutes between the start of whatever happened to those people and the Deathlords arriving," Dunscar said. "In that time, as best we can tell, they all succumbed to whatever it was that had affected them."

"If what occurred there happened throughout the station, that would explain why they did not send out a distress signal," Gebhard commented grimly. "Were you able to recover anything else from other parts of the station?"

"I still have people going through the databanks, but most files have either been wiped or corrupted," Dunscar replied. "This was the first video file with enough fragments left over to reconstruct. It seems the Deathlords were careful to cover their tracks."

"In an effort to keep whatever weapon they used here a secret?"

"Most likely," Dunscar replied. "Unfortunately, we were also unable to recover the sensor logs from the operations center, so there's no way to know what may have caused the attack. My team will keep searching for clues, but I believe this video to be important enough to share with I.I.S. headquarters on Omnicron, as well as the I.I.A."

"Agreed," Gebhard said. "If this is indeed a new Deathlord weapon they are testing out here in the Rim, the central government needs to know of it straight away. In the meantime, we should probably notify all outposts and colonies to enact emergency protocols at the first sign of any unidentified sensor contact."

"I believe that to be a wise decision, my Lord."

"Very well. Keep me updated should you find anything new," Gebhard said. "And send me a copy of that video. I wish to review it further."

Dunscar nodded. "As you wish, Lord Skyborn."

When the call ended, Gebhard sighed. He got up from his seat and moved to the small bar in his office, pouring himself a stiff drink. The footage of what had occurred on Altimac 7 was indeed disturbing. But even more disturbing to him was what could have caused such a thing. Missiles, plasma cannons, even

Planetkiller ships he could understand. But something that could drive people to become so terrified they'd mutilate themselves and others? That was something he had a hard time wrapping his brain around.

Gebhard sat down and leaned back in his chair, nursing his drink as he reviewed the disturbing video again. Gebhard watched it and rewatched it, questions running through his mind as he saw the gruesome scene play out over and over. What could cause such behavior? Is it really a new form of weapon? If so, how was that weapon deployed? And more importantly – was there any way to defend against it? As Gebhard pondered these questions, a notification on his screen appeared, alerting him that his aide wished to speak to him. Gebhard paused the video and answered the call.

"Pardon the interruption, my Lord," Sorensen said, "but we've received a message for you over the ultrawave which I believe you'll want to hear."

"The ultrawave?" Gebhard said. "Shouldn't all official communication be broadcast through our dedicated subspace channels?"

"This is not an official communication, my Lord," Sorensen said. "It's from the head of a mercenary band who is insisting on speaking to you."

"A mercenary?" mumbled Gebhard. "And why do you feel I'd want to hear something from the likes of him?"

"Because, my Lord, it concerns the Earthman."

That certainly piqued Gebhard's interest. Despite his reservations on dealing directly with such a dubious individual, anything relating to the Earthman and his whereabouts needed to be heard. "Very well," said Gebhard with a sigh. "Put him through."

Sorensen's image was then replaced with that of a man with a bionic eye and scars from burns covering half his scalp.

"This is Lord Gebhard Skyborn. You wished to speak to me concerning the Earthman?"

"Aye, that's right," said the man, his voice gruff and scratchy. "Name's Copperhyde, m'Lord. I run with the Durasteel Raiders, out tha Boro sector."

"What do you have to report, Mr. Copperhyde?"

"We got us one of the Earthman's companions. The Rognok. We'd like to arrange a hand-off to ya."

"If you have captured one of the Earthman's crew, you should go to the closest Peacekeeper office or I.P.D.S.[16] outpost and turn him in. I am not in the business of collecting on bounties."

"Yeah… here's the thing though…" said Copperhyde, looking a tad nervous. "He says he'll only allow himself to be turned in if we take him to the Maxima system."

"You're letting a prisoner dictate the terms of his incarceration?"

"All due respect, m'Lord… you ever deal with a Rognok before?"

"Can't say I have."

"Right… let's just say me and mine are woefully ill-equipped to make him do anything he don't wanna do," Copperhyde replied. "Now, I know you probably think I'm the type that's beneath you dealing with, m'Lord. But so far, this is the only member of the Earthman's crew to be captured, and he may know where they're going and where the Princess is. We're comin' to Maxima regardless if you want this beast or not. The only question is… are we gonna dump him on your doorstep? Or are you gonna send out an Alpha Force squad to take him off our hands?"

Gebhard thoughtfully tapped his fingers on his desk as he considered the man's proposal. "Very well," Gebhard finally replied. "I'll have one of our Alpha Force squads meet you and take custody of the prisoner."

A look of relief washed over Copperhyde's face. "Oh, praise RNGsus[17]!" he muttered.

"Hang on. I'll transfer you back to my aide, and she'll coordinate the details."

"Thank you, m'Lord! Thank you!"

Gebhard put the man on hold and contacted Sorensen once more. "Ellyn," he said. "I need you to coordinate with this mercenary concerning a prisoner transfer."

"A prisoner transfer, my Lord?"

---

[16] I.P.D.S. stands for Imperial Peacekeeper Deputy Service and it is the governmental department responsible for coordinating with bounty hunters and paying out on bounties.
[17] RNGsus is the god of random number generation. Followers of the Church of RNGsus of Pre-Determined Destiny believe that through random numbers they can be guided toward doing what they need to do to in order to follow the path fate has laid out for them.

"Yes, for the Earthman's Rognok companion. It will require one of our Alpha Force squads, so have one assigned to the task. And notify Wilvelm and Fredreek. Have them accompany the soldiers."

"Do you feel it wise to send them to meet with such a dangerous alien, my Lord?"

"They know the Earthman personally, perhaps that will assist in the transfer of the prisoner," Gebhard said. "Besides, Urion Goldstone wanted me to find more things for them to do. Escorting a prisoner from point A to point B under the protection of an entire Alpha Force squad shouldn't be too dangerous for either of them. Wouldn't you agree?"

"Yes, my Lord. I'll begin working out the details with this mercenary right away."

"Oh, before you go," said Gebhard, "get me Casgor on the subspace. I need to speak with him."

"As you wish, my Lord."

It was a few minutes before Gebhard's screen transitioned to being on hold for the Office of the Director, and a few more before Casgor answered the call. "Gebhard," Casgor said, looking and sounding tired. "To what do I owe the pleasure?"

"I have some news that might lift your spirits, Uleeg."

Casgor raised an eyebrow. "Oh? By all means... lift away!"

"I just got off a call with a mercenary who's managed to capture one of the Earthman's companions."

That news made Casgor sit up at attention. "Is that so? Which one?"

"The Rognok."

Casgor frowned, his shoulders slumping. "Blast it," he muttered. "That big dumb beast barely talks. Interrogating him would most likely be futile."

"Regardless, it's a break that must be followed up on," Gebhard said. "I'm having an Alpha Force squad take custody of the Rognok here in Maxima. I would appreciate it if you would coordinate with the I.I.A. and any other agency you need to about taking this thing off my hands."

Casgor nodded. "Consider it done," he said. "Have your office send mine all the relevant information about where the Rognok will be picked up and held. I'll have my people arrange for a transport to the deepest gravity cell we've got."

"Much appreciated, Uleeg," Gebhard said. "You'll be hearing from my office shortly. Skyborn out."

★ ★★ ★★

Casgor shut off his call with Gebhard and leaned back in his chair. *So, we have the Rognok, eh?* he mused. Casgor himself knew that capturing the massive beast was insignificant in the larger scheme of things, but he did know one person who would find this news particularly interesting. And after their last meeting, Casgor knew he needed a few points of merit to get back in that person's good graces.

Casgor typed in the subspace code for the Maguffyn offices and before long, Hylda Whaller's face appeared on the screen. "Greetings, Director Casgor," she said. "How may I help you today?"

"I need to speak to your boss," Casgor said.

"I'll transfer you to Mr. Virtuoso right away—"

"Not that boss," Casgor said. "The other one."

Whaller frowned. "Hold, please," she said.

Whaller then closed her eyes. After a few moments, when she reopened them, they were pure white.

"Yes?" she asked, her voice deep and queer.

"Tell me, Verrutus," Casgor said, smiling smugly. "How badly do you want to kill a Rognok?"

CHAPTER  20

Professor Green looked down at Jack with concern as the boy lay upon the observation table in the Earthship's medical bay. *Poor boy,* he thought. *Please be okay! I do not wish to lose you as I did Shepherd.*

Jack remained motionless, his eyes closed. Though Jack had not had any further episodes since Shanks had healed him, Professor Green couldn't help but worry. He felt responsible for Jack, just as he felt responsible for the well-being of the Earthship. And seeing the boy suffering from such a grievous injury caused him to fret to no end.

The sound of the medical bay's door opening caused Green to turn to see Scallywag enter the room. "Came by ta tell ya we're exiting hyperspace soon," Scallywag said. "How's he doin'?"

"The same," Green replied. "The ship's medical scans all say he's okay… but they said the same thing about Shepherd, did they not?"

"Well, yeah, they did," Scallywag confirmed. "But yer Paragon buddy was flailing all about despite tha readings. At least Jack don't seem ta be sufferin' anymore."

"Regardless, I'd feel far better if he were to regain consciousness," Green muttered.

"Tha monk said ta give 'im time," Scallywag replied, trying to sound comforting. "And if tha healers in the Conclave are as good as ya all say, then I'm sure if he's not up and about by the time we get there, he will be in short order."

Green nodded. "Let us hope so," he said. "Without Jack… well… I don't know what we'll do. Especially now that we've lost Heckubus and Grohm."

"Tha lad has come in handy from time ta time," Scallywag agreed. "Though the robot and tha Rognok ain't around no more, he's still got us… for all the good we are. But now that we have Mourdock on our side, I'd say we have ourselves a better than average chance of saving tha Princess. And that's what the lad would have wanted."

"Please, dear fellow. Don't speak of him like he's dead."

"Sorry. I just meant… y'know…"

"Yes, I know," Green replied with understanding. "And I do appreciate your efforts to be optimistic, my friend. I know it is hard for you."

Scallywag nodded. "Bein' cynical means yer never disappointed," he said. "Guess runnin' with you lot has gotten me used ta disappointment."

"Thanks... I think," replied Green.

It was then that Dan entered the room carrying some duffle bags. "Ah! Master Green!" he said. "I have done as you requested and packed up the Earthman's belongings, as well as some of your own."

Green nodded in acknowledgement. "Thank you, Dan. I appreciate your doing that."

Scallywag eyed the luggage Dan was carrying. "Oy, ya really think we need ta bring all that much stuff with us?" he asked.

"Oh, most definitely," Green replied. "The Conclave is a rather... unique place, my friend. You shall certainly need to pack for an extremely extended stay."

Scallywag gave Green a lopsided frown. "Right," he muttered. "Can't we just make a run back to tha Earthship if'n we need anything once we're there?"

"That would not be recommended," Green said. "Best to bring as much with you into the Conclave as you can."

"If you would like, Master Scallywag, I can assist you in packing for the trip," Dan offered. "If you take note, I have packed all of Master Jack's clothes, as well as some toiletries, and other personal items, such as a few books from his room, posters from his wall, as well as the ceremonial batons the Royal Vanguard gifted him. Admittedly, Master Jack did not have many possessions, so it was a simple task to determine which items to—"

"Yeah, yeah," Scallywag replied. "Sounds good. Why don't ya go ta me chambers and pack up some clothes and me weapons."

"Weapons, sir?"

"Aye. Never leave home without 'em," Scallywag replied. "And don't forget me lowbacco box. Or me Loquir deck fer that matter. Oh – and rum. Lots o' rum. Not takin' a chance this Conclave place don't have alcohol."

"Very well, sir. I shall get on that right away!"

With that, Dan shuffled out of the room to carry out his assigned task. Green gave Scallywag an odd look. "I do not believe you'll be needing your weapons in the Conclave, my friend," he said.

"Best let me decide where I be needin' me weapons, greenskin," Scallywag replied. "Now, let's go join Mr. Future Emperor on the bridge. We should be exiting hyperspace any minute now."

Mourdock and Hasatan were both at the ship's control panels when Scallywag and Green entered the bridge of the Skyborn Corvette. Shanks was there, as well, standing to the side, leaning heavily on his elderwood walking staff. The monk had begun to look rather drawn and weathered since his effort to heal Jack, but whenever Green tried to broach the subject of how Shanks was feeling, the monk simply shrugged it off, telling the Professor he was simply tired.

Mourdock swiveled his chair around to look at the two as they approached. "How's Jack?" he asked.

"Unchanged," Green replied.

"Do not worry. The Earthman will be fine," Hasatan interjected.

"How can ya be so sure?" Scallywag asked.

"Because I have faith in your Luminadric friend over here."

Scallywag looked at Shanks who nodded his head in response. "Give it time," Shanks said. "I have no doubt Jack will recover, eventually."

"I'll be sure to have the Conclave's healers attend to him once we're safely inside," Mourdock said.

"Oy, I hope you lot are right about this," Scallywag said. "Be mighty nice not ta have ta be dealin' with that browner of a Deathlord Supreme anymore."

"If your theories of the slythru being unable to take control of those with Paragon training are true, there can be no safer place," Hasatan offered. "More than that, since the Conclave exists in a separate universe, it is highly unlikely whatever connection this Verrutus has to the Princess will be able to exist once we cross the tether into it."

"I pray you are correct, Master Hasatan," Shanks said. "Without the Deathlord Supreme there to interfere, we may just have a chance of reaching the Princess and separating her from her tormenter."

"Don't worry," Mourdock replied. "I will not rest until Anna is finally safe. Once we're in the Conclave, I'll have the best healers available with her around the clock."

"Sounds good ta me," Scallywag said. "The sooner she's better, the sooner she can lift these bloody bounties off all our heads."

A notification on Mourdock's console beeped, causing him to turn back to it. "We've reached the Regalus system," he said.

The Skyborn Corvette dropped out of lightspeed and flew out of hyperspace. On the viewscreen, a bright white sun shined at the center of the system. The ship's long-range sensors marked the positions of the visible planets in orbit around the star on the screen. Scallywag leaned against the back of Mourdock's chair and eyed the image before him.

"So, this is tha Regalus system, eh?" Scallywag said. "Ta think... it weren't too long ago this was considered ta be the center o' tha universe."

Green frowned. "Yes," he said. "Hard to believe that in just ten short years this went from being one of the most populated systems in the galaxy to possessing only a few remaining colonies."

"Without Regalus Prime to support them, the system expansions simply weren't able to sustain themselves," Mourdock noted. "As if losing all the natural resources the planet produced weren't bad enough, without a working portgate in the system, trade was crippled. Most of the hyperspace lanes were diverted, and without the space traffic, commerce quickly dried up. Most of the system's population immigrated elsewhere. But even though the Regalus system has been all but abandoned, there's still one important thing that remains..."

Mourdock called up an image on the ship's viewscreen. It was a modest sized space station, with a large domed top that tapered down into a long cylindrical body. The station was nestled within an asteroid field in the system's habitable zone.

"Remnant Station," Mourdock said, "built among the remains of Regalus Prime, around the tether to the Conclave universe."

Scallywag eyed the image. "Bein' from tha empire next door, I've heard a lot o' stories about this place," he said. "Can't say I rightly believe most of 'em, though."

"Whatever you've heard, it's most likely true," Mourdock said.

"So ya say."

"Surely even the Visinis must have some knowledge about the Conclave," Mourdock said.

Scallywag shrugged. "My people don't place much importance on Paragons or yer 'free mind' hocus-pocus," he said. "Ain't never been a Visini Paragon in all o' history. And it ain't as though we be welcome guests this deep inta Imperial space. But we still heard the tales of a mystical gateway inta a different universe where Paragons are made."

"I don't know if 'mystical' would be the word I would use," Green said. "I mean, don't get me wrong, it is amazing! But the tether between the pocket universe of the Conclave and our own actually has quite a firm basis in science—"

"Whatever," Scallywag said. "All I know is that the portal survived the destruction of the planet, and the Paragons then built Remnant Station around it so they could keep makin' new Paragons."

"Well, you're not wrong," Mourdock replied. "The tether used to be housed in the Temple of Arcturus, around which the royal palace was built. Somehow, after the Deathlords destroyed Regalus Prime, it remained. When this was discovered, the Paragons in our universe and the ones trapped in the Conclave coordinated their efforts to construct Remnant Station so that the Conclave's lifeline to the prime universe would be preserved."

"I say, the station has certainly gotten bigger since I last saw it," Green mused. "It would appear the Paragons have been expanding it over the years."

"They've had to," Mourdock said. "Maintaining a space station among the debris field of a former planet is quite tricky."

Green looked over at Shanks, who was quietly studying the image of the station on the viewscreen as he leaned heavily on his walking stick. "Have you ever been to the Conclave before, Brother Shanks?" Green asked.

Shanks shook his head. "My training took place in the Temple of Light, on the planet of Ettib," he said. "That is where Nameer and Paragon Darwyn founded the Luminadric Monks after the Starfall War. I have, unfortunately, never stepped foot in the Conclave."

"Well, Brother Shanks, that is about to change," Mourdock said as he hailed the space station.

Within minutes, the image of a stout looking Corkron appeared. His entire bald head was littered with tiny tattoos, and his brilliant ochre colored eyes were narrow and beady.

"Paragon Skyborn," he said, "this is an unexpected surprise."

"Greetings, Paragon Patton," Mourdock said. "Forgive me for not alerting you to my visit prior to arriving, but I am here on an urgent matter concerning the security of the Empire. I shall need to meet with the Order of Peers immediately."

"I'll clear a docking bay to receive you and will notify the Order of your arrival," Paragon Patton replied.

"I have prepared a video message for the Order concerning the nature of my visit," Mourdock said as he tapped some buttons on his console. "I am transmitting it to you now. I would appreciate it if you would forward it on to them before we land."

"I shall do so right away," Paragon Patton replied. "See you soon, Paragon Skyborn."

"The Order o' Peers too busy ta take yer call directly?" Scallywag asked after the transmission ended.

"Not exactly," Mourdock replied. "The nature of the Conclave makes direct real-time communication impossible. All communication has to be done through recorded messages."

"Oh? And why's that?"

Mourdock smiled. "Scallywag, we have about thirty minutes before we dock with Remnant Station, and I'm not sure that is enough time to properly explain it to you."

Scallywag looked over to Professor Green, who shrugged. "I told you... the Conclave is a rather unique place," Green said.

After the Skyborn Corvette had docked in one of Remnant Station's hangar bays, the group disembarked, transporting Jack atop a hovering medical gurney and the Princess strapped onto a hovering chair. Scallywag looked around at the hangar as they exited the ship, not sure what to make of what he was seeing.

"Oy, what's with all the stone?" he asked Green as they walked, referring to the sandstone material of which the hangar seemed to be comprised.

"Primarily an aesthetic choice," Green said. "Though the station is built using highly advanced materials, the Paragon Engineers who designed it wanted to keep the interior stylistically consistent with that of the Conclave."

"So... they made the inside of a space station look like the inside of an Ancient temple, eh?" Scallywag muttered. "And just when I thought livin' in space couldn't get any more depressing..."

 ~ 189 ~

A small group of Paragons had assembled in the bay to await the group's arrival. Clad in full body armor, they appeared to be an escort of some type. Among them was Paragon Patton, who was adorned in a bright orange robe.

"Paragon Skyborn and friends," Patton said with a slight bow, "welcome to Remnant Station."

"Thank you, Paragon Patton," replied Mourdock. "What was the reply from the Order concerning my message?"

"They have granted you and your companions access to the Conclave," Patton answered. "We are here to escort you there forthwith."

"You will not escort me anywhere except back to Omnicron Prime!" said Anna, forcefully. "These men have abducted me against my will! Do you have any idea who I am?"

Paragon Patton sighed, not bothering to look at the Princess. "Admittedly, this is a most unusual situation, Paragon Skyborn," he said. "I have no doubt it will cause complications between the Empire and us, but for now the Order wants you and the Princess in the Conclave. I trust they will get to the bottom of what is going on and will decide upon the best course of action."

"On that, I have no doubt," replied Mourdock. "The Order of Peers is wise. If ever there were a situation that required guidance and insight from those who comprise it, it is this one."

"Indeed," Patton said. "I'll have my men tend to your ship. Now, if you'll follow me…"

The group followed Paragon Patton out of the hangar bay and through the station. Though the architecture of the station did indeed resemble that of an Ancient Temple, there were many of the station's parts that were obviously made of metal and alloy, hinting at a mechanical foundation beneath its simple stone façade.

Eventually, they came to a large door that opened to a circular room. In the center of the room was a strange, swirling vortex – like a ripple in a pool of water. Only instead of water, this ripple was on the plane of reality. The vortex existed between two tall stone pillars, and the light from the room that passed through it was refracted, causing ribbons of light to dance across the walls, like sunlight reflected from a pool.

Scallywag whistled. "What tha blazes is that?" he asked.

"That, my friend, is a tether to another universe," Green said, smiling in awe at the sight.

"I seen a portal to tha Nexus[18] before," Scallywag said. "It didn't look nothin' like that."

"I believe the two are quite different," Green said. "Theoretically, a portal is a gateway to another place within our own universe. We call this a tether because it is a bridge connecting two entirely separate universes."

"Aye. And ya can come back from this one, whereas tha Nexus is a one-way trip."

"Yet another important distinction, for sure," agreed Green.

Paragon Patton gestured toward the tether. "The Order will meet you on the other side," he said.

Mourdock nodded in acknowledgement before leading the group through. He was followed by Hasatan pushing Anna in her chair and Dan, saddled with all the luggage, pushing Jack on his gurney. Shanks was next, and then Scallywag and Green.

Passing through the tether was a disorienting experience. For a moment on the other side, Green wobbled, feeling as though he were drunk. The room shifted to-and-fro before he was able to get his bearings as the effect quickly wore off.

Scallywag vigorously shook his head, blinking his eyes to make them focus. "So, that's what travellin' to another universe feels like," he said. "Call me crazy, but I think I prefer hyperspace."

The group found themselves on a large, circular stone platform, the swirling tether behind them, once more flanked by two large ornate pillars. The room they were in was cavernous with many different platforms both above and below them and various stairs, bridges, and connections leading from one platform to another. A welcoming party was already there to greet them as soon as they passed through. At its head was a Tygarian with majestic white fur with black stripes, his eyes a brilliant gold color. He was clad in a pristine, flowing white robe and appeared kind and gentle despite his large and intimidating frame.

To the Tygarian's right was a blue-robed Regal with dark hair styled in a simple bowl cut. He seemed young – at least compared to the others in the group,

---

[18] The Nexus is an inescapable "nightmare" dimension into which the galaxy deports their worst criminals.

particularly to the man on the left of the Tygarian. This man was extremely old, with patchy cotton-colored hair thinning atop his head and loose and wrinkly skin under his weak chin. He, too, was wearing a white robe, though his was not as pristine as the Tygarian's.

"Paragon Skyborn," the Tygarian said with a slight bow, "welcome back to the Conclave."

"Master Highclaw," Mourdock said in response. "Thank you. It is good to be back. I take it you received my message?"

"Of course," Highclaw said. "We've been preparing for your arrival for some time."

"Some time?" Scallywag muttered. "We just got here."

Green chuckled. "To us, yes," he said.

Scallywag rolled his eyes. "Right. This place is 'unique'," he muttered. "Now I know how Jack must feel all tha time."

"Marvus Hasatan, my old friend!" the old man to the left of Master Highclaw said as he approached Hasatan. "So good to see you again! When I heard you'd be returning, I simply had to come and greet you myself," he said, happily shaking Hasatan's hand.

Hasatan looked blankly at the old man, as though he did not recognize him. "Er… yes, thank you. It is good to see you, too."

"Come now, don't tell me you've forgotten about your old study buddy!" the old man said. "I'm the one living in the time constriction! It's supposed to be the other way around!"

"I have not forgotten about you… Paragon Brunwahld," Hasatan said awkwardly. "I just did not expect you to still be alive."

Paragon Brunwahld laughed heartily at that. "Ah! That's the Marvus I remember!" he said with a broad smile. "Oh, how I've missed your ribbings! Soon we shall have to sit down and catch up. I've been working on a great number of things I'm eager to get your thoughts on, particularly my farsight studies…"

"Yes, some other time," Hasatan said, dismissively. "Right now, we have more pressing matters to attend to."

"Yes, the Princess," Highclaw said as he turned his gaze upon Anna, who glared back at him defiantly.

"I demand you release me," Anna said. "These men are holding me against my will."

"Don't bother," Mourdock said to her. "I already explained the situation to Master Highclaw in my message. He knows everything."

"Lies," Anna insisted, looking at Highclaw. "By the authority of Legacy Prime, I command you release me and arrest these men."

"I fear the authority of Legacy Prime does not carry much weight here, your Highness," Highclaw replied. "The Conclave is its own sovereign entity. We are not part of your Empire."

"My ancestors built this place!" Anna snapped. "Legacy Prime created the Paragons!"

"And if you'll recall, they created Paragons as equals," Highclaw said. "There is a reason Arcturus named the Order of Peers as he did. Though he was Emperor, he saw those in the Order as his equals. He may have ruled the galaxy, but here in the Conclave, there were no rulers – only colleagues and friends."

Anna scowled at Highclaw, who then looked over at the medical gurney Jack was on.

"And this must be the Earthman," he said.

"Yes," Mourdock replied. "I'm afraid he has yet regained consciousness from his trauma."

"We have already prepared healing chambers for your friend and the Princess," Highclaw said. "If you'll follow me, I'll take you to them."

As the group followed Highclaw, the blue-robed man lingered behind. Professor Green approached him, smiling broadly. "Eldrich Pennywise!" Green exclaimed. "It has been far too long! Even by non-Conclave standards!"

The man returned Green's smile before giving him a friendly embrace. "Thaddius," Pennywise said. "It is good to see you, as well."

"Yes, it is good to be back! Though I wish the circumstances surrounding my return were different."

"Indeed. A number of us were greatly disturbed at the news contained in Mourdock Skyborn's message."

"I can assure you, it is all true, old friend," Green said, sadly.

"I'm sure there are a great many things you can tell me about what is going on in the prime universe. And frankly, I'm eager to hear them. But despite the

circumstances surrounding your arrival, it is most fortuitous that you are here. I am in need of your expertise."

"You are?" Green asked, surprised.

"I know you must attend to your companions, but if I could borrow you for a few moments, it would be greatly appreciated."

Green nodded. "Of course. Lead the way!"

Professor Green began to follow Pennywise as he led him through the sandstone hallways of the Conclave. "I heard you discovered another Great Seal in your travels," Pennywise said as they walked.

"You heard correctly," Green replied. "Quite a wondrous thing. It had created a multi-dimensional planet, if you can believe it."

"Did you happen to get much of a chance to study it?"

"Unfortunately, no," Green said with a frown. "As a point of fact, I did not even get to lay eyes upon it. I was rather busy sneaking into a Deathlord mothership at the time."

Pennywise raised an eyebrow in curious surprise. "Come again?" he asked.

"It's… a rather long story," Green said. "Suffice it to say, the Great Seal was destroyed before I had any opportunity to examine it. But I'd hoped, with its destruction, some here in the Conclave would be able to uncover the knowledge that it harbored."

Pennywise nodded. "Yes, Master Highclaw has been leading meditation groups in an effort to try to discover what knowledge was contained within the Great Seal of the Ghost Planet ever since we received word of its destruction," he said. "Though the prevailing theory is that the Great Seals somehow block discovery of the knowledge they use to manifest their wonders, there are some here who are worried that even if the knowledge is now accessible by those with free minds, it may be so advanced, that it is nearly impossible to rediscover. Many would have preferred you to have preserved the Seal, rather than to have destroyed it."

"I completely understand that sentiment," Green acknowledged. "And had there been any other way to stop the Deathlords, I can assure you, we'd have done that. As it stands, well… there were no better options, I'm sorry to say."

"Knowing how passionate you are about Ancient technology and the study of the Great Seals, I believe you, my friend," Pennywise said. "We still use many

of the papers you wrote during your time here at the Conclave as reference in the ongoing study of our Great Seal, in fact."

"You do?" asked Green, surprised to hear that.

"Yes, a number of your theories are quite fascinating. There's a small circle of researchers here who would even go so far as to say you're on the forefront of Great Seal theory, and many wish you had stayed to pursue your studies."

Green couldn't help but feel a little pride upon hearing that. "Well, as much as I would have liked to have continued my research here, I felt helping the Princess search for more Ancient artifacts was a better use of my time, considering how much was lost when the Deathlords destroyed Regalus Prime."

Pennywise nodded. "If I'm being honest, I was skeptical when Shepherd recruited you for the Princess's project. Not to say I didn't believe you were the best person for the job, mind you. It was just that you always struck me as more of an academic than a field researcher."

Green laughed at that. "You are not incorrect in your assumption, my good man. I do prefer sitting behind a desk over traipsing around the galaxy. But by leaving, I've gotten to see some incredible things I never in my wildest dreams could have imagined. And almost all of them have had to do with the Ancients."

Pennywise nodded as he stopped in front of two large stone doors with the engraved image of an all-seeing eye within a pyramid upon it. "I hope the things you've seen have helped to deepen your understanding of Ancient technology, Professor," he said, "because right now, everyone in this temple is in desperate need of such insight."

Pennywise placed his hand on the door, and immediately it rumbled open. The two stepped inside a grand amphitheater, much like the one that contained the Great Seal on the Sunshell of the Ancients. The massive room had a large domed ceiling as well as stadium benches all around it, with stairs leading down to a circular floor area. A triangular wall extending forward onto the floor harbored a Great Seal.

As Green followed Pennywise down the stairs, he eyed the scene before him curiously. There were a number of Paragons at work stations set up around the Great Seal. Mostly they consisted of those wearing blue robes and green robes, but there were a few Paragons clad in white robes, as well. Some were meditating on the benches of the stadium. Others were analyzing readings their computers were taking from the Seal. Even though Green had been involved in research projects concerning the Conclave's Great Seal before, he'd never seen such an intense and elaborate set up for one.

"My, my… this is quite an extensive operation you've got here," Green noted.

"It's gotten bigger over time, I'm afraid," Pennywise said. "We first noticed an anomaly with the Great Seal about three years ago, prime universe time…"

"An anomaly?" asked Green.

"Yes. And since then, the anomaly has grown. As it has increased, so have our attempts to discover what it is. Whatever is afflicting it is beginning to affect the Conclave's pocket universe, and we are concerned its effects might get stronger over time."

"Oh, dear," muttered Green. "That sounds rather serious."

"It is," replied Pennywise. "It's to the point now that until we're able to determine exactly what's happening, we've sealed off the chamber to everyone but the research team and the Order of Peers."

As Green got closer to the Great Seal, he could see it had changed since he'd last seen it. Before, the circular sandstone with the engraving of the all-seeing eye had been pure and clean. However, now it was riddled with pale veins that appeared in shades of dull red, green, and purple. The veins were most prevalent at the outer edges of the Seal and disappeared about a quarter of the way in toward its center.

Green approached the Great Seal and looked with concern at the veins that afflicted it. "Oh, dear," he said. "What… what's wrong with it?"

Pennywise frowned. "That, my old friend, is what I was hoping you could tell me."

CHAPTER ✹ 21

Master Highclaw led the group down a sandstone hallway where two open chambers awaited them. Mourdock and Hasatan took Anna into one, while Scallywag, Shanks, and Dan took Jack into the other. The chamber was a large, well lit, egg-shaped room with a bed in its center. The Paragons escorting the group helped to move Jack from the gurney onto the bed and then left them to wait, sealing them inside.

Scallywag paced around the room restlessly while Shanks took a seat in a chair next to Jack's bed. Scallywag studied the smooth white walls, which were noticeably different from the coarse sandstone bricks he'd seen everywhere else. Beyond that, the chamber contained no extra bells, whistles, art, or decoration. I was just a simple, bland room.

"Oy, robot," Scallywag said to Dan, "break out some o' that rum ya packed fer me. I'm guessin' we're gonna be here a while."

Thus, Scallywag plopped himself down on the floor and nursed a bottle of Claxagaar rum while they waited for what seemed a rather long time. Much to Scallywag's annoyance, every time he felt as though he were getting a nice buzz going, for some reason, it disappeared rather quickly.

"Danny-boy," Scallywag said, "this rum ya packed... ya got it from me chambers, right?"

"Most certainly, Master Scallywag," Dan replied.

"I'd be about three thrusters to tha wind 'bout now, having drank this much," Scallywag said, holding up the bottle and sloshing its contents about. "But it ain't havin' no effect. Did ya accidentally have tha ship manifest some watered-down swill?"

"It is not the alcohol at fault. It is the room," Shanks said. "I am sensing a large amount of energy being emitted from the walls of this chamber. No doubt it is meant to assist in the healing of whomever is within it. Likely, your body is being healed before the effects of intoxication can take hold."

Scallywag frowned before capping the bottle and tossing it back to Dan. "Great," he grumbled. "Well, that explains me. What about you, monk? Yer lookin' as worn as ever."

"I am fine."

"So ya say, but ever since ya healed Jack, you've looked like death."

"It was a most difficult procedure," Shanks admitted. "It took a great deal out of me. I simply need time to recover."

"Yeah, but shouldn't this healin' chamber have an effect on ya? We've been sittin' here fer hours, and ya don't seem any better for it."

"I appreciate your concern," Shanks replied. "However, with how time works here in the Conclave, I am not sure I have actually been in this room long enough to benefit from its effects."

"Oy, there's that 'uniqueness' everyone speaks about again," Scallywag said. "Is someone gonna get around ta explainin' to me what tha blazes is goin' on around here?"

Before Shanks could reply, the door to the chamber opened. Green entered, accompanied by Paragon Pennywise, and a green-skinned Viridian[19] with slicked back bright red hair and a large, bushy, bright red beard to match. His face was hard and weathered, and he appeared rather gruff and burly. He, too, wore a blue robe.

"About time someone showed up," Scallywag said as he got to his feet. "I was beginnin' ta think we'd been forgotten."

"Apologies, my friends," Green said. "There were some other matters we had to attend to. But we're here now! And we've brought the greatest medical mind in the temple!"

"Allow me to introduce Master Paragon Grendal Savage," Pennywise said, gesturing to the man beside him. "He is a member of the Order of Peers, Head of the Water Ring, and our Master Healer here at the Conclave."

Savage wasted no time with pleasantries and moved to Jack's bedside. He looked at Jack intensely, the Paragon's gaze scanning Jack's body up and down. "I sense nothing physically wrong with him," Savage said as he gently laid his hands on Jack's chest. "However... his spiritual energy is in great turmoil. That distress is certainly having an effect on him."

"Ya don't say," grumbled Scallywag.

Savage raised an annoyed eyebrow at the Visini. "What happened to him?" the Paragon asked.

---

[19] Viridians are a species of green-skinned humanoid aliens with bright red hair, known for being extremely social, academic, and promiscuous.

"We was ambushed by a particularly nasty bounty hunter," Scallywag explained. "Then Jack shot a ghost ball out of his hand and saved our rears. That's about tha time his jimmies got all rustled."

Paragon Savage looked at Scallywag in surprise. "A ghost ball?" he said.

"Yeah, like the Deathlords do," Scallywag replied. "Only... y'know... smaller and not as scary."

Savage looked down at Jack in alarm. The Paragon instinctively removed his hands from Jack's chest, as though he'd touched a hot surface and burned himself. He eyed Jack suspiciously, a worried look locked upon his face.

"The boy suffered from a soul severing," Shanks added, getting to his feet and leaning upon his staff. "I did my best to mend it, but he has not regained consciousness since."

Savage did not respond. He merely continued gazing at Jack, his face hard and cold.

"Oy," said Scallywag, trying to get Savage's attention. "Will the lad be okay?"

Savage frowned before nodding. "In time," he muttered. "A soul severing is an extreme trauma. It is usually fatal. But whatever the monk did seems to have saved him. All we can do now is wait for the boy's spirit to settle. Once that happens, he should regain consciousness." Savage then turned and looked at Shanks. "And you..." he said.

"I am not of concern," Shanks interrupted. "Right now, the only people who matter are the Earthman and the Princess."

Savage pursed his lips, looking at Shanks with a measured gaze before finally nodding. "Very well," he said. "Take me to Her Highness."

Pennywise then led Savage and the others to the Princess's healing chamber. It was exactly like the one where Jack was being kept, except instead of a bed in the room, a chair, into which Anna had been strapped, stood in the center. Master Highclaw was sitting on the floor before Anna, meditating. Mourdock and Hasatan were sitting off to the side but rose to their feet when the others entered the room.

Master Savage met Anna's contemptuous gaze as she glared at him. "What are you sensing?" Savage asked Highclaw.

The Tygarian opened his eyes and looked at Anna thoughtfully. "I can sense nothing wrong with her," he said. "If it were not for the insistence of the others, I would think she were perfectly normal."

"That's because I am perfectly normal!" Anna insisted. "How many times must I say it? I have been kidnapped!"

"If that is really the case, then you'll be released," Master Savage said as he moved back behind Anna and placed one hand on her shoulder and the other over her heart. "But until such time, we will need to examine you…"

"Don't touch me!" Anna hissed.

Despite her objection, Savage squeezed her shoulder more firmly to keep her from moving as he closed his eyes. After a few moments, he opened them back up and looked at Highclaw. "I sense nothing, as well," he stated.

"Master Savage," Hasatan said. "The nature of the Princess's affliction is… unique to the Deathlords. Of all the people here at the Conclave, I believe you are the most qualified to diagnose such a thing."

Savage frowned at Hasatan before looking back to Highclaw, who gave him a subtle nod. Savage grimaced but repositioned himself to focus his gaze on the back of the Princess's head. His pupils grew large for a brief moment before he shut his eyes and shook his head, appearing agitated by what he'd just done.

"Blast it…" he muttered.

"What did you see?" Highclaw inquired.

"Assemble the Order," Savage grumbled before heading for the door. "I shall meet you in the Chamber of the Five Rings."

With that, Savage made a hasty exit. Scallywag watched him go with a curious look. "Oy, what's with him?" he asked.

"Master Savage is a most disciplined man," Highclaw said as he got to his feet. "His duties can weigh heavily on him, which at times can affect his bedside manner."

"At times?" muttered Scallywag. "Or all times?"

"Paragon Pennywise," Highclaw said, "do be so kind as to let Masters GorJiro and Hodapp know the Order is assembling."

Pennywise bowed. "At once, Master," he replied before leaving.

Highclaw then turned to the others. "I'm inviting you all to attend our meeting in the Chamber of the Five Rings," he said. "I am sure you'll want to hear Master Savage's findings just as we do. Please, follow me."

The group followed Highclaw as he led them up a seemingly unending flight of stairs. Though the Paragon seemed unfazed by the climb, the others were getting an unexpected work out as their legs burned and cramped from the arduous ascent. Finally, the stairs led into a grand hallway, ending at two large stone double doors. As Highclaw approached, the doors opened. The room beyond it had a golden floor with a large circle etched into it. Within that circle were five rings inlaid into the floor, each a different color. They went from black, to orange, to blue, to green, and finally to white. Within each ring was a luxurious chair.

The walls of the room were transparent, each one rising up into a pyramid shape. Beyond the walls was just darkness, but within that darkness were subtle, multi-colored swirls fading in an out. As far as Scallywag could tell, however, there were no stars anywhere in sight.

Master Highclaw took his seat in the chair within the white ring, before promptly closing his eyes and meditating. The group followed Mourdock and Hasatan as they stood outside the edge of the largest circle on the floor and awaited the arrival of the others. Paragon Pennywise entered the room and bowed to Master Highclaw before joining the others in waiting.

"Oy, not that I don't mind climbing tha stairs o' infinity just to be made ta wait with me hands in me pockets fer hours on end," Scallywag grumbled. "But it would help to know what we're waitin' for."

"The members of the Order of Peers are assembling so they can all hear Master Savage's findings and determine what to do with the Princess," Pennywise explained. "All major decisions concerning the Conclave are made by committee. The members of the Order can only make unilateral decisions concerning their own rings."

"Rings? Ya mean those things in the floor?"

"The Conclave is made up of five different schools," Green said. "Each school is associated with a different colored ring. It's just a way to identify the different subjects the Paragons train in."

"Right, glad we got that cleared up," Scallywag muttered. "Who we waitin' on?"

"Master Hodapp should be here shortly," Pennywise said. "Master GorJiro was training, but he should be here soon, as well. Master Savage will join us once he's finished his meditations."

"Oy, the meditating couldn't wait until we were done?"

"Apparently not," Pennywise replied. "We don't typically question the decisions of the Order. They're all considered to be Masters for a reason."

The first to arrive was a Scollum[20] in a large mechanical exoskeleton which lumbered into the room on its heavy feet, making its way to the chair in the green circle. Upon hearing the clanking of the exoskeleton, Master Highclaw opened his eyes. "Master Hodapp," he said.

"Master Highclaw," Hodapp replied before his exoskeleton lowered onto the chair within his ring. "Sorry I'm running late. One of my students got a tad overzealous with testing a transdimensional slooping fluxxor and almost unraveled all of reality."

"I trust everything is under control now?"

"Depends. You haven't seen any evil doppelgangers of yourself walking around have you?"

"I have not."

"Then it most likely is."

"Do I even wanna know?" Scallywag muttered to Green.

"I'm not sure any of us does, good fellow," Green replied.

The next one to enter was a tall and muscular Tassari[21] with rust colored skin and no nose. His eyes were as dark as his hair, which was pulled into a ponytail falling between his shoulder blades. Long wisps of hair from the corners of his mouth formed a droopy moustache on his face. He wore an ornate orange robe with golden trim and walked with purposeful strides toward his chair in the orange ring.

"Master GorJiro," Highclaw said in greeting.

"Master Highclaw," GorJiro replied curtly before taking his seat.

---

[20] Scollums are an alien race resembling slugs, distinctive for their one large eye and ability to communicate using odors.
[21] Tassaris are an alien race stemming from a warrior culture and are known for being exceedingly durable in regards to aerobic/physical activities.

Master Savage was the last to arrive, taking his seat within the blue circle. The only chair left empty was in the black ring. Once Savage had sat down, Highclaw spoke. "The Order has assembled," he stated. "We are here to discuss the matter of Princess Glorianna of Legacy Prime, as requested by Master Savage. Master, do you wish to share your findings?"

Master Savage leaned forward in his seat, his face dour. "I have concluded that the Princess is, indeed, infected by some type of parasite, which has spiritually attached itself to her."

"You were able to see this parasite?" Master GorJiro asked.

"I was," Savage replied.

"Then the report Paragon Skyborn sent before his arrival has merit?" Highclaw inquired.

"It would seem so," answered Savage.

"Very well. Then we should begin enacting a plan to assist the Princess and Paragon Skyborn's companions immediately," stated Highclaw.

"Unfortunately, as far as the Princess is concerned, I fear she is beyond our help," Savage said. "There is nothing we can do to improve her condition."

"What???" exclaimed Mourdock.

Mourdock wasn't the only one who looked surprised upon hearing Master Savage's statement. Highclaw appeared troubled, as did Shanks and Green.

"Whatever has attached itself to the Princess has successfully melded with her spiritual energy," Savage stated. "Removing it would kill her."

"I do not believe that to be true," Shanks replied, stepping forward.

Savage eyed Shanks with a hard stare. "Are you questioning my diagnosis?" he asked.

"In my meditations, I have made contact with the creature that is afflicting the Princess," Shanks said. "I believe there is a way to kill it without inflicting a mortal wound to the host."

"Master Savage, is this true?" Highclaw asked. "Is there a possibility the creature can be killed off without harming Princess Glorianna?"

Savage frowned and sighed deeply. "There is... a way," he begrudgingly admitted.

"Oy, then why did ya just say there wasn't?" Scallywag asked, perturbed.

"Because it is beyond the ability of any in this temple to perform," Savage replied.

"Master Savage, is that true even of you?" inquired Highclaw.

Savage hesitated for a long moment before answering. "I'm sorry. I can't help her," he said.

Scallywag's eyes narrowed. "Can't? Or won't?" he asked.

"Either way, the result is the same," Savage replied, before getting up and exiting the room.

"Charming bloke, that one," Scallywag said as he watched Savage go.

Mourdock approached the remaining members of the Order, his face heavy with concern. "Masters," he said, "we cannot simply give up on the Princess. The fate of the galaxy is tied to her. *My* fate is tied to her. Please... there must be something we can do."

Master GorJiro got to his feet. "I fear healing is not my strong suit. I will be of little use in that matter. However, I will attempt to have further words with Master Savage. Though I doubt anything I say will change his decision, I can try."

"Thank you, Master," Mourdock said before GorJiro exited the room.

"I'll see if I can develop some new equipment to see this parasite and analyze it further," said Master Hodapp to Highclaw. "I'll get my best pupils on it. Perhaps with the right tools, we'll be able to treat her."

"That is a fine idea, Master Hodapp," Highclaw said. "I, too, shall assemble a team to meditate over her. Perhaps we may be able to recreate the monk's results and tackle the problem that way."

After Master Hodapp left, Highclaw approached the group. "I am sorry, my friends. I know you'd hoped we could do more."

"Oy, it sounded like that Savage bloke could do more, but he chose not to."

"Master Savage has his reasons for making such a decision," Master Highclaw replied. "Though I do not agree with it, I must respect it."

"Perhaps it would be better to respect the well-being of the only living member of Legacy Prime," Shanks said, also sounding frustrated with the situation. "If Master Savage really can help her, then he should be ordered to do so."

"That is not how the Order of Peers works," Highclaw replied. "We cannot order each other to do things. For now, we must find another way of tackling this problem."

"Oy, we've tried other ways. So far, none of them have worked!" complained Scallywag. "You mean to tell me that in this entire bloody temple, ya ain't got one Paragon who can help the Princess?"

"Other than Master Savage, I fear there are no other Paragons here at the Conclave with the necessary skills to deal with the Princess's affliction," Pennywise replied. "However, outside the Conclave… there may be options."

"What sort of options?" Scallywag asked.

"There is another Master Healer who may be able to assist the Princess," Pennywise said. "She has a specialty in spiritual healing. If there is anyone besides Master Savage equipped to help the Princess, it is she."

"And who is this healer you speak of?" Shanks asked.

"Her name is Sawbones MacCrusty," Pennywise replied. "A Stonehooligan[22] Paragon of great renown."

Shanks nodded his head. "Yes, I'm familiar with Paragon MacCrusty," he said. "I studied alongside her at the Temple of Light when she came seeking advanced spiritual instruction. Her mastery of spiritual healing is held in great regard among those in my order."

"Topper!" Scallywag said. "Get a message to her and ask her ta get her rear back here and fix the lass up."

Master Highclaw frowned. "I fear it is not that simple," he said.

"Of course not," Scallywag grumbled with a shake of his head. "Tell me, what makes recalling yer doc so blasted complicated?"

"Her last communique alerted us that she was dealing with a plague outbreak near the Great Border[23]," Highclaw explained. "The planet on which she is stationed has since been quarantined."

"Bloody squick…" Scallywag muttered under his breath.

"Well, surely we can recall her for such an important matter," Green suggested.

---

[22] Stonehooligans are a humanoid alien species that resemble Dwarfs.
[23] The Great Border is the area of space where the Visini and Regalus Empires meet.

"The situation we find ourselves in is a... delicate one, at best," Highclaw said. "To retrieve Paragon MacCrusty from the quarantine, we need the assistance of the Imperial Government. Unfortunately, because of the nature of this request, we do not believe Director Casgor will agree to it. At least, not without us agreeing to hand all of you over to Imperial custody and freeing the Princess."

"Which most certainly cannot happen," insisted Shanks.

"Regardless, I fear the Order of Peers cannot officially help you in this matter," Highclaw said. "Though we are happy to grant you asylum, our power and influence ends on the other side of that tether. Barring some other option, I fear we must wait until the quarantine is lifted and Paragon MacCrusty can freely return here to the temple."

Scallywag shook his head. "Aye. And how long will that take?" he asked.

"I fear I do not know," Highclaw admitted. "But should you come up with a better solution to the dilemma, I can promise we shall grant you any support it is within our power to give."

With that, Master Highclaw turned and left. Scallywag seethed. "So... guess that means he expects us ta come up with a better option, then," he muttered.

"It would appear so," Shanks said. "If we are to save the Princess, then it will be up to us to retrieve Paragon MacCrusty from this planet she has been quarantined on."

"So much fer layin' low for a while," Scallywag said bitterly, before looking at Pennywise. "Oy, do ya happen ta know which planet this Paragon of yours be on?"

"I believe it is called Eionmeer," Pennywise responded.

"Ah! Eionmeer!" Professor Green said with a smile. "I've been there before!"

"Have ya now?" asked Scallywag.

"Why, yes! As a matter of fact, I spent quite a bit of time on the planet during my tenure in the Imperial Exploratory Service," Green replied. "A group of us had a theory that there may have been an Ancient Temple located there, and I was part of a team that went searching for it. We'd found some readings which indicated a portgate might have existed on the planet, but nothing ever came of it, unfortunately."

"But ya know tha planet well enough, eh?" Scallywag asked.

Green nodded. "I lived in the Twin Rivers settlement for a couple of months. Got to know the city quite well, actually."

"And how many settlements does tha planet have?" Scallywag asked.

"Just the one, if I recall correctly."

"Good. That means it'll be easier ta find this Paragon doctor."

"I take it that means you know of a way to get past the quarantine?" Shanks asked.

"Ain't no different than smugglin' goods past a blockade," Scallywag replied. "I done that enough ta know how ta keep from gettin' nicked. But if we're gonna pull this off, we're gonna need help."

"What type of help?" Shanks inquired.

"Normally, I'd say I reach out to me old pirate crew and enlist them," Scallywag said. "But they ain't been answering me dead drop messages. Got no idea where they all might have gone. So we'll need ta enlist another crew. One with experience in these types o' things."

"Do you have one you can trust?"

Scallywag frowned. "Might be I do," he muttered. "But even if we can smuggle ourselves past tha quarantine, I see two problems that ain't gonna be easy ta overcome."

"And what might those be?" Shanks asked.

"First, we gotta find this Paragon and convince her ta come with us."

"That will not be an issue," Shanks stated. "I know Paragon MacCrusty quite well. She'll most likely be at the epicenter of the fight against whatever is plaguing the planet. We will just need to find the most active hospital in the area. If given the chance to speak with her and explain what is at stake, I have no doubt I can convince her to join us."

"Right," Scallywag replied. "But that ain't tha problem that worries me. What worries me is what we do after we convince her. Getting past the quarantine and onto tha planet is one thing. Getting us off and back here to tha Conclave is another headache entirely."

"Well, what about the Earthship?" offered Green. "Perhaps we can simply use the Entanglement Engine both to get past the quarantine and to make our escape?"

Scallywag shook his head. "Tempting, but I don't think it'll work. Quarantined planets have a constant sensor scan goin' on from orbit. If tha Earthship shows up anywhere in their range, tha Empire is gonna know we're there in a heartbeat. And that's not taking into account Virtuoso's little gadgets that track quantum fluctuations. If anythin', using tha Earthship will just put a bigger target on our backs."

Green frowned. "I see," he said. "Well, then, that is quite a problem, isn't it?"

"Pardon me for interrupting, sirs," Dan interjected. "But I do believe I may have a solution to your issue."

The group looked at the robot. "Yes, Dan?" Green said. "What would your solution be?"

"I happened to have learned a great deal about hacking teleportation arrays, thanks to Master Heckubus and his use of abandoned teleportation platforms on Omnicron Prime," Dan explained. "If Eionmeer is a typical Imperial colony, then it will most likely have a geosynchronous space port in orbit above it. Is that not correct?"

"It is!" replied Green. "There is a space port above the planet – Port Overlook, I believe."

"If that is the case, then it has a teleportation network linked to the colony on the planet," Dan said. "Spaceports usually act as a way of transporting personnel and cargo between the planet and the station. If I am able to hack into the port's teleportation network, I could successfully teleport all of you off the planet when you are ready to leave."

Scallywag raised his eyebrows at that. "That a fact?" he said. "And would ya be able ta bypass teleporting us back to tha station and onto, say... a starship instead?"

"As long as that starship is within range of the teleportation apparatus of the space port, and it is not moving, I believe so, Master Scallywag."

"So... I get us on tha planet. Greenskin shows us around until we find the Paragon. The monk convinces her ta leave with us. And tha robot gets us to our getaway ship," Scallywag said, stroking his chin thoughtfully. "Oy, that might just work. 'Course, it'd be better if we had a few of those fancy Warrior Paragons with us as back up."

Pennywise frowned. "I fear the Order would not agree to assist you in that fashion," he said. "And if I were not involved in such important work here, I'd offer my assistance. However, I am afraid I'm unable to leave the Conclave at this time."

Scallywag then looked at Mourdock. "What about you, Ascendant?" he asked. "Ya came in pretty handy at Port Somewhere."

"My place is with Anna," Mourdock replied. "I cannot leave her, or Jack for that matter. They both need me."

"And my place is with Mourdock," Hasatan said.

"However, I can offer you the use of my ship," Mourdock said. "It's designed to be operated with minimal crew, and no one is looking for it. Surely, that will be of some help."

Scallywag nodded, then looked at Shanks. "Well, monk... hope that vow o' non-violence is still on hold, 'cause we may need ya ta watch our backs if'n we get inta another scrape."

Shanks frowned but nodded. "I will do my best. For the sake of the Princess."

"Right..." Scallywag muttered. "Well then, we best get movin'. Tha sooner we save her royal Highness, the sooner we can all get back ta normal."

As the group dispersed, Green patted Scallywag on the shoulder. "Do not fear, old chum," Green said, encouragingly. "This is a good plan."

"Yer right. It is good," Scallywag replied. "Which is why I'm expectin' everything that could possibly go wrong to do just that."

CHAPTER ✹ 22

Heckubus sauntered across the tarmac of the auxiliary spaceport of Capitol City on Stratum 50, making his way toward the hanger in which *The Shamrock* was parked. He was not used to walking about so freely in public and found his hologuise was a welcome change from skulking around the network of secret tunnels he had in the city. Though the sight of an antique mining-bot might draw unwanted attention, the sight of a creepy old man in quasi-futuristic clothing hobbling about seemed to draw no notice whatsoever.

As he approached the ship, he could see Buchignani and his crew around it. Buff and Siv were sitting on some nearby containers playing cards, Buchignani seemed to be tinkering with an access panel on the ship, and Kamm supervised a few maintenance-bots attending to the vessel.

Kamm saw Heckubus approaching and gave a whistle to catch Buchignani's attention. Buchignani smiled when he saw Heckubus and pulled himself away from his tinkering to approach the robot in greeting. "Ya came back," Buchignani said. "And within the timeframe ya set, too."

"Was there ever any doubt?" Heckubus replied.

"A little," said Kamm as he approached.

"We've had charters try and skip out on us before," Buchignani said. "It's a real pain havin' ta hunt them down at times."

"Then perhaps you should insist on payment up front?" Heckubus said.

"I guess that's how the core-worlders would do it. But out on the Frontier, a man's word has gotta mean somethin'. So I'll believe ya when ya tell me you're going to pay me, and you'd better believe me when I say I'll be comin' for ya if ya don't."

"A noble philosophy," Heckubus replied. "Moronic. But noble."

Buchignani shrugged. "In the criminal world, all ya got is your reputation," he drawled. "If your reputation is good enough, people don't muck with ya."

"And believe me, people don't muck with the Wild Ones," Kamm stated.

"I must admit, I am not accustomed to working with such competent and reliable Henchmen. From what I can surmise, your reputation is well deserved. That is why I am here to pay you the remainder of our agreed upon fee,"

Heckubus said as he took out his datapad. "Good work deserves good pay, does it not?"

"It sure does," Kamm replied as he took out his datapad and wirelessly linked it up to the one Heckubus held.

Heckubus tapped on his screen and transmitted the payment. "There," he said. "Pleasure doing business with you."

"And with you, old-timer," Buchignani replied.

"Hold up," said Kamm, studying the read-out on his datapad. "He's short."

"Short?" said Heckubus, incredulously. "I resent the accusation. I may be evil, but I am not cheap!"

"How's he short, Kamm?" Buchignani asked.

Kamm held out his datapad so Buchignani could see the readout. "He left out a share," Kamm replied.

"Ah, I see," said Buchignani, turning to Heckubus. "Ya forgot about Aneel's share."

"Aneel's share?" replied Heckubus.

"Yeah. The fifth member of our crew?" reiterated Buchignani. "He's gotta eat, too."

"Ah, now I see the use of an invisible crewmember," Heckubus said. "This is a way to extort more money from those you do business with! A bigger crew means a larger fee…"

"Look, old-timer," said Buchignani, "I know ya don't exactly believe in Aneel, and frankly, I can't say I blame ya. But he's as real as you or me, and he's a part of this crew. That means he gets paid his fair share…"

"Yes, yes, you don't have to justify your petty extortion scheme to me. If anything, it only makes me respect you more," said Heckubus as he again fished out his datapad. "Your loyalty to your imaginary friend is quite admirable. Therefore, I shall play along. After all, it's only money…"

Heckubus promptly transferred another payment to Kamm's datapad. Kamm gave it a look and nodded to Buchignani in approval.

"Well, I appreciate your uprightness, old-timer," said Buchignani as he gave Heckubus a tip of his hat. "Was afraid things might have had ta get nasty there for a minute."

"Speaking of getting nasty, how would you lot like to earn double what I just gave you?" Heckubus inquired.

Buchignani and Kamm exchanged a curious glance. "Double you say?" replied Buchignani, his interest piqued.

"How nasty we talkin' about getting?" Kamm inquired.

"As yet to be determined," Heckubus answered. "I will simply say that my work here on Omnicron has only just begun, and I will be requiring a good amount of muscle going forward. Muscle which I trust you and your crew could adequately provide. I must admit, I'm not very familiar with you Frontier types, but from what I've seen, you appear loyal enough and have a satisfactory work ethic. Thus, I am willing to enlist your services for the foreseeable future, if you don't mind getting your hands a bit dirty."

"Dirty hands never bothered us much," Buchignani said, "so long as your digicredits are good."

Heckubus tossed Kamm his digicredit card. "A criminal genius, such as I, never lacks for funds," he boasted. "Stick with me, and you shall all be rich men. But decide quickly. Time is of the essence, and I must proceed with my plan posthaste."

Kamm and Buchignani looked at each other. Kamm regarded the digicredit card for a moment before giving Buchignani a nod. Buchignani smiled at Heckubus. "Alright, partner," he said, "ya got yourself some muscle. How ya want to flex it?"

Heckubus twiddled his fingers. "Tell me," he said. "How familiar are you with Stratum 12?"

Boozskeller Winchester was as sordid an establishment as one could find on Stratum 12 of Capitol City. Though the stratum boasted of all kinds of questionable businesses, the boozskellers, which catered to the numerous unsavory patrons frequenting the stratum, were of a particularly seedy variety.

Heckubus glanced around the establishment as he entered. With its cracked and flickering digital windows, cheap and rickety furniture, metal grate flooring, and terrible lighting, Boozskeller Winchester was indeed one of the most poorly kept bars he'd ever seen. It didn't even take long for a brawl to break out among some *Loquir* players in the corner. No one even bothered to break up the fight, with the winner robbing the loser and leaving him a bloody, unconscious mess on the floor.

"What a charming place," Heckubus cheerily said to himself before approaching the bar.

"What can I get you?" grumbled the Karkovian[24] bartender.

"I wish to purchase a great deal of illegal goods and contraband!" Heckubus said loudly.

The bartender frowned. "Um… we have beer."

"And I have money!" replied Heckubus, flashing a handful of digicredit cards in the most unsubtle way possible. "Lots and lots of money! Which I wish to spend on numerous items of ill repute!"

"So… 'no' on the beer?"

"If by 'beer' you mean black-market merchandise, then yes! Lots and lots of it!"

The bartender shook his head in annoyance. "He's all yours," he muttered before tending to other barflies. Heckubus turned and saw that during his rather unsubtle conversation, he'd been surrounded by a number of big, beefy goons, all wearing tight red shirts and glaring at him.

"Well, hello there," Heckubus said, not the least bit intimidated.

"You're being awful loud over here, old man," grumbled one of the goons.

"That's because being quiet never draws enough attention," Heckubus replied. "I was told this was the place to go if one wanted to acquire certain hard to acquire items, which is what I wish to do."

"Oh? And who told ya that?"

"Various sources, which I consider to be reliable. Now, which one of you is this 'Thugnificent' fellow I've heard so much about?"

The goons all exchanged glances. "We don't know who you're talking about," one of them said.

"Then take me to someone who does," Heckubus replied, slipping a digicredit card into the goon's pocket.

---

[24] Karkovians are humanoid aliens with six arms.

The goon pulled out the card with a curious look and slid it through his datapad. He showed the result to one of his companions, who nodded. "Wait here," he said, before heading off to the back.

Heckubus sat at the bar patiently until the goon returned and told Heckubus to follow him. All six of the thugs fell in around Heckubus as they walked to the room located in the rear of the boozskeller. A door opened to reveal a large and gaudy office filled with knock-off furniture, matted carpets, and over-sized holo-paintings of the Izard who was lounging on a ridiculous golden throne atop a small dais.

"Uh'hurro, *oldboi*," Xao said in greeting as Heckubus entered the room and the goons all fanned out around him. "Xao hear you come seeking audience with *the Thugnificent!*"

"I take it that's you?" inquired Heckubus.

"You tell me!" replied Xao, lightly clapping his hands.

"All hail Xao the Thugnificent," the goons all reluctantly chanted. Xao cleared his throat and looked at the goons expectantly. After a few eyerolls, the goons continued. "King of thieves and outlaws. Master of stratum 12. Boss of all bosses. Hail. Hail. Hail."

Xao giggled giddily as though savoring the forced adoration of his minions. "You see?" he squealed. "You meeting with the top guy, *oldboi*. Xao the BIG boss around here!"

"Then you are indeed the one to whom I wish to speak," Heckubus said. "I've heard you run quite the smuggling operation and can reliably deliver any number of illicit and controlled items."

"You heard correctly," Xao boasted. "Xao got hook-ups all over the galaxy! Anything you need, Xao can get – for the right price."

"And you can assure delivery? No issues with Imperial patrols, blockades, or customs stations?"

"Xao in with allllllll the right people, *oldboi*. No need to worry."

"Well then, it would seem what I've heard about your criminal network is true. And if I may say, what you've been able to build is quite impressive."

"Thank you," said Xao with a smile. "Now, Xao's minions have told Xao you have quite a bit of digicredits to spend. Shall we get down to business?"

"We shall," said Heckubus. "But first, I must ask… is that the new Overlord 5000 you're resting upon?"

Heckubus nodded toward the massive golden throne on which Xao lounged. Xao stroked the arm of his chair, smiling broadly. "You like?" he asked.

"I've always preferred Overlord brand thrones to lord over others with," Heckubus admitted. "Not only are they garishly over-the-top, but they also offer a surprising amount of lumbar support."

"Xao know!" Xao giggled. "This one has built-in massage features, too!" Xao opened a panel on his armrest and hit a button. A low hum emanated from the chair as it vibrated, causing Xao to sigh contently.

"Impressive," Heckubus said. "I commend your choice in single-seat furniture meant to intimidate and establish authority."

"Thank you," Xao replied before turning off the massage feature. "So nice to meet someone who can appreciate Xao's excellent taste in décor."

"I assume this model is like other Overlord thrones in that it has a control panel to operate various deathtraps around the room in which we are currently located?"

"But of course!" cried Xao, giddily. "Xao grew tired of glitches walking in here, thinking they better than Xao and threatening him. Xao got the full deathtrap package! Xao spared no expense!"

"The full package?" asked Heckubus, impressed. "You mean with the incineration pits, dematerializer beams, and genitalia-targeting punching arms?"

"Xao even spring for the flesh-eating goo add-on!" Xao exclaimed. "No one muck with Xao in his house no more! Nyah, nyah, nyah."

"Yes, well, despite all the fine features the Overlord 5000 has, I'm sorry to tell you that no true self-respecting villain would ever actually use one."

That comment made Xao raise an eyebrow. "Oh?" he asked. "And why's that?"

"Because for all their benefits, the Overlord brand has always had a single glaring flaw," Heckubus said as he produced his datapad from his pocket. "You see… they're incredibly easy to hack."

With a tap of his datapad's screen, Xao's group of thugs were suddenly gone, having fallen through trap doors, de-materialized, melted by flesh-eating goo, or passed out from being hit by genitalia-targeting punching arms. Before Xao knew it, all his goons had been dispatched.

"Mwuahahaha," Heckubus chuckled.

Xao's narrow eyes grew wide with surprise. He quickly opened another panel on his chair and began frantically tapping buttons.

"Don't bother trying to enable any more of your deathtraps," Heckubus said. "I've disabled your chair completely."

"Well, there something you forgot to disable, *smartboi*," Xao said with a sneer as he reached behind him and pulled out a gold-plated plasma pistol that he aimed at Heckubus. "This!"

"Oh, dear," Heckubus said, raising his hands in mock surrender. "It would seem I've brought nothing but a datapad to a gun fight."

"Yeah!" cried Xao, jumping out of his chair. "Who the smart one now, *muggahugga?*"

Then, the sound of plasma blasts rang out from within the boozskeller. Xao looked past Heckubus to the entrance of the office with a growing look of concern on his face.

"Probably the one who brought the most guns with him," Heckubus said.

With that, the door to Xao's office opened and the Wild Ones came walking in, each one training a plasma pistol at Xao. The Izard quickly tossed his weapon aside and put his hands in the air. "Don't shoot! Don't shoot!" he cried. "No need for violence! We friends!"

"Yes, yes, bosom buddies," said Heckubus. "Siv, be so kind as to show the Thugnificent how we treat our friends."

Siv lumbered over to a cowering Xao and grabbed him by the neck, lifting him up so Xao's tiny legs peddled in the air as he hung helplessly in Siv's grasp. "What... what you want???" Xao asked while trying to breathe.

"I should think that would be obvious by now," Heckubus replied as he sat in Xao's throne. "I'm taking over your operation."

"You can't!" Xao wheezed. "Xao... connected!"

"Yes, so I've heard," Heckubus said. "I briefly considered doing business with you because of that, but I ultimately decided it would be more efficient to simply cut out the middleman and get what I need directly. Oh, and you being a complete incompetent idiot also factored heavily into my decision. Not that I don't appreciate your unique brand of sniveling ambition, but your mismanagement of this so-called criminal empire you've somehow built in this city is, frankly, insulting to my rather considerable intelligence."

"You don't know... who you're... mucking with!" Xao gasped.

"Trust me, I have a very good idea. Now, let us get to the part where you reveal your various smuggling connections to me so I can begin co-opting them for my own purposes. Siv, every time he refuses to give one up, tie him into a different knot."

Before the interrogation could begin, the door to the office opened and a metal orb was tossed inside. The orb hit the ground and rolled to the center of the room, its crevices glowing a bright orange color as a high-pitched hum signaled it was now armed, immediately dominating the group's attention.

Before Buff had a chance to react, a cybernetic arm punched him in the face, causing him to drop his plasma weapon. Then, he was grabbed and used as a shield between the new arrival and the rest of the group.

Buchignani and Kamm both trained their weapons on the man, but he'd already gotten his blaster out and was aiming it right at Heckubus. Though he was a large and muscular fellow, enough of him was hidden behind Buff to prevent the others from getting a clear shot. The cybernetic eye in the middle of his forehead was open and glowing red.

"I've got a firing solution on all four of you," the man stated.

"Ya think you're quick enough to take us all out before we take you, partner?" Buchignani asked.

"Don't have to take all of you out. Just the ringleader," the man replied. "That thermal charge there will handle the rest of you. It's linked to my arm and is designed to detonate the second my heart stops beating."

Buchignani and Kamm both glanced at the metal orb on the floor in concern. Heckubus then began a slow clap of appreciation. "Bravo! Bravo!" he said. "And here I was, thinking we'd dispatched all of this idiot's muscle. Who might you be?"

"Name's Banjax," the man replied.

"Well, Banjax, as commendable as your loyalty to your employer is, I'm sure I could make you a better offer. I can always use more competent henchmen."

"Not that I give two flips about that sniveling farragut[25] you have dangling by the neck there, but my job is to protect him. The people I work for want him alive and in business, so that's how things are gonna stay."

---

[25] A farragut is an unhygienic animal that's a cross between a weasel, a rat, and a fox.

"Then it appears we are at an impasse," Heckubus said. "You can't kill all of us before we kill the both of you, and we can't kill you without killing ourselves."

"It would appear that way."

"Thusly, a humble end to my hostile takeover," Heckubus said, whimsically. "Very well. Let us say we release the Izard, everyone sets down their weapons, and we all agree to play nice and do business like civilized criminals."

"I can get behind that," Banjax replied. "But that thermal charge is staying armed 'till I'm satisfied you're not trying to pull anything."

"Agreed," Heckubus said, signaling to Siv to let go of Xao.

Siv released the Izard who fell to the ground and rubbed his neck. He got back to his feet and walked toward Banjax, a scowl on his face. "What took you so long???" Xao demanded.

"I was finishing my lunch," Banjax replied as he released Buff and pushed him toward his friends.

"Whatever!" Xao said. "Kill these glitches, and let's get out of here!"

Banjax holstered his plasma gun. "I say we hear them out."

"WHAT???" cried Xao. "That muggahugga just tried to take over my business!!!"

"Yeah, and he would have succeeded, too, if I hadn't showed up," Banjax said. "That kind of play at least warrants an audience."

Xao seethed. "Fiiiiiine," he relented. "We hear him out, *then* kill him!"

"So… who exactly are we speaking with?" Banjax asked.

"Allow me to introduce myself!" said Heckubus, getting up from Xao's throne. "I am the infamous Doctor Verhooven Verbootun Nefarious the third. Criminal genius extraordinaire."

"Infamous, huh?" muttered Banjax, unimpressed. "Never heard of you."

"Psh! Silly henchman!" chided Xao, slapping Banjax on his chest. "He not famous! He *in*-famous! No one ever hear of people who are *infamous*, dumb-dumb."

"That is very much incorrect, but regardless, I'm quite a big deal," stated Heckubus.

"What type of doctor are you?" Banjax asked.

"Why, a doctor of EVIL, of course! What other type is there?"

"Medical, psychiatric, sociological…"

"Yes, but those all make for poor criminals," Heckubus replied. "My fields of study lean more toward grand larceny, extortion, torture, murder, and my personal favorite – mass genocide."

"Eeeh," squealed Xao. "What kind of school teaches that???"

"It's a vocational one," Heckubus said, off-handedly. "But enough about my degrees. Let us get down to business, shall we?"

"We're listening," said Banjax.

"I am seeking a number of items that are frustratingly hard to come by," Heckubus explained. "After asking around, it would seem you lot are the only smuggling network I was able to find that could conceivably provide everything I am looking for."

"And what are you looking for, exactly?"

Heckubus took out his datapad and tossed it to Banjax. Banjax caught it and looked at the contents of its screen before showing it to Xao. Xao whistled. "*Oldboi* ain't kidding. That some heavy stuff right there. Reeeeeally hard to come by."

"But not impossible," Heckubus said.

"Not impossible," Xao agreed. "But not cheap neither."

"Money is not an issue. What *is* an issue is whether or not you can get it?"

Xao stroked the wispy hairs of his long moustache thoughtfully. "Xao can get most of it," he said. "At triple rate, for you glitches trying to take over Xao's operation."

"Fair enough," said Heckubus. "And what is it you are unable to acquire?"

"Says here you need ten ounces of unstable glyceryl trinitroxate," Xao said. "That some highly controlled weapons-grade gunk. But Xao know someone who can get it."

"And who might that be?"

"Another big boss on the stratum. Some *playboi* named Goldpinkie."

"Goldpinkie? You mean Golddigit?" asked Heckubus.

"Yeah, yeah, gold-something," muttered Xao. "He into all this crazy dangerous stuff. Always building things to try and take over the planet and other silliness."

"Yes, our paths have crossed on more than one occasion," Heckubus said with a frown. "But you are correct, Golddigit undoubtedly has access to that material. I take it you could broker its acquisition on my behalf?"

"For double commission."

"Very well," said Heckubus, approaching Xao and offering his hand. "You have yourself a deal."

Xao smiled maliciously and shook Heckubus's hand. "Don't be so happy, *oldboi*. Xao still may kill you after deal is over."

"Thanks for the warning," Heckubus replied. "But just know… if I'm to die, I'll be taking you with me."

Xao's smile disappeared.

"Henchmen!" Heckubus said. With that, the Wild Ones began to file out of the room, each one giving Banjax the evil eye before leaving. Heckubus handed Xao a digicredit card. "Here's a down payment. And in the high likelihood you are thinking of trying to double-cross me, I'd recommend you don't."

"And why's that?"

"Because I'm much smarter than you," said Heckubus as he made for the door.

"Hey," said Banjax before Heckubus left. "What do you need all this stuff for?"

"That is none of your concern," Heckubus replied.

"Might be I'm making it my concern," Banjax said. "From the looks of this list, I'm tempted to say you're building some type of weapon. And who you plan on using it against might be cause for a great deal of concern."

Heckubus chuckled. "You needn't worry yourself, Mr. Banjax. I only intend to kill one person. And I'm sure neither you, nor the Thugnificent, will care that he's gone."

Banjax watched Heckubus and his crew leave the boozskeller before deactivating the thermal charge he'd tossed into Xao's office. Xao paced around the room, irate. "That muggahugga thinks he gonna get away with this?" Xao ranted. "Xao no do business with that glitch! Xao kill him and keep the money!"

"No," said Banjax. "You'll do as he asks."

"WHY???" shrieked Xao. "Why we care about that silly old man and what he wants?"

"Because…" said Banjax, turning to Xao to reveal the white eyes of Verrutus. "I'm quite curious to know who he intends to kill."

CHAPTER ✹ 23

Jack was sitting in a vast black void. He had no idea where he was or how he'd gotten there. He felt disoriented and found it hard to concentrate. He knew something had happened to him. Something bad. But no matter how hard he tried, he couldn't remember anything.

Across from him sat Anna. Her posture was straight and her gaze unwavering. Her mouth moved, as though she were talking to him.

"Anna? What are you saying? I can't hear you..."

Anna continued trying to speak, but no sound came from her. Jack turned his head and saw that Shanks was sitting between Anna and him, at the head of a triangle the three of them formed.

"Why can't I hear her?" Jack asked.

"Because you are not yet listening," Shanks replied.

The monk reached out his left hand. Anna took hold of it, a brilliant light emanating from where their hands met, sending a warm, golden glow up their arms and to their hearts. Shanks then offered his other hand to Jack.

"The trinity must be completed," Shanks said. "Mind must touch body. Body must touch soul. Soul... must be shared."

Jack nodded. He wasn't sure he understood, but a part of him already felt the connection which the monk was speaking of. Jack reached out and took Shanks' hand, a light growing between them, as well, moving from their hands to their hearts and connecting the monk to both Anna and him.

Anna then reached out for Jack. She smiled at him. He smiled back. Jack reached out and took hold of her hand, and the moment they touched, the energy of all three combined. Within the triangle formed by their arms, a great, all-seeing eye opened, light shining up from it brightly.

Jack looked down at the eye and met its gaze, hearing a voice whisper in the darkness...

Edil Meldilorn[26].

---

[26] Eldil Meldilorn was the mantra of the Ancients. In the Old Solar language, it translates to "Free Your Mind."

Jack felt himself fall into the light of the eye, which wrapped around him like a cocoon.

And that is when he opened his eyes.

Jack's head throbbed. His mouth was dry. His vision was hazy, and his muscles ached. He looked around at his surroundings. The room he was in was shaped like the inside of an egg, with friendly white walls and a stone floor. Jack tried to get up, but the moment he moved, a sharp pain shot through his head, and he hissed as he grabbed his temples.

"Careful," came a voice. "You must take it easy."

Jack turned and saw a man in blue robes sitting next to his bed. The man had a kind smile on his face, but Jack was nonetheless alarmed. "Who are you?" Jack asked. "Where am I?"

"You are someplace safe," the man said. "My name is Paragon Eldrich Pennywise. I am a friend of Thaddius Green and Paragon Shepherd."

Jack relaxed a bit at the sound of those names. "You... you knew Shepherd?" he asked.

"Very well," Pennywise replied. "We grew up together, in fact. His wife, Casca... she was my sister."

Jack frowned. "Oh..." he said. "I'm sorry."

Pennywise nodded. "I was told you were quite affected by his loss, as well."

"Yeah, he... uh... he was a good teacher. And a friend."

Pennywise acknowledged that in silence. Jack slowly sat up, his head still hurting, but the pain was slowly subsiding as his body began to awaken. Despite all that, there was a part of him that felt strange. Jack didn't know how to describe it. It felt as though there were something within him that hadn't been there before, like a new organ or bone. However, Jack knew it was just a feeling, albeit an odd one.

"Last thing I remember, this crazy bounty hunter was trying to capture me..." Jack said. "Then, after that... I think I dreamed or something, but... I really don't recall what it was about."

"Yes, you suffered quite a trauma in that altercation," Pennywise replied. "You almost died."

Jack's eyes went wide. "Really?" he asked.

"Luckily, Brother Shanks was able to save you, and your friends were able to bring you here."

"And... where is here? Exactly?"

"The Conclave."

Jack blinked at Pennywise. "Uh... you gonna give me anything more to go on than that?"

Pennywise tilted his head to the side. "Have you never heard of the Conclave before?"

Jack shook his head. "Should I have?"

Pennywise smiled, good-naturedly. "Well, then, my young friend... allow me to show you around."

Pennywise stood and held out his hand. Jack took it and slid off the bed. A door opened and Pennywise motioned for Jack to follow him. The Paragon led Jack out into a long hallway made from what looked like sandstone bricks.

"Are we in an Ancient temple?" Jack asked as they walked.

"We are indeed," Pennywise replied. "You've been to Ancient temples before?"

"Yeah. There was one on my home planet. And there was sort-of one on this Ghost Planet. And there were these weird chambers on this place called the Sunshell."

"My, my," mused Pennywise. "You've certainly been around."

"I guess," Jack said. "They all pretty much look the same. You've seen one, you've kinda seen them all."

"If that is indeed the case," Pennywise said as he approached a door at the end of the hallway, "I fear you'll probably find the Conclave rather... boring."

Pennywise placed his hand on the door, which rumbled open. When Jack stepped through the opening, he froze, looking at his surroundings in awe. Before him was a massive, multi-tiered room, so cavernous it appeared to stretch on forever. Majestic pillars rose up from a seemingly bottomless pit below, holding up different tiers of floors, which connected to one another through stairs and bridges. The tiers were decorated differently. Some contained ornate etchings on their floors. Some were adorned with arches. Some had large crystals, which glowed in different colors, jutting from them. Some sported gardens, pools of water, and even fountains.

The tiers all seemed to lead to different levels of the structure, branching off to various openings and exits. High above, hovering in the air, was a brilliantly glowing orb at the center of a spinning gyroscope, which seemed to mimic a sun's illumination, its light shining down and causing the crystals to shimmer. There were a great number of people around. Some were traversing the tiers, travelling to different levels. Some were lounging around, reading books, and eating lunch. Others were participating in activities and playing sports.

Jack had never seen anything like it in his life.

"Dude," he said. "What is this place?"

"This is the Crystal Concourse," Pennywise replied. "It's the central area of the Conclave. You can get to practically anywhere within the temple from here."

Pennywise began to descend the stairs before them toward a platform below. Jack followed, still trying to take in the majestic scene as he walked.

"I've... I've never seen anything like this before," Jack said.

Pennywise chuckled. "The Conclave is quite a unique place," he mused.

"I can tell," Jack replied.

"Trust me, my young friend, you really can't. Not yet, anyway."

Jack followed Pennywise to another door that opened before them. It led to another sandstone hallway, which eventually gave way to what appeared to be a mechanical door. It opened to reveal an orb-shaped pod built of transparent plastic. Beyond the pod stretched a long tunnel. Pennywise sat down on one of the benches within the pod, and Jack sat opposite him. Before long, the door leading to the pod closed, and they were sealed inside. Then, the pod began to move, whisking down the tunnel at great speed.

"Where are we going?" Jack asked.

"To the outer ring," Pennywise replied. "I believe it is wise to give you an idea of exactly where you are."

"The temple has an outer ring?"

"It does indeed," Pennywise said. "It was manufactured... oh... about a thousand years ago, I believe. Around the time the Order of Peers decided to begin exploring the pocket universe in which we're located."

"Pocket universe?"

"Yes," replied Pennywise. "You see, the Conclave exists in a different universe than the one you're used to."

Jack rubbed his head. "I'm not sure I understand."

"If you think of the universe as a large quilt, a pocket universe exists within one of its patchwork layers."

"Like another dimension?"

"No, not exactly. Another dimension would be its own quilt, you see. A pocket universe exists within the greater universe we live in, only it contains a different set of natural laws than the primary universe."

"You mean, things don't work the same way here as they do somewhere else?"

"Precisely," Pennywise replied. "It's believed that the Ancients created this pocket universe with an entirely different set of natural laws as a way to assist other species in achieving enlightenment. Without the Conclave, it may very well be impossible for average beings to become anything resembling a Paragon within their lifetimes."

"Okay," Jack said, still trying to wrap his brain around the concept of a universe within a universe. "So… what's different here?"

"A great many things. But the biggest change is how one perceives the passage of time."

"What do you mean?" Jack asked. "I don't notice anything different."

"No, you wouldn't," Pennywise agreed. "However, while in this universe, you're experiencing a phenomenon known as a 'time constriction.' Tell me, are you familiar with the concept of time dilation?"

"Nope."

"Time dilation is a difference of elapsed time between two events as measured by observers who are either moving relative to each other or are situated differently from a gravitational mass," Pennywise explained. "The weaker the gravitational potential, or the further you are from the source of gravity, the faster time passes. So if you were to orbit a supermassive black hole, time would move more slowly for you there while you are under the influence of its gravity. A few minutes to you may actually be hundreds of years to those outside of the black hole's gravitational influence."

"Are you saying time moves faster here in the Conclave?" Jack asked.

"In a sense," Pennywise said. "There is no time dilation effect here. In fact, time at the Conclave is directly connected to normal time in the greater universe. An hour there is equivalent to an hour here. The difference is how we here in this universe experience that hour. To us, an hour here feels as though two days have passed."

Jack shook his head. "That doesn't make any sense," he said. "How can we experience two days' worth of time in an hour if time isn't any different?"

Pennywise shrugged. "It's all a matter of perception," he said. "Think of it like this… when you're having fun, time seems to move more quickly, does it not? And when you are bored, time seems to move more slowly. Waiting in line feels like it can take ages, whereas performing an exciting activity can feel as though it has taken seconds. It is all a matter of how our brains have perceived the passage of time. Here in the Conclave, that type of perception is persistent. We believe this was intentional, because learning to free one's mind takes a great deal of time. However, simply speeding up time would be counter-productive, since the natural lifespan of average beings would expire long before they had a chance to take advantage of the accelerated timetable. Thus, our bodies continue to age in synch with the prime universe. However, our minds mature at an incredibly accelerated rate, allowing us to reach our fullest potential within our lifetimes."

"Okay…" said Jack as he began to understand what Pennywise was telling him. "So that means if I leave here after a month, I'd have only aged a day, even though I remember a month's worth of stuff?"

"Essentially, yes."

"That's awesome!"

"It is quite an impressive feature of this universe," Pennywise said in agreement. "And quite necessary for the creation of Paragons. Without it, it's highly unlikely any of us would be able to come close to being able to free our minds."

Jack felt the pod they rode in slow down, and soon, the transparent casing around them rotated and a hatch opened before them. He followed Pennywise out and into a long tubular corridor, lined with extended stretches of windows looking out into space.

"The outer ring extends around the entire temple," Pennywise explained as they walked. "This is where we test out new ship designs and new propulsion systems, or we simply study the outside of the temple and the pocket universe in which we live. But one of its best features… is the view."

Pennywise gestured to a window, and Jack gazed out in awe at the Conclave temple. The temple was shaped like a diamond, looming as large as any city Jack

had ever seen. The bricks from which it was constructed glowed as though reflecting the rays of a sun, even though there was no star in sight.

"The Conclave is its own ecosystem," Pennywise continued. "We do not know how it is possible, but the bricks it is made up of provide our air, our heat, our gravity… everything that's needed to survive in this pocket universe is generated by them. Even out here, in the dark emptiness of space, the temple provides light. And what it does not provide, we have learned to make for ourselves. The Conclave is entirely self-contained. Independent. A model for the Paragons it breeds and sends out into the galaxy."

Jack gazed out at the strange backdrop that made up the Conclave's universe. Unlike the outer space he was used to, there were no stars dotting the empty void. Instead, there were tiny swirls of color – almost like oil on top of water – slowly moving against the darkness.

"What's out there?" Jack asked. "Why does it look like that?"

"No one really knows for sure," Pennywise said. "Unlike the normal universe, the Conclave's universe is rather finite. Those colors you're seeing out there mark the boundary where our pocket universe ends. Some believe they are a result of this universe pressing up against the greater one, like an air bubble under water."

"Um… what happens if the bubble pops?"

"Best guess? It would be like two universes colliding – the natural laws of one impacting with those of the other causing a catastrophic collision, resulting in the utter annihilation of both universes and all they contain."

Jack's eyes went wide at that. Pennywise chuckled.

"Or nothing happens at all," he added. "It's hard to say. Perhaps the natural laws of the greater universe would override this one's and would incorporate its contents as a part of itself. It's all theoretical, which is one of the reasons why we study such things."

"That's crazy," Jack said. "So… this universe is finite? Like, how big is it?"

"Not very, compared to the prime universe, anyway," Pennywise said. "We estimate its radius is approximately 250,000 miles, with the Conclave existing at its center."

Jack whistled. "Seems pretty big to me," he said.

"Well, considering the time it would take for a modern spacecraft to traverse that distance, it's really not very big at all."

Jack glanced down the long, circular ring they were in, spotting all the different, small spacecraft that were docked there. "Is my ship here, somewhere?" he asked.

"No," replied Pennywise. "When they departed, your friends left your ship docked at the space station on the other side of the Conclave's tether to the prime universe. But do not worry. The Paragons who guard Remnant Station will keep it safe."

Jack looked at Pennywise, curiously. "Wait – my friends are gone?"

"They are. They left on a mission to find a healer who would be able to help the Princess."

Jack eyed the Paragon suspiciously. "My friends wouldn't have just abandoned me," he said.

"They did not abandon you. They left you in my care," Pennywise replied. "You must understand, Jack, your injury was of a very serious nature. We were not sure when you would recover from it. Your friends did not make the decision to leave the Conclave without you lightly."

"When did they leave?"

"Months ago."

"So… a couple days normal time, right? I could still catch up to them."

"Jack–"

"Take me to my ship," Jack said. "I'm awake now. I need to go join them."

Pennywise frowned but acquiesced. "Very well. Follow me."

Jack followed the Paragon back to the pod, and they returned to the Crystal Concourse. Pennywise took Jack to the platform leading to the tether, which swirled between its two pillars. Pennywise gestured toward it.

"Your ship is on the other side of that tether," he said. "If you'll wait for a few minutes before going through, we can send a message to those on Remnant Station to be expecting you. However, as your caretaker, I would suggest you not leave quite yet. You are still recovering from the effects of your wound and must take more time to heal."

"I'll be fine," Jack replied. "My friends need me. And if what they're doing can help Anna, I need to be with them."

"I understand," Pennywise said. "Your friends left the subspace channel of your robotic companion. Before you leave, I'd recommend sending them a message to let them know you are okay. Then you can wait for their response before you venture out of the Conclave."

"But… wouldn't it take, like, months for them to respond?"

"It could. At least it would seem like that while you are here. But it would also allow you more time to recover."

Jack hesitated for a moment, unsure of what to do. He looked at the swirling portal of the tether. He still felt like complete crud, and he'd had that strange feeling ever since he'd awoken, which was making him disoriented. *Maybe taking a bit more time to recover isn't such a bad idea,* he thought.

"Yeah, okay," said Jack. "I'll send them a message first."

Pennywise nodded. "Before we do that, would you permit me to show you one more thing?" he asked.

"Sure," Jack replied.

Pennywise led him through the Crystal Concourse and up a seemingly never ending flight of stairs that made Jack regret agreeing to the Paragon's request. Eventually, they came to a room with transparent walls and a floor inlaid with colored rings.

"This is the Chamber of the Five Rings," Pennywise said. "This is where Emperor Arcturus established the first Order of Peers, at the very top of the Conclave's temple. This is where the Conclave, as we know it, was born. And this is where, to this day, the Order of Peers assemble for meetings."

"Cool," muttered Jack, not sure why it was so important for Pennywise to show him this room.

Pennywise turned and looked at Jack. "Before he left, I had the opportunity to sit down and catch up with Professor Green," he said. "He told me that before Shepherd died, he had agreed to take you on as an apprentice and teach you to be a Paragon."

The memory of that promise flashed into Jack's head. It felt like it had happened a lifetime ago. "Yeah," Jack replied. "He felt guilty that my planet got destroyed and promised to help teach me how to fight the Deathlords. But after he died, well… it's kinda hard for him to keep his promise now."

"But does that offer still interest you?" Pennywise asked. "If given the opportunity, would you choose to become a Paragon?"

"Well, yeah. Of course I would."

"And do you understand what it means to be a Paragon?" Pennywise pressed. "Not just the part about fighting Deathlords. But what it truly means to dedicate yourself to an ideal? To shed that which limits you, to free your mind, and to become the pinnacle of what this universe has to offer?"

"I'm guessing... no?" Jack replied, sheepishly.

Pennywise chuckled at that. "Come here," he said, gesturing for Jack to stand next to him among the rings inlaid into the floor. "I wish to explain this to you."

Jack moved to Pennywise's side as the Paragon referred to the five rings on the floor. "There are five essential aspects of being a Paragon, just as there are five essential elements to the universe," Pennywise explained. "To attain mastery in all five of these aspects is to achieve a truly free mind, but becoming proficient in any one of them will make you a Paragon of great skill and ability. Each aspect is associated with a ring – an infinite loop – which is entwined with the others. These aspects each contain their own unique properties, just like the essential elements of the universe, and are, thus, associated with them."

Jack looked down and saw the white ring light up, glowing brilliantly.

"The Wind Ring encompasses the spirit. This is where Paragons are able to study things such as religion, belief, harmony, morality, enlightenment, and the supernatural. Those with mastery of the Wind Ring are great philosophers, wise leaders, and sage advisors. They dedicate themselves to discovering the power that lies within themselves and others, and the wonders that lie within the realm of spirituality."

Next, the blue ring glowed, rippling like water in a pond. It was followed by the green ring, which gave the impression of leaves rustling in the wind.

"The Water Ring encompasses life. Without water, there can be no life. This ring focuses on preserving and protecting life. It focuses on medicine and healing. The Ground Ring encompasses creation. All creation springs from the ground – plants, animals, minerals. To us, this is the creation not only of these things but also of art, music, literature, and invention."

Then, the orange ring lit up, shimmering and looking like molten lava.

"The Fire Ring encompasses conflict. Here, one studies action, fighting, and movement. Fire gives one mastery over his own body and actions, which can be used to great effect in battle and the defense of others. Fire Ring is where warriors are bred. And finally, we have The Void..."

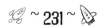

Jack looked at the final ring. Unlike the others, it did not glow. Instead, it was an inky black color that looked different and out of place among the other rings to which it was connected.

"The Dark Side..." Jack whispered to himself.

Pennywise raised an eyebrow upon hearing Jack's utterance. "Beg your pardon?" he asked.

"The Void is the Dark Side, right?" said Jack. "That's the part that contains all the evil, forbidden knowledge that turns people bad, isn't it?"

Pennywise gave Jack a questioning look. "Why would you say that?"

Jack shrugged. "Well, the guys that control the Deathlords are called the Lords of the Void," Jack replied. "And there's always a Dark Side, right?"

Pennywise chuckled. "I cannot say I know much about these Lords of the Void that you speak of, but I can say that The Void is not evil. Nor is it good. None of the five rings is good or evil. The rings simply are. Knowledge is a tool, my friend, and tools cannot be good or bad. Their uses are entirely dependent upon those who wield them. Fire gives us heat, and it can be used to cook and create, but it can also be used to burn, destroy, and consume. Water is essential for life, but too much of it can drown you. The ground gives us bounty and supplies the building blocks of wondrous creations, and yet it can bury us and crush us beneath its weight. Air is needed to breathe, but when a strong wind blows, it can cut as sharply as any knife and tear down even the sturdiest wall. All five of the rings of knowledge have the potential for great good and terrible evil. But part of being a Paragon is knowing how to use knowledge to bring about the best qualities in the universe – not just in yourself but in others, as well. That is why the Conclave is so important. It is here where people train, not only to wield great power... but also to understand the responsibility of doing so."

Pennywise looked at Jack. "Every year within the prime universe, we bring in a new class of candidates to train as Paragons," he continued. "Some of them are invited. Some are recruited. Some volunteer. But all of them are taught these five aspects, in the hopes that they will unlock their potential and follow the path of the Free Mind. The new season of training is set to begin very soon, and I took it upon myself to include you in it."

Jack blinked at the Paragon. "You included me?" he asked.

Pennywise nodded. "Shepherd may not be around to keep his promise, but I know he'd have wanted me to follow through if he could not. I am of the Water Ring. Fighting is not my strong suit, so I would be a poor candidate for you to

apprentice with. But by joining the new season of candidates, you'll have the opportunity to enter into Paragon training and to choose the Ring in which you wish to specialize. However, if you choose to leave, you will not be able to participate."

Jack frowned. "So… you're saying I can either help my friends or train to be a Paragon, but not both?"

"The way time works here, if you leave, you will never make it back in time to participate in the new season," Pennywise explained. "You could wait until next season, if you wish, but it comes down to how you think you can best help your friends. If you were to learn the skills of a Paragon, would you not be able to assist them better? Would you not be better able to help the Princess? If your friends have need of you, they know how to contact us. But in the time it takes for them to return with the healer they are seeking, you could conceivably have the equivalent of years of training under your belt. Knowing how to fight, knowing how to heal, knowing how to create, gaining wisdom and experience… is that not a better use of your time than chasing after those who do not currently need your help?"

Jack was quiet for a long moment as he mulled over the Paragon's words.

"What you say makes sense, but… I can't just abandon my friends," he said.

"You're not abandoning them," Pennywise replied. "Mourdock Skyborn is still here at the temple, as is Princess Glorianna. As you train, you can also take part in the efforts to heal the Princess. And should your friends need you, you will be better equipped to help them when necessary."

Pennywise approached Jack and laid a hand on his shoulder, looking down at him with an understanding gaze.

"You have a decision to make, Jack," he said gently. "And it is a life-changing one. Those decisions are never easy, but they can be rewarding. I'm offering you this opportunity to follow in Shepherd's footsteps and fulfill the promise he made you. The only question now is… will you accept it?"

Jack hesitated, struggling to make a decision. His instincts were telling him to go after his friends, but every other part of him saw the wisdom in Pennywise's reasoning. Jack thought about Shepherd. He thought about Anna. He thought about his friends and all the times they could have used the abilities Pennywise was offering him. The Paragon looked at Jack, expecting an answer, and Jack finally had one to give.

Jack met Pennywise's gaze and nodded.

"Heck yeah," he said.

CHAPTER ✺ 24

ack sat in a communications chamber before a large, bulky, antiquated subspace array. He thought the boxy machine looked like something an '80s movie would consider high-tech. Luckily, it wasn't too complicated to figure out how to use. All he needed to do was use the boxy camera that was attached to the array to record a message and then type in the subspace channel to which he wished to send it.

"Hey, guys, it's me," Jack said after enabling the camera. "I'm okay! Well... I'm awake, at least. Still feel like I just got hit by a train. Anyway, thanks for saving my life and getting me to the Conclave. It's super weird here, but it's nice not being on the run for a change. Wish you guys could have stuck around. I miss all of you. I know it probably doesn't seem like much time has passed to you, but here, well... it feels like it's been weeks since I last saw any of you. Anyway... I guess while you're all off on your mission, I'm going to be here training to be a Paragon, if you can believe it. So maybe by the time you get back, I'll be able to fight bounty hunters without almost killing myself. One can hope, right? But, just so you know, I'm here if you need me. Just say the word, and I'll hop on the Earthship and fly to the rescue, or whatever. So... yeah... I guess that's it. Good luck finding that healer! Peace."

Jack cringed as he reviewed the recording, but he doubted he could do another take that felt any less awkward. He typed in the subspace channel Dan had provided Pennywise and uploaded the video. Once it was completed, Jack sat there for a moment, as though expecting an immediate response.

It was a silly notion, of course. Pennywise had explained to him that due to the time constriction of the Conclave, it would be quite some time before Jack would likely receive an answer. Even if his friends had gotten the message as soon as he'd sent it, to Jack it would probably seem like days before he would get their response. Jack supposed that "days" would be optimistic. Most likely he wouldn't hear from his friends for weeks, or possibly months, depending on what they were up to and how often they checked Dan's subspace communicator.

As Jack left the communications chamber, he began feeling tired once more. He still hadn't fully recovered from his accident at Port Somewhere and had needed to rest in his healing chamber quite often. He could only hope this feeling would go away before the start of his training. He had just started shuffling back toward his chamber when he heard Pennywise's voice.

"Jack," Pennywise said.

Jack turned and saw the Paragon headed toward him. One look at Pennywise's face and Jack could tell something was wrong. "Oh, hey," Jack said. "Um... everything okay?"

"I need you to come with me," Pennywise responded, a sense of urgency in his voice. "We need to go to the Chamber of the Five Rings immediately."

"Why? What's going on?"

"The Order of Peers has been called to meet. They're going to vote on whether to kick you out of the Conclave."

Jack's eyes widened. "What? Kick me out?" he said, shocked. "But... I thought they gave me asylum, or something..."

"That was before they learned of your intent to enroll in the new training season," Pennywise said. "Now, some members of the Order want you gone."

Jack frowned as he walked hurriedly alongside Pennywise. "What difference does that make?" Jack asked. "Why would me wanting to train here mean I can't stay?"

"I guess we'll find out soon enough. Now, hurry. We must get to the chamber before the Order votes on the matter."

As they made their way toward the Crystal Concourse, they passed another Paragon in the hallway, a Regal woman with short, dark blonde hair and kind green eyes. She wore blue robes, just like Pennywise, and moved to intercept him. "Eldrich, there you are," she said. "I got your message that you wished to see me."

"Yes, Frenesca, I need your help," Pennywise said, without breaking stride. "I need you to track down Mourdock Skyborn. Check the healing chamber where the Princess is being kept. Tell him he needs to come to the Chamber of the Five Rings right away. His friend Jack needs his help urgently."

Frenesca nodded. "May I ask what this is about?" she inquired, concerned.

"I shall have to explain later. Just, please, do as I ask."

"Very well," she responded. "I'll do my best."

"Who was that?" Jack asked, once Frenesca had hurried off to carry out her task.

"A colleague," Pennywise said.

Jack got the impression there was more between the two than simply being "collegues," but he didn't ask about it further. When they arrived in the Chamber of the Five Rings, it appeared as though Masters GorJiro, Hodapp, Highclaw, and Savage had all just begun to assemble. Master Savage turned and gave them both a disapproving look as Jack and Pennywise approached. "Paragon Pennywise," Savage said, "how did you know of this meeting?"

"I told him," said Master Highclaw.

Savage looked at Highclaw in disappointment. "And why would you feel it necessary to do that?"

"Paragon Pennywise is the one sponsoring the Earthman into training," Highclaw replied. "I felt it appropriate he should be made aware of this vote you have called."

"Very well, he is aware," Savage said. "But he is not a member of the Order, so his presence here serves no purpose."

"I feel I should be given the chance to make a case for the Earthman, Master," Pennywise said. "After all, is it not fair that the Order hear his side before such a vote is to be had?"

"I am of a mind with Paragon Pennywise on this matter," Highclaw stated. "The Conclave is a place of learning. We should weigh all information if we are to take a stance on whether or not one will be permitted to partake in what this place is meant for."

Savage frowned. "Very well," he grumbled. "Make your case, Paragon Pennywise."

Pennywise bowed to Savage and took a moment to prepare himself as the members of the Order sat in their appropriate seats. Once the Order had officially convened, Pennywise began.

"Esteemed Order," he said. "I am here before you today to petition for the inclusion of Earthman Jack Finnegan into the new round of Initiates to be trained here at the Conclave this season. Despite the controversy surrounding him in the prime universe, I believe he has proven himself to be one of great character, skill, and bravery. He has put his life on the line many times, not just for Princess Glorianna, but for the entire galaxy. He already showcases many of the traits we teach those who wish to become Paragons. But beyond all that, a former member of the Order of Peers, Paragon Shepherd, also believed in him. For that reason alone, he should be permitted to train to free his mind."

"As highly as I regarded Paragon Shepherd, he is not here to confirm or deny any of his thoughts regarding the Earthman," Savage said. "There is no way for us to be certain whether or not he had affection for the Earthman as you say he did."

"That is not true, Master. I was told by Professor Thaddius Green that Paragon Shepherd, before his demise, intended to take Earthman Finnegan on as an apprentice. I believe his word on the matter to be trustworthy."

"Trustworthy or not, Paragon Shepherd is not here to confirm it," Savage insisted. "Beyond that, an apprenticeship requires a Master, and Paragon Shepherd has unfortunately passed away, meaning such a thing is no longer an option."

"This is why I am petitioning for the Earthman's inclusion into the general class," Pennywise said. "Absent Paragon Shepherd's involvement, I believe he would have wanted the boy to be trained in the ways of the Free Mind."

"And without such a respected Master to guide him, we cannot know if he can be trusted left to his own devices," argued Savage. "Which is why he should not be permitted into the general class and should be removed from the Conclave posthaste."

"What are you talking about, dude?" interjected Jack. "What's your problem with me?"

Savage scowled at Jack. "My problem is that you've proven yourself to be both dangerous and undisciplined, as evidenced by your condition when you arrived here."

Jack was about to object further, but Pennywise put a hand on his shoulder to stop him. "Master Savage," Pennywise said, "the circumstances surrounding the Earthman's arrival here are rather unique. They should not be used to judge his worthiness as a candidate for training."

"And yet, do we not take into account the circumstances surrounding other candidates who apply for training?" responded Savage. "Character has a large role to play in the forging of a Paragon. And need I point out the boy is a fugitive?"

"That is of no concern here," Highclaw replied. "The Conclave is not beholden to the laws of the prime universe."

"Then let us address the laws of our universe," Savage countered. "The boy performed an act of Servuchur. A discipline which is strictly forbidden here."

"An act of what?" Jack blurted. "I don't even know what you're talking about!"

"Are you denying you are capable of manipulating the life energy of living beings, as the Deathlords do?" demanded Savage.

Pennywise put a hand on Jack's shoulder to quiet him before he could respond. "Jack is young and ignorant about our rules, Master Savage," Pennywise said. "He performed the act you are referring to unknowingly, and it almost killed him."

"Regardless, one with such skills should not be taught how to become more powerful," Savage replied. "I do not believe I need to remind the Order what happened the last time trained Paragons attempted to master such a discipline."

"Again, the Earthman was unaware of what he was doing," Pennywise interjected. "Surely, not allowing one with such abilities to train to control them is far more dangerous than teaching him that such abilities should not be used."

"It is an interesting conundrum," commented Master Hodapp. "Paragon Pennywise makes a good case as to why the Earthman is a worthy candidate. Yet, Master Savage also makes a good case as to why he might be a danger."

"I believe this is no different from the reason we expel those who wash out of Fire Ring and prevent them from receiving further training," GorJiro stated. "The skills we teach in Warrior training can be used to devastating effect, making those with even a rudimentary understanding of them extremely dangerous. Limiting their training further keeps them from reaching a level they are not prepared for. If they wish to advance, they must apply again in a new training season and prove, once more, they have what it takes before they can continue. We have no issue prohibiting training in that scenario. Why should we have an issue in this one?"

"I would argue because the Earthman has not yet proven himself to be a danger, Master GorJiro," Pennywise said.

"Except to himself," countered Savage.

"I believe that logic to be unfair, Master Savage," Pennywise replied. "Paragon training can be a perilous endeavor. It is very common to be hurt or injured, and in some cases killed, in the pursuit of new skills."

"And how much injury could one with the power of a Deathlord inflict on those here at the Conclave, do you suppose?" Savage asked.

"I don't have the power of a Deathlord!" objected Jack. "I don't even know what happened with that bounty hunter who was trying to kill me! I barely remember any of it!"

"Those who were there had quite clear memories of what occurred," said Savage. "What further evidence does this panel need to see the threat this boy poses?"

"Leave it to Grendal Savage to be threatened by a child..." came a voice.

All eyes went to the entrance to see a tiny Harvshodd[27] hobbling into the chamber. No more than three feet tall, he was dressed in dirty and faded black robes and relied on a walking staff that was taller than he was. His bare feet were big and hairy, sporting cracked and blackened toenails. His dark, greasy hair was pulled back into a short pony tail. His face was flattened and framed by a scraggly and coarse looking beard. His skin was an ashy grey color, and his nose was long and pointy with an ugly wart on it. As if the sight of him weren't odd enough, he also wore a cloth blindfold tied over his eyes.

"Master Ravencrow," Highclaw said, a hint of surprise in his voice. "We were unaware you had returned from your travels."

"Well, that explains why there was no welcome celebration upon my arrival," Ravencrow muttered as he continued hobbling toward the group with what seemed to be great difficulty. "I take it you have not filled my seat in my absence?"

"The seat is still yours," Highclaw replied.

"Shocker," Ravencrow said as he moved to the chair in the black ring and climbed onto it. Jack noticed Master GorJiro seemed to stiffen as the tiny Harvshodd took his seat, but Jack wasn't sure if that was because GorJiro didn't like the alien, or because the strange squeaking noise Ravencrow had made when he sat down had actually been a fart.

"The Order of Peers would like to officially welcome back Master Moon Ravencrow to the Conclave," Highclaw stated.

"Does Master Ravencrow know how long he will be staying this time?" GorJiro asked, stiffly.

"Just short of 'long enough', most likely," Ravencrow grumbled. "Depends on how much more annoying you all have gotten in your old age. And judging from the bickering I heard when I entered, I think it's safe to say it's quite a bit

---

[27] Harvshodds are an ugly alien race that are short in stature and resemble trolls.

more. So... what pressing business has brought the Order together today, hmmmm? A change in the lunch menu? A consensus about how itchy the robes everyone here is forced to wear are? Come now, the suspense is killing me."

"We have assembled to decide on whether or not a wanted criminal who performed an act of Servuchur should be admitted to the new season of training," Savage stated.

"Well, now... the Initiate pool has certainly gotten far more interesting since I was last here," Ravencrow said with a chuckle.

"If I may be permitted to restate my case for Master Ravencrow's benefit..." Pennywise began.

"No need," Ravencrow said. "I'm bored enough as it is. Has the Order voted on the matter yet?"

"We are still debating the subject," said Highclaw.

"Enough debating," Ravencrow replied. "If any of you hasn't made up your minds by now, you never will. Let's vote on this so I can get back to more important things, like trimming my toenails and discovering new smells."

"I second the call for a vote," Savage said. "Let us put this matter to rest."

"Very well," Highclaw said with a heavy sigh. "I do not see the harm in accepting the child. I vote to allow him into the new class of Initiates."

"As do I," Hodapp said. "This is a place of learning. Let him learn!"

"I am against," Savage stated. "The Earthman is dangerous and has no place here."

"I, too, am not comfortable with granting him entry," GorJiro said. "From what I have heard, trouble seems to follow this Earthman wherever he goes. In that respect, training him to harness the power of a Paragon could be disastrous. I am against."

"The tally is two against two," Highclaw stated, turning his gaze toward Ravencrow. "Master Ravencrow, the vote comes down to you."

Jack looked at the gnarled little alien as Ravencrow's face scrunched up in thought. *Please, please, please, please!* Jack thought, as he awaited Ravencrow's response.

"Against," Ravencrow finally said.

"What?" cried Jack, not believing what he'd just heard. "Why?"

"I don't like the way you smell," muttered Ravencrow.

Jack was about to protest again when Pennywise stopped him. "Esteemed Order," Pennywise said. "I would urge you to reconsider. Surely the endorsement of both Paragon Shepherd and myself in the Earthman's favor must count for something?"

"Your support of the Earthman has been taken into account, Paragon Pennywise," Savage said. "However highly we may regard your input, it does not change the fact that you are not a member of the Order."

"But I am," came a voice.

Jack turned and saw Hasatan entering the chamber. All eyes went to the old Paragon as he stood by Jack's side. "Last I checked, anyway," Hasatan continued. "I may not be a sitting member, what with my duties mentoring the Emperor Ascendant, but I am present now. Does that not entitle me to a vote on this matter?"

"As a member of the Order of Peers, you are, of course, entitled to vote on any issue you are present for when the Order is assembled," Highclaw said.

"Then I vote to include the Earthman," Hasatan stated. "Let him train. If he succeeds, then it proves Paragon Shepherd's instincts about him were correct. If he fails, the only thing wasted is time. And here at the Conclave, we have nothing but time, do we not?"

"Whether or not we are wasting time training an Initiate is not the issue here," Savage objected. "The issue here is whether or not the boy is too dangerous to be trained in the first place."

"Oh, he's dangerous all right," came the sound of Mourdock's voice. Jack turned to see Mourdock entering the chamber, coming to a stop next to Jack. "Dangerous to the Deathlords, anyway. Because of Jack, the planetkiller fleet was destroyed, the portgate network was saved from destruction, and Princess Glorianna was rescued before the slythru could take complete control of her. All this without any type of training. Given the proper instruction and skills, I shudder to think what he'd be capable of against our enemy."

"So, the Earthman now has the support of two esteemed Paragons and three members of the Order," Highclaw stated.

"Support from Paragons Skyborn and Pennywise do not count toward the vote of the Order," Savage argued. "The vote now stands deadlocked, three to three. And until the Order can come to a consensus, the Earthman cannot be permitted to train, regardless."

Mourdock stepped forward. "Master GorJiro," he said, gaining the Paragon's attention. "Aside from Master Hasatan, you know me better than any in the Order. I trained by your side for most of my life. You know the respect I have for you and your teachings, and I hope I have made you proud in my actions as a Paragon. I would ask that now, you place your trust in me, and believe me when I say Jack deserves the opportunity to train here. If my opinion means anything to you, Master... I ask that you change your vote and give Jack a chance to prove he is worthy of your teachings."

GorJiro regarded Mourdock for a long moment. All eyes were on the venerated master before Hasatan stepped forward, as well. "This is the right decision, Master GorJiro," he stated. "If you do not fully trust your own pupil's word, then trust mine."

GorJiro frowned but then nodded his head. "Very well," he said. "Upon the recommendations of my former student and my colleague, I am changing my vote to permit the Earthman to train."

Savage scowled at the decision but did not object. Ravencrow looked bored and remained silent.

"The vote is now four to two," Highclaw said. "The matter has been resolved. The Earthman will be permitted to attend the new season of training."

Upon hearing Highclaw's words, Jack's heart leapt, and he was able to breathe easily once more. Pennywise patted his shoulder in congratulations, and Mourdock turned and smiled, shaking Jack's hand.

"Thanks," Jack said.

"Anytime, compatriot," Mourdock said. "We're friends. It was the least I could do."

Before Jack knew it, Master GorJiro was standing in front of him, looking down at him with a stern and intimidating expression. "Do not make me regret this decision, Earthman," GorJiro stated. "I expect a great deal from you."

Jack nodded, nervously, in response. "Yes... yes, Master... sir."

As GorJiro left, both Master Hodapp and Master Highclaw approached. "Congratulations, youngling!" said Hodapp. "I look forward to seeing you in class."

"As do I," Highclaw said with a kind smile. "Judging by the praise and faith your friends have put in you, Initiate Finnegan, you have a great deal to live up to."

"I'll try my best, sir. I mean, Master."

"Do, or do not. There is no... well, we all know how that saying goes," replied Highclaw. "Rest up, Initiate. You shall need to be at your best before the season begins."

After they left, Master Savage came up, looking at Jack with a sour expression. "I'll be watching you, Initiate," he said bitterly, before leaving, as well.

"I must apologize for Master Savage," Pennywise said, once he'd gone. "He has strong opinions and can be quite passionate about them."

"Yeah, well... at least he's straight up as to why he's a jerk," Jack replied. "That's more than I can say for that dude." Jack looked over at Ravencrow, who was the only one remaining in his chair. The Harvshodd made no effort to get up, simply sitting there quietly, the hint of a smile on his face. "He voted against me without knowing a thing about me."

"Do not take it personally, Jack," Pennywise said. "Master Ravencrow is known to be quite... unconventional."

"Well, I think that's enough drama for one day," Mourdock said, slinging his arm around Jack. "How are you feeling, compatriot?"

"Like crud, still."

Mourdock chuckled at that. "Come on. Let's get you back to your healing chamber. You're going to need to be rested for the New Season Celebration."

"Um... yeah, I could use some sleep," admitted Jack as the group began to head for the door.

As they all made their way out of the Chamber of the Five Rings, Jack turned and caught one last glimpse of Master Ravencrow. Though the Harvshodd was blindfolded, Jack could have sworn the small alien was glaring directly at him.

And for some reason, that gave Jack a very uneasy feeling.

After travelling with the others to return the Earthman back to his healing chamber, Zarrod excused himself and made his way to his own room under the excuse of being tired – which was not far from the truth. Keeping up the guise of Hasatan tended to wear on him. It was a good thing he had been with

Mourdock when that Frenesca woman had found them. Having the Earthman expelled from the Conclave would have complicated his plans, particularly since he'd yet to figure out why the Earthman's injury had seemingly also affected *him*.

There is some connection between us, Zarrod thought. *There has been ever since the Great Seal broke on the Ghost Planet. But I've yet to understand just how deep that connection goes.*

Zarrod's pain had disappeared the moment the monk had healed the Earthman. And though Jack appeared to still be suffering the effects of the soul severance, Zarrod was completely back to normal. But it did concern him that he could be made to suffer if the Earthman sustained an injury. Until he could determine how this was possible, he wanted to keep Jack close to him.

Zarrod opened the door to his chambers, but stopped in the doorway before entering. There was someone in his room, waiting for him in the dark. "I was wondering when you'd come see me," Zarrod said as he stepped into the room and sealed the door behind him.

"You should not be here, Hasatan," the figure replied.

"Why not? It's my chamber."

"You know what I mean."

Zarrod smirked. "My place is beside young Mourdock," he responded. "If he is here, I must be, too. Or have you forgotten the part he has to play in the grand design of our Lords?"

"I have toiled away for what has felt like eons, working to bring about that grand design," the figure said, its voice low and stern. "And now that my part of the plan is so close to being fulfilled, you appear and bring with you... complications."

"You speak of the Earthman?" Zarrod asked.

"Among other things," the figure responded. "However, he does not worry me as much as the presence of young Skyborn, or the Princess."

"Skyborn is ready. You have nothing to worry about on that front," Zarrod reassured his mysterious visitor. "I have continued manifesting the corruption within him, as was my task."

"It is not enough," the figure insisted. "I have been spreading the corruption among those who reside in this place for a very long time. Even now, I am preparing to spread it to the new crop of Initiates so that they, too, shall join us when the time comes. But Skyborn has been too long away from my sight. He may be able to resist my call."

"If that is the case, it won't be for long," Zarrod said. "I can assure you, he is as vulnerable as we need him to be."

"And the Princess? Why is she here and not with Verrutus?"

"She was being wasted on Verrutus. The Earthman had her locked away on his ship. She will be far more useful for your purposes."

"So… you brought her here to deliver her to me?"

"You now have access to two with Ancient blood, one of which has no problem accessing Ancient technology. Her mere presence here will allow you to spread the corruption within the Great Seal more rapidly. And when it comes time to raise the Dark Temples, the Princess will be at your disposal, as well."

The figure was silent for a long moment. "I do not appreciate you taking it upon yourself to modify my plans without first consulting me."

"I can understand that, but the nature of the situation did not lend itself to such a thing. I had to improvise."

"Why do I get the feeling you are doing more here than improvising?"

"Probably because you are a wise and talented Paragon," Zarrod replied. "I will not lie to you. I am also here because I need your assistance with something."

"And what would that be?"

"I need to gain access to the Forbidden Archives. I wish to learn the Conclave's teachings on Servuchur."

Zarrod didn't need to see the figure's face to know it was displeased. "Why would you need such a thing?" the figure asked.

"It is necessary for Mourdock's continued corruption," Zarrod lied. "I have instructed him in what I can, but my knowledge of Servuchur is limited. If he is to reach his full potential, he will need such teachings."

"What you are proposing is risky," the figure stated. "The Forbidden Archives are highly secure. There is a chance that accessing them could lead to my discovery."

"If anyone can get them, unnoticed, it is you."

The figure was quiet for a long moment before speaking. "Very well. I shall help you with this one thing."

Zarrod couldn't help but smile. Getting access to the Servuchur research so he could regain his mastery of it had been the entire motivation behind steering the Earthman and his companions to the Conclave. And now that his mysterious ally had made contact, Zarrod felt that goal was finally within his grasp.

The figure made its way toward the door of the chamber, stopping briefly beside Zarrod. "If I find out there is more to this than you say, there will be consequences."

"You give me far too little credit," Zarrod replied. "We both serve the same masters. We both want the same things."

"Perhaps," the figure said as it moved to the door and opened it. "I will be in touch again once I've accessed the archives. Until then... no more surprises."

Zarrod watched the figure go, a sly smile on his face.

"As you wish... Mellegogg," he said.

CHAPTER ✵ 25

n the Boro sector of space, which contained the Great Border between the Regalus and Visini Empires, was a hyperspace junction collectively known to the galaxy at large as "The Bazaar." Established not long after the hostilities of the Great Border War ended and trade developed between the two populaces, merchants and traders began frequenting this location due to the fact that important hyperspace routes from both empires led to this particular point in space. And for most of those engaged in intergalactic commerce between empires, it became far easier to set up shop at this location than to continually hop back and forth across the border.

Because there were no planetary bodies in this area of space capable of being colonized, a loose collection of mercantile vessels eventually came to establish the Bazaar. These ranged from small transport freighters all the way to salvaged capital ships, permanently parked in space with their prospective owners operating various businesses out of them. Over time, the Bazaar attracted more and more entrepreneurs eager to cash in on the hyperspace traffic and the convenient location between the Visinis and the Regals. And because the start-up cost of beginning a business here essentially amounted to the cost of a space-worthy vessel, the Bazaar was a veritable cornucopia of capitalist initiative.

The space platforms here ranged from groups of transport containers strung together and retrofitted with life support systems and berthing docks, all the way up to state of the art shipping vessels the size of small cities. Though admittedly, this made the Bazaar a bit of a jumbled eyesore, it also made it quite a convenient marketplace where travelers could find pretty much anything they wanted to buy, sell, or trade.

Of all the various businesses being run at this location, probably one of the biggest and most popular was known as I-sembly, the corporate headquarters of which were located on a massive blue and yellow space vessel shaped like a cube. I-sembly was owned and operated by a race of beings known as the Bjorg, which was actually a collection of species that had been turned into cybernetic organisms functioning as drones in a hive mind collective. Though the Bjorg started off as a threating entity, which had its sights set on the attainment of "perfection" through the forcible assimilation of diverse sentient species, technologies, and knowledge, they eventually changed their goals after assimilating a rather friendly species known as the Greedish that fervently believed in hard work, the free market, and the accumulation of material wealth.

After assimilating the Greedish people, the Bjorg collectively agreed that "the Greed are good" and quickly decided it was far easier and more profitable to design and sell ready-to-assemble modern style furniture, appliances, and home accessories than it was to systematically assimilate the entire universe. Thus, they set their sights on becoming the galaxy's largest furniture retailer, including products for storage, lighting, kitchen appliances, and pet care. Fueled by their collective knowledge and efficient workforce, the Bjorg took the universe by storm, supplying countless worlds with stylish furniture and home decorations.

Making I-sembly products was one thing, but delivering them was another. As things turned out, the Bjorg did not care to venture too far from their corporate headquarters and, thus, outsourced the shipping and delivery of their products to independent contractors – such as Glimmer of House Brightstar, for instance.

Though Glimmer had started out as a pilot for one of her father's many trade ships, she quickly struck out and began her own import/export operation at a surprisingly young age. Unlike most blue-skinned ladies from great houses, Glimmer preferred the exciting and transient life of a spacefarer, taking pleasure in exploring the cosmos, interacting with other cultures, and running with a distinctly un-ladylike crowd.

Though her father didn't always approve of her choices, Glimmer had always been able to turn a profit and had grown her small company into a rather formidable shipping operation, which at least had temporarily alleviated the pressure from her family to settle down and marry, as most other attractive blue Visini women did. Indeed, by Visini standards, Glimmer was quite a beauty, even if she did have a propensity for scandalous hair colors, such as the current pink hue she sported. Her culture had a tendency to look down upon the fashionable use of certain colors, but Glimmer had always had a fondness for red. And as long as she kept bringing in money for her house, she had the freedom to be as single and scandalous as she pleased.

Glimmer stood in the massive hangar of the I-sembly headquarters supervising the loading of her various ships, as her first mate – a granite colored Recklec named Gage – went over the manifest with her. Their Bjorg liaison (all of whom answered to the name 'Bjorg') was with them.

"*The Hopskipper* is fully loaded," Gage said. "She'll be headed to the Corrino sector within the hour, scheduled for three stops. *The Bellwether* is still waiting for delivery of the units of office desks, but we expect to have her on her way to the Richese sector by tomorrow. *The Lilywhite* is on her way back from the Cobalt system. Should return in a week or so."

"What do you say, Bjorg?" Glimmer asked. "You guys going to have those shipments of coffee tables ready by then?"

"We are the Bjorg," Bjorg replied. "You will be satisfied. Assembly is required."

"Great Jouromir's ghost," Glimmer muttered as she looked at the manifest. "Forty thousand units? The people on Cobalt sure do love their coffee tables, don't they?"

"Considerin' these coffee tables actually make ya coffee, yeah, I can see how they'd be popular," Gage replied.

"Well, how about that. Coffee tables that make coffee," mused Glimmer. "What will you Bjorg think of next, eh?"

"We are the Bjorg," Bjorg replied. "You will be satisfied. Assembly is required."

Glimmer handed her datapad containing the various manifests back over to Gage. "Keep me updated. Let me know if there are any problems. Let's see if we can get all our ships launched on time."

"Sure thing, boss lady," Gage replied. "Where you off to?"

"The cafeteria for lunch," Glimmer said with a smile. "Didn't you hear? They're serving Greedish meat orbs today."

"They're always serving Greedish meat orbs," Gage grumbled.

"Why change what works?" Glimmer said. "After all, you know the Bjorg..."

"You will be satisfied," Glimmer and Gage both said.

"Assembly is required," Bjorg chimed in.

"I'll be sure to let the chef know that," Glimmer replied, jokingly, before heading off toward the cafeteria.

If Glimmer hadn't been hungry before setting off for lunch, she was certainly working up an appetite traversing the massive warehouse-like interior of the I-sembly ship on her trek to the meal area. Many different alien species were making their ways through the efficiently designed showrooms of the ship where they could see the various products the Bjorg offered for sale while catchy synthpop music played over the ship's loudspeakers. It was so crowded, that Glimmer decided it would be quicker to take a more roundabout route to the cafeteria.

She had just taken a turn down one of the nonpublic corridors of the ship when she passed a scruffy-looking Regal spacer who spoke to her. "You've changed yer hair," the man said.

Glimmer stopped and turned toward the man, her eyes narrowing with suspicion. "What did you say?" she asked.

The spacer turned and smiled at her. "You've gone pink," he said. "Last time I saw ya, it were white."

Glimmer raised an eyebrow. "I haven't had white hair in quite some time," she replied. "And I don't believe I know you."

"Oh, ya know me quite well, Glimmer," the man said as he tapped his wristband, his holographic disguise abruptly fading away.

Glimmer's eyes widened. "Scally?" she said in surprise.

"'Ello there, lass," said Scallywag, with more than a bit of swagger. "Miss me?"

Glimmer smiled. "Madly," she replied, before promptly slapping him across the face as hard as she could.

Scallywag stumbled from the surprise blow but quickly shook it off. "Right," he said, nursing his cheek. "I deserved that."

Glimmer immediately slapped him across the other cheek, even harder.

"Prolly deserved that, as well…"

Glimmer reeled back for another slap before Scallywag caught her wrist.

"Oy," he said, "a man only deserves so much."

"Oh, you deserve way more than a couple of stung cheeks, you scoundrel," Glimmer replied.

"Without a doubt," retorted Scallywag. "But ya know me motto. Get what ya want, not what ya deserve."

That made Glimmer smirk. "Aye. And what is it you want, pray tell?"

"Your help."

Glimmer laughed at that. "The nerve of you," she said. "Considering I could turn you in to the Regals for a reward big enough to buy a new fleet of

ships ten times over, you are making a mighty big assumption about how far my affection for you goes."

Now it was Scallywag's turn to smirk. "Not that big o' an assumption, considerin' all the times ya coulda turned me in ta the Visini fer a reward, and ya never did."

"That was before what you did to me on Toshi Station," Glimmer said.

"Aye, but it was also long after what I did ta ya on Veilspring Moon," Scallywag responded.

"Neither of those memories is helping your case, Scally," Glimmer stated, flatly. "But for the sake of our history together, I'll give you sixty seconds before I break your face and turn you over to the authorities."

"Fair enough. But just so ya know, ya won't just be helpin' me. You'll be helpin' tha heir ta the Regalus Empire herself."

Glimmer raised an eyebrow in curiosity. "Is that so?"

"It is," said Scallywag. "See, she's been infected by a brain worm—"

"Yeah, I've seen the holo of the Earthman and his little conspiracy theory," Glimmer replied. "What of it?"

"Well, if I'm gonna clear me name, I gotta detach this brain worm thing from her," Scallywag explained. "And the only way ta do that is ta get this Paragon healer and bring her back to the Princess."

"Sounds easy enough," Glimmer replied. "Why do you need my help? Didn't I hear the Earthman had some fancy spaceship you've been gallivanting around the universe in?"

"There be a couple reasons why that's not an option fer us. But all that aside, turns out the Paragon we need is stuck on a planet that's been quarantined because of some weird plague. And we need a way ta smuggle her out o' there."

"So let me get this straight," Glimmer said. "You want me to smuggle you through a quarantined planetary system, so you can kidnap a Paragon healer away from a planet where some deadly virus is on the loose, possibly exposing countless people – including me and my crew – to it in the process, all to rescue the leader of the Visini Empire's greatest adversary? Is that what you're asking?"

"Well, when ya put it like that, it don't sound all that appealing," Scallywag responded.

"And how would you put it, exactly?"

"That ya owe me a solid after stealing me ship."

"Ah," said Glimmer with a disappointed nod. "So that's why you're really here."

"Ain't no better vessel I can think of ta smuggle something in than tha *Reaver*," Scallywag replied. "And considering me old crew has up and vanished on me, there are precious few people left in this universe that I trust. You happen ta be one o' them."

"Of course, I am. I'm a Blue," Glimmer said, holding up her hand as if to point out the color of her skin. "You can always trust a Blue. A Red, however... well, let's just say there are precious few people in this universe *I* trust... and you are definitely not one of them."

Scallywag frowned. "Glimmer, I know I done ya wrong. And believe me, if I had any other options available, I'd be usin' 'em. I'm between a rock and a hard place here. If it were just about me saving me own hide, I'd respect yer decision to tell me ta kiss off. But this is bigger than me. The entire universe is hangin' in the balance."

Glimmer shook her head. "Leave it to you to make covering your hide sound so grandiose."

"Glimmer, please... I'm beggin' ya... if you ever had any feelings fer me, help me out here."

Glimmer frowned. Despite her instincts to the contrary, she wanted to believe Scallywag. Something about him seemed genuine for a change. And, as mentioned before... she always did have a fondness for the color red.

"What is it you need from me, exactly?" she asked.

"I need a ship with a legit I.D. code and an emergency medical clearance," Scallywag said. "Something that can get us through the Visini side of a planetary quarantine. I then need you to dock with an orbital space port, unload some cargo with me and me mates hidden inside, wait for us at a fixed location until we can teleport back aboard your vessel, and then high-tail it outta there."

"That's an awful big 'ask' you have there, Scally," Glimmer muttered, not happy with what she was hearing.

"Big ask, big reward," Scallywag said. "You do this, I've worked out a deal with Mourdock Skyborn himself to award you an exclusive minerals shipping contract in the Maxima system. And if we end up saving the Princess, you'll get your choice o' the juiciest government contracts the Regals have ta offer. This could make ya the biggest trader in the entire Visini Empire. And just to show ya I'm serious, I got a mighty nice Maxima Corvette I'm willin' ta offer as collateral."

Glimmer puckered her lips. "How do I know any of this is true?" she asked.

"Don't take me word for it. Take the word o' the next Regalus Emperor," Scallywag said as he produced a datapad and handed it to her. "Skyborn himself sent along the contract. It's officiated and everything, contingent upon the delivery of the Paragon we're off to pick up."

Glimmer looked over the contract. The encryption on it appeared official. "Humph," she said. "You've certainly made some interesting friends since we last saw each other."

"Aye, that's an understatement if ever there was one," Scallywag replied. "So waddya say, lass? Ya up fer a bit o' adventure?"

Glimmer hesitated, weighing the pros and cons of the offer. The risk was indeed great. But the proposed reward certainly made it worth it. "My father has some connections with the Space Authority. It may take a few days, but we can get an emergency medical clearance. The real question is how you plan to teleport off the planet and back onto my ship."

"We're gonna hijack the planet's spaceport teleporter ta beam us all to yer location."

Glimmer raised an eyebrow. "Well… that's certainly novel."

"Yeah, you know me. I like ta think outside tha box."

"It wasn't your idea, was it?"

"Not even a little," Scallywag admitted. "But the bloke who came up with the idea is pretty confident he can pull it off."

"And if he can't? If we should run into trouble?"

"Now, I been thinkin' about that," Scallywag said. "If'n we do, however unlikely that may be, we should have a ship with us that is capable of scrappin'. A ship that's reliable in a fight, but one that's still fast and maneuverable. So, what if… and bear with me here… just what if—"

"We took *The Reaver?*" Glimmer finished for him.

"There's yer lolly," Scallywag said with a wink and a smile.

Glimmer rolled her eyes. "For a bloke who claims to think outside the box, you are mighty predictable, Scally."

"What can I say? I miss me ship."

"*My* ship," Glimmer corrected. "And it just so happens she recently returned from a cargo run, so she's available."

"This mean yer on board?"

Glimmer looked back at the Skyborn contract and thoughtfully tapped the datapad against her palm. "Let me see this Corvette of yours," she said. "If it checks out, I'll consider it."

"Fair enough," Scallywag said. "But first, I wanna see *The Reaver*."

"Very well. Follow me."

Scallywag re-engaged his hologuise and followed Glimmer back to the hangar bays. Even without looking like himself, Glimmer could tell he was excited to see his ship once again. She found the obvious eagerness cute, but she reminded herself not to fall for Scallywag's roguish charm.

"There she is," Glimmer said.

"Where?" asked Scallywag, looking around. "I don't see her."

"Right there," Glimmer replied.

Glimmer pointed toward a boxy six-story freighter that was five hundred feet in length. The exterior had been painted a light sky-blue color with golden trim. Scallywag eyed the vessel for a long moment, his mouth open in disbelief.

"Blimey," Scallywag muttered. "What did ya do to me ship???"

"First off, it's *my* ship," Glimmer said. "Secondly, I had to make a few cosmetic modifications to help disguise it. I had a few casings installed and painted it to make it look more like a freighter. Military-class Man of War vessels tend to draw unwanted attention on cargo runs."

"That's because tha *Reaver* ain't meant fer bloody cargo runs!" Scallywag said in distaste. "She's meant ta be a scrapper! Tough enough to take a few hits ta get in close, and vicious enough ta snare-winch her prey so tha crew can board it."

"That's true, for battle and piracy," Glimmer replied. "But she's also fast, maneuverable, and now has a rather large reinforced equalarium-lined cargo hold, courtesy of the idiot that first stole it from you. That makes *The Bluebell* one of my best transports, particularly for risky jobs."

Scallywag blinked at Glimmer. "*The Bluebell?*" he muttered. "Tell me ya didn't rename the deadliest pirate ship ta ever grace tha galaxy some pansy name like *The Bluebell!*"

"I think it's pretty," Glimmer said with a shrug.

Scallywag sighed. "Oy, lass... of all tha things tryin' ta kill me, you just might be tha one that succeeds."

Glimmer smiled coyly at Scallywag. "You always did know how to sweet-talk a girl," she chided.

Scallywag returned her smile. "I do, don't I?" he said, with a modicum of bravado. "Look at us. You and me, on *The Reaver*, gettin' up ta no good... it be just like old times."

"I haven't agreed to the job, yet."

"Well, ya ain't broken me face or turned me in yet, neither," Scallywag said. "I'd say things are lookin' hopeful."

"Looks can be deceiving."

Scallywag sidled up to Glimmer, giving her a playful glare. "C'mon, lass. You really gonna tell me yer happy shippin' furniture across the galaxy?"

"It's good money."

"That's not what I asked," Scallywag said as he reached up and ran his fingers over some of Glimmer's pink hair. "Ya always did like ta run with a bit o' red. And I think yer dyin' ta have a bit o' fun."

"You know me so well, don't you?"

"'Bout as well as you know me," Scallywag replied, leaning in close enough to kiss her. "So what do ya say, lass? Care ta get a bit crimson with yer old sweetheart?"

Glimmer locked eyes with Scallywag. She'd forgotten how much she'd missed his banter. How intoxicating his presence could be. How he always brought out the wild side in her, and she loved every second of it.

"I say..."

Their faces were inches apart, and for the briefest of moments, Glimmer was tempted to give in.

But only for a moment.

She swiftly kneed Scallywag as hard as she could in the groin, causing him to double over before dropping to his knees.

"Oh! Me jimmies!" Scallywag whined.

"You may not get what you deserve, but I'll be getting what *I* deserve for a change," Glimmer said, smiling down at Scallywag with a cocky grin. "I'll smuggle you to your little plague planet in exchange for your ship and your contracts. And if anything should go wrong, or I get even the slightest hint you're trying to swindle me, I'll turn you in for that reward in a heartbeat – if I decide not to kill you first. Oh, and just for future reference..."

Glimmer kicked Scallywag across the face, splaying him out onto the ground.

"You'll refer to me as *Captain* from here on out. I'll contact you when *The Bluebell* is ready to leave. Until then, don't let me see you around – or I'll show you just how red I can *really* run. Savvy?"

With that, Glimmer turned and walked away, leaving Scallywag writhing in pain on the ground.

"Well..." Scallywag muttered, "that went better than expected."

Scallywag gingerly picked himself up, unsure what hurt worse – his pride or his crotch.

CHAPTER  26

"J ack..." came a voice.

Jack stirred, lingering in the blissful haze between unconsciousness and awareness, not wanting to wake up.

"Jack?" the voice said again. "Hey, Jack..."

Finally, Jack opened his eyes, looking up at the face of Mourdock Skyborn. "Huh?" replied Jack, groggily.

"Wake up, compatriot," Mourdock said. "It's almost time for the party."

Jack blinked. "Party? What party?"

"The New Season Celebration," Mourdock said. "I told you about this. It's the big party that's thrown at the start of each training season to welcome the new Initiates. This is going to be your chance to meet your fellow classmates."

Jack sat up and rubbed his neck. Though he'd been sleeping a lot, he still felt exhausted, and that bizarre feeling he'd been experiencing ever since his fight with Stalker Crux really didn't put him in a partying mood. "Um, is it important to go to this thing?" he asked. "I just... I don't know... don't really feel up for it."

Mourdock frowned. "Well, if you're not feeling up for it, you can obviously skip it. But speaking from experience, I do think it's important to go. Once your training starts, you won't have a lot of time to unwind or do things that are social. The New Season Celebration is going to be your best chance to make friends before your classes begin."

Jack sighed. "Yeah, okay," he muttered as he slowly got off his bed. "But I may not stay all that long."

A smile returned to Mourdock's face. "Whatever you feel like, compatriot. Shall we?"

Jack and Mourdock exited the healing chamber and began walking down the sandstone corridor leading deeper into the temple. Jack trudged alongside Mourdock, feeling lethargic and cruddy. "So, where is the party being held?" Jack asked.

"In one of the activity chambers on the recreation level."

"Activity chambers?"

"Yeah, they're kind of like all-purpose rooms for activities and events," Mourdock replied. "You can use them for anything from poetry readings to gravityball games."

"The Conclave has gravityball courts?"

"Well, not in the traditional sense," Mourdock said. "Gravityball courts utilize a couple of different artificial gravity generators. Here, the students are the ones who are tasked with maintaining the different gravity levels."

"They're what now?" Jack asked, confused.

"Paragons can learn to manipulate gravity," Mourdock explained. "They learn the basics by maintaining different graviton levels during gravityball games here."

Jack wasn't exactly clear on everything Mourdock was saying, but he got the gist of it. "So... is that how you learned to do those gravity pulse things you do?" he asked.

Mourdock chuckled. "Yeah. I can't tell you how long I had to sit around on gravityball duty before I had enough experience not to kill myself with the gravity pulses. They are extremely dangerous if you don't know what you're doing."

Just then, a group of children, led by an aged woman in a white robe, came around the corner. A young Regal girl who couldn't have been much more than eight years old squealed when she saw Mourdock, her eyes going wide at the sight of him.

"Mourdock!" she cried. "Everyone! It's Mourdock!"

Mourdock laughed as the group of children all cried out and ran toward him. Jack stepped to the side as Mourdock scooped up the girl who'd cried his name and hefted her onto his shoulder. "Is that Relli?" Mourdock said with a smile. "Great Observer! You've gotten big!"

"Mourdock! Mourdock! Look what I can do!" cried another child who promptly did a backflip.

"Wow!" said Mourdock. "That was great, Xanpher!"

"Mourdock! Look! Watch!" said another who manifested a small ball of water, which then dropped to the floor with a splash.

"Impressive, Yanesh," Mourdock said. "I wasn't able to manifest anything until I was 10."

The kids continued to clamor for Mourdock's attention before the woman in the white robes walked up. "Now, children, let's not bother the Emperor Ascendant," she said, smiling at them warmly. "I'm sure he has places to be."

The kids all voiced their displeasure with that statement, but the woman clapped her hands and the kids all fell back in line.

"Don't worry, everyone," Mourdock said. "I'll stop by soon and play with all of you."

"Promise?" asked Relli.

"Cross my heart," Mourdock replied as he traced an "X" over his chest with his finger and mussed the little girl's hair.

The kids all waved good-bye to him as they continued down the hallway. The older woman in the white robes nodded her head toward Mourdock. "That's very kind of you, Paragon Skyborn," she said. "The children do so love your visits."

"It's my pleasure, Master Fareia," Mourdock replied. "I also enjoy them a great deal."

"Off to the celebration, I assume?" Master Fareia asked.

Mourdock chuckled. "Indeed I am. My friend Jack will be participating in the new season. I wanted him to experience the party, as well."

Master Fareia smiled at Jack. "Ah, to be young again," she said wistfully. "I'm sure you'll enjoy yourself. The new season celebrations are always quite fun."

After Master Fareia had left, Jack began to follow Mourdock once more. "So..." Jack said as they walked, "you're a celebrity here, too, huh?"

"In a manner of speaking, I guess," Mourdock replied. "Obviously, some people want to buddy up to me because I'm the future Emperor. Others have heard of my prowess as a Paragon and want to learn from me."

"And those kids?"

"Those are what we call Boarders. They spend most of their childhood living here at the Conclave. They usually have some gifts which make it easier for them to eventually become Paragons, so they're given special tutors and training until such time as they're ready to become Initiates."

"I take it you're one of those special tutors?"

"I am, when I'm around," Mourdock replied. "I, too, was a Boarder, way back when. It always meant a lot to me when real Paragons came by and taught us things, so I make it a point to give back when I can."

"That must have been tough, being a kid here with the time constriction and everything," Jack said. "Does that mean you were, like, a hundred years old by the time you turned ten?"

Mourdock laughed at that. "Fortunately, no," he replied. "No one really knows why, but the time constriction doesn't seem to have the same effect on children as it does on those of us who've reached puberty. Their mental states stay pretty consistent with the regular time in the prime universe. But the older one gets, the more of an impact the time constriction has. Some think the Ancients designed the Conclave this way on purpose, to allow young people who enter it to retain their childhood. The theory holds that children don't need as much help freeing their minds as older people do."

Jack nodded. "I guess that makes sense," he said as they approached a set of stairs and began to ascend them. After a couple of flights, Jack was starting to become winded. Mourdock, of course, didn't look fazed in the slightest. "Uh… is it much further?" Jack asked, his legs aching.

"Just one more level," Mourdock reassured him.

"So what's a Paragon party like?" Jack asked as they finally reached the floor to which they'd been travelling. "Does everyone sit around in a circle and meditate? Do they play 'truth or dare' with their manifestation powers? Is there cake?"

Mourdock gave Jack a curious look. "Have you never been to a school function before, Jack?"

"Not really. I was going to go to my school's Homecoming dance back on Earth, but… you know."

Mourdock gave Jack a knowing smile as they approached a large stone door. "Well, let's just say, Paragons know how to have a good time."

Mourdock placed his hand on the door, which rumbled open. As Jack stepped inside, he looked around wide-eyed. The activity chamber had to have been five stories tall. Multicolored orbs hovered throughout the room, flashing brightly as tiny, soundless fireworks flared, sprinkling the air with beautiful sparks. Strobe lights flashed randomly, turning different parts of the room different colors.

Hundreds of students were packed into the chamber. Some were milling about, chit-chatting. Some were dancing in front of a stage where students in green robes were waving their hands, dance music emanating from them. A layer of water hovered in the air, with people leaping up into it from the floor and others diving down into it from diving boards erected above it. Some kids were chasing each other around on jetpacks, while others were playing drinking games.

"Whoa…" said Jack, completely overwhelmed by what he saw.

"See?" Mourdock said, patting Jack on the back. "Told you."

Jack's gaze drifted to the stage where the students in the green robes were waving their hands in the air, like they were trying to hit something in front of them to the beat of the music. "What's going on up there?" Jack asked.

"Those are musicians from the Ground Ring," Mourdock said.

"But they don't have any instruments."

"That's because they're practicing a discipline called ethermincy," Mourdock explained. "It's the manipulation of air to create sound without instruments."

"Awesome!" Jack said, completely blown away by how good the music was. Indeed, the entire atmosphere had a wild, crazy, chaotic feel to it, almost like depictions of college parties in the funny movies he used to watch back home after his mother went to sleep.

A giant pig-like Gourvine[28] sniffed at Jack and grunted as it walked by. To the side, two Karkovians were arm wrestling each other with all six of their arms as a group of spectators cheered them on. Female Oreans[29] were on scattered stages around the room, making impassioned speeches. And Jack swore he saw someone get thrown through the air from a catapult.

Off to the side of the room were stacks of large wooden barrels, sporting small spouts at their bases. Groups of students were milling around them, filling mugs with the barrels' contents. In a giant barrel at the center of it all was an odd creature, which jutted up from the open top of the container. Its skin was a bubbly, frothy mess, and it had a long beak. On top of its head sat two dome shaped eyes with irises that seemed to jiggle around haphazardly as the creature

---

[28] Gourvines are large aliens that resemble pigs, and are known for their ability to regenerate tissue and eat almost anything.
[29] Oreans are humanoid aliens with acute vision who primarily communicate with body language. They also have garish taste in fashion.

moved and spoke. All-in-all, Jack thought it looked an awful lot like a massive sock puppet.

"What the heck is that?" Jack asked.

"Oh, that's Belcher, the Conclave's master brewer," Mourdock said. "He's the king of the yeasts."

"King of the what?"

"Yeasts," Mourdock said. "You know, the fungi that are used to make things like beer and bread?"

"Yeasts have a king?"

"According to Belcher, they do," Mourdock said with a shrug. "Apparently he's been ruling over the yeasts here at the Conclave for over seven thousand years. Gets them to produce all types of crazy beverages you can't get in the prime universe. Wanna try some?"

"Um, depends," said Jack. "They're not gonna make me black out and act like a jerk, are they?"

Mourdock laughed at that. "Don't worry, I'll babysit you," he said, putting his arm around Jack and guiding him toward the crazy yeast King. "Hail, King Belcher, Lord of the yeasts!" Mourdock said, waving as they approached.

"Well met, Paragon Skyborn!" King Belcher replied, his voice high-pitched and bubbly. "'Tis been a Gonza's age since I last saw ye!"

"Well, I have returned, good King," Mourdock said. "Allow me to introduce my compatriot, Earthman Jack Finnegan."

Jack waved at King Belcher. "S'up?" he said.

King Belcher loudly burped at Jack, spraying froth and foam all over him and Mourdock, the expulsion of powerful air lasting an uncomfortably long time. "Well met, Earthman!" King Belcher said after the burp had subsided. "What can I get thee to quench thy thirst?"

"Uh… I dunno," said Jack as he brushed off the foam King Belcher had sprayed on him. "What do you have?"

"Ah! We have ourselves a fine selection of quality beverages! A libation to suit all types of revelry!" replied King Belcher, before burping once more. "Do ye fancy yourself a warrior, Earthman?"

"A warrior?" asked Jack. "Well… I've fought people before…"

"Then perhaps you'd like to partake in some of our Belligerence Beer!" said King Belcher as he gestured toward a large wooden keg with red markings on it. "'Tis guaranteed to start all manner of roughhousing!"

Jack turned to see two students in orange robes standing in front of the keg, each one swaying drunkenly as the Belligerence Beer sloshed from their cups.

"Whaddid ya call me?" slurred one of the students.

"I called ya a son of a motherless goat!" replied the other one.

"I don't even know what that means!"

"ME NEITHER!"

At that, the two students tackled each other and began rolling on the floor, punching each other's lights out. Jack frowned. "Um... not really into the roughhousing," he said.

"Then mayhaps ye would care for some of our Amorous Ale?" suggested King Belcher, referring to a wooden keg with pink markings on it. The keg was surrounded by students who were all laughing and shouting and making out.

"I love you, man!" cried one student.

"I love you, too!" replied another.

"I LOVE EVERYONE!" shouted a female Orean before the whole group erupted in a unanimous "WOOOOOOO!"

"And if ye aren't in a mood for revelry, we also have our Melancholy Malt, for those who prefer a more somber feeling," said King Belcher, referring to another keg with black markings on it. All the students drinking from that keg looked depressed, angry, or were simply weeping quietly as they drank.

"No one loves me..." muttered one female student as she hiccupped between sobs. "I'm going to die alone!"

"Life is pain!" cried another student. "Anyone who says otherwise is just trying to sell you something!"

"Jeez," muttered Jack. "Don't you have anything less... I don't know... emotional?"

"Ah! If ye are simply looking for a fine beverage of which to partake, then ye can do no better than our patented 'Mere Mead!" King Belcher said as he gestured to a keg with blue markings on it.

"What the heck is 'Mere Mead?" asked Jack, just as an extremely fat student waddled up from the keg, drinking a mug of the aforementioned mead.

"HEY! HEY YOU!" shouted the fat student, pointing at Jack.

"What?" Jack asked.

The fat student then motioned for him to come closer. "C'mere..." he slurred, before passing out and falling on his face. Indeed, it seemed everyone who was drinking 'Mere Mead was simply stumbling around, haphazardly telling anyone closeby to "c'mere" and gesturing with their fingers for them to approach.

Jack looked at the scene before him, not sure what to think. Mourdock laughed. "King Belcher," he said, "would thou be so kind as to serve us two Backward Brews, if it pleases you."

"It would please me greatly!" King Belcher said, before burping loudly.

A nearby keg with green markings produced two robotic hands from its top, holding out mugs of frothy liquid toward Mourdock who took them and raised them in salute to King Belcher. "My thanks, good King!" Mourdock said.

"Go forth and be libatious!" King Belcher replied, before burping once again.

Jack looked at the mug curiously as Mourdock handed it to him. "And what's this do?" Jack asked, almost afraid to hear the answer.

"Relax," said Mourdock with a chuckle. "It's Backward Brew. If you drink too much of any of the other drinks, a cup of this will sober you up and return you to the way you were before you started drinking. Beyond that, it's actually quite tasty." Mourdock then clinked his mug against Jack's. "Cheers!" he said, before taking a swig.

Jack took a tentative sip of his drink. The froth on top clung to his lip, and the liquid had a rich, sweet, butterscotch taste to it. Overall, Jack thought it was actually quite delicious! And oddly enough, the more he drank, the more normal he began to feel. The odd sensation he'd been experiencing since awakening from his fight with Stalker Crux slowly started to subside. Before long, Jack found himself happily drinking the concoction as he followed Mourdock through the commotion of the celebration.

Jack and Mourdock skirted the dance floor where lots of students were showing off their dance moves, and Oreans were having conversations. Suddenly, someone from the dance floor bumped into Jack, causing him to stumble into an exceptionally tall and muscular woman who was standing nearby with other similarly tall and muscular women. The woman turned, gazing at Jack with a disapproving sneer, her stern face framed by her long dark hair.

"Watch where you're going, patriarchal-man-oppressor!" the woman hissed.

"Sorry," Jack replied, stunned at the woman's hostility. "I didn't mean to bump you."

"What do you mean 'bump you'?" asked another of the muscular women, stepping forward combatively. "We do not accept your patronizing and objectifying innuendo, tiny man-mongrel!"

"We do not need unwanted romantic attention from your kind to be happy!" stressed another, pushing Jack back from them. "Pack up your misogyny and take a hike, chauvinist swine!"

"WE ARE NOT INTERESTED IN YOUR REPRODUCTIVE ORGANS!" shouted another, angrily.

Jack's eyes went wide, not quite sure what to do as the massive women began to crowd around him. Luckily, Mourdock stepped in between him and the scary females before things escalated further. "Forgive my friend, he has not yet learned all men are awful," Mourdock said. "Girls rule!"

"GIRLS RULE!" the women all replied, holding up their fists in acknowledgement.

"Be sure to teach this one to know his place!" said the woman Jack had originally bumped into, pointing to him as Mourdock began ushering him away. "Disrespecting someone because of their gender will not be tolerated! MEN SUCK!"

"Men suck!" called back Mourdock, before stifling a laugh.

"Dude... what the slap was that???" asked Jack when they were safely away. "I was afraid those chicks were going to beat me down!"

"They probably were," Mourdock replied. "You have to be careful around Femezons. In their culture, men are rude and obnoxious bullies they only put up with so they can propagate their species."

"Femezons, eh?" muttered Jack. "What do they call their men? Menezons?"

"Oh, so you're familiar with them."

Jack raised his eyebrows. "Dude, I think the universe just entered a whole new level of ridiculous."

Mourdock chuckled. "Trust me, Jack, you haven't seen anything yet."

Just then, a voice cried out: "Ohmigosh! It's Mourdock Skyborn!"

Before Jack knew it, a throng of students rushed forward, all greeting Mourdock, shaking his hand, and patting him on the back. While Mourdock entertained his adoring fans, Jack found himself pushed off to the side. He sighed. The party was indeed amazing, but he was feeling very out of place. Much like on Omnicron, everything just seemed so strange to him. He didn't feel like he belonged at the party, let alone at the Conclave. Jack took the opportunity to slink off to a far wall, nursing his drink as he watched everyone else have a blast.

"A bit overwhelming, huh?" came a voice.

Jack turned and saw someone standing next to him. His pointy ears gave away that he was a Regal, but he had dark hair, a beard, and was very much overweight. He, too, seemed to be nursing a mug of Backward Brew. As far as Jack could tell, the man appeared to be at least ten years older than he was.

"Yeah, you could say that," replied Jack. "Never been to a party with a floating swimming pool before."

The man nodded. "Just wait," he said. "Eventually, someone is going to get drunk enough to fly into one of the people keeping the pool's gravity at zero, and it's going to collapse and drench everyone on the dance floor."

Jack laughed at that. "Well, that's one reason not to leave early, I guess," he said, before extending his hand. "I'm Jack."

The older man shook Jack's hand. "I know," he said with a smile. "You're only one of the most famous people in the galaxy right now."

"Oh, uh… don't believe everything you hear," Jack replied.

"Well, considering you're palling around with the man whose fiancée you're accused of kidnapping, I'm guessing the part about being a criminal isn't exactly true?"

Jack smiled. "Not exactly, no."

"Must be one heck of a story," the man said. "I'd love to hear about what really happened, sometime. You know, after I'm done partying down." The man jiggled his body in a mimicry of dancing that was so goofy, Jack had to laugh. "Sorry, that was embarrassing," the man said. "I'm not very good in social situations, in case you haven't guessed."

"You seem fine to me," Jack replied. "At least, you know, you haven't tried to kill, capture, or patronize me yet. That's always a plus."

"Well, the night is still young," the man joked.

Jack chuckled at that. Whoever this guy was, he seemed cool. Jack guessed he had to be an instructor or something, just based upon his age and his manner. "I never got your name," Jack said.

"Oh! Right," the man said, looking embarrassed. "Apologies, I didn't think to introduce myself when you did. My name's—"

"Screw Up!" shouted a voice.

Jack looked toward the source of the yelling and saw three guys walking toward them, led by a tall, blonde, muscular meathead with a stupid looking grin on his face. "Screw Up! That you?" the meathead said. "You back again?"

"Name's Krupp," the man said after a roll of his eyes. "Scofeld Krupp. But some people around here call me—"

"Yeah, yeah, I got it," Jack said as the group of men walked up.

The group's leader gave Krupp a slap to his belly, causing Krupp to flinch. "What's this make, Screw Up? Eight times? Nine? What's the count?"

Krupp frowned. "Ten," he muttered.

"Great balls of gravity!" the meathead cried. "Ten seasons? When ya gonna face it, compatriot? You just don't have what it takes to be a Paragon."

One of the meathead's companions with extremely muscular arms eyed Jack and then tapped his friend's shoulder. "Hey, Tannyn," he said. "It's the Earthman."

Tannyn turned his attention from Krupp and looked at Jack as if seeing him for the first time. "Well, well, look at that," he said, eyeing Jack up and down. "So the rumors of you being here were true. Funny, I thought you'd be taller."

"Thinking doesn't seem to be your strong suit," Jack replied.

Krupp's eyes went wide at that, and Tannyn's companions both raised their eyebrows. But rather than seem insulted, Tannyn simply laughed and slapped Jack on the chest. "Thinking's not my strong suit! Good one!" he said. "No wonder you're a Hero of the Empire! Bet you have witty things to say to bad guys before you vanquish them, too. Am I right?"

"Uh…"

"Tell me what you think about this one," Tannyn said as he slung his arm around Jack's shoulder and started leading him away from Krupp. "Right before I fight my first Deathlord, I'm going to say this: 'I hear you can't die. But by the time I'm done with you, you'll wish you could!' Eh? That's good, right?"

"I guess," Jack replied, jealous he hadn't thought of that one first.

"If you liked that, just wait – I got a million of them," Tannyn said. "Name's Tannyn, by the way. Tannyn of Legacy Hillvalley. These here are my friends, Gunshow and Headbasher."

Jack looked at Tannyn's two companions, curiously. "Your names are really Gunshow and Headbasher?"

"Nah, that's just what I call them," Tannyn said, answering for his friends. "Headbasher likes to bash things with his head. I swear, his noggin' must be made of metal because he can hit anything with it. And Gunshow has some mighty fine guns on him. Show him, Gunshow."

Gunshow then flexed his incredibly well-defined and muscular arms.

"Pew! Pew!" Tannyn said as he mimicked shooting off lasers with his pointer fingers at Gunshow's arms before laughing like it was the funniest thing ever. "See what I mean?"

"I do," replied Jack. "Very creative names."

"I know, I came up with them myself," Tannyn said, snapping his fingers toward Headbasher who handed him a cigarette, which Tannyn took a puff of before offering it to Jack. "Dreamleaf?" he asked.

"No thanks," Jack said, remembering what happened last time he'd smoked Dreamleaf[30].

Tannyn shrugged before handing the Dreamleaf cigarette off to Gunshow. "Listen, Hero," he said, squeezing Jack's shoulder. "This may be my first season as an Initiate, but I was a Boarder here at the Conclave for a long time, so I know a thing or two about how stuff works around this place. Let me give you some advice... pick your friends carefully."

"What's that supposed to mean?" Jack asked.

"I'm just saying," Tannyn replied, "if you hang out with losers, you're going to be a loser. Losers drag you down. Know what I mean? Like Screw Up back there. Did you know this is his tenth time trying to train as a Paragon?"

"So?"

"So?" replied Tannyn, surprised Jack didn't think anything of that little fact. "That fat sack of failure has washed out nine times! And the only reason the

---

[30] Dreamleaf is a plant that alters brainwaves to mimic REM sleep while allowing the users to remain conscious, letting them perform activities without the need to sleep.

Order of Peers keeps allowing him to return is because on his first attempt, he somehow managed to pass the Manifestation exam, only to be kicked out of Fire Ring almost immediately after. Since then, he's failed the Manifestation exam every single time he's come back! I mean, how do you just forget how to manifest stuff? So I ask you – is that really the type of guy you want to hang around with?"

"As opposed to who?" Jack asked. "You?"

Tannyn smiled and patted Jack on the cheek. "That's right, Hero. Me. You think Mourdock Skyborn is a great Paragon? Just you wait. I'm going to be the greatest warrior to ever come out of the Conclave. I've been training for this my whole life, and if you stick with me, you'll be a winner, too."

"I think I've done pretty well on my own so far."

Tannyn shrugged. "If you say so. But if you're planning to train in Fire Ring, you gotta know there's no room for failure. You wash out there, you're banned from further training until the next season… and that's only if you can get past the Manifestation exam." Tannyn held out his hand and manifested a mug of beer, chugging its contents before tossing the mug away. "After all, if you can't pass Manifestation, you just don't have what it takes."

Tannyn gave Jack a hard slap on the back, and then motioned for his friends to follow him toward the dance floor.

"See you tomorrow, Hero!" Tannyn said to him as he walked away. "Good luck at the Assignment Ritual! Fingers crossed you don't end up like your new buddy and get placed in the Unlikelies! Be a shame for a Hero of the Empire to wash out so early!"

Tannyn and his goons laughed as they disappeared into the crowd on the dance floor. But before he completely lost sight of Tannyn, Jack saw him manifest a ball, which he proceeded to throw directly at one of the students who was maintaining the gravity of the pool. The ball hit the student in the head, and immediately, the part of the pool directly above Jack fell, drenching him and everyone around him.

Jack stood there, dripping wet and none too happy.

"Jack?" came Mourdock's voice. Jack turned to see Mourdock – completely dry, of course – looking at him, concerned. "You okay?" he asked.

Jack sighed. "Yeah, just making new friends," he replied.

Jack turned and looked at the dance floor where Tannyn had grabbed a few girls and had begun to dance obnoxiously.

And new enemies, he thought, bitterly.

CHAPTER ✹ 27

For once, Jack had awakened without feeling like complete crud. Though the bizarre feeling he'd been experiencing was still with him, it wasn't as noticeable as it had been. Jack suspected that may have had something to do with the Backward Brew he'd drunk the night before, but he also held out hope that maybe he was healing and that strange feeling would soon go away.

Paragon Pennywise had stopped in to check on Jack and to bring him some fresh clothes, which essentially amounted to a drab, grey jumpsuit that apparently all the Initiates wore until they chose their specialization.

"So, what's this 'Assignment Ritual' all about?" Jack asked as he changed clothes.

"It's a system that was devised once the Conclave began accepting large groups of students for training," Pennywise explained. "It's essentially a way to group students based on their aptitude so that they can be properly trained. More naturally gifted students are given less rigorous classes, while those less predisposed are given more intensive ones to try and bring everyone to the minimum skill level required to advance."

"I see," said Jack. "And how do you guys determine that type of thing? Is there a test we have to take or something?"

"In a manner of speaking," Pennywise responded. "You're analyzed by the evaluation crystals, and they will place you into the group they feel you best belong."

Jack raised an eyebrow. "Evaluation crystals?"

Pennywise chuckled. "Do not worry. When the time comes, you'll simply have to stand there and the crystals will do all the work."

"And what if… you know… the crystals decide I don't have what it takes to be a Paragon?"

"It's important to remember, Jack, that no one can decide what you are capable of, other than you," Pennywise said, reassuringly. "The assignment ritual is simply about assigning you to a program that will increase the likelihood of unlocking your potential. Nothing more."

"Well, I heard that if you fail the Manifestation exam, that's it. You're expelled."

Pennywise nodded. "Expelled maybe isn't the best way to describe it," he said. "Freeing one's mind is a very difficult process, Jack. Not everyone is able to accomplish such a feat – even those who may have an aptitude for doing so. If, after all the training we provide, students can still not achieve the basic cornerstone of what it means to be a Paragon, they are not permitted to proceed further as a way to ensure those with the ability to free their minds get the proper attention. Paragons are a rare breed, you see, and those who choose to stay in the Conclave and train others are rarer still. Thus, the system that is in place is meant to get the most out of the trainers so that more students can advance. But just because one fails the Manifestation exam does not mean the Initiate can never attempt to come back. After all, students can continue their training outside the Conclave."

"Yeah, but what are the odds of learning that type of thing without all the benefits the Conclave gives you?"

Pennywise sighed. "Admittedly, not very good. It may take most of one's life to unlock such abilities."

"So if you fail, you're basically out of luck."

"Try not to think of it like that," Pennywise said, attempting to be reassuring. "There are many people who have left the Conclave, unable to train as a Paragon, who have gone on to do great things."

Jack frowned. "Yeah, it's just... I really want to be like Shepherd, you know? I need to be able to fight and protect people and be a superhero, like he was."

Pennywise smiled with understanding and gave Jack a pat on the shoulder. "May I let you in on a little secret, Jack?" he asked. Jack nodded. Pennywise leaned down and whispered in Jack's ear. "Shepherd was a superhero, long before he had superpowers."

Jack smiled at that. "You're saying it's who he was that made him great, not what he could do."

"Exactly."

"But the superpowers helped."

Pennywise laughed at that. "You should get going," he said. "The ritual will be starting soon."

Jack sighed. Despite the Paragon's reassurances, he was still incredibly nervous as he made his way toward the Crystal Concourse. For some reason, he'd allowed that Tannyn jerk to get in his head, and now he was paranoid about something bad happening at the ceremony.

When Jack finally arrived, lots of students had already assembled in the open area before the arch leading to the platform known as the Crystal Tier, which contained large outgrowths of crystal pillars around its edges. Masters Highclaw, Savage, GorJiro, and Hodapp were all standing on the elevated area under the arch, chit-chatting with one another as the students continued to file in from around the temple.

Jack didn't exactly know what to do, so he simply waded through the hundreds of students who were coalescing, waiting for the ceremony to begin. Some of them looked just as nervous and confused as he felt – which didn't exactly make him feel any better. To make things worse, he didn't recognize any faces from the night before, and Mourdock, his only friend, was nowhere to be seen. This made Jack feel very alone and extremely out of place.

"Hey Jack," came a voice.

Jack turned and saw Krupp nearby, waving at him. Though he didn't know the guy all that well, it was a relief to see someone with whom he was at least familiar. "Oh, hey dude!" Jack said. "Sorry I disappeared on you last night. After dealing with that Tannyn guy, I didn't really feel much like mingling."

"Don't worry about it," Krupp said, with a dismissive wave of his hand. "I've had to deal with Tannyn every time I've come here. I know what an obnoxious little snot he can be."

Jack chuckled at that. "Yeah, he didn't exactly make a great first impression."

"Just wait. Each subsequent impression only gets worse."

"Yet another thing to look forward to," Jack said dryly. "His friends seemed like real tools, too. Does the Hillvalley system just specialize in breeding dumb meatheads or something?"

"Actually, it's known for breeding soldiers and military heroes."

"For real?" Jack asked, surprised by Krupp's answer.

"Oh, yeah. See, the Hillvalley system is located really close to the Visini border," Krupp explained. "It was a major area of conflict during the Great Border War. Almost everyone in Tannyn's Legacy has a military background, and a great number of citizens from that system enter into the Imperial Army. They place a great deal of importance on being a warrior there."

"Doesn't give him the right to be a jerk," Jack stated.

"I'm not trying to defend him. But part of freeing one's mind is understanding and accepting the differences between people. Knowing where Tannyn comes from may help you to deal with him going forward."

"I know how to deal with bullies," Jack said. "You stand up to them. If you don't, they just get worse and worse."

"Well, if you end up going into the Fire Ring, you're going to get ample opportunity to stand up to the guy."

Jack smiled at that. "Yeah, that's my plan. I want to train to be a warrior. What about you? What do you plan on specializing in?"

"The same," Krupp said. "Fire Ring for me, too."

"Really?"

Krupp chuckled. "What? Think I'm too old and fat to be a warrior?"

"No, no, it's just… you don't strike me as the type."

Krupp frowned at that. "Well, you wouldn't be the first to say such a thing."

"I'm sorry, I didn't mean I don't think you could do it," Jack explained. "And who cares what other people think, anyway? You do what you want to. More power to ya."

Krupp nodded. "That's always been my philosophy. That's why I keep coming back, even though everyone tells me I'm a lost cause. I just know I have it within me to be a Paragon."

"Yeah, I heard you passed the Manifestation exam once."

Krupp sighed, wistfully. "Yes, a long time ago. I was able to manifest a single drop of water. It wasn't much, but it was enough to get me through. Unfortunately, that seemed to be the only time in my life I've been able to manifest anything. Part of me still wonders if it weren't just some sweat from my palms or something."

"Well, you know what they say," Jack said, encouragingly. "Tenth time's the charm!"

Krupp laughed. "Let's hope what they say is right. I'm getting awfully tired of my Unlikely status."

"Yeah, I heard about that from Tannyn last night," Jack said. "What's it mean?"

"Didn't anyone explain to you how the Assignment Ritual works?"

"Just that it's about putting people into categories to figure out how to best train them."

Krupp snorted at that. "I guess that's the official stance, yeah. But to the Initiates, it's just a way to tell who's most likely to become a Paragon and who isn't."

"I'm not sure I understand."

"There are three groups Initiates are sorted into," Krupp explained. "You have The Gifted, who are the ones most likely to free their minds and progress to become Paragons. Then, you have The Normals, who have a fifty-fifty chance of succeeding. And lastly, you have The Unlikelies. They're the ones with the least chance of success. If you're placed into The Unlikelies, it essentially means you have no shot of completing your training. In fact, about 80% of those sorted into that group just withdraw immediately and go back home."

"You mean, they just give up? They don't even try?"

Krupp shrugged. "Some try to prove they have what it takes, like me, for instance. But 99% of the time, the crystals are correct. Those in The Unlikelies are thought to be just wasting everyone's time, including their own."

"But that can change, right?" Jack asked. "Just because you're an Unlikely doesn't mean you can't become a Paragon."

"Theoretically, yes. But it's extremely rare for Initiates placed in the Unlikely group to do so. I still hold out hope that this season will be different. But then again, I'm always hoping that."

Jack nodded. "Well, I'm rooting for you, dude. I hope it's different for you this time around."

"Thanks, I appreciate that," responded Krupp. "If the stories I've heard about you are true, then you should get into The Gifted group, easily."

"Stories?" asked Jack. "What kind of stories have you heard?"

"Oh, you know... you fought a Deathlord Supreme single-handedly, you have a magic spaceship, you battled the Royal Vanguard, you outflew a Starkeeper ambush... the usual."

Jack chuckled at that. "Nothing about downloading an Ancient language database into my brain, absorbing the energy from a Great Seal, entering into Equilibrium, or ripping off part of my soul?"

Krupp raised his eyebrows. "Uh… what?"

"Nothing," Jack replied. "Just that, now that you mention it, I guess I shouldn't have been worrying so much about getting accepted."

A melodic ringing echoed throughout the concourse, quieting the noise of the chatter from the students. They all turned their attention toward the raised area where Master Highclaw stood beneath the engraved arch. When everyone had fallen silent, Master Highclaw spread his arms and started to speak.

"Welcome to the Conclave," he began. "This is a place of learning. A place of discovery. A place where you can become the person you've always wanted to be. As Paragons, our motto is that anything is possible. But the Conclave has its own motto. It is the motto Emperor Arcturus I developed when he originally discovered this sacred place, thousands of years ago. And that motto is '*All Things. No Teachers.*' Though we offer you guidance, instruction, and counselling when necessary, here at the Conclave you are your own teacher. You learn what you want, at your own pace. The path to a Free Mind is different for everyone, and it will be up to you to discover yours. There will be help when you need it, but no one will ever be able to help you more than yourself. You must forget your old prejudices. You must shed your old limitations. You must unlearn what you have already learned. Only then will you be able to free your mind. And this is the place where you will be able to do that."

Highclaw looked out over the gathered students of all shapes, sizes, and races, his golden eyes seeming to sparkle.

"Today, we partake in an old and honored ceremonial exercise," he continued. "One by one, you will be called and placed into chapters that will assist us in helping to guide you in your training to free your mind. These chapters are meant to help tailor your training to maximize your potential going forward. Once you've proven you have what it takes to open your mind to the possibilities of the universe, you will be admitted as a full Initiate and will begin training to become a Paragon. The road ahead will be difficult. Some would even say it is impossible. But things are only impossible until they are done. And here, in this sacred place… *anything* is possible."

Master Highclaw then gave the stage over to Master Savage. "When your name is called, please walk into the circle at the center of the Crystal Tier and stay there until your chapter is assigned to you," he said, his matter-of-fact tone noticeably different from Highclaw's inspirational one. "You will be placed in either chapter Arcturus, chapter Regalius, or chapter Tantalis. When your chapter is assigned, please move to the appropriate tier and join those who have also been sorted into your chapter. Let us begin."

As Master Savage began calling names to enter the Crystal Tier, Krupp leaned over to Jack. "Chapter Arcturus is where The Gifted are sorted into," he whispered. "Chapter Regalius is for The Normals. Tantalis is where you don't want to end up."

Jack nodded. "I've heard of Arcturus before, but I don't recognize the others."

"They were early Emperors," Krupp explained. "Regalius was Arcturus's son. He was the one who united Regalus Prime after his father had conquered all of it. And Tantalis was the first Emperor to unlock the portgates, which allowed travel to distant worlds, setting the stage for the Age of Conquest."

"So... why are the Unlikelies sorted into his chapter?"

Krupp shrugged. "Not really sure. Tantalis is known as 'The Explorer Emperor' because he personally led the first expeditions through the portgate on Regalus Prime. He was often the first to set foot on planets no one had ever known about. Maybe those who are placed in his chapter are put there because they need to explore their potential more? I don't really know. I've never bothered to ask why the chapters are named what they are."

Jack then heard Tannyn's named called. He watched as the meathead bounded up the stairs to the Crystal Tier, waving at his friends with confidence as he did so. He passed under the arch and moved into the circle that was inlaid in the floor of the tier. The large, multicolored crystals around him lit up shortly after he entered the ring, and eventually they all changed to a warm, golden color.

"Chapter Arcturus," Master Savage declared.

Tannyn clapped his hands and let out a victorious cheer. His friends in the crowd cheered along with him as he made his way to the tier where others who'd been sorted into his chapter were waiting to greet him. Jack frowned.

"Well, he's certainly gifted at being a jerk," he said.

Krupp chuckled. "Boarders always have an unfair advantage when it comes to training to be Paragons," he said. "Growing up here in the Conclave, they see the kind of things that are possible. Their minds aren't usually set in their ways like the rest of us. Many of them are able to manifest things by the time they're eight or nine. I guess you could say that makes them a bit... cocky?"

"Mourdock isn't like that. He grew up here."

"You mean Mourdock Skyborn? Yeah, that guy is a Legend! He's the type of Paragon I'd like to be."

Jack looked at Krupp. "If you wanted to be a Paragon so badly, why didn't you ask your parents to let you be a Boarder?" Jack asked. "I'd think people would be lining up to have their kids become Paragons."

"Oh, there are lots of factors that go into being a Boarder," Krupp said. "You usually have to be in a Legacy, related to another Paragon, have some ties to the Ancients, or some other indication that you might be predisposed to freeing your mind. As for me, I didn't decide to become a Paragon until ten years ago."

"Why? What happened ten years ago?"

Krupp frowned. "Um... the Deathlords blew up Regalus Prime," he said.

"Oh, right..." Jack replied, feeling stupid. "Sorry. I forgot."

"It's okay. Before that I wanted to be a teacher. Never even thought of becoming a Paragon."

Jack smiled. "A teacher?"

"Yeah. Early childhood education. I always liked working with kids. My mother was a teacher, too. I guess I got that from her. I had just started at the Central Galactic University when she died, along with the rest of my family..."

Krupp trailed off, looking sad. Jack knew how he felt. "They all lived on Regalus Prime?" Jack asked.

Krupp nodded. "When I lost them, being a teacher wasn't enough for me anymore. I wanted to avenge them. I wanted to fight the Deathlords and make them pay for what they'd done. I've never been fit enough to join the military, but you don't need to be fit to be a Paragon. Here, at the Conclave, anything is possible – even a fat nerdy kid becoming a warrior. That's why I refuse to give up. I owe it to my family to fight for them. And this is the only way I know how to do that."

"Initiate Scofeld Krupp," Master Savage's voice boomed.

"This part always gives me a headache," Krupp muttered before smiling at Jack. "Wish me luck!"

"Good luck, man," Jack said as Krupp made his way through the crowd.

Jack watched as Krupp walked up to the Crystal Tier and entered the circle. He stood still as stone, his eyes shut in concentration as the large crystals which lined the outer edges of the tier all glowed.

Please, not Tantalis, Jack thought to himself. *Please, please, please!*

Then, all the crystals came to glow a deep red color.

"Chapter Tantalis," Master Savage declared.

Jack saw the look of disappointment on Krupp's face as the man let out a deep sigh, as though he'd been holding his breath the entire time. Jack felt really bad for him, especially after hearing his story. Krupp turned and began making his way toward the tier where others from Chapter Tantalis awaited. The sound of clapping could be heard from those in Chapter Arcturus, led by Tannyn.

"Screw Up!!!" they chanted as Krupp walked. "Screw Up! Screw Up! Screw Up!"

"Enough!" admonished Master Savage, his voice immediately putting an end to the chant. Though the chuckles of ridicule continued.

The sorting continued as Jack watched each Initiate enter into the ring of the Crystal Tier and be assigned to the chapter which best suited them. As the ceremony dragged on, Jack began to wonder when he'd be called as the crowd around him grew thinner and thinner. Finally, everyone's name had been called except Jack's, and he stood there alone as all those from each chapter looked down on him.

Master Savage gazed at Jack with a frown before finally saying, "Initiate Jack Finnegan."

Jack made his way up the stairs to the Crystal Tier, feeling awkward as everyone watched him. The large platform of the tier seemed so much bigger now that he was actually standing on it. He passed under the arch, walking to the center of the inlaid circle.

Jack looked around at the large crystals and the three branching tiers where the other Initiates all stood. *Okay, what now?* he thought.

Suddenly, Jack's surroundings descended into darkness, as though someone had shut off all the lights. Then, the circle beneath him glowed with brilliant illumination. Two hoops rose up from the circular inlay in the floor and began to spin around Jack, one of their edges always making contact with that of the other, a melodic hum emanating from where they touched.

A cavalcade of images played out before Jack's eyes, moving so fast that it gave him a headache. From what he was able to see, it was like he was looking at his memories as they were projected before him. He saw images of his mother. Images of Shepherd. Images of Anna. Images of his spaceship. The Earth exploding. Fighting Zarrod. Breaking the Great Seal on the Ghost Planet. Trying to rescue Anna from Verrutus.

Jack began to feel dizzy as the avalanche of information continued. He saw himself fighting Stalker Crux and then screaming in agony. He watched as Shanks healed him. He saw flashes of his father and some of Zarrod. Images of the grand majesty of the universe stretched out before him and pulled back until it became a mosaic of a single, great all-seeing eye…

Then it all disappeared.

Jack stood frozen, unable to move or talk. From the darkness in front of him, four large heads became illuminated, each one shifting to a different color. The first head had a beard; the second head was female; the third head was bald and fat; the fourth head had a pointy cranium and angular eyebrows.

"What have we here…" muttered the head with the beard. "Jack Finnegan, from Earth, eh? Well now, he's a curious one, isn't he?"

"I like him!" said the giant female head.

"Be quiet, ZeeZee. You like everyone," grumbled the big, bald, fatty head.

"I don't like you, TauTau," ZeeZee retorted. "My mother was right about you."

TauTau rolled his eyes. "This is the last time I date within the workplace," he muttered.

"His thoughts are so juvenile," complained the big pointy head.

"That's because he *is* a juvenile, GumGum," the bearded head said.

"Yes, BarBar, but he's even juvenile for a juvenile!" GumGum replied. "I like movies about ninjas and jokes about bodily functions as much as the next guy, but honestly, this is a tad much."

"And yet, despite all that, there is a great deal of maturity here," noted BarBar. "This one has seen much tragedy and known great loss. He has had to overcome significant hardship in his short time of existence."

"Perhaps that is why his aura is so chaotic," ZeeZee said. "His nature is that of a child, yet he has been forced to become more than that. The two aspects are in conflict with one another."

"We are not here to assess his nature. What of his Trinity?" inquired GumGum. "That is the true measure of a Paragon."

"Hmmm…" said TauTau, ponderously. "His body has potential, but his spirit is weak."

"His spirit is injured, not weak," corrected ZeeZee. "That can heal in time. There is a powerful strength in this one."

"Still, his mind is rather… odd."

"Yes," agreed GumGum. "I have never before seen so many images of pretty girls in swimwear and professional wrestlers performing sweet moves in the mind of one being before."

"That is not what I meant," said TauTau. "His mind should be simple and closed off, yet… it is as though it is getting help. Like a flower being forced to blossom before it is ready."

"His body has been altered, as well as his mind," said BarBar. "He is strongly connected to many other beings who are influencing him, but I cannot see who they are."

"I sense great potential in this one," said ZeeZee. "However, that sense comes and goes. He could be great, or he could be insignificant. It is hard to tell."

"Too many unknowns," stated BarBar. "The Void surrounds this one."

"Agreed," said TauTau.

"Agreed," said GumGum.

"Then we have reached a decision?" asked ZeeZee.

"We have…" replied BarBar.

"Chapter Tantalis," Master Savage declared.

Jack opened his eyes, not realizing they'd been closed. Everything was suddenly back to normal. He could move once more, but he felt disoriented. Jack stood still for a moment, not sure he'd heard the declaration correctly. Indeed, everyone watching from the other tiers seemed surprised as there was a moment of absolute silence before Jack started to hear people chuckling.

Jack looked around him and saw all the crystals were glowing a deep red color. He frowned, then started to make his way toward the appropriate tier. As he walked, he heard Tannyn shout.

"Hero of the Empire!"

There was some laughter before people began to chant "Go Hero, Go! Go Hero, Go! Go Hero, Go!"

Jack looked back toward Master Savage, expecting him to put an end to the chants like he had before. But Master Savage simply returned Jack's gaze stoically, not bothering to say anything. A feeling of embarrassment swept over Jack as he grimaced and continued to walk toward the awaiting Chapter Tantalis Initiates, the chant continuing to grow louder and louder.

This doesn't make any sense, Jack thought. *All the things I've been able to do... how can I be placed here?*

When Jack finally ascended the stairs to his tier, Krupp was there waiting for him, a sad smile on his face.

"Hey, Jack," he said. "Welcome to the Unlikelies."

CHAPTER ✺ 28

Amadeus sat at the head of the briefing table in the Emerald Tower war room, which was filled with the system's top military commanders. General Rustwave, a seasoned-looking Nakkota with light skin and greying hair, led the briefing as head of Redwater's System Defense Agency.

"Long-range sensor scans have given us a good idea of the 3rd fleet's blockade position, my Lord," Rustwave said as he referred to a representation of the system being projected holographicly over the briefing table. "As you can see here, the fleet is running its warships in two concurrent orbits around the x-axis and y-axis of the system, with constant fightercraft patrols on random schedules filling in the gaps. We've positioned our ships in a defensive posture in tune with the system's fourth planet, Rorfyn, and its orbital path around our sun. Because Rorfyn is so close to our asteroid belt, we're using that as a de facto boundary at which to hold the Starkeeper fleet at bay. So far, it's working. Drucker is keeping his forces on the outskirts of our system for now, giving us a neutral buffer zone in the vicinity of our fifth planet, Bulgar."

"I take it that buffer zone will not be lasting long?" Amadeus asked.

"If Drucker sticks to protocol, it will not," Rustwave admitted. "Right now, the system patrols are meant as a show of force, as well as a way for them to secure all hyperspace lanes into and out of the system. As we speak, the 3rd fleet is seeding our hyperspace territory with defense matrix platforms meant to cut us off from intergalactic travel. Once he has secured hyperspace, we believe Starkeeper Drucker will then begin directing his ships to specific settlements, working his way from the outside of the system inward, until he eventually meets with our fleet."

The holographic map changed to showcase what Rustwave was explaining, with the growing areas of the system eventually controlled by the 3rd fleet glowing in red.

"And what happens when the blockade eventually meets our fleet?" Amadeus asked.

"That, my Lord, is the real question," General Rustwave said, with a frown. "Scenario One is that Starkeeper Drucker respects the boundary we've established and halts his advance, opting to secure our outer colonies and wait us out. Scenario Two involves him ignoring our boundary and our ships, continuing to press forward with expanding the blockade, and essentially daring us to engage him and to be the first to fire."

"And Scenario Three?"

"He attacks."

Amadeus nodded, thinking that none of those scenarios sounded very appealing to him. "And if it should come down to a fight between our two fleets? How is that expected to play out?"

"Not in our favor, my Lord. Though our fleet is indeed formidable, it pales in comparison to the full strength of the 3rd Quadrant Fleet. They have bigger capital ships and far more starfighters than we do. In every simulation we've run, our fleet is eventually overwhelmed and defeated. There are things we can do to slow their advance and inflict a great deal of damage to them, but ultimately, we estimate our chances of a military victory to be extremely unlikely."

"That is not a very encouraging picture you've painted for me, General," Amadeus said gloomily.

"No, my Lord. It is not," he acknowledged. "There is a reason why the Regalus Empire is a force to be reckoned with in this galaxy and why it has emerged victorious in every major conflict it has entered into. Its military is the most advanced in the universe and its resources are practically limitless. Without support from other Legacy fleets... I'm afraid this is a fight we are not going to be able to win."

Before a sense of depression and dread could fully take hold over Amadeus, the door to the briefing room opened and Kimlee entered while texting on her datapad, her high heels clomping as she walked. "Hello, boys!" she said, barely looking up from her datapad's screen. "Sorry I'm late. I had to do my hair, and I must have gotten stopped for autographs, like, twenty times between here and the parking lot."

Amadeus rubbed his forehead in exasperation as Kimlee plopped herself down in a chair against the wall behind him, next to a disapproving Okotah. Kimlee was even chewing on a piece of gum, her lips smacking loudly as all her attention was focused on her datapad. The looks on the faces of the Generals in the room pretty much reflected what Amadeus was feeling.

"Gentlemen," Amadeus said to his advisors, "would you give me a moment, please?"

General Rustwave nodded his head. "Take whatever time you need, my Lord."

Amadeus then stood and moved to where Kimlee was sitting. Okotah got up and offered Amadeus his seat, which he accepted. "Would you put that away?" Amadeus asked, tersely.

"In a sec," Kimlee said, blowing a bubble with her gum that popped loudly. "I've got over a trillion followers who are going to love this selfie I took on the way here."

Amadeus reached out and put his hand over the datapad, forcing Kimlee to look at him. "This is a briefing about the defense of our star system," Amadeus said sternly. "I agreed to include you in these important meetings after my failure with the World Leaders because you said you wanted to help. I assumed that meant you'd know to show up on time."

Kimlee sighed and rolled her eyes. "Please, like I need to be on time to listen to the Generals tell us how borked we are," she said. "The schedule Okotah sent me said we're going to be going over our defensive options in a few minutes. I'm here for that."

Amadeus frowned. "Would you at least, for the love of Nameer, please try to act a little more professional? We need to be projecting strength right now, especially to our military leaders."

"*You* need to be projecting strength. I'm a woman who sings songs about partying that their kids listen to. There's no way I could act that would make these men think I'm strong."

"But there is a way you can act to have them further lower their opinion of you."

Kimlee chuckled. "Fine, I'll behave. I'll just be quietly badmouthing Uleeg Casgor to my adoring fans on the ultraweb while you guys plan your war. You won't even know I'm here."

Kimlee then removed Amadeus's hand from her datapad and went back to typing, blowing another bubble as she did so. Amadeus sighed and got back to his feet, taking his seat at the head of the briefing table once more. "General Rustwave," Amadeus said, "let us continue."

"We will now be looking at our defensive options against the Starkeeper fleet, my Lord," General Rustwave said once the rest of the advisors had reconvened. "Fortunately, your father had been preparing for a war with the Deathlords for some time, so we are not without options when it comes to a military engagement with Imperial forces. In fact, we have a great number of weapons we've been researching to assist us in fights against a superior foe."

Thank you, father, Amadeus thought to himself. "That's encouraging to hear, General. What do we have that may help us in our current situation?"

"To explain that, I've brought in the head of the System Defense Agency's Research and Development department to brief you," General Rustwave said. "He's been the one on the forefront of our weapons design and is best suited to answer any of your questions."

Rustwave nodded toward one of his aides who opened the door to the conference room and led in a rather skinny man with a bulbous bald head. He was wearing a white lab coat along with thick infoglasses and appeared quite anxious.

"Lord Evenstar, let me introduce Lead Technician Seqoia Saroquell," General Rustwave stated.

"Technician Saroquell," Amadeus said in greeting. "What do you have for us, today?"

Saroquell fidgeted uncomfortably, glancing nervously from Amadeus to the Generals and around the room. He looked as though he were trying to figure out something to say but didn't quite know how to say it.

"Is there a problem?" Amadeus asked.

"Please, forgive me, Lord Evenstar," technician Saroquell finally said. "It's just… I hesitate to brief you on our developments because of what you're planning for the weapons we've been designing."

"I will not have any plans for their use until I know what they are."

"Well, it's just that… your father intended these weapons to be used on Deathlords," Saroquell said, "not on other members of the Empire."

Amadeus frowned at the suggestion. "My father intended for these weapons to be used against our enemies, no matter what form they took."

"True, but I cannot, in good conscience, assist you in any way when it comes to harming members of the Imperial military. I know saying so may cost me my position, Lord Evenstar. However, I cannot be party to such a thing."

Amadeus had to resist the urge to sigh in exasperation. Walking the fine line between defending his system and an all-out war with the 3rd fleet was difficult enough without his top weapons technician fighting him on it.

"I can assure you, Mr. Saroquell, no one has any wish to harm citizens of the Empire, despite what you might have heard. In fact, we are here today to attempt to find options which will avert bloodshed, both of our people and the Empire's."

"What my brother is trying to say," said Kimlee, chiming in, "is that if you don't want us to hurt members of the Imperial military, then help us find a way not to. Because if we're forced to engage them, and you have done nothing to prevent such a thing, you're just as much at fault as we are."

Saroquell blinked at Kimlee, processing her words. Amadeus smiled. He may not have put it as bluntly as his sister had, but sometimes the direct approach was the preferable one. Saroquell cleared his throat. "Well… just as long as we all understand each other's positions," Saroquell said. "If our ultimate goal is the avoidance of bloodshed, then I have no issue briefing you on what we've been developing."

"Good," said Amadeus. "Now, if you please, tell me what we have."

Saroquell linked up his datapad to the conference table and projected a series of holographic images above it. The briefing was rather in-depth, covering experimental weapons and a bevy of other offensive tactical solutions. Some were of more practical use than others, but they were all quite impressive achievements and gave Amadeus some hope that, with their use, the picture General Rustwave had painted earlier might not be as dire as he had thought.

Finally, the holographic image of a large canister the size of a coffin appeared, slowly rotating as data about its specifications appeared underneath it. "Lastly, we have project 'Deep Sleep'," Saroquell said. "This is a high frequency electromagnetic pulse superbomb. It was developed to disable the entire Deathlord Planetkiller fleet should they have ever entered into the system."

Amadeus raised an eyebrow. "Did you say the *entire* fleet?" he asked.

Saroquell nodded. "It is an extremely potent and far-ranging EMP blast, my Lord. We figured with such a large enemy fleet, we needed some type of weapon that would be able to do maximum damage across its groupings. Even disabling a handful of the Planetkillers might prove to be useful, should it ever come to that. However, it's hard to say if its practical application matches its theoretical one. We have yet to test it."

"Why haven't you?" inquired Kimlee. "Seems to me such a powerful weapon would have extreme value in the event of an invasion."

"You are correct, Lady Evenstar," replied Saroquell. "However, there are certain issues with the prototype that made us question whether or not we should continue to develop it."

"What sort of issues?" asked Amadeus.

"Numerous ones, my Lord. There is a danger of the EMP blowing back on those using it, making it just as dangerous for us as it is for the enemy. And then, there's the question of delivery. I fear this bomb would never make it past the Deathlord fleet's point defense array."

"Point defense array?" asked Amadeus.

"Yes, my Lord."

Amadeus and Kimlee exchanged annoyed looks. "Mr. Saroquell," Kimlee said. "Forgive me, but I am not very well-versed in technical terminology. Perhaps you'd be so kind to explain this to me as though I were a child who has no knowledge whatsoever of space combat?"

Saroquell's eyes widened as he realized he'd been talking over the heads of his superiors. "Forgive me. I get too caught up in shoptalk sometimes," he said. "Large capital-sized spacecraft are often outfitted with numerous plasma cannons on all sides of the vessel. Though they can be used for offense, they can also be used for defense. When these cannons all fire at once, they create a radius around the ship which intercepts incoming missiles, bombs, projectiles, and enemy fightercraft. The terminology for such an array of weapons is known as 'point defense'. It makes it very difficult for anything to get within range to damage larger spacefaring vessels."

"So you're saying a bomb with as large of a blast radius as this one would never get close enough to inflict any damage?" asked Kimlee.

"In all likelihood, no," Saroquell responded. "Not to mention that the bomb takes time to charge up in order to reach its maximum radius. If it is somehow destroyed before it has time to complete its charge, it would be quite useless."

"So just charge it before you launch it," said Kimlee. "Seems like an easy enough solution to me."

"That is a wise suggestion, Lady Evenstar," replied Saroquell, nervously, "except that... well... once the bomb reaches full charge, it will automatically detonate. An EMP of this magnitude is not something that is easily contained. You cannot simply hold it back until it is ready to be released. Part of what makes the blast radius so large is that we are essentially overloading the core of the bomb to the point at which the electromagnetic field that is being generated can no longer be contained."

"Aren't most military vessels equipped with EMP shielding?" Amadeus asked.

"You are correct, Lord Evenstar. They are indeed. Specifically to prevent this type of attack from disabling them. However, the nature of the high frequency of this EMP allows us to bypass any shielding a vessel may have, at least temporarily. You see, the nature of this pulse sends out electromagnetic discharge on a frequency equal to that of gamma rays, which allows for ionization. This means certain materials affected by the blast will hold the charge of it, thus, facilitating a continued disruption of electrical systems, at least until the charge wears off."

"And if we were to use such a weapon against the Starkeeper fleet in order to subdue them? What would happen, exactly?"

"The ships would, indeed, be disabled. However, the pulse would only disrupt the core systems' shielding, not the actual systems themselves. Once the charge on the shielding would wear off, the systems would function normally once more. This would mean the ships would only be disabled for a short period of time, as opposed to permanently."

"How short a period?"

"Hard to say without testing, my Lord. It's very much dependent on how advanced the shielding is and how long it would possess the electromagnetic charge. Twenty minutes, maybe? Ten? I honestly couldn't tell you."

"Still, disabling a Starkeeper capital ship for ten to twenty minutes could be valuable, particularly if we need to mount an evacuation," Amadeus said. "I would like you to pursue this prototype of yours, technician Saroquell. We may have need of such a thing very soon."

Saroquell nodded. "I will do my best, my Lord. Now, if there is nothing further, that is the conclusion of my briefing."

After Saroquell was escorted out of the room, General Rustwave once again took command of the briefing. "Apologies for technician Saroquell, my Lord," he said. "Had I known he feels as passionately as he does about the situation, I'd have brought in someone better suited for this meeting."

"That is okay, General," Amadeus said. "He simply vocalized what I'm sure all of us are feeling right now. This is a difficult situation all around, and I certainly understand his frustration with it. Despite his objections, I found much of what technician Saroquell had to say very encouraging. If we can beef up our current forces with some of this new technology, we may be able to give ourselves a fighting chance should the 3rd fleet attack. How long would it take to retrofit our fleet with the new armaments technician Saroquell briefed us on?"

General Rustwave looked thoughtful for a moment. "The system's shipyard is well within our defensive zone. It can accommodate up to five ships at a time, so... best guess would be a week if we automate the process around the clock. That timeframe, of course, depends on what is to be installed."

"And what of hull enhancements? How long would those take?" Kimlee asked.

All eyes in the room turned toward her. General Rustwave gave her a curious look. "Hull enhancements, my Lady?"

Kimlee shrugged and ditzily twirled her hair with her finger. "Yeah. What if we wanted to increase our fleet's armor? How long would that take?"

"That would be most impractical, my Lady," General Rustwave replied. "It's far easier and more effective to increase the quality of a ship's shield generator—"

"Yeah, but I'm asking about a ship's hull," Kimlee responded. "How long?"

Amadeus frowned, then nodded toward the General to humor her. General Rustwave sighed. "Again, it depends on the type of armor that's to be installed. For the entire fleet, it could take months."

"And what if it were for just a handful of ships?"

"My Lady, why would we increase the armor of just a handful of ships?"

"Some is better than none, right?" Kimlee replied. "You said the shipyards can handle five ships at a time? So how long would it take to bulk up the hull of five?"

"Working around the clock, automated... probably a few days. Again, that depends—"

"On the material being installed, yes, I got that part," Kimlee said, before tilting her head to the side and smiling brightly. "Thank you, General."

"You're welcome, Lady Evenstar," General Rustwave said with a bow of his head. "Is there any particular reason you're suggesting we increase our fleet's armor?"

"What? Oh, no, I wasn't suggesting we actually do that," Kimlee said, off-handedly. "I mean, that's a stupid idea, right? Why increase armor when shield generators are so much more effective!"

The advisors all nodded, though it was obvious they all felt Kimlee had just wasted their time with such a silly line of questioning. Even Amadeus gave Kimlee a curious look, knowing his sister was smarter than to press such an insignificant issue at a system defense briefing.

"Yes, well... I would like an operational plan to outfit as many ships as possible to properly defend against the 3rd fleet," Amadeus stated.

"I'll have one put together for you right away, my Lord," replied General Rustwave with a salute.

"Thank you, gentlemen," Amadeus said, getting to his feet. "Let us continue to hope for the best as we prepare for the alternative."

As the briefing ended, Kimlee followed Amadeus out of the room, continuing to tap away at her datapad. Once they were clear of the Generals, Amadeus glared at his sister. "What was that about?" Amadeus demanded as they walked. "It was like you were playing up your stupidity for the cameras, only there weren't any cameras around."

"Maybe I'm just stupid."

"You and I both know that isn't true."

Kimlee raised an eyebrow at Amadeus. "Well, you're half right," she said, pointedly. "Now if you'll excuse me, I have to be getting back home. I'm scheduled to do an interview in a few hours."

"Why are you doing an interview? I thought you'd decided to stay out of the public eye."

"Wars are waged on many fronts, little brother," Kimlee said as she walked away. "While you worry about Starkeeper Drucker, I'm going to be applying a little pressure on our least favorite member of the Directory."

"Kimlee..." Amadeus started to object.

"Laters!" Kimlee cheered as she waved her hand without looking back.

Amadeus sighed and shook his head. "Great Observer," he said, looking upward, "please don't let me survive facing off with a Starkeeper only to have my sister be the one to kill me."

On the ride back to the Evenstar compound, Kimlee sat quietly, mulling over the information from the briefing. The spark of an idea had begun to gestate within her mind when the technician had been explaining the options they had available to them. That idea had begun to burn hotter and brighter the more Kimlee thought about it.

It's crazy enough that it just might work, she thought.

She had held back telling Amadeus about her meeting with Devorian, knowing that her little brother would not only throw a fit about her doing something so risky, but also because Kimlee knew he'd never trust Devorian or his offer. Amadeus was smart, but he wasn't nearly as cunning as he needed to be if they were going to win this fight. Her chat with Devorian had made Kimlee realize Redwater had stopped being a part of the Empire the moment Princess Anna had made her decree to abolish Legacy Evenstar. A fact that Amadeus had yet to accept.

This meant that Amadeus would never entertain any plan other than one which somehow prevented open rebellion. But Kimlee knew war was all but inevitable, and that in the end, they would either have to surrender or declare independence. Frankly, Kimlee would rather go down fighting than give up everything her family and her ancestors had worked for.

No, Amadeus isn't ready to hear this plan just yet, Kimlee decided. *But when he is, the pieces will need to be in place to enact it. Quickly.*

That's when Kimlee made the decision. She'd be the one to do what her brother was not willing to. She was going to fight the Empire. And she was going to win.

Kimlee pulled out her datapad and made a call. Within seconds, Devorian's holographic image appeared above her screen. "Lady Evenstar," Devorian said. "Have you come to a decision regarding my offer?"

"Actually, Mr. Westlake, I am in need of your other service at the moment," Kimlee responded. "I need you to smuggle something off Redwater."

Devorian raised a curious eyebrow. "And what is it you need smuggled off planet, my Lady?"

Kimlee smiled.

"Me," she replied.

CHAPTER ✺ 29

Krupp had been right about the fallout of the Assignment Ritual. The vast majority of those who'd been dubbed "Unlikely" had simply quit, heading back out through the tether and returning to their normal lives the very next day, their dreams of becoming Paragons having been forgotten. But there were still quite a few others who were determined to give it a shot, Jack being among them.

A great portion of the Conclave was dedicated to residential chambers, and shortly after the Assignment Ritual, the new Initiates had been designated quarters. These were mostly grouped according to the category the crystals had given them. All the Gifted had their own hall, as did all the Normals. There weren't nearly as many Unlikelies, so they were all grouped into an area that had numerous smaller rooms leading into a large common room.

The living quarters weren't much to look at. There were no visual displays, no computers, and barely any furniture – just a few wooden tables, chairs, and bunkbeds. Jack had chosen to room with Krupp, but they shared their quarters with two other Unlikelies. One was a Trundel[31] who introduced himself as Scrappy. He was about Jack's height, with green skin dotted with yellow patches, the most notable of which was around his right eye. He had a long thin neck, which made his large head bob when he talked, and short curly red hair that ran around the back of his head. He seemed friendly enough, if not a bit nerdy, and reminded Jack of Professor Green in more ways than one.

Jack's other roommate was an Egoi by the name of Snodgrass. Jack was unfamiliar with Egois and found Snodgrass's lack of a mouth rather off-putting at first. He was a tall, lanky fellow with pale brown skin, a noticeable potbelly, and dark black hair tied up in a small topknot. Probably the strangest thing about Snodgrass was that when he spoke, Jack heard Snodgrass's voice in his mind. Krupp explained to him that Egois communicated through telepathy, and that they consumed knowledge instead of food. Their bodies were made up of the same material as their brains, so it was as though every part of them was neural tissue. Because the main part of their brains was located in their stomachs, the

---

[31] Trundels are humanoid aliens who resemble turtles, and are known for their good memories and skills at science and engineering.

fatter an Egoi was, the smarter he was said to be. Based on that logic, it seemed Snodgrass was not considered to be all that smart.

Though there were maybe thirty or so others living in the rooms off the common area, Jack didn't really get to know them all that well. The one exception was an Orean girl by the name of Flitter, who cheerily danced around introducing herself to anyone and everyone, and then chatting their ears off, whether they wanted to talk to her or not. She had the typical light orange skin and large dark eyes of an Orean, with half-blonde half-brown hair through which she'd strung all types of ribbons and beads. She seemed to have taken a liking to Jack after he'd demonstrated he knew her language, making it almost impossible for him to go anywhere without her following.

The other exception was Morosa, who happened to be the Femezon Jack had accidentally bumped into at the New Season Celebration. It seemed everyone except Flitter stayed away from her, but being the social butterfly that she was, Flitter tried to include Morosa in her activities, which immediately brought the large Femezon into Jack's orbit – much to the chagrin of both Jack and her.

One of the major adjustments Jack had to make while living within the Conclave was the concept that everything one needed in order to live had to come from a self-sustaining ecosystem within the temple itself. Most things Jack had taken for granted previously – like food, clothing, and other things he utilized on a daily basis – had to be created as opposed to simply being provided to him.

To this extent, the Conclave used the Initiates who had not yet passed their manifestation exams as a workforce to assist in the daily activities that benefited the entire temple's population as a whole. This was how Jack found himself – along with the rest of his class of Initiates – in the Willowhite Orchard on one of the Conclave's agricultural levels.

Paragon Cheffini, a massively large Gourvine with pink skin and a large brown spot over one of his eyes, was the head of the Conclave's Food and Beverage department and oversaw all the food production and meal creation the Conclave offered its residents. This day, the pig-like alien was instructing the Initiates on how to extract milk from the Willowhite trees.

"Now pay attention, liebchens," the Gourvine said as it walked among the students, the massive alien easily a foot bigger than Jack even on all four of its legs. "Today we be milking the Willowhites, yah? Without Willowhites, we be having no milk to drink or cook with. <snort snort> Cheffini no like that, yah? To extract zee milk, liebchens simply screw spigot into tree, and allow tree to lactate into bucket. Is easy, no?"

"Lactating trees," Jack muttered. "Guess that gives a whole new meaning to the term 'Mother Nature', eh?" Jack laughed and looked around to see if any of the others were amused by his remark. When all he saw were confused stares, Jack awkwardly stopped chuckling and sighed. "No one gets me," he muttered, before sticking the spigot into the Willowhite tree in front of him and collecting the milk that drizzled from it into his bucket.

Frankly, the last thing Jack wanted to be doing right then was collect milk from the tall, white trees that dominated half the level of the temple. After what felt like ages of settling into the workforce routine forced upon him and his classmates by the Conclave, their first day of actual classes was about to start. To Jack's surprise (and relief) it appeared there was only one class they were scheduled to take:

Manifestation 101.

According to Krupp, Manifestation 101 was the only class Initiates had to worry about until they took their Manifestation exam. After an Initiate had proven he could perform the most fundamental skill of a Paragon, he'd then be allowed to pursue a more focused discipline. But no matter what the discipline was, the idea that Jack was going to learn how to create anything he wanted, simply with the power of his mind, was incredibly exciting.

I'm going to create armor, and guns, and glowing swords, and flying cars, and all sorts of awesome, Jack thought as he excitedly made his way back to his chambers once workforce duty had ended. Indeed, all his classmates were excited about their first Manifestation class, discussing their different theories on how it all worked as they got cleaned up in preparation.

"I'm so excited to finally learn something!" said Flitter. Her body gyrated with barely controlled nervous energy, her blond and brown hair swaying as she spoke in her high-pitched cadence. "First thing I'm going to manifest are some comfy shoes! Oh – or maybe a nicer pillow! OH! Or maybe –"

"Earplugs," muttered Morosa during Flitter's nonstop chatter. "I shall definitely manifest earplugs."

"I'm looking forward to metals the most!" said Scrappy. "And wood! And plastics! And alloys! Oh, the things I'll be able to build with all that…"

"<I am most excited about manifesting knowledge,>" Snodgrass proclaimed. "<I shall discover so much, I'll be the fattest Egoi ever!>"

"Large and in charge, that's the way to live, buddy," Jack said.

"What about you, Jack?" asked Flitter. "What are you going to manifest?"

"A TV, a stereo, a Gamerbox 3000 – anything to have some fun with!" Jack proclaimed. "Not that living like a homeless person and milking trees all day isn't a blast, but if the rest of Paragon life is this boring, I may not want to pass the manifestation exam."

It wasn't long before the group had all gotten ready and had begun their trek to what their datapad maps called the "Wall Room" for their class. Upon entering the Wall Room, Jack stopped short. It was a fairly simple room, similar to many of the other ones in the Conclave, with sandstone floors and walls. However, the wall at the opposite end of the room was made of red brick. But that wasn't its most noticeable difference from the other walls in the room. That distinction belonged to a long, luxurious-looking white beard growing from the brick and hanging all the way down to the floor.

"That... that wall has a beard," said Jack, dumbfounded.

"Yep," replied Krupp.

"Why does that wall have a beard?"

Krupp shrugged. "I guess if it didn't have a beard, we'd have to call it 'old Wall' instead of 'old Wallbeard'."

Before Jack had a chance to pursue his line of questioning, a voice rumbled through the room.

"Take your seats, okay-yeah?" it boomed.

Jack looked up and saw that the wall at the front of the room now had eyes and lips to go along with its beard. The large eyes darted to-and-fro, glancing at all the students in turn. "Come along. Chop-chop. We don't got all day, dontcha know," the Wall said.

The Initiates all took their seats on the floor. Jack simply gazed in utter disbelief at the big talking wall with a huge beard. When everyone had settled in, the Wall spoke once more.

"Well, hello dere, class. Welcome to Manifestation 101. Muh name is Fargo. Fargo Nor'Dakota. You may also address me as Master Fargo, or Master Nor'Dakoda, dontcha know. What you may not address me as is Wallbeard, Master Wallbeard, or anything having to do with the joining of the words 'Wall' and 'Beard', okay-yeah?"

"Okay, yeah," the class responded, in unison.

"Well, okay then. In this here class, I will be instructing ya all on how to manifest your thoughts into reality. The ability to manifest objects into reality is

the cornerstone of what it means ta be a Paragon, dontcha know. Without the ability to manifest your thoughts, you're no different than normal people. And until you master this skill, you will not be able to progress in your training. In fact, those of you who are unable to perform manifestation will be asked to leave the Conclave, until such time as you are able to demonstrate you can sufficiently free your mind enough to do this most basic of Paragon skills. Okiedokey?"

"Okiedokey," the class replied.

"Okay, then! Now, before we begin, are there any questions?"

Jack raised his hand.

"Yes, you there," Wallbeard said.

"Um… why do you have a beard?" Jack asked.

Wallbeard blinked at Jack. "You touched, son? I say I'm going to teach ya how to manifest anything ya can think of, and you just want ta know about muh beard?"

"Well… what if I want to manifest a beard?"

"Hmmmm. Good point," Wallbeard replied. "Very well. I'll answer yer question. I have a beard because I don't like to shave. Next?"

Jack was about to follow up his question when Flitter popped up beside him. "Ooh! Ooh!" cried Flitter, her hand shooting up and waving around furiously. "Master Wallbeard! Master Wallbeard, sir?"

"Uff-da!" sighed Wallbeard, his big eyes rolling upward. "See here, now. What'd I say about calling me Wallbeard? Just because I'm a wall with a beard doesn't mean I don't have a name, dontcha know? How would you like it if I started calling you lot 'Regal Face' or 'Bi-pedal pimples?' Don't be strange, now."

"Sorry, Master Fargo," replied Flitter. "When I get excited, I tend to forget things."

"It's okay, child. Now, what's your question?"

"Why don't you like to shave? Is it because you don't have hands?"

"Yes," replied Wallbeard. "Any more questions?"

Almost all the students in the room raised their hands.

"Any more questions that don't have to do with the fact that I'm a wall that has a beard?"

All the hands slowly lowered.

"Good. Then let's get started, shall we?" Wallbeard said. "The first thing you all gotta accept, before we make any progress here, is the Biocentric Theory of the universe. This is the cornerstone of the Paragon belief system, and it is this theory upon which we base all our teachings. Raise yer hand if ya know what the Biocentric Theory is."

A few people in the class raised their hands.

"A few of ya. Good ta know. For the rest of ya, here's the Biocentric Theory in a nutshell... it states that life and biology are central to being, reality, and the cosmos. This means that consciousness creates the universe rather than the other way around. The Biocentric Theory asserts that current theories of the physical world do not work, and can never be made to work, until they fully account for life and consciousness. While physics is considered fundamental to the study of the universe, and chemistry fundamental to the study of life, biocentrism claims that biology must be placed before all other sciences to produce a coherent theory of everything. Ergo... living things create the world in which they live, and nothing would exist without life to first create it. Not the other way around. Ya get me? Yah?"

"Yeah," the class responded.

"Yah. Okay then. So with this in mind, it is our consciousness which constructs our reality. And if we can control our consciousness, we will be able to manipulate and adjust the reality that we, and others, experience. This means we will be able to create objects out of thin air. Perform acts of incredible physical ability. Change the very nature of reality and break the laws of physics... all by using our minds."

"Cool..." Jack said.

"You betcha it's cool!" Wallbeard replied with a smile. "But it's also really honkin' difficult, if ya know what I mean. Manifestation isn't a simple proposition of thinking about something really hard until it comes true. Oh, no. It's a process by which one must use their mind, body, and soul to alter their reality and the reality of others. That being said, difficult doesn't mean impossible. Any living thing that possesses a mind, a body, and a soul has the capability to manifest anything it wants. It's simply a question of whether or not that living thing can free its mind from its constraints so that it believes in the new reality it wishes to create, as opposed to the old one it has spent its entire life believing in. That's what it means to 'free your mind', dontcha know? To have the ability to believe in anything so strongly that it becomes your reality. Now, who wants to learn to do this?"

The students in the room excitedly raised their hands. Wallbeard laughed at their enthusiasm.

"Never had a class where no one raised a hand when I asked that," he said. "Okay, then. Let's get started. Does anyone here know what a filmstrip is?"

"Yeah," replied Jack. "It's images on a transparent strip of film. Like the kind you watch at a movie theater."

"Yah, a bit archaic, but correct, dontcha know," Wallbeard responded. "When you pass light through a filmstrip, its image is projected onto a wall or a screen, and others can experience the image that is on the strip."

The air before the class rippled as Wallbeard manifested an old movie projector in front of him. It began to whir as the film on its reels ran through it, projecting onto one of the room's walls the image of a bustling town.

"Well, manifestation works much the same way. Think of your body as the projector and your mind as the filmstrip. Your mind is what contains the image of what ya wish to manifest, okay? And in order for other people to experience that image, you must first pass a light through it in order for it to be projected into reality. Anyone care ta guess what that light would be?"

"Your soul," Krupp answered.

"Oh, we got a smart one here!" Wallbeard said with a smile. "Forget that I've seen you in this class a hundred times by now. You're still correct. Your soul is the light that must be projected through your mind in order to manifest yer thoughts into reality. Now, keep in mind that yer body has the ability to manifest yer thoughts through your actions. This is how art is created, after all. However, to manifest objects that did not previously exist into reality, the mind and the soul must work together ta bring that to fruition. Yah, you with the nervous ticks, you got a question?"

Flitter put her hand down. "Yes! Um – what do you mean by 'soul', exactly? Do you mean the scientific definition or the religious definition, and if it's the religious definition, which religion? Oh! And—"

"Yah, yah, yah," interrupted Wallbeard. "Without gettin' bogged down in details, the soul is simply the energy your body harbors that makes you who ya are. Some call it electromagnetic, some call it spiritual, but at the end of the day, it's simply the spark of consciousness that resides inside yer body which makes ya unique to the universe. The issue here is that most people – heck almost all people – don't know how ta harness the power of their soul. And if they do, they don't always know how to make it work in tandem with their mind and their body. But here in this class, I'm going to show ya how to do all that. Yah?"

"Yeah!" the class replied.

"Yah. Okay then. Here's the good news. Your brains are already well trained on how to create the reality around you. Part of the Biocentric Theory is that our consciousness constructs the universe around us. This room, the bodies of the people in it, the air in it – everything in it is constructed by our minds. See, the very atoms that make up matter are sensitive to our living consciousness. Through the simple act of observing, we can make atoms respond to us. Thus, the first step in learning manifestation is to learn ta understand the building blocks of reality. In short, ya gotta understand atoms."

Jack frowned. This was starting to sound like a science class, and he always hated science class.

"So here's what we're gonna do," Wallbeard said. "We're gonna do what's called a Guided Meditation. This is where you all meditate, and I help you to understand a thing-or-two about the universe while yer in a meditative state. So what I need from ya all is fer you to close yer eyes, relax, empty yer minds, and allow yerselves ta go along with what I'm goin' ta share with ya, okay-yeah?"

The other students all closed their eyes. Jack followed suit. He tried to do what Shanks had taught him about meditation. He slowed his breathing, emptied his mind, and focused on his Source. However, it wasn't as easy to connect to his Source as it had been in the past. Jack had a hard time finding the flow of his energy. So hard a time, in fact, that he started to get worried. Jack peeked open an eye to see that everyone around him seemed to be in a deep, meditative state. He closed his eye once more and tried again to empty his mind. He struggled to calm his emotions and find some type of inner peace to settle in on.

There ya go… he heard in his mind. *Just relax. Ya don't need ta do anything special, dontcha know.*

When Jack opened his eyes, he was surrounded by darkness. He looked around, confused.

"Where am I?" Jack asked.

Suddenly, the disembodied eyes and beard of Wallbeard appeared before him, smiling. "Yer deep inside yer mind, yah?" Wallbeard said. "There's a place inside all of us where the subconscious part of our mind exists. We call these places 'constructs'. When we're able ta get in touch with our subconscious, we can merge with it to consciously exist in a place created by our own minds."

"I... I think I've been somewhere like this before..." Jack said, remembering the place back in the Sunshell where he'd seen Anna before being attacked by Verrutus.

"Judging by how hard it was for ya ta find it this time around, I'm guessin' ya haven't been here lately," Wallbeard said. "But, yer here now. So what's say you and I get started, yah?"

A strange, circular, blue cloud appeared before Jack. The cloud seemed to shimmer slightly, the particles that comprised it as fine as grains of sand, all swirling in an almost hypnotic fashion. At its center was a small orb that pulsed with a faint pink light. "Whoa," said Jack, looking at the strange cloud in awe. "What is that?"

"That, is an atom," Wallbeard said. "Made large enough for ya ta see. A typical atom is about a ten-billionth of a meter in size, so they're essentially invisible. But if ya know what one looks like, it will help ya visualize it when ya go about manifesting things."

"But... it looks like a cloud. I didn't think atoms looked like that."

"Neat, eh?" Wallbeard said, his disembodied face hovering around Jack's shoulder. "That cloud is where the electrons rotate around the nucleus, which is made of protons and neutrons."

"Kind of like how a planet orbits a sun?"

"You betcha. Electrons are negatively charged particles, which are attracted to the positively charged particles called protons in the nucleus. The number of electrons orbiting the nucleus of an atom is equal to the number of protons it has. And the number of protons in the nucleus determines what element the atom is a part of. This here is the atom for gold. Its atomic number is 79, which means it has 79 protons in its nucleus and 79 electrons orbiting around it."

Jack gazed at the atom before him, curious. "So... this is what gold is made of?"

"Oh, yah. Atoms are the basic building blocks of matter, see? Gold is made up of atoms that look like this one. The atom itself has the properties of gold, and because of this, the atoms of the element gold cannot be broken down further."

"So, everything has its own type of atom?" Jack asked.

"All the basic elements do, yah," Wallbeard replied. "But sometimes, different types of atoms combine to form what's called a molecule, which is basically more than one type of atom joined together. Like this one…"

The atom before Jack disappeared and was replaced by three new ones. They seemed to have their electron clouds joined together, and Jack could see the number of protons in their nuclei were different.

"This is the molecule H_2O, more commonly known as 'water'," Wallbeard said. "See how the two hydrogen atoms have bonded with the oxygen one? Together, they create a liquid. But if ya were ta break them apart, ya'd get hydrogen and oxygen gas. But ya can't break hydrogen and oxygen down any further, because those are basic elements. Ya get me?"

Jack nodded. "Yeah, I think I understand."

"Good," said Wallbeard, right before disappearing.

Jack opened his eyes and noticed everyone else seemed to be coming out of their meditations. All their attention turned back to Wallbeard.

"Ya all have now seen protons, neutrons, and electrons, and how they form ta make an atom," Wallbeard said. "Now that ya know what they look like, it's time for ya ta learn which is which."

In front of each student, a piece of paper appeared with the periodic table of elements on it. Jack picked it up and looked at it. It was similar to the one he remembered from his high school science textbook, but it was much larger and more detailed -- not to mention all the elements weren't named the same things as they were back on Earth.

"You'll want ta familiarize yourself with as many different elements as ya can," Wallbeard said. "Learn their atomic make-up. Start with the elements colored in white on your sheet. They're the easiest. The ones in green are more complicated, and the ones in red are the hardest. Eventually, you'll want ta know every element by heart, but fer now, keep it simple, yah?"

"Do we really have to memorize all this?" Jack asked. "Can't we start learning how to manifest stuff right away?"

"Whoa, now. Slow down there, speedy," Wallbeard replied. "Walk before ya start running, dontcha know. Ya gotta know tha basic elements before ya even think of manifesting things! Remember that ya can only manifest something if ya truly understand what it takes ta make it exist. Thinking of a sword won't make it manifest itself. However, thinking of the metal that comprises the sword will. If ya don't know how to build something from the atomic level on up, ya won't be able to manifest anything. Okiedokie?"

"Okiedokie," the class responded.

"Okay, then. Off with ya! Learn yer elements. Next time we meet, we're going ta start working on how ya focus yer soul to start manifesting these elements into reality. See you all in a few days. Buh-bye, now."

With that, Wallbeard's eyes and lips disappeared, leaving only his beard behind. The class all got to their feet and began filing out the door. Jack frowned at the periodic table he held in his hands, looking at it, glumly. "I forgot how much I hate homework," he muttered. "We gotta memorize all these elements? I suck at memorizing stuff!"

"Just worry about the easy ones for now," Krupp said. "You'll need to know more as you attend higher level classes. But memorizing them is the easy part."

Jack raised an eyebrow. "What's the hard part?"

Flitter tapped Jack upside the head. "Actually *manifesting* them, dummy!" she said, with a giggle.

"She's right," Krupp said, with a nod. "It's one thing to know what they look like. It's another thing to actually make them come together and form something based on the power of your beliefs."

"But, they'll show us how to do that, right?" Jack asked.

"They'll try," Krupp said with a sigh. "Look around, Jack. Ninety percent of the people in this class won't make it past the exam. And that's being generous."

Jack glanced around him at the myriad of faces. For some reason, it had never occurred to him that most of the people who were there now may not make it through.

"Really?" asked Jack. "That many?"

Krupp shrugged. "If it's like any of the previous seasons," he said. "Could be less. Could be more. Sadly, the reality is that most people are just too stuck in their ways to free their minds enough to manifest anything. And if you can't manifest things, you can't be a Paragon."

Jack left the room feeling a lot less excited than he had been when entering it. He'd pulled off some things he had never believed he'd be capable of in the past. But he'd never tried manifesting anything out of thin air before.

In the back of his mind, Jack harbored one terrifying thought that had wormed its way into his brain and now wouldn't disappear. What if he couldn't do it? What if he were part of the ninety percent who were dismissed?

What if he didn't have what it takes to become a Paragon?

"I really hate school..." Jack muttered as he made his way back to his chambers.

CHAPTER 30

At the top of the smoking remains of the Nakatomi Tower building in Los Angeles, one fateful Christmas Eve night, Zarrod and his henchmen were hurriedly gathering millions of dollars in bonds when they were suddenly interrupted.

"Zarrooooood!" came a pained voice.

Zarrod turned to see Jack limping toward him with an automatic rifle in his hands. It was obvious Jack had come for a final showdown, but Zarrod had one last ace up his sleeve. Before the Earthman could fire, Zarrod grabbed the gun from his belt and pulled a captive Anna in front of him as a human shield. Anna looked at Jack, wide-eyed and frightened, as Zarrod held his gun to her head. Anna gazed at the rough state Jack was in as he limped ever closer, aghast at how beaten up he was.

"Jack..." Anna whispered.

"Hi, honey," Jack replied, looking at the bags of bearer bonds Zarrod had lying around. "So that's what this was all about? A stupid robbery?"

Zarrod moved back toward the windows, careful to keep Anna between him and Jack. "Put down the gun," Zarrod warned in his classy German accent.

"Why'd you have to nuke the whole building, Zarrod?" Jack asked.

"When you steal six hundred dollars, you can simply disappear," Zarrod replied. "But when you steal six hundred million, they will find you unless they think you're already dead. Now put down the gun."

Jack looked at Anna's frightened face and reluctantly dropped his weapon. Jack then held his hands behind his head in a gesture of surrender. "You got me," he said.

"Still the cowboy, Mr. Finnegan," Zarrod mused. "How Americans are all alike. Well, this time John Wayne does not walk off into the sunset with Grace Kelly."

"It's Gary Cooper, jerkface," Jack replied.

"Enough jokes," Zarrod sneered.

"You'd have made a pretty good cowboy yourself, Zarrod."

"Ah, yes… what was it you said to me before?" Zarrod asked. "Yippee ki-yay… Mr. Falcon?"

Jack suddenly began to laugh. It was an odd laugh. Unexpected. Zarrod looked at Jack curiously, but the humor of the exchange finally found him and he, too, began to laugh. But unlike Jack's laugh, which seemed to be a resigned acceptance of his fate, Zarrod's laugh was one of condescension.

Normally, at this point, Zarrod would point his gun at Jack, planning to kill him before finishing off his hostage. But for some strange reason, he decided not to do it in that order.

"Happy trails, Earthman," Zarrod said, holding his gun to Anna's temple.

With that, Zarrod pulled the trigger.

"NO!" cried Jack, rushing forward as Anna's lifeless body fell to the ground.

When he got close enough, Zarrod grabbed Jack and pushed him through the window behind him and over the side of the building, sending the boy falling through space.

"This is not the way this movie eeeeeeeeends!" cried Jack as he fell in slow motion to the ground below.

Zarrod smiled smugly before straightening the tie on his John Phillips suit. "It's the way my movie ends," the Deathlord said before rushing to his helicopter and flying away with millions in stolen bearer bonds, laughing victoriously the entire time. He found he was rather enjoying himself until he opened his eyes, at which point the dream ended and the fuzzy haze of consciousness settled in.

Another bizarre dream, the Deathlord thought, bitterly. *Oh, how I hate those things…*

Sleeping and dreaming was not something Zarrod was used to. Back when he was a Deathlord Supreme, he did not do such things. But after his exposure to the Great Seal on the Ghost Planet, he found it was something he seemed to require. And if that weren't bad enough, the dreams he had were always of the strangest nature, as if they were somehow based on stories he should know but with which he was unfamiliar. Furthermore, he always felt as though they were toned down to a ridiculous degree, as if to make them more acceptable for general viewing audiences.

Zarrod checked the hologuise emitter on his wrist. Though it was designed to project its holographic disguise for long periods of time, it still needed to be recharged occasionally. But he dared not turn it off while in the Conclave. The risk of discovery with all the Paragons around him was too great.

Zarrod's patience was beginning to be strained as it appeared his mysterious friend had forgotten about their arrangement. At least, it certainly seemed that way. The passage of time in the Conclave was enough to drive one mad. It felt as though everything moved at a snail's pace, and the longer Zarrod was forced to wait for what he wanted, the more irritated he grew.

However, upon arriving in this new universe, Zarrod had discovered that one of the unique properties of the Conclave was that simply being in the temple assisted in facilitating the opening of one's mind. Though he had absorbed Hasatan's knowledge and skills when he'd killed the Paragon, he hadn't exactly mastered how to use such things. Now that he had so much time on his hands, and he was in a place that assisted in the development of those skills, Zarrod had taken to practicing them, as well. Though his ultimate goal was to regain his mastery over Servuchur, he could not deny that acquiring the skills of a Paragon could be useful, too.

He'd only recently found he was able to manifest objects into reality. It was still a clumsy and difficult endeavor for him, yet he persisted. His first success had been an odd, misshapen piece of clay. But he continued to practice and was slowly discovering how to manifest more objects with greater accuracy.

After a rigorous session in which he practiced manifesting cups, plates, and spoons, Zarrod needed to take a break. He decided he'd check in on Mourdock. Ever since arriving at the Conclave, Mourdock did little but tend to the Princess, meditating over her with the other Paragons in a futile attempt to cure her. Zarrod also knew the efforts of the Earthman's companions would be fruitless, since he was quite confident that once the slythru joined with its host, it would be nearly impossible to remove. Yet, he allowed the farces to play out. It was good to have everyone's attention focused elsewhere while he pursued his goals.

Zarrod opened the door to his chamber and stopped when he noticed a small envelope at his doorstep. He reached down and opened it to find a passcode scrawled on a scrap of paper inside.

So… you finally came through, Mellegogg, he thought.

Excited by this development, Zarrod wasted no time making his way to the Conclave's Chamber of Knowledge, a library supposedly dwarfed only by the one the Central Galactic University maintained. The cavernous room contained an overwhelming mixture of paper books and data servers. It was one of the most

heavily frequented chambers in the Conclave, with students from all Rings going there to read, study, and research.

Zarrod walked among the long rows of computer terminals, looking for a free one to access. One of the trickier parts of accessing the Forbidden Archive was that it had to be done from the Chamber of Knowledge. One could not simply connect to it remotely. Though the Conclave had a very open policy on the sharing of knowledge, there were a few subjects deemed too dangerous, destructive, or advanced to make publicly available. These topics were heavily guarded and usually accessible only through the blessing of the Order of Peers. Even then, the study of these topics was heavily supervised by the temple's most skilled Paragons.

After finally finding an empty terminal, Zarrod typed in the passcode he'd received into the command prompt. He was then granted access to a secure directory where his dark ally had left a copy of the Conclave's research on Servuchur. Zarrod could barely contain his excitement as he plugged a datastick into the workstation and began downloading a copy of the folder. He was so eager, in fact, that he opened the file to glance at its contents while it was downloading.

What he saw stunned him.

This… this cannot be…

As a Deathlord Supreme, he'd believed his Lords had granted him full mastery of Servuchur. However, the contents of this file proved that he'd only been granted a fraction of the power such a discipline offered. The contents of the research before him were vast and comprehensive. Some information was so advanced, he did not understand it, even with his extensive knowledge of its art and practice.

Zarrod rapidly scanned through the folder's contents, looking at all the aspects of Servuchur of which he'd previously been unaware.

SPIRIT ARMOR:>> THE USE OF SPIRITUAL ENERGY TO ENCASE A PHYSICAL BODY, FORMING A NEARLY IMPENETRABLE OUTER SHELL.

SOUL STEPPING:>> THE REMOVAL OF ONE'S SPIRIT TO ACT INDEPENDENTLY AS THE BODY REMAINS FUNCTIONING, CREATING TWO ENTITIES CONTROLLED BY THE SAME MIND.

SOUL SIPHONING:>> THE ABILITY TO FORCIBLY EXTRACT KNOWLEDGE AND MEMORIES FROM ANOTHER BEING.

SOUL LEACHING:>> THE HARNESSING OF ANOTHER'S SPIRITUAL ENERGY TO GRANT ENHANCED STRENGTH, SPEED, AND HEALING ABILITY.

The list went on. As he read, Zarrod grew more and more angry. What else had his Lords lied to him about? What else had they denied him? How could he have been so blind and content to wallow in ignorance? His growing rage was unexpectedly interrupted by the sound of a voice.

"Ah! Hasatan, my old friend!" said Paragon Brunwahld, cheerily. Zarrod turned to see the doddering fool of a man approaching him, carrying a number of thick, leather-bound books with him. "I almost didn't see you there! What brings you to the ol' Chamber of Knowledge today?"

Zarrod quickly exited out of the folder he'd been viewing the contents of and shut off the monitor as the download was finishing. "Just... exploring a few theories on how to help the Princess," he lied.

"Ah, yes. Poor thing," replied Brunwahld. "Is there any progress concerning her condition?"

"None, I'm afraid."

"Pity. If you like, we could retire to my chambers and bounce some ideas off one another over tea. It would be like old times!"

"Perhaps another day," Zarrod replied, rapidly growing annoyed with the old man. "I fear I have much work to do."

"Sadly, as do I," Brunwahld said, referring to the books in his hands. "I was finally able to track down the three Volumes of Prophesy that have been lost on the shelves here for ages. I am in for some heavy reading tonight, I assure you!"

Zarrod gave Brunwahld a curious look. "Volumes of Prophesy?" he asked.

"Yes, written two thousand years ago by Paragon Ridlick," Brunwahld explained. "It was his attempt at creating a written history of the Aedion race."

"I am not familiar with such a race."

"Fascinating species," Brunwahld commented. "They experience time backward, you see. Age in reverse, move in reverse, speak in reverse – it's really all quite confusing, actually. To them, the future is the past, and the past is the future. Ridlick theorized that by documenting their history, he might be able to predict future events."

"Is that so?" asked Zarrod, his interest piqued. "Did he succeed?"

"In a sense. Many believe he predicted the arrival of the Deathlords and the destruction of Regalus Prime. However, his writings are so confusing due to the nature of the Aedion people, that whether he actually did or not is open to interpretation."

"And why is it you are so interested in Paragon Ridlick's writings?"

"Just another way to delve deeper into my study of farsight."

"Yes, you mentioned that before," Zarrod said. "Does this mean farsight has something to do with prophesy?"

"I suppose you could say that," replied Brunwahld with a chuckle. "It's really about unlocking the future! If you get a chance, I'd be happy to tell you all about it sometime."

Zarrod subtly removed his datastick from the computer terminal and slid it into the sleeve of his robe as he stood up. "How about now?" he asked.

"I thought you were busy?"

"Our little chat has suddenly made me nostalgic for the 'good old times'," Zarrod replied. "Does your offer for tea still stand?"

Brunwahld lit up. "But of course!" he exclaimed. "Come, follow me."

Zarrod followed Brunwahld out of the Chamber of Knowledge and back to the Paragon's quarters as the old man talked his ear off. Though Zarrod found the old fool insufferable, this 'farsight' discipline he kept mentioning was intriguing him. At least, for the time being.

Brunwahld's chamber was well lived in and cozy. Classical holopaintings adorned its walls, books and datapads were stacked everywhere, and two well-worn, high-backed leather chairs were situated next to a fireplace. "Please, have a seat!" Brunwahld said as he gestured toward one of the chairs before setting the tomes he'd lugged from the Chamber of Knowledge atop an already precarious stack of books balancing on an end table.

Zarrod sat down as Brunwahld rummaged through his small kitchen and set a kettle of water to boil on his stove. "I am so glad we're finally getting a chance to catch up!" he said, cheerily. "I realize things have been crazy since the Princess's arrival, but it has felt like eons since I last saw you."

"It doesn't feel to me as though it's been that long," Zarrod said.

"Heh. Indeed," Brunwahld mused as he shuffled back to the fireplace carrying a tea platter. "Blasted time constriction. Sometimes I think I'm spinning my wheels here at the Conclave while the universe passes me by." The doddering old Paragon poured some steaming tea from his kettle into two cups and offered one to Zarrod.

"No, thank you," Zarrod answered. He didn't require any food or drink to survive, but he could consume it. However, he wasn't sure how well his hologuise would hold up if he were to attempt to do so.

"Hmmmm. Never known you to turn down a cup of tea," Brunwahld commented. "It's my elderberry frostblossom blend. Sure you don't want any?"

A perturbed feeling took root in Zarrod's chest. He knew from Hasatan's memories such a tea was his favorite. Turning it down would indeed be suspicious. "Well, if it's the elderberry frostblossom blend, how can I refuse?" Zarrod replied.

Brunwahld smiled and handed the second cup of tea to Zarrod before settling down in his leather chair opposite the Deathlord. Zarrod held the teacup but did not partake as he watched the old Paragon take a sip and smack his lips as he enjoyed the steaming brew.

"Ahhhhhhhhh, good stuff," Brunwahld said with a satisfied smile. "Picked a good crop to make this. There's this Initiate in the Ground Ring – Soneheim I believe his name is. Has a real talent for botany. Really knows how to get a full bloom from the frostblossoms and grows some of the fattest elderberries you've ever seen! Yes, yes, yes… I foresaw that he would have an excellent yield on his latest batch and was able to swoop in and get my choice of his bounty before it got raided by anyone else."

"Yes," replied Zarrod, glad it would be easy to transition to what he really wanted to talk about. "Tell me more of this new 'farsight' technique you are developing."

"Wouldn't exactly call it 'new', necessarily," said Brunwahld with a good-humored smile. "It's been a Paragon discipline for many thousands of years. It's just so difficult that few have ever truly been able to use it beyond parlor-trick status. However, seeing as how we are at war with such a ruthless enemy, I thought it might be a good idea to take the discipline a tad more seriously to see if we could give the Imperial military a way to anticipate Deathlord strategies."

"And have you been able to do so?"

"Yes and no. I believe I have made great advances in the farsight discipline. In fact, if you'd permit me to brag a bit, I'd say that I am the foremost Farseer in the entire Conclave. My visions have averaged out to about a 70% accuracy rating, which is quite good, all things considered. There have been Paragons in the past who have had higher averages than that, though. If memory serves, Paragon Nostradamas got as high as 90%, but I fear to reach that level. At that point everything becomes so predictable, life becomes dull, don't you know?"

"Still, effectively predicting the future 70% of the time is quite an achievement," Zarrod said. "I'm sure the Imperial military is quite interested in retaining your services."

"Yes, well… to be perfectly honest, that accuracy rating I just shared with you is a tad… oh, how would you put it? Skewed?"

"How do you mean?"

Brunwahld sighed. "Well, to understand the limitations of farsight, one must first understand how it works. It's less about actually seeing the future than it is about *predicting* the future. The discipline helps one to see various potential outcomes, based on the information one possesses. It creates a type of hyperawareness of details, I guess you could say. And from those details, one can pick the most likely scenario to occur."

"What type of details are you talking about, exactly?"

"Well, let's say you see a banana peel on the ground, and someone who hasn't noticed it is walking toward it," said Brunwahld. "Using farsight, one would take into account the type of floor the banana peel is on, how fresh the peel is, the length of the strides the person is taking, the trajectory of the path he is on, and so forth. From all that information, one can make a prediction as to whether that person is going to slip on that banana peel or not. Farsight will give you all the potential scenarios of a given situation and help you to choose the one that is most likely to occur."

"And how is it that your results are skewed?"

"Because that rather high accuracy rating I shared with you is based on small scale predictions. They are predictions I made based on a great deal of information I had about the situations or people whose future I was trying to determine. The great limitation of farsight is if one does not possess all the information he needs to make accurate predictions, then the outcome he's determined is most likely to happen *might* occur but is not guaranteed to *actually* occur. Also problematic is the fact that longer term predictions are far more difficult to make accurately than are shorter term ones. This means that predicting the immediate future of people I'm familiar with can be quite accurate. But more wide-ranging predictions, particularly of the Deathlords, are far more

difficult to make. Especially when we have such limited information about who the Deathlords are and what their plans may be."

Zarrod nodded, digesting the information the Paragon was sharing with him. "But let's say you had a great deal of information about the Deathlords," he ventured. "Let us say, hypothetically, that you knew everything there was to know about them and what their intended actions are. If one were to use farsight in that instance, would it be possible to stop or alter their plans?"

"Oh, without a doubt!" answered Brunwahld. "Information is the fuel upon which farsight feeds! The more information one possesses, the farther out he can predict events, and the greater the accuracy of the predictions. Not to mention if a farseer is familiar with the individuals involved in the events one is trying to predict, he could achieve even greater accuracy. Unfortunately, due to the nature of the universe, it is always impossible to have all the information necessary to be correct in one's farsight 100% of the time. But that doesn't mean one can't get close."

"I must admit, it does indeed sound like an impressive achievement, even with its limitations," Zarrod said. "Have you taught it to many students yet?"

"No, not really," Brunwahld said with a frown. "It's a rather difficult discipline, I'm afraid. It requires a great deal of concentration and a level of mastery over one's Trinity that only advanced Paragons possess. There have been a few Initiates who have come to me expressing interest in learning how to become Farseers, but nowadays most Conclave recruits just want to be Warriors. For now, it makes no matter. I'm still trying to perfect my mastery of the discipline and am keeping copious notes concerning my study of it for posterity. Even though I feel as though I've lived for an extremely long period of time, I fear my age is indeed starting to catch up with me."

Brunwahld chuckled at that and took another sip of his tea. Zarrod studied the old man for a moment, before speaking. "Tell me, old friend," he said. "Can you use farsight to predict your own death?"

Brunwahld raised an eyebrow. "Yes, of course," he replied. "Many Farseers in the past have. But honestly, why would anyone want to know such a thing? To have that knowledge hanging over one's head would surely put a damper on life. Personally, I'd prefer not to know. When my time comes, I feel it is best for it to be a surprise."

A wicked smile grew on Zarrod's face as his eyes met those of the old Paragon's.

"Well then… surprise!" the Deathlord said.

Zarrod reached his hand out toward Brunwahld and ripped the Paragon's soul from his body before the old man even got a chance to react. A pathetic squeal escaped from Brunwahld before his body went limp, his lifeless eyes gazing upward as the teacup he'd been holding fell to the floor with a dainty crash, breaking apart as the tea within it splashed onto the ground.

Zarrod absorbed the man's life force, feeling that dizzying high he got every time he used Servuchur to consume another living soul. The Paragon's memories flooded into Zarrod's mind, playing out an entire lifetime of experiences in the blink of an eye before finally settling down. Zarrod took a deep breath as he reflected on what Brunwahld's soul had taught him. He now had all the old man's skill in farsight.

And he intended to use it.

There was no better time to make use of the skills and memories of a soul than immediately after the soul had been harvested, when its essence was still fresh in Zarrod's mind. The Paragon had bragged that he was the best at the farsight discipline, but with the knowledge Zarrod possessed, the Deathlord was sure he could beat the accuracy rating to which Brunwahld had laid claim.

Zarrod set aside his teacup and then proceeded to enter into the meditative state farsight required. Even with Brunwahld's knowledge of the discipline, it took Zarrod a great deal of time to align himself in order to access the talent. Aligning his Trinity in such a way made Zarrod feel uncomfortable. Deathlords were not meant to have such abilities. But, then again, Zarrod was no longer a mere Deathlord.

Zarrod could feel his consciousness shift when he'd finally entered the farsight state. It was a disorienting feeling. He suddenly became hyper-aware of all his memories. Everything he knew about his Lords and their plans for the universe was laid out before him in picture-perfect detail. All his knowledge of Verrutus, Mellegogg, and Ashtoroth was added to that mosaic, as was his knowledge of the Earthman, the Princess, and all those who allied themselves with them.

All this began to combine, interacting with one another and playing out in different scenarios. So many, in fact, that it was almost too much for him to deal with. However, Zarrod maintained his focus, and eventually, a picture began to form that was clearer than any other. The scenario that was most likely to manifest itself played out before him, in excruciating, step-by-step detail.

Zarrod then focused solely on that eventuality, slowly adding in decisions he wished to make to see how they would affect it. Finally, he found an outcome that was precisely what he wanted. An outcome that would give him everything he desired. A perfect vision of the perfect future – a future in which Zarrod was the ultimate victor over all his enemies.

The Deathlord opened his eyes. He suddenly felt very tired, as though the process of using farsight had drained him. He looked at Paragon Brunwahld, who slumped limply in his pathetic old chair. Zarrod couldn't help but smile at the man.

"Thank you, old friend," he said, getting to his feet. "You have been most helpful in allowing me to figure out what needs to be done."

Zarrod then turned and began to exit the living quarters, a determined look on his face.

"Now, I simply must do it," he said.

CHAPTER ✺ 31

Alabaster eyed Paragon Ordrich Velden as the old man sat before the desk in Alabaster's office, looking over the datapad Alabaster had supplied him. Paragon Velden was the Chief of the Royal Corps of Paragon Engineers and had been the one tasked with helping to retrofit Capitol City when the Empire had moved its seat of power to Omnicron. He'd overseen construction of over half the supertowers in the city, as well as the Megabases and the defense rings around the planet. If anyone were qualified for the task Alabaster needed to be completed, it was Paragon Velden.

The old Regal scratched at his neatly trimmed white beard as he read through the proposal on the datapad. The crow's feet at the edges of his light eyes grew deeper as he processed what he was seeing, before finally looking up and meeting Alabaster's gaze. "This is quite an unusual request, Chief Alabaster," the Paragon said.

"I am well aware of that, Paragon Velden," Alabaster replied. "But I would not be making it if it were not of great importance."

Velden sighed. "Very well. What do you need from me?"

"The first thing I need to know is if it is doable."

Velden turned his attention back to the datapad's display. "I believe so, but it will require at least four Paragon Engineers. Ideally, a team of ten."

"The more Paragon Engineers we siphon away for this project, the more attention it will draw," Alabaster said. "How long will it take with four?"

"Hard to say," Velden replied, stroking his beard thoughtfully. "Depends on how well versed they are with the technology. A week or two, maybe?"

Alabaster nodded. "Obviously, the quicker it can be completed, the better," he said.

"Obviously," Velden agreed. "If you'd like, I could pull in a few regular engineers and mechanics. It would speed up the process without drawing undue attention."

Alabaster shook his head. "No, we can't take the risk of someone infected by a slythru gaining access to the project. The staff must consist of Paragons only. That is of the utmost importance."

Velden nodded. "Understood," he said, getting to his feet. "I'll begin approaching those I feel are best suited for this project immediately."

Alabaster also rose and shook the Paragon's hand. "Thank you, Paragon Velden," he said. "The Empire is counting on you."

"I will not disappoint, Chief. After all, it's not every day a Paragon Engineer gets to build... well, something like this."

The two men chuckled. "I don't imagine so," Alabaster said. "And please, remember to keep the circle of those you tell about this small and tight. Secrecy is of paramount importance."

"Do not fear, Chief. This is not my first secret project. I'll keep all details strictly 'need-to-know'."

Once the Paragon had left, Alabaster sat back at his desk and took a moment to clear his head. It was part of his job to juggle multiple tasks and oversee the intelligence apparatus of a galaxy-spanning government, but all the cloak-and-dagger machinations that were required sometimes wore on him. And with the stakes as high as they were, with the Princess in jeopardy and the Deathlord Verrutus lurking in every corner, Alabaster found himself far more stressed than usual.

"Pardon me, Chief," came the voice of Alabaster's secretary over the intercom at his desk. "I have your next holo-conference appointment on hold, sir."

Alabaster took a moment to check the calendar on his datapad to see that he was scheduled to have a briefing with a professor from the Central Galactic University concerning the Deathlords. "Remind me what this is concerning again?" Alabaster said into the intercom.

"An Egoi Professor named Riortrain believes he's discovered important information regarding the Deathlords from the reports of the Earthman's rescue of the Princess," his secretary explained. "He submitted a report a week ago concerning his findings, and you requested a meeting so he could brief you on the matter further."

Alabaster nodded. He remembered the report this Professor Riortrain had submitted. It was concerning the Deathlord Supremes, which the Princess and Professor Green had heard Zarrod mention when they were his captives, and some link they had to an extinct alien race. The report had not been very detailed, but it had caught Alabaster's attention and made him curious to know more about Riortrain's findings.

"Right," Alabaster acknowledged. "Please put the Professor through."

The viewscreen on Alabaster's desk was suddenly filled with the image of an exceptionally fat Egoi, his dark hair tied up in his race's traditional chonmage, with a long, bushy beard that went from below his nose down to his chest. Alabaster always found the lack of mouths on Egois disconcerting but did his best not to show it.

"Professor Riortrain," Alabaster said, "thank you for taking the time for this briefing."

The Egoi nodded his head. "<You are most welcome, Chief of Imperial Intelligence Alabaster,>" he responded, his telepathic communication being translated into a digital voice. "<It is my pleasure to be of service in this most difficult time.>"

"I appreciate that," Alabaster said as he called up the Professor's initial report on his datapad. "The report you submitted was quite an interesting read. You say that you've found specific references to the known Deathlord Supremes in an historical text?"

"<That is correct.>"

"Ever since Princess Glorianna returned from her trip to Earth with intelligence about the Deathlords, I've had my people combing through everything they can to see if we can glean any more insight into our enemy. So far, your discovery of the names for the known Deathlord Supremes is the only lead we've been able to turn up. What can you tell me about them?"

"<What I can tell you stems from an anonymous Paragon tome called *The Lanterne of Light*,>" Riortrain explained. "<Though its true authorship is under dispute, it is widely attributed to Wyclape Crumpe, an Egoi Paragon and theologian and the leading historian regarding Halcyonian culture.>"

Riortrain hit a few buttons on his console, calling up text from the *Lanterne of Light* on Alabaster's screen.

"<It is believed that Paragon Crumpe stumbled upon this knowledge during one of his many meditations, transcribing one of the lost Halcyonian religious texts as his mind opened to their culture. This led Crumpe to devote a great deal of his life to the study of the Halcyonian people, though many of his writings and conclusions about their culture and society are not backed up by historical proof. Thus, a lot of his writings are ignored by respected historians.>"

"And yet, you give it credence?"

"<Though it can often be hard to distinguish fact from fiction when it comes to Paragon meditative writings, my study of Crumpe and other Halcyonian academics leads me to believe that a great deal of what we know about Halcyonian culture may be accurate, though terribly incomplete.>"

Alabaster nodded as he scrolled through the pages of text on his screen. It was a large book, written in the Halcyonian's religious language, with which he was unfamiliar. The translation also didn't appear to be incredibly accurate, but that was to be expected with such a long-dead language and a little-known book.

"Tell me, Professor," Alabaster said. "What does an ancient religious text from an extinct culture have to do with the Deathlords?"

"<There is not much, from what I can surmise,>" Riortrain replied. "<Much of the text is dedicated to doctrine meant to teach the Halcyonians how to live, as many religious texts are. There is no mention of the Deathlords or any race like them within the text itself… at least, not until the names of the Deathlord Supremes come to light.>"

Riortrain called up what looked to be the final chapter of the book, entitled "The Book of Annihilation." Alabaster pursed his lips when he saw it. "Charming," he muttered.

"<The last chapter of the *Lanterne of Light* describes what the Halcyonian's believed to be the end of the universe and its rebirth as paradise. The Halcyonians did not believe in an afterlife as many cultures do. Their belief was that their souls remained trapped in this plane of existence, and they would be reincarnated into a paradise formed by the three Great Masters of Creation. But in order for paradise to be created, the old imperfect world must first be annihilated.>"

"So, a 'burn it down and build it back up' philosophy," Alabaster noted.

"<So it would seem. It's all fairly typical religious prophesy, up until we get to the Harbingers.>"

Riortrian called up a few pages on the screen, each containing illustrations of different, god-like beings. Each were humanoid in appearance, but they had no features to speak of – only different auras surrounding them.

"<The text states that there are five Harbingers of Annihilation who shall bring destruction to the universe and pave the way for paradise. You may recognize some of the names of these Harbingers.>"

The software translated the text from the Halcyonian language and formed a list, which Alabaster did indeed recognize. Four of the names were those Professor Green and Princess Glorianna reported as being Deathlord Supremes.

"<The first name, Zarrod, means 'bringer of conflict' in the Greater High Halcyonian language,>" Riortrain said. "<According to Paragon Crumpe, this Harbinger is associated with War. Zarrod is the architect of conflict. His job is to perpetuate a state of hostility, battle, and antagonism on an ever-growing scale.>"

Alabaster nodded. That seemed in line with what they knew about Zarrod. As commander of the Planetkiller fleet, he is the one who had initiated the war with the Empire and had sparked the most armed conflict with the Deathlord race to date.

"<The second name is Verrutus, which means 'bringer of weakness',>" Riortrain continued. "<This Harbinger is associated with Decay, which in this context means the process of rotting or decomposition. His task is to break down and weaken all life, making it easier for it to be consumed by the other Harbingers.>"

Alabaster felt a cold chill run up his spine. If what he knew about Verrutus was true, then this was indeed an eerily accurate description of the Deathlord. He'd been working in secret to undermine the entire Regalus Empire for quite some time, breaking it down from the inside. He was the rot that was causing the foundation of the Empire to crumble.

So far, the two Deathlord Supremes, with whom the Empire had experienced direct contact, seemed to match their counterparts in this *Lanterne of Light* book. It made Alabaster curious as to the others it mentioned. "Tell me about this next one," Alabaster said. "Mellegogg."

"<His name means 'bringer of disease', and he is tasked with Corruption,>" Riortrain replied.

Alabaster frowned. He didn't like the sound of that one bit. "Disease you say? What kind of disease?"

"<It is not very clear from this text,>" Riortrain responded. "<The Halcyonians attributed all sickness to a corruption of some kind, be it physical, mental, or spiritual. They believed the corruption of the mind or spirit could be just as harmful as one of the body. So things like depression, hopelessness, fear, anger… these are all forms that corruption can take. But in regards to this Mellegogg, his is a wide-spread corruption meant to blanket all of creation, in mind, body, *and* spirit.>"

Alabaster quickly made a note of that. Of all the Deathlords so far, this one troubled him the most, especially since he had yet to reveal himself. "I'm almost afraid to ask about the next one," Alabaster muttered.

"<Ashtoroth, bringer of famine,>" Riortrain continued. "<In this context, 'famine' is meant to embody a drastic, wide-reaching shortage of essential resources. It is the task of Ashtoroth to deny all that is consumed or relied upon to sustain life as we know it.>"

"So, food, water, things like that?"

"<That and more,>" replied Riortrain. "<Anything we rely upon. The air we breathe, the medicine we take, the technology we use... Ashtoroth could very well take it all away from us.>"

Alabaster sighed. *Grimmer and grimmer*, he thought. "And what of this last one? You said there were five Harbingers, yet our reports only name four Deathlord Supremes."

"<Yes, the fifth Harbinger of Annihilation is Moredread, whose name means 'bringer of destruction',>" Riortrain explained. "<He is said to be the embodiment of Wrath, which in this context translates to uncontrolled feelings of hatred and anger. Wrath, in its purest form, presents self-destructiveness, violence, and hate that can provoke feuds, which can go on for centuries. It is said that his arrival will mark the beginning of the end, and he, along with the other Harbingers, will annihilate all of creation.>"

"I don't suppose this text describes how they plan to do that?" Alabaster inquired.

"<Not in detail, I am afraid,>" responded Riortrain. "<According to Halcyonian religious texts, the five Harbingers of Annihilation will spread war, decay, corruption, famine, and wrath across the universe, all of which will combine to form what is referred to as 'The Great Death', in which everything in existence will die – from the lowliest insect to the brightest star. From this, the three Great Masters of Creation will remake existence into the Grand Paradise, and all Halcyonians will be reincarnated to live for eternity in bliss.>"

"Well, I guess the good news is that it has a happy ending," deadpanned Alabaster.

"<Indeed. It is actually theorized that the Halcyonians, as a culture, wished to usher in The Great Death to hasten the creation of the Grand Paradise. And there are quite a few references indicating that the Halcyonians worshipped and revered the Harbingers as gods themselves. Though the Harbingers' tasks are

quite awful, the Halcyonians saw them as the sign that a new beginning would be starting soon, and since all Halcyonians would be reincarnated in paradise, the Harbingers were not to be feared, but welcomed.>"

"Are there are any clues in the text as to what these Harbingers look like or where we may find them?"

"<Unfortunately, I have not come upon anything like that in my research. The closest thing to a description mentioned in the text is that the Harbingers take many forms. No two are alike, and they can inhabit various different likenesses to suit their purposes.>"

"So… in regards to the Deathlord Supremes, that means they may not look like actual Deathlords as we know them," noted Alabaster. "The Supremes could all be quite different from what we have encountered so far."

"<I would say that is a logical assumption, Chief Alabaster,>" Riortrain said. "<The Halcyonians seemed to believe that the Harbingers' true forms would be unknowable until they finally revealed themselves. Because of this, all references as to how the Harbingers may look are quite vague.>"

Alabaster tapped his finger on his desk, his mind processing this new information. "Professor, is there any more information about these Halcyonians? Their civilization, how they lived, what they looked like… how they became extinct?"

"<Again, I fear there is very little, Chief Alabaster. What we do know about them has been gleaned from ruins found on what is believed to be their home planet of Shadowsphere.>"

"Shadowsphere?"

"<Yes, named because of the constant cloud cover over the planet, which keeps it perpetually dark. It was discovered a couple hundred years ago by members of the Imperial Exploratory Service while mapping new hyperspace routes in the Herbert sector. Though some expeditions have been mounted to study the ruins of the Halcyonian civilization, there has not been great interest in the culture beyond certain academic circles. Thus, very little is truly known about them.>"

"And yet, entire religious texts from the species are being written by Paragons," Alabaster noted.

"<Yes, Chief Alabaster. But Paragons often tune into many strange types of knowledge during their meditations. Frankly, until the intelligence from the Earthman, there was very little reason to pay much attention to the Halcyonian

culture at all. Had I not done a focus in theological studies and previously researched their religious texts myself, I would never have even made this connection.>"

Alabaster nodded. "Professor, if I may ask… what would it take to discover more about these Halcyonians?"

Riortrain stroked his beard thoughtfully for a moment. "<Short of mounting an expedition to Shadowsphere? Not much that I can think of.>"

"Would you have any interest in leading such an expedition?"

"<Why, yes, Chief Alabaster! I would find that most exciting!>"

"Good," Alabaster said. "Anything you need – ships, supplies, manpower, funding – let me know. I'll ensure you get it."

"<That is quite a generous offer. I shall make up a detailed list and submit it to you, along with any and all research we currently have on Halcyonians.>"

"Do that. Thank you for your time, Professor. This briefing has been most enlightening."

After ending the call with the Professor, Alabaster's mind raced. This felt like the first real break in figuring out the vexing puzzle that was the Deathlords. If they are indeed somehow connected to this Halcyonian race, that means there could be clues as to whom the Deathlords really are and where they come from.

Beyond the Halcyonians, Professor Riortrain had given Alabaster some insight into the more immediate threats facing the Empire. According to the Earthman, Zarrod had been defeated, and Alabaster was already working on taking down Verrutus with the help of Heckubus Moriarty. That left three more Deathlord Supremes to worry about.

Alabaster looked over his notes from the briefing. The final Deathlord Supreme, Moredread, would be the hardest to find. After all, how does one track 'wrath'? Alabaster supposed he could look into any feuds that could be occurring in the universe, but then again, there were always feuds. However, famine and corruption had very specific signs that might help him track down the final two Supremes, and hopefully give him enough time to stop them.

"Computer," he said. "Call up any reports of famine from within the Empire. Include shortages of food, water, medicine, and essential supplies."

After a few moments, the computer replied. "I am sorry Chief. I am not finding any reports of famine from within the Empire. Matter replication makes shortages of any essential supplies virtually impossible."

Alabaster frowned at that. "Monitor all reports for shortages or theft of essential supplies," he ordered. "If there is even a hint of a famine, I want an alert."

"Alert for famine created, Chief."

"Now call up reports for any type of widespread disease," Alabaster continued. "I want to know about any type of sickness that could be affecting large populations."

"There are close to seven million reports of widespread disease within the Empire," the computer responded.

"Filter out all outbreaks that have known cures."

"Filtered," said the computer. "There are now four million reports of widespread disease."

"Filter out any that are race specific. Focus only on outbreaks that appear to infect any species."

"There are now 726,942 reported cases of widespread disease within the Empire."

"Now filter based on the population size of the infection," Alabaster commanded. "Eliminate all diseases or illnesses that have infected less than ten thousand people. Give priority to any pandemic diseases."

"There is one reported case of widespread disease that matches your search criteria, Chief," the computer responded.

Alabaster raised his eyebrow. He hadn't expected to have just one result. But if that were indeed the case, then it might be a good bet that wherever this disease was occurring, this Mellegogg character would most likely be behind it.

"What is the location of this disease?" Alabaster asked.

"The planet of Eionmeer," the computer responded.

CHAPTER ✥ 32

limmer sat in the Captain's chair on the bridge of *The Reaver* as it travelled through hyperspace. She ran her fingers over the cracked leather padding of the armrest, smiling to herself. Though she'd renamed the ship and changed how it looked on the outside, there was no mistaking it. This was and would always be *The Reaver* – the scrappiest fightercraft of the Great Border War, the deadliest pirate ship in the Visini Empire, and the ship that had changed her life such a long time ago.

"Fifteen minutes from destination, Captain," her Karkovian pilot, Tweak, said.

"Acknowledged. Let our passengers know our E.T.A.," Glimmer replied.

Because of the nature of this job, she'd had to choose her crew wisely. Glimmer only brought those she trusted the most. Tweak was one of her best pilots. Pops wasn't the best engineer in her employ, but the grizzled old Visini had been with her a long time. Airabelle was surprisingly good at math for an Orean, which made her a good navigator. Quess had patched Glimmer and her crew up enough times for her to know the Wezden[32] medic wouldn't do anything to endanger anyone's lives. And Smash may have been a Rattan thug, but he was Glimmer's thug, and had proven his worthiness performing security on many jobs.

When she'd explained the mission to her crew, she'd gotten mixed reactions, but all of them agreed to come on board. The only one who fought her on it was Gage. Normally, she'd have left Gage behind to run her business while she was away, but Glimmer was also afraid he might do something stupid and alert the authorities after she left in a misguided effort to protect her. She ultimately decided it was better to have him on the job by her side.

Gage approached the Captain's chair, gazing at the countdown to their destination on the bridge's main viewscreen, the displeased look he'd worn since leaving The Bazaar still plastered on his face. "Captain," he said, "may I just point out, yet again, that I think this is a bad idea."

"Your objection has been noted. Many times," Glimmer replied.

---

[32] Wezdens are red-hued humanoid aliens with stout rounded bodies, big eyes, and antennae that sprout from their foreheads.

Gage frowned. "I just don't see why we're risking our necks for this lot. The Red alone is worth a fortune, not to mention the bounties on the other two. Why risk getting caught and losing everything you've worked so hard for?"

Glimmer sighed and gave Gage an understanding look. "As tempting as it may be to collect on their bounties, I happen to believe there's more going on here than we know. Scallywag isn't one to risk his neck lightly. If he's willing to sneak onto a quarantined planet for the sake of rescuing the Princess of the Regalus Empire, then that tells me he believes everything the Earthman's been saying on the holonet."

"Even if that's the case, what's it to us?"

"It's one of those rare opportunities where we get to do the right thing, Gage. And in doing so, we get to help ourselves. It's a win-win."

"Doing the right thing is overrated."

"Then perhaps you should work for someone whose skin isn't blue."

Gage frowned. "I'd follow ya through a black hole and out the other end, Captain. I just don't understand why you'd have so much faith in a Red."

"I don't have faith in Scallywag, Gage," Glimmer said with a smile. "Just a lot of history."

It was then that the door leading to the bridge opened, and Smash led in Scallywag and his companions. The bristly black hair of the Rattan was standing on end as he kept one of his hands on the blaster pistol in his holster while eyeing Scallywag and the group for any sign of trouble. Scallywag frowned when he saw Glimmer sitting in the Captain's chair. She knew it would drive him mad seeing someone other than himself sitting there, but she took a perverse pleasure in annoying him.

"Comfy?" Scallywag asked.

"Extremely," Glimmer purred. "It's as though this seat were *built* for me."

Scallywag rolled his eyes. "Go on. Have yer fun. I'll be back in that chair soon enough."

Upon exiting hyperspace, Eionmeer loomed large before them. The planet displayed on the viewscreen appeared dry and arid, dominated by yellow landmasses and only small bodies of water.

"Oh, my," Green said upon seeing the image on the viewscreen. "What's happened to the planet?"

"Is something the matter, Professor?" inquired Shanks.

"The Eionmeer I remember was quite lush," Green said. "From the looks of things now, though, it would appear the planet is… dying."

"Well, they quarantined it fer a reason," Scallywag said.

"Yes, but… how could a plague literally be affecting the whole planet?" Green wondered aloud.

"According to the latest update of my cultural databases, Master Green, it would seem Eionmeer has been suffering from an ecological decline for quite some time," Dan informed him, "so much so, the colony located on the planet had to have terraforming generators installed around it to keep the settlement habitable."

"Oy, ya couldn't have given us that update before we left the Conclave?" Scallywag asked. "The planet dyin' may affect our plans."

"Forgive me, Master Scallywag, but I did not deem it relevant to our mission. And while at the Conclave, I was rather preoccupied with completing the upgrades Master Heckubus had recommended for me. If it is of any consolation, though Eionmeer is indeed facing an ecological crisis, it is not estimated to be uninhabitable for at least another two to three years."

"That seems like an awfully short period of time," Green muttered. "I was here with the Imperial Exploratory Service not five years ago. I remember talk that the planet was experiencing some strange ecological anomalies back then, but to have the whole planet be affected so drastically in such a short timespan…"

"Hey, greenskin, focus," said Scallywag, snapping his fingers to break Green out of his overanalyzing. "We ain't here ta save tha planet. We're here ta save the Princess. It don't matter if Eionmeer is a jungle or a dry rock. The only thing we're here for is tha Paragon. Savvy?"

"Captain, we're being scanned," Gage informed Glimmer. "We have a Visini vessel moving to intercept."

"On the screen, please," Glimmer said.

The image on the bridge's viewscreen changed to show that of a massive capital ship. It was extremely long, with a curved underside to its hull, and four wings – two in the front and two in the back – with large engines attached to them. A structure toward the back of the vessel jutted upward, ending in a rectangle shape that overlooked the expanse of the ship's top deck. The name on its side read: *V.I.N.V.*[33] *Megavolt*.

"What tha bloody blazes is that?" Scallywag asked, looking at the image with curiosity.

"One of the new Terranda-class capital ships," Glimmer said. "Highly advanced, state of the art, and almost as big as your ego."

Scallywag smiled at that. "Almost," he agreed. "So tha Visini navy has been busy buildin' itself up, eh? Why dispatch such a fine specimen o' spacecraft fer quarantine duty?"

"Probably because a single Terranda vessel can do the job of three Variant-class ships," Glimmer said. "With this ship guarding the Visini side and the Regal vessels guarding the other, my guess is the planet is pretty well secured."

"Aye. With the added bonus of showing off our navy's new tech and rubbin' it in tha Regal's faces."

"I'm sure that played a part in the decision, as well," Glimmer said with a smile.

"Captain, we're being hailed," said Airabelle.

Glimmer turned to her passengers. "Time for those fancy disguises of yours, gentlemen," she said.

Scallywag and the others all enabled their hologuise emitters before Glimmer answered the hail. A light blue-skinned Visini with a neatly trimmed grey beard appeared on the bridge's viewscreen. "Merchant vessel *Bluebell*, this is Rintin of House Richmarr, executive officer and first lieutenant of the Visini Imperial Naval Vessel *Megavolt*. You are to turn back immediately. This system is under quarantine."

"I'm sorry, Lieutenant Rintin, but we are here to deliver some much needed medical supplies and relief aid for the Twin Rivers settlement," Glimmer replied. "We are submitting our emergency medical clearance credentials now."

Rintin checked the credentials as they were transmitted. "Acknowledged, *Bluebell*," he said. "Credentials received and verified. Please direct your ship to the *Megavolt* and dock for inspection."

Glimmer raised her eyebrows. "Inspection? Did you not just say our credentials were checked and verified?"

---

[33] V.I.N.V. stands for Visini Imperial Naval Vessel.

"Captain Eisenwolf has ordered all ships delivering supplies to the planet be inspected before proceeding to Port Overlook."

The sound of the Captain's name gave Glimmer pause. "Did you say... Captain Eisenwolf?" she asked.

"Yes. He is the commanding officer of *The Megavolt*."

Glimmer frowned. "Surely we're to be inspected at the port, Lieutenant. Why must we submit to such a thing twice?"

"Captain Eisenwolf does not trust the Regals running the port to be diligent enough in their duties."

"And what is the Captain afraid will get through? People want to escape a quarantine, not sneak into one."

"The situation on the planet lends itself to a lucrative black market," Rintin replied. "We've intercepted attempts to smuggle illegal drugs and other contraband to the surface."

"And is my word as a Blue and our verified credentials not enough for you to believe we are not smugglers, Lieutenant?"

"If it were up to me, that would be sufficient," Rintin said. "But it is not sufficient for Captain Eisenwolf."

Glimmer sighed. "Very well. Please forward us the docking instructions."

Once the transmission ended, Scallywag and the others disengaged their hologuises. Glimmer looked at Scallywag, visibly unhappy. "Eisenwolf?" she said. "Of all the people to be commanding that ship, it's *Eisenwolf*?"

Scallywag frowned. "Relax, lass. It ain't like he knows we're comin'."

"I'm sorry, do you know this Eisenwolf fellow?" Green asked.

"Eisenwolf the Blue of House Maestro," Glimmer said. "Son of the great Admiral Steppenwulf the Purple, hero of the Great Border War and casualty of Harkon's rebellion, courtesy of one Scallywag the Red."

Shanks frowned. "You are responsible for his father's death?" he asked, looking at Scallywag.

"I'm responsible fer the deaths of lots o' fathers," Scallywag replied. "But not all their sons hunt me across tha galaxy. Eisenwolf's been on me tail ever since he got his first command. Took what I did personal."

"Can't imagine why," Glimmer muttered.

"It was war, lass," Scallywag argued. "Things happen in war. Ya deal with 'em and move on."

"I'm sure Northstar would agree with you."

Scallywag's face darkened upon hearing his brother's name. "Just because Eisenwolf has himself a fancy ship doesn't mean we're in trouble here," Scallywag insisted. "We let 'em do their inspection and stick to the plan. He don't know I'm here, and it's gonna stay that way. Savvy?"

With that, Scallywag turned and marched off the bridge. Glimmer watched him go, a sinking feeling in the pit of her stomach.

"Captain?" Gage asked. "Everything okay?"

"It's fine, Gage," she replied. "Bring us in for inspection."

Upon docking in one of *The Megavolt's* hangar bays, Glimmer and her crew waited patiently for what seemed like an abnormally long time as their ship was scanned by the hangar's sensors. Eventually, they were ordered to open their boarding ramps to allow an inspection team aboard, led by First Lieutenant Rintin himself. Glimmer joined him in the cargo bay as his men searched through the containers.

"I noticed on your shipping license you are of House Brightstar," Rintin said. "That house sounds familiar to me. Is there somewhere I'd know it from?"

"We are one of the lesser Great Merchant houses," Glimmer said. "We operate many shipping fleets."

"Yes, perhaps that's it," Rintin said as one of his men approached and saluted him.

"All cargo has been inspected, sir," the Visini soldier said. "They're clear."

Rintin nodded in acknowledgement and glanced down at his datapad. "We've checked your credentials, cargo manifest, and crew roster. Everything appears to be in order. You are now free to proceed to Port Overlook."

Glimmer was able to breathe easier once Rintin had led his soldiers away, and the ship had been able to launch from *The Megavolt*. When she returned to the cargo bay, Scallywag seemed to have noticed her tense demeanor.

"Relax, lass," he said. "The worst is behind us now."

"Easy for you to say," grumbled Glimmer. "I don't like complications. And Eisenwolf has always been a major complication."

"Aye, but the bloke may have done us a favor. If those on tha port know we've already been searched by the Visinis, chances are they ain't gonna look too closely at us. My guess is it's smooth sailin' from here on out."

Glimmer was still concerned about Eisenwolf's presence in the system, but she had to admit Scallywag had a point. She looked at Scallywag and his companions and sighed. "This better be worth the trouble, Scally," she said.

"You wouldn't be here if'n it wasn't," Scallywag replied with a wink.

Glimmer resisted the urge to smile. For some reason, Scallywag's bravado never failed to get to her.

Scallywag turned to his companions. "Right, so here's how this is gonna work, gents," he said as he moved to one of the cargo containers. "We didn't have ta hide anything from the Visinis, but we do from tha Regals. These here containers look standard issue, but they got themselves a false bottom. The Professor, the monk, and meself are gonna be hidden in our own containers. Standard procedure for these customs transports is a sensor scan. Sometimes they may do a visual inspection of the container's contents, but that's usually only if they're suspicious about something."

"Will we not be detected by the sensor scan?" asked Green.

"The very bottom o' these crates has an equalarium lining in the casing," Scallywag said. "It'll prevent any sensor readings from being picked up. Just try not to move too much when the scans occur. Anyway, while we're packed away, the android will be hacking inta the port's teleportation array. Ain't that right, robot?"

"That is correct, Master Scallywag!" Dan replied. "I shall need to establish a direct link to the port's systems, but once I have successfully accomplished that task, I will then be able to access the array remotely."

"Once Danny-boy has his link established, Glimmer will pack him away in another container to be teleported down to tha planet," Scallywag said. "Her and her crew will then head to tha rendezvous point and wait for us ta teleport back onboard."

"Waiting for you will be trickier now that we know Eisenwolf is in the system," Glimmer said. "He's very diligent about his patrols."

"Aye. If'n ya need ta change anythin', just send us a message ta Dan's communicator," Scallywag said. "Gettin' down ta the surface will be tha easy part. Gettin' off will be tha real challenge. We gotta do whatever it takes to make our escape, so if we need ta improvise, so be it."

"We are on approach to Port Overlook, Captain," came Gage's voice over Glimmer's communicator.

"Acknowledged," Glimmer replied before looking to Scallywag. "It's showtime."

"Right," said Scallywag. "You heard her, gents. Up and at 'em."

"This is so exciting!" said Green as he climbed into his container. "I've never been smuggled before!"

"You never forget your first time," said Glimmer dryly, as she helped secure the false bottom on top of Green.

Once the group had all been secured in their crates, Glimmer led Dan down to the boarding ramp where Gage and the other members of her crew were waiting. "Try not to draw too much attention to yourself," Glimmer instructed Dan. "We'll keep the technicians as occupied as we can, but if you get caught, we'll be in a very bad position."

"Do not worry, Mistress Glimmer," Dan replied. "I happen to excel at being overlooked. I consider it one of my specialties."

"Good to know," Glimmer muttered as she felt the ship come to a landing.

"We've successfully docked with the port, Captain," came Tweak's voice over Glimmer's comm.

Glimmer signaled Gage to open the boarding ramp. When it had fully lowered, there was a young Regal customs agent in a beige uniform waiting to greet them. "Welcome to Port Overlook!" the man said. "My name is Drayke. I'll be the one overseeing your delivery today."

"I'm Captain Glimmer of *The Bluebell*," Glimmer said as she descended the ramp and handed Drayke a datapad. "This is my crew. We're here to deliver emergency medical supplies and aid packages to the planet."

"And they are desperately needed, for certain," Agent Drayke replied as he looked at the manifest on the datapad. "I tell you, it's been a nightmare ever since this quarantine was instituted. Most of the planet's natural resources have dried up, so all supplies on the ground have had to be replicated. It's putting a real strain on the power generators of the colony. Most of our normal supply ships aren't able to make it through the blockade, especially on the Visini side. Frankly, I'm amazed you got past *The Megavolt*."

"Why is that?"

"The Visinis have been incredibly strict about the quarantine protocol. Normally we're the ones who decide what makes it to the planet's surface, but ever since *The Megavolt* showed up, the Visinis have been throwing their weight around and intercepting most of the system's space traffic. I've heard talk the ship's captain is a real hardcase. Apparently, he was supposed to be taking part in the manhunt for the Earthman but got assigned this duty at the last minute, so he's determined to make everyone as miserable as he is. Not that those on the planet don't need to be any more miserable, mind you."

That certainly sounds like Eisenwolf, Glimmer thought. "Isn't the Regal contingent of the quarantine able to do anything about that?" she asked.

Drayke shrugged. "If they are, they don't seem to be. With all the resources focused on recovering the Princess, the Empire has only sent us three frigates to enforce the quarantine. Bare minimum, you know? Ever since the Great Border War, Eionmeer has been a point of contention between the Visinis and the Empire, so I'm guessing the Regals are under orders not to do anything that might provoke them, even though the Visinis seem to be looking for any excuse to throw a fit."

Drayke handed the datapad back to Glimmer. "Looks like everything is in order," he said as a group of worker-bots boarded the ship to transport the cargo from it. "You and your crew can head to the concourse level if you want. There are some nice restaurants there if you're hungry. I can also recommend lodgings if you're not planning to stay on your ship."

"We would actually prefer to supervise the delivery to the planet surface," Glimmer said. "I want to make sure these supplies actually get to those who need them."

Drayke nodded. "That shouldn't be a problem. Follow me."

Agent Drayke led Glimmer and her crew through Port Overlook as the cargo from *The Bluebell* was transported through customs. They followed Drayke through a long corridor which led to a large room containing a massive teleportation platform. There were a few technicians loitering around, looking bored, when the group entered.

"You lot seem busy," Gage noted.

"Yeah, it's been slow ever since the quarantine started," Drayke replied. "Used to be there was a lot of trade happening around here. We'd be transporting cargo and personnel to and from the planet all day. But now, well… let's just say my job has gotten much easier."

"If possible, I'd like these containers teleported to the surface first," Glimmer said, referring on the manifest to the containers in which Scallywag and the others were stashed. "They are the ones with the most needed medicine and should be given priority."

Drayke took note of the containers and nodded. "Those have already been checked through the sensor scans. I'll get them loaded for transport right away."

Glimmer watched as the worker-bots arrived with the cargo containers from her ship, loading them onto the teleportation platform one by one. The process was rather slow for her liking. She kept watch on Dan out of the corner of her eye as the robot milled around, looking for a place to connect to the port's computer systems. However, the abundance of inactive technicians seemed to be making it difficult for him to find an opportunity to do so.

Just as the third crate had been loaded onto the platform, the doors to the room opened and a large group of Visini soldiers – all of them armed – came rushing inside, taking everyone by surprise. "NOBODY MOVE!" they shouted as they spread out with weapons drawn, covering Glimmer's crew and the spaceport's technicians, all of whom immediately raised their hands in surrender.

Lieutenant Rintin entered with even more soldiers following him, his face stern. "In the name of the enlightened Emperor Maxmillen, I order you to stop this transport immediately," he said to Drayke.

Agent Drayke looked at Rintin, wide-eyed. "What? Why? You have no authority here."

"Under subsection nine of clause twelve of the emergency cooperation pact between our two empires, we have the authority to take command if we feel there is an imminent threat to the integrity of the quarantine," Rintin stated.

"I... how do I know that's even true?" Drayke asked, obviously in over his head.

"Go to your supervisor if you do not believe me," Rintin replied, "and take your men with you. For the time being we are securing this teleporter and taking the crew of *The Bluebell* into our custody."

Agent Drayke frowned but did not argue. He gave Glimmer an apologetic look before he and his co-workers made a hasty exit. All those who were with Glimmer were immediately disarmed and patted down, the soldiers keeping weapons trained on them all the while.

"What is the meaning of this?" demanded Glimmer.

"It turns out I have heard of your house before, Lady Glimmer," Rintin responded, "at least, in regards to you and known sympathizers of war criminals. Once I realized who you were, we were forced into this course of action."

"I have no sympathy for war criminals," Glimmer insisted.

"Tell that to him," Rintin said, before turning to look expectantly down the corridor behind him.

The sound of heavy boots meeting the metal of the hallway rang out. A Visini with deep blue skin and dressed in the proud navy blue uniform of an officer, complete with golden epaulets, walked purposefully into the room. His silver hair was slicked back on his head, his white-gloved hands were clasped behind his back, and his piercing yellow eyes were hard and cold as he met Glimmer's gaze. He stopped before her, looking her up and down briefly before settling on an expression of abject disdain.

"Lady Glimmer," Eisenwolf said, his voice hard as steel.

"Captain Eisenwolf," Glimmer responded. "I demand to know what you think you are doing!"

"Detaining you and your crew for questioning," he stated.

"On what grounds?"

"On the grounds of your connection to Scallywag the Red."

"It has been years since that scoundrel abducted me," Glimmer protested. "I've not had contact with him since!"

"That is not what I have heard," Eisenwolf replied.

"Then you have heard wrong," Glimmer countered. "There is no justification for this unlawful detainment. I have committed no crime. Even your own inspections cleared us."

"Yes, about those inspections…" Eisenwolf said, producing a datapad from his pocket. "Upon closer analysis, we found some interesting developments concerning your ship." A holographic image of *The Bluebell* was projected from the datapad. The ship's outer casing was pulled away to reveal a sleeker ship beneath it. "It would appear your vessel is actually a Visini Man of War class Frigate, disguised as a freighter."

"There is no law against flying a repurposed spacecraft," Glimmer replied.

"Still, it is curious. Especially when the spacecraft appears to be none other than *The Reaver*."

"The ship's name is *The Bluebell*."

Eisenwolf shut off the projection and took a step toward Glimmer, staring her down and looming over her menacingly. "Do not play games with me," Eisenwolf growled. "I'd know that ship anywhere. I've hunted it across the galaxy and back. It's Scallywag the Red's. And you will tell me how you came to be in possession of it."

"I don't know what you are talking about," Glimmer said, not allowing herself to be intimidated. "Check the ship's I.D. transponder. There's nothing there but what's on the registry."

"We shall check it thoroughly, I assure you, once we've impounded it and taken it into *The Megavolt*."

"You can't do that!" Glimmer objected.

"You'd be surprised at what I can do, Lady Glimmer," Eisenwolf said before snapping his fingers at his men and pointing to the containers on the teleporter platform. "Take the cargo, as well," he ordered. "I want everything that was on that ship."

As his men moved to take the containers, Glimmer rushed up to the platform to put herself between the men and the cargo. "These are emergency medical supplies for the crisis taking place on the planet!" Glimmer said. "They contain desperately needed philanthropic aid sanctioned by the Visini government! You must not prevent their delivery!"

"If they are as you say, they will eventually be delivered to the settlement," Eisenwolf stated. "But seeing as how *The Reaver* is a known pirate and smuggling vessel, it must be assumed any cargo transported by it is either stolen or contraband."

"Your men already inspected all of it," Glimmer protested. "They found nothing!"

"Nothing via a cursory visual inspection and sensor scans. But I believe a more thorough inspection to be in order."

With that, two of the Visini soldiers flipped over one of the containers, spilling its contents onto the floor, along with Shanks. The monk tumbled onto the teleporter platform and before he could get to his feet, one of the soldiers smashed him in the face with the butt of his plasma rifle. The blow caused Shanks to drop his staff, which one of the soldiers promptly kicked away from him before stepping off the platform, keeping his weapon trained on the monk from a safe distance. Shanks cried out in pain, clutching at his chest as he lay on the ground.

"No!" exclaimed Glimmer.

Another container was tipped over and Professor Green fell out. "Oh, dear," he muttered as the soldiers trained their weapons on him.

Two more soldiers opened the container Glimmer was protecting, only to be promptly shot by purple rays, causing them to fall off the platform and onto the floor. Before anyone could react, Scallywag leapt out of the container and fired at the Visinis who'd tipped over the other containers, stunning them, as well.

Eisenwolf's eyes grew wide at the sight of Scallywag. "You!" he cried.

"Tha one and only!" replied Scallywag before taking a shot at Eisenwolf.

Rintin moved in front of his Captain and took the blast, crying out and falling to the floor as more soldiers rushed forward, their rifles at ready. Scallywag suddenly grabbed Glimmer, using her as a shield as he put a blaster to her temple. Eisenwolf's men immediately trained their blasters on him.

"Put 'em down!" barked Scallywag. "Or I swear on Osiris, I'll kill her!"

"What are you doing?" muttered Glimmer quietly, not liking the position she was in one bit.

"Just trust me," Scallywag whispered back.

Eisenwolf eyed Scallywag carefully. "You think I won't order them to shoot?" he asked.

"I think you getting a Blue lady of a big house killed wouldn't exactly help yer career."

"That 'Blue lady' is a smuggler."

"She didn't know we were here," Scallywag lied.

"I don't believe you."

"Believe what ya want, so long as ya lower yer weapons and back away."

None of Eisenwolf's men moved. Green looked on nervously as Eisenwolf and Scallywag stared each other down. "Oh, dear," he muttered. "They don't appear to be cooperating..."

"Thanks fer the update," Scallywag grumbled. "Monk, ya wanna jump in here at some point?"

Shanks was visibly trembling. He tried once more to reach for his staff, but the Visini soldiers nearby focused back on him immediately. "I fear... I am unable to help..." Shanks said through gritted teeth.

"You will release your hostage, drop your weapon, and step off the teleporter immediately," Eisenwolf said, his voice icy cold.

"Or what?"

"Or I'll kill all of you," Eisenwolf stated.

Scallywag frowned. He knew Eisenwolf wasn't bluffing.

"Don't do it," Glimmer whispered. "He'll kill you anyway."

"I know he will," Scallywag whispered back. "But I ain't gonna have you die on my account."

"Scally…"

Before Scallywag could release Glimmer, the teleportation platform lit up. Eisenwolf's eyes widened in surprise. "What's happening???" he demanded.

Scallywag looked past Eisenwolf to see Dan had linked himself up to a control panel unnoticed while the stand-off was occurring. "I fear I will not be able to accompany you on your mission, my friends," Dan said. "However, considering the alternative, I do feel this is the best course of action. Good luck."

"NO!" Eisenwolf cried as the hum of the teleporter grew louder. Scallywag saw him draw his own weapon and aim it at Glimmer. Scallywag immediately moved her aside as Eisenwolf fired, right before the flash of the teleporter.

And like that, they were gone.

Eisenwolf glared at the empty teleportation platform, seething, as his men rushed toward Dan and yanked his connection from the teleporter console. "Oh, my," Dan said as the Visini soldiers manhandled him.

"What are your orders, sir?" one of the soldiers asked.

Eisenwolf looked at the remainder of Glimmer's crew, all of whom were being held at gunpoint by his men. "Take them to the brig, and put them with the others," he said.

"And the robot?"

Eisenwolf looked at Dan, who gazed back at him with his large ocular orbs. "I do apologize for hindering your efforts to capture my companions, sir," Dan said. "However, my programming dictated—"

Without wasting another moment, Eisenwolf raised his weapon and shot Dan in the head. The plasma blast caused the side of Dan's head to erupt in a small explosion as the machinery within melted, and the robot's remains crumpled to a smoking heap on the floor.

 ~ **339** ~

"Take it to Maintenance," Eisenwolf grumbled. "Have them scrap it for parts."

"Right away, sir."

As his orders were carried out, Eisenwolf stepped forward and glared at the teleportation platform his prey had just been on moments before.

"You won't get away," Eisenwolf swore. "I'll be coming for you, Scallywag… and I won't stop until I *get you!*"

The group materialized in a field of dead grass on the other side of a chain-link fence on the outskirts of the settlement. Scallywag, who'd been moving when the teleporter engaged, fell to the ground, crying out as he grabbed onto his arm.

"Scally!" exclaimed Glimmer as she rushed to his side.

Scallywag grunted as he looked at his forearm where Eisenwolf's blast had landed. "Bloody squick…" he grumbled, gritting his teeth in pain.

"You'll be okay," Glimmer said as she looked at the wound. "It looks like it just grazed you."

"Aye, and melted me blasted hologuise wristband in the process…" Scallywag lamented as he inspected the damage the plasma blast had done.

Professor Green moved to Shanks' side as the monk quickly recovered his staff, seemingly able to breathe easier the moment he took hold of it.

"Brother Shanks," Green said. "Are you alright?"

"Yes…" Shanks replied as Green helped him up. "Now I am."

"What happened up there?" demanded Scallywag as he got to his feet. "We coulda used some of yer hocus-pocus right then!"

"I… was unable to concentrate," Shanks replied.

Scallywag sneered, not happy with Shanks' response, but he didn't press the issue. Glimmer looked up at the hazy image of Port Overlook high in the sky. "Eisenwolf has my people," she said. "We need to get them back!"

"Oy, that'll have ta wait," Scallywag said. "We got bigger problems at tha moment."

"Bigger than being hunted by the most ruthless commander in the Visini fleet?" snapped Glimmer.

"Aye," replied Scallywag. "In case ya don't remember, that android was our bloody escape plan!"

"Oh, dear," muttered Green.

"Yeah, that's putting it mildly," said Scallywag as he turned and looked at the sorry state of the Twin Rivers settlement which stretched out before him. "Congratulations, everyone," he said. "We've just been stranded on tha bloody plague planet."

CHAPTER 🪐 33

t didn't take long for Jack's life at the Conclave to fall into a routine, which essentially was broken down among workforce duty, his manifestation classes, and study time. The lack of distractions in daily life at the Conclave also began to wear on Jack. There was no television, no ultranet, and no video games. The only real forms of entertainment were on the recreation level, where the Conclave's residents would put on talent shows, concerts, lectures, and various other activities and events. But other than sleeping, there wasn't much else to do besides work and study.

Jack's manifestation classes had been progressing, but the further along in the curriculum he went, the more obvious it became as to why the Unlikelies had been grouped together as they had. Wallbeard was indeed a good teacher, but all the Initiates in Jack's class seemed pretty hopeless. No one had been able to successfully manifest anything yet, which drove them to study harder and harder as the day for the manifestation exam grew closer. Jack felt like he'd been studying for months with no real progress. And he wasn't the only one getting frustrated. The stress of impending failure was definitely starting to take its toll. More people dropped out and went home, making the living quarters seem emptier and sadder than it had previously. Only Flitter seemed immune to the malaise, and she continued to try to keep everyone's spirits high by being her usual annoying self – which, as one could imagine, didn't do much to actually keep spirits high.

After a long study session during which Jack had stared at his periodic table for so long his vision had gone blurry, he couldn't take it anymore. He needed to do something that didn't involve thinking about atoms for a while. When he entered the common area, Flitter was dancing around the room, which was simply her way of reciting in Orean all the names and atomic numbers of elements she'd memorized. Scrappy was surrounded by books about chemistry, and the others all appeared to be meditating.

"Hey," Jack said. "I'm going to take a break and head up to the recreation level. Anyone want to come with?"

"I would! But I really have to get my radioactive elements down," Flitter said as she twirled around and continued dancing.

"I'm good," Scrappy replied, without looking up from his books. "I'm on my fifth memorization of all the elements, and I'd like to get a sixth in sometime today."

Jack raised an eyebrow. "You've memorized all the elements five times?" he asked.

Scrappy glanced up at him. "You mean you haven't?"

Jack sighed, then nudged Krupp, who was sitting cross-legged nearby, trying to meditate. "What about you, dude? What's say we cut loose for a bit? Recharge our batteries?"

Krupp sighed and opened his eyes. "It's tempting, but I really need to stay focused. I'm determined not to have to come back here an eleventh time."

Jack nodded. When it became clear no one else was interested in taking a study break, he set out on his own, taking a stroll up to the recreation level to see what was going on.

Jack smiled as he entered one of the chambers and saw some students playing a game of gravityball. The court was very similar to the one on which he'd played back on Omnicron, but there were numerous students sitting on the edges of the different levels, watching the game intently. Jack could only assume those were the ones practicing their gravity manipulation skills.

According to the scoreboard, the current game was almost over, and Jack was eager to see if he could get in on the next one. A fun activity was exactly what he needed to forget about the pressure of the impending exam and his complete inability to manifest anything.

"Hey, Hero!" came a voice. Jack glanced behind him and saw Tannyn and his friends entering the chamber. They were all clad in their gravityball gear. Tannyn had a huge cocky grin on his face as he spun his helmet in his hand. "Shouldn't you be studying? Big exam coming up, you know."

"Figured I'd take a break from studying and clear my head," Jack said. "Do you know where I can get some equipment to play?"

Tannyn's group laughed at that – with Tannyn laughing the loudest. "You want gravityball equipment, Hero, you got to make it yourself!" Tannyn replied. "This is the Conclave! You may be used to having things handed to you, but here, everyone is responsible for providing for themselves. Don't worry, I'll get you started!"

Tannyn then manifested a gravityball and tossed it to Jack. The ball was, of course, set at its heaviest gravity and catching it knocked Jack down. Tannyn and his group chuckled as they walked away. "Good luck on the exam, Hero!" Tannyn called. "Hope to see you at the start of classes – however *unlikely* that may be!"

Jack scowled at the group as they laughed at him one more time before heading onto the court. Jack pushed the heavy gravityball aside and picked himself up off the floor. *Guess gravityball is out of the question*, he thought with disappointment. *Not like I'd want to play with those jerks anyway.*

Jack wandered around the recreation level for a bit longer, looking for something to do. There were some poetry readings going on, some band practices, and even an Orean debate team, but nothing that really captured Jack's fancy. Eventually, he sullenly left the area and made his way to the Crystal Concourse.

The gyroscopic artificial sun shined overhead as Jack meandered through the different tiers of the concourse. He passed by ornate fountains, lush gardens, and majestic crystals. He even passed by the welcoming arch with the Conclave's motto on it. *All things, no teachers*, Jack thought as he read the arch's inscription. *Kinda wish there were a few more teachers available right now, to tell the truth...*

Eventually, Jack found himself on the tier leading down to the Conclave's tether. The portal rotated between its two stone pillars. There was something peaceful about its movement, which prompted Jack to sit down on one of the steps leading to its platform. Jack sat there, staring at the tether, the ripples in the fabric of reality swirling hypnotically. He glanced over at some students lounging around, studying. The sight made him think of study hall with Shepherd, and that made him think of the advice the Paragon had given him back on Earth.

I feel so helpless. Am I playing the victim again? Jack asked himself. *Am I just letting this place tell me what I have to do, instead of taking control and determining my own destiny? Is that why I'm struggling so much?* Jack sighed and picked at his pant leg. *I miss my friends. I wish they were here. I wish my ship were here! Being on it always made me feel better.*

It was then Jack felt the back of his head tingle. He glanced back up at the tether and smiled. *I can still feel you, even when I'm in an entirely different universe, huh?*

Jack's head tingled again, as though the Earthship were answering him through the tether. It comforted Jack to know his ship was out there, even if he couldn't see it.

"I can jump out of supertowers, fight Deathlords, and outfly entire fleets of ships. But I can't do the one thing I need to in order to be a Paragon," Jack muttered. "How is it I'm able to do all this amazing stuff, but the things I *want* to do, I can't?"

There was another tingle in the back of Jack's head, and memories of his friends appeared in his mind. Scallywag, Grohm, Professor Green, Heckubus, Shanks, Anna, Shepherd – even Dan – all appeared. It was then Jack realized what the Earthship was trying to tell him.

"I've never done it alone…" Jack realized. "I've always had others there to help me figure things out. To guide me."

Jack smiled and got to his feet.

"Good talk," Jack said to the tether. "We should do this more often."

The Earthship made Jack's head tingle again, as if to say: *My pleasure. You know where to find me.*

Jack began making his way back to his chambers, thinking over his new revelation. His normal companions were not around, but he had new ones here in the Conclave. And though they weren't the group most likely to succeed, Jack had to admit he was never part of groups that were. But by working together, somehow, they always seemed to pull it off. When Jack re-entered the common room, every one of his friends was still studying. He clapped his hands to get their attention, interrupting their meditations.

"Guys!" he said. "Guys! Listen up. I've got an idea…"

"Not now, manling," Morosa said. "Take your testosterone-poisoned idea elsewhere!"

"<To put it more civilly than Morosa, Jack, we are busy studying,>" Snodgrass said.

"Yeah? And how's that working out for you?" Jack asked. "We've all been studying. For ages! And we're no closer to manifesting anything than we were when we started."

"I understand you're frustrated, Jack, but I don't need that kind of negative thinking around here," Krupp said.

"But that's just it – I'm not being negative," Jack countered. "I'm just pointing out that what we've been doing hasn't been working! So why do we keep trying to do what doesn't work?"

Everyone gave each other curious looks.

"Well… what else can we do?" asked Scrappy.

"Yeah, we're just following Master Wallbeard's teachings," Flitter said.

"But don't you guys see? We've been trying to do it separately!" Jack said. "We're each doing our own thing and struggling because of it. We need to shake things up! Try something different. Let's work on this together!"

"Work on it together?" Krupp said, looking confused. "You mean, like, study as a group?"

"I mean bring our own unique skills to the table and help strengthen each other where we're weak," Jack said. "All of us here have things we're good at individually, so let's combine our efforts and help one another out! I've learned about meditation from a Luminadric Monk, Krupp's manifested stuff before, Scrappy knows all the atoms, Snodgrass has telepathy, Flitter can keep us from getting discouraged, and Morosa… well… she's really good at giving orders."

"What do you mean by 'giving orders'???" Morosa demanded.

Jack rolled his eyes. "Just saying girls are better leaders than men," he muttered.

"I accept this explanation," Morosa declared.

"Anyway, I know we're all struggling here," Jack continued. "And maybe it's true that as individuals, we're unlikely to make it. But I've faced the impossible before, and if I've learned anything, it's that when people come together and work as a team, they can do the impossible. So what do you guys say?"

The group was quiet for a moment before Flitter jumped to her feet. "Let's do it!" she cheered. She then looked at everyone else, encouraging them to join her.

"Well… I suppose it couldn't hurt to try," said Scrappy.

"<I can think of no better alternative,>" Snodgrass stated.

"I will not allow this glass ceiling to defeat me!" Morosa claimed. "Even if it means partnering with filthy man-animals to do it!"

Jack met the gaze of Krupp, who smiled and nodded in agreement. "Well, you know what they say. Tenth time's the charm."

Jack smiled. "Alright, team. Let's huddle up!"

The group came together and sat on the floor in a circle. "So, how is this supposed to work?" inquired Krupp.

"Well, when my friend Shanks taught me how to meditate, it was all about getting your spiritual energy to connect to your mind and to the energy of others," Jack said. "So… if we all join hands, and try to connect our energy, we should be able to enter into a shared vision together."

"Kind of like Master Wallbeard does with the guided mediations?" Flitter asked.

"Yeah, kinda," Jack said. "I mean, we've all been meditating, right? The only difference here is we'll focus on connecting to each other rather than on thinking about atoms and stuff."

"Must I be forced to hold your hand?" Morosa asked. "I find your masculine touch repugnant."

"Um, I don't think it'll work if you don't," Jack replied.

Morosa sighed in exasperation. "Very well," she said. "But if this is simply a ploy to molest my palm, I shall break you."

"Noted," answered Jack. "Okay, everybody ready?"

With that, the group all joined hands and closed their eyes. "Find your energy," Jack said, trying to remember how Shanks had instructed him. "Feel how it flows through you. Notice where it goes. Notice where your own life's energy goes. Can you feel its Source? The place it comes from?"

"Um… maybe?" Flitter said, unsure.

"<I feel something, but I am unable to tell if it is spiritual energy or a stomach ache,>" Snodgrass said.

Jack opened one of his eyes and peeked at the group, all struggling with his guidance. "Uh… try focusing on your chest, under your ribs. That's the genesis of your spiritual energy. Feel its connection to your mind, body, and spirit. Discover how those three aspects interact with one another. Become aware of them."

Jack tried following his own advice. He was able to make contact with his Source, feeling the pulsing glow of his spirit in his chest. However, it appeared that the others in the group were having difficulty.

"I'm not feeling anything," muttered Krupp.

"I had better be the only one focusing on my chest," grumbled Morosa.

"<This isn't working…>" Snodgrass lamented.

"Stay focused, everyone! We can do this!" encouraged Flitter. "I think I can, I think I can, I think I can!"

Jack's frustration with the situation was building within him, but he was determined not to let it break his concentration. *Get centered,* he told himself. *Don't let this get to you. We can do this. We can do this! Even if I have to do all the work for them, we are going to do this!!!*

Jack took a deep breath. He cleared his mind. He relaxed his body. He tried to focus on his Source, that part within him that Shanks had shown him – where his spiritual energy resided.

Focus, Jack thought. *Focus...*

He made contact with his Source and slowly pulled it forth, sending it through the hands of those he was holding.

Focus...

He continued to work his energy through all the others, feeling the flow of their energy as his mingled with theirs. Finally, the two ends of his energy reached each other and reconnected.

Suddenly, Jack was standing in a wide open grassy field, with a light blue sky overhead and a warm sun behind him. He looked around, surprised. His friends were all there, as well, standing in a circle, looking just as bewildered as he did.

"Where are we?" Krupp asked. "This doesn't look like a subconscious construct."

"<What's it matter?>" Snodgrass asked. "<We did something!>"

"Yay! Something!" cheered Flitter as she jumped up and down.

"I don't believe it... we're all in a shared meditation!" Scrappy said with excitement.

"But what do we do now that we are here?" Morosa asked.

Jack looked out at the horizon, feeling a cool breeze waft over him as the grass rustled gently. He'd never seen this place before, but for some reason, it felt like home to him. "Um... Scrappy, can you think of an atom? Something solid? Like gold?"

"Of course!" Scrappy said. "Gold is only 79 protons and electrons. That's easy!"

"Great," said Jack. "Now, Snodgrass, can you help the rest of us see what Scrappy is visualizing?"

"<I will attempt to use my telepathy to do so now,>" Snodgrass replied.

Soon, a gold atom appeared in the center of their circle, its electron cloud glowing blue, and its nucleus pulsing pink.

"I see it!" exclaimed Flitter.

"Okay," said Jack. "Krupp, how do we make this real?"

Krupp frowned. "I… I don't know…" he said.

"How did you do it before? With the drop of water?"

"I just… I don't know. I thought of water, and it appeared."

"Well, try thinking of gold," Jack suggested.

Krupp tentatively stepped toward the atom, looking at it with a mixture of curiosity and trepidation. He closed his eyes and slowly reached out his hand, touching it.

"Gold…" he whispered.

Other gold atoms appeared, swarming together and shrinking as they did so. Jack and the others watched, transfixed, as the atoms eventually formed into a hunk of sparkling golden rock in the palm of Krupp's hand. Krupp opened his eyes and looked at the gold he held, amazed at the sight of it.

"You did it!" Scrappy said. "You got the atoms to form their element!"

"Now we must bring it into reality," Morosa said. "But how?"

Jack stepped forward and placed his hand atop the golden rock Krupp was holding. "Together," he said.

The group all stepped forward and placed their hands atop each other's. Jack could feel the merging of their energy as one by one they added their hands to the pile. The sun seemed to glow brighter as they did so, and in the back of Jack's mind, he felt that familiar tingle he always felt when he made a connection to the Earthship. Only this time, the connection was with his friends.

Eldil Meldilorn he heard a voice whisper in his mind.

With that, the sun shone so brightly that the group was entirely enveloped in light. When the light cleared, they were all back in their chamber, holding hands and sitting on the floor just as they had been.

"Guys… what just happened?" Scrappy asked.

"Look!" exclaimed Morosa.

She pointed to a hunk of gold on the floor before them at the center of their circle. It was the same hunk of gold Krupp had created in their vision.

Scrappy gasped. Krupp gazed at the gold in shock. Snodgrass blinked his eyes to make sure they weren't playing tricks on him. Flitter hopped up and down, clapping her hands excitedly. "We did it!!!" she exclaimed.

"We... we did it," Krupp said, amazed.

"We did it?" Scrappy, Morosa, and Snodgrass all said.

Suddenly, a laugh escaped from everyone. It was a laugh of relief. Of amazement. Of hope. None of them could truly believe that they'd been able to accomplish together something each had almost given up on. They all looked at one another in excitement. Jack looked at each one of his companions in turn, smiling.

"Let's do it again," he said.

Encouraged by their initial success, Jack and his friends continued to practice their group manifestation until they became familiar enough with the process to attempt it on their own. Though the act of manifesting new objects into reality had become familiar to them all, it was still difficult. Eventually, the group settled in on a strategy of specializing in manifesting just one thing, since that was all that was needed to pass the upcoming exam.

Jack's friends began to experience modest success at manifesting materials on their own. However, Jack had yet to achieve any success by himself, which began to worry him as the day of the exam grew closer. When his friends were around to help him, Jack discovered he was actually quite adept at manifesting many basic elements. However, the second he tried to do so alone, he faltered.

This was probably why Jack was such a bundle of nerves the day the manifestation exam finally arrived. He'd never been very good at passing tests, but the added pressure of having so much on the line made this exam even more difficult for him. So much was riding on his becoming a Paragon. If he were to pursue his quest of saving Earth, of defeating the Deathlords, and of protecting Anna, he'd need the skills Shepherd had promised to teach him. With Shepherd gone, the training the Conclave offered was the only option left.

Jack had decided to skip sleep and practice through the night before the exam. He stayed in the common room and tried to manifest something – anything – so that he'd be able to be admitted to the Paragon training. For a kid who hated school, Jack found it ironic that he was working so hard to try to get accepted into one.

"Any luck?" Krupp asked as he emerged from the bedroom to find Jack still practicing.

"Sometimes I think I'm just about to do it," Jack said. "There's a funny feeling I get... like I know something's there, even though it's not."

"Yeah, I know what you mean," Krupp acknowledged. "I feel that, too. It's like thinking you've just seen a ghost."

Jack gave up on practicing for the moment and looked at Krupp. "What about you? Are you ready?"

"I hope so," Krupp said with a sigh. "It's hit or miss. Sometimes I can do it, and I think I've got it locked down. Then other times I struggle, and no matter how hard I try, it just won't work."

"Well, at least you're batting fifty-fifty. My score remains a big fat zero."

"Keep at it, my friend," Krupp said, giving Jack a reassuring pat on the shoulder. "Without you, none of us would even have a shot right now."

Despite his last-ditch attempts to try to continue practicing, a growing sense of defeat was starting to build within Jack as the time came for the group members to make their way to the Chamber of the Five Rings for the final exam to see who would be admitted to train as a Paragon. Jack had almost resigned himself to his fate as he and the rest of Chapter Tantalis travelled through the Conclave to the temple's apex.

The door to the chamber was already open when Jack and the rest of his chapter arrived. Those from Chapter Arcturus and Chapter Regalius were already crammed into the room, chattering excitedly and practicing their skills up to the last minute.

The five members of the Order of Peers sat in chairs in the center of the room, forming a semicircle around a small wooden table. Master Savage looked as dour as ever. Master GorJiro was his usual stoic self. Though Masters Highclaw and Hodapp appeared happy to be there, Master Ravencrow seemed to want to be anywhere else, sitting slumped in his chair, a disinterested frown on his face.

"You think he'll take his blindfold off for the exam?" Jack asked, referring to Ravencrow.

"No idea," Krupp replied.

"I thought you've been through this, like, a billion times. Shouldn't you know everything about how this exam is supposed to go?"

"Honestly, in all my time here, this is the first I can remember Master Ravencrow ever being present," Krupp said.

"What's his story?" Jack asked. "He's a member of the Order, right? Where's he been all this time?"

"I have no clue," Krupp answered. "I'd never even heard of him until he showed up this season. Apparently no one other than the members of the Order seem to know who he is. He sure seems to make them uncomfortable, though. Just look at the way Master GorJiro is sitting next to him."

Indeed, Master GorJiro did seem rather uncomfortable sitting next to the dirty little Harvshodd. Considering how uptight GorJiro always appeared, though, it was a bit hard to tell. But there was definitely some tension between the two.

"Attention! Attention!" Master Savage said, clapping his hands and quieting the room. "The final exam is about to begin."

Highclaw then stood up, slipping his hands into the sleeves of his white robe and looking around at all the Initiates in the room.

"Welcome, all of you, to your first trial of initiation into the sacred order of Paragons," he said. "This is where the concepts of science and magic meet. Where quantum physics ceases to be theory and becomes reality. Thoughts are things waiting to materialize. If you know much about physics, you recognize that matter can neither be created nor destroyed. It simply changes from a solid form to energy, and visa-versa. This brings us to the concept that our thoughts create our reality. For some time now, you have all been training to change how you perceive your reality. This one incredible skill is what separates a Paragon from a normal being. In the age of Arcturus, in the Age of Empire, Paragons were thought to be mystical beings capable of creating anything out of thin air. But a true Paragon is more than a magician. He is a scientist. An artist. A healer. A fighter. A philosopher. True Paragons are all these and more. They are the pinnacle of what it means to be living beings. To be a Paragon is to be the best this universe has to offer. And as you come before us today to prove you are capable of being a Paragon, all we ask of you, is that you do your best."

Highclaw took his seat once more as Master Savage spoke up. "When your name is called, please come forward. To pass this trial, you must prove you have the ability to manifest something of substance into our reality. You will be judged by this panel, not simply on your results, but also on the control you have over your ability, and on your potential moving forward. That said, let us begin."

As the Order began summoning Initiates forward to showcase their skills, Jack shifted on his feet nervously. Each passing second felt as though he were getting closer and closer toward failing. The only solace he took was in looking at his new friends around him and knowing that even if he didn't make it, some of them might.

Everyone in the Gifted class passed with flying colors – including Tannyn, much to Jack's dismay. A good portion of the Normal class — at least 60% — passed, as well. But there were still a number who choked under the pressure or completely failed because they simply didn't have the ability. The Unlikelies were last, and as expected, one by one, those that remained approached the Order of Peers and failed to manifest anything.

"OhMeeGee, OhMeeGee, OhMeeGee!" Flitter said as she nervously shuffled from foot to foot. "I'm up next! Wish me luck!"

"Good luck," Jack said, before Flitter skipped over to where the Order was waiting.

"Initiate Flitter DeFlurr," Master Savage said, "are you prepared to manifest an object from your reality into ours?"

"I think so!" Flitter said excitedly. "I mean – yes, Master Savage! I'm ready!!!"

"Very well. Proceed."

Flitter took a deep breath and clenched her fists. Her large, dark eyes were fixated on the table before the Order. The air close to the surface of the tabletop rippled slightly, and a tiny puddle formed on it.

"What have you manifested?" Master Savage asked.

"Water, sir! I mean, Master!" Flitter said. "Just like the Ring I want to go into!"

For some reason, that made Master Savage smile. He looked at his companions. "Well?" he asked.

"It does appear to be water," Master Hodapp said.

"It seems so," Master GorJiro answered, stiffly.

Master Ravencrow snorted, looking bored.

"Congratulations, Initiate DeFlurr," Master Highclaw said. "You may now train to become a Paragon. I'm sure you will be a welcome addition to the Water Ring."

"YIPPEE!!!" Flitter cheered, before composing herself. "I mean – um… thank you, Masters!"

Flitter then rushed back to the group, who all congratulated her eagerly. Scrappy, Snodgrass, and then Morosa went up afterwards, and in turn, each one successfully manifested something small. Scrappy manifested a sliver of wood, Snodgrass a strip of paper, and Morosa a small pile of sodium. They were all admitted to Paragon training, with much fanfare from their classmates.

"Initiate Krupp, approach," Master Savage said.

Krupp took a nervous breath at the sound of his name. Jack patted him on the back. "You got this," Jack said with encouragement.

Krupp smiled at him and approached the Order. When he came to stand before the table, Master Savage gazed at him sternly. "Initiate Scofeld Krupp," Savage said. "This is the tenth time you've appeared before this panel. And though you've passed the exam once before, we feel that by now you should be able to manifest something more than a single drop of water in order to advance. Therefore, we have decided that if you fail to manifest anything of substance today, you will not be permitted to reapply for admittance for Paragon training until you can prove you are ready."

Krupp turned pale upon hearing that announcement. "Oh…" he said. "I… I see…"

Way to spring it on a guy, dude, Jack thought, scowling at Master Savage. *No pressure.*

"You may proceed, Initiate Krupp," Savage stated.

Jack crossed his fingers as he watched Krupp close his eyes. It was obvious he was concentrating hard. Krupp held out his hand and opened his eyes. He gazed intently at the table before the Order. Then, the air above the table grew hazy. There was a small ripple in reality, and a tiny rock appeared on the table's top.

Krupp exhaled sharply, a look of pride and achievement on his face as he lowered his hand and smiled broadly at the Order, who were appraising the rock.

"And what is this?" Savage asked.

"That, Master Savage, is gold," Krupp replied.

A robotic arm extended from Master Hodapp's exoskeleton and picked up the rock, holding it up to the Scollum's massive eye as a magnifying glass extended

to give him a closer look. "Hmmmm. It is indeed gold!" Master Hodapp said with a smile.

Master Highclaw nodded and smiled at Krupp, who looked at him excitedly. "Congratulations, Initiate Krupp. Late is better than never. You may now train to become a Paragon. Again."

The group of remaining Unlikelies cheered as Krupp hopped in the air, pumping his fist in celebration. He rushed back to the group to a round of hugs and pats on the back. Jack could see tears of happiness welling in his friend's eyes as he shook his hand.

"I don't believe it…" Krupp said. "I couldn't have done it without your help, Jack! Thank you!"

"Hey, this was all you, buddy. You earned it," Jack replied. "Guess tenth time really is the charm!"

They both laughed at that. Once the celebration had died down, Master Savage's voice rang out once more.

"Initiate Jack Finnegan."

The sound of the Paragon's voice sent a nervous chill up Jack's spine. All eyes were now on him. He approached the Order, feeling as though he were marching toward an execution. He came to a stop before the table, trying his best not to fidget as he stood before the men who were to decide his fate.

"Are you prepared to manifest an object from your reality into ours?" Master Savage inquired, his hard stare doing nothing to settle Jack's nerves.

"I believe I am," Jack replied.

"Proceed."

Jack took a breath to calm himself and closed his eyes. He held out his hand toward the table and tried to make contact with his Source. But his nerves were getting the better of him, making it hard to concentrate.

Come on… come on… he thought.

He felt that strange feeling he'd had since his fight with Stalker Crux flare up suddenly. Whether it had been caused by nerves or something else, Jack couldn't say, but it succeeded in making him lose his concentration. Jack was suddenly aware of the long period of time that had passed since he'd started to try to manifest something, and he could hear whispers of concern coming from the onlookers as he floundered in his efforts.

Jack grimaced and opened his eyes. He felt the heavy weight of failure settle in the pit of his stomach.

No... he thought, desperately. *I can't fail! I won't fail!*

Finally, Master Savage spoke up. "Very well, I believe we've seen enough," he said.

"No, wait," objected Jack. "I can do this!"

"Then do it," Savage said, "or stop wasting our time."

Jack glanced at each member of the Order in turn. Highclaw and Hodapp were both looking at him patiently. GorJiro was stoic. Savage looked annoyed. Ravencrow appeared as though he were asleep.

Jack took a deep breath and closed his eyes. *Help me...* he prayed, to no one in particular. *Help me do this...*

Jack felt the back of his head tingle. He was suddenly in a wide open field, sitting across from Shanks. To his right sat Shepherd. To his left, his father. His dad smiled at him.

"Mind," his father said.

"Body," said Shepherd.

"Spirit," said Shanks.

"Eldil Meldilorn," they all said, in unison.

The buzzing in the back of Jack's head intensified as he opened his eyes. In his mind, he saw a hunk of clay morph into a majestic urn, with a great all-seeing eye etched upon it. He reached out his hand as if to pull the picture of what he saw into reality.

Eldil Meldilorn! he heard, echoed in his mind.

The air above the table grew hazy as reality warped. There was a collective gasp from his classmates. Highclaw leaned forward in his chair. Savage frowned. Even Ravencrow tilted his head, as though he could sense what was happening.

Feel it... believe it... manifest it! Jack ordered himself.

Then, somewhere in Jack's mind, something clicked. And to him, it was as though he'd been staring at the object he'd wanted all along...

Well, kind of.

There, sitting on the table before him, was a strangely shaped piece of clay that looked like something a three-year-old had molded into what resembled a cup – a far cry from the expertly crafted urn Jack had seen in his head.

Master Hodapp leaned forward, his single large eye looking at the object, a tad bit confused. "What... is this?" he asked, curiously.

"Ummm..." said Jack, sheepishly. "An... ashtray?"

"It looks like a piece of misshapen clay," Master Savage said.

"Where I'm from, that's what ashtrays are," said Jack, though even he didn't sound like he believed what he was saying.

"There is no skill on display here," Master Savage objected. "From the looks of things, he meant to manifest one thing and ended up with... whatever this is."

"And yet, he was able to manifest something," Master Highclaw said. "That means he has the ability. Skill will come over time."

"I just don't see it," argued Savage. "He was sorted into the lowest class for a reason. This *Earthman* is nothing but a waste of our time and resources."

"Is that so?" Ravencrow said, suddenly piping up. "Tell me, Savage, what was the first thing you ever manifested, besides a foul stench?"

Savage scowled at Ravencrow. "I don't see how that's relevant," Savage said, tersely.

"I seem to remember you eking out a crooked stick of wood no bigger than my finger," Ravencrow said, lifting his hand to show Savage that his middle finger was extended in a rather crude gesture. "Seems to me if you were judged by the standards to which you're holding the Earthman, you wouldn't be here now. How's that for relevance, eh?"

"I was under the impression you didn't approve of the Earthman being here either, Master Ravencrow," Savage said with a sneer.

"Considering how little I approve of in this life, that's not saying much," Ravencrow muttered. "A Paragon must be able to manifest reality. Well, the Earthman just proved he can do that. So whether you like it or not, he should be admitted."

"Agreed," said Master Hodapp.

"He's proven he has the gift," GorJiro stated, matter-of-factly. "Now, we must train him to use it. Admit him."

Savage grimaced and turned his hard gaze toward Jack. "Very well," he said, begrudgingly. "He shall be admitted."

Master Highclaw nodded and looked at Jack, who could barely contain his smile.

"Congratulations, Initiate Finnegan," Highclaw said. "You may now train to become a Paragon."

CHAPTER ✷ 34

ilvelm looked at the faces of all the Alpha Force soldiers as he and Fredreek sat among them in the rear of the transport ship. Wil could tell they all had seen some action and some of them even had the scars to prove it. But despite their friendly demeanor as they joked with one another during the voyage, Wilvelm could see that familiar look the military types would always get in their eyes when he and Fredreek were around.

Namely, the look that communicated the soldiers all believed they were on 'babysitting duty'.

All the Alpha Force soldiers were already clad in their bulky power armor, sitting in the rows of jump seats lining either side of the inner cabin. The quarters were cramped, since a hefty gravity vault had been hastily installed to contain the passenger they were on their way to pick up. Wilvelm uncomfortably tugged on the harness that was holding him in his seat. Fredreek sat beside him, not even attempting to hide the flask of Poshretrain Whiskey from which he was drinking. Yet another reason the soldiers probably thought the two Legacy heirs weren't to be taken seriously.

Wilvelm and Fredreek had seen their fair share of combat battling Deathlords alongside Mourdock, but they'd never really been front-line fighters. Mourdock was always the one leading troops into the fray, using his Paragon skills to make short work of the enemy. Both Wil and Fred were lucky to get a few blaster shots off from the rear before the battles were usually over. Their presence on the field of battle was more of a resume builder, allowing them to say they'd fought the Deathlords without being put in any real danger – something both Wilvelm's father and Fredreek's father no doubt insisted upon.

Sometimes Wilvelm resented the fact that he never really had much of a role to play in combat. His Legacy was descended from a long line of military soldiers, and he'd even been trained as one in the military academy back on his home planet of Darkrock after washing out at the Conclave when he was younger. But his position as heir of Legacy Blackfyre meant it was necessary that he be protected from any real combat. Thus, he was often relegated to being Mourdock's cheerleader and assigned missions that typically translated to "go fetch this" or "report back what you see."

Though their lack of importance in the grander scheme of the Deathlord war bothered Wilvelm, it didn't seem to faze Fredreek in the slightest. He was often all too content to let others face the dangers the Deathlords represented (though when he hit the bars, his tales would make one think he'd been fighting the war single-handedly). Not that Wilvelm thought Fredreck was a coward or inept in any way. In fact, he trusted Fredreek with his life, because when push came to shove, Wilvelm knew Fredreek would always stand up and do the right thing in the end. But then again, few people knew Fredreek as well as Wilvelm did. Even Mourdock didn't seem to always have a great deal of confidence in Fred's abilities.

Wilvelm again studied the group of Alpha Force soldiers around him. Though each soldier's bulky armor bore an official nameplate, it was common for the soldiers to answer to nicknames they'd earned while in the squad. There were eight members in total, led by Lieutenant Graysen Monroe who everyone referred to as 'L.T.' There was a big guy called Roadblock, a skinny guy called Skinny, a woman called Lucky, an Endolan nicknamed Double-R, a Frontier-type called Drifter, a young-looking guy known as Missionary, and a shifty guy called Skeptic.

"Yo, L.T.," said Roadblock as he fiddled with what looked to be a large weapon of some type. "You've dealt with Rognok's before, haven't ya?"

Monroe nodded. "That's right," he replied. "Back on Ostelara. Had one go berserk in the middle of a city. Leveled half of it before we were able to put him down."

Roadblock whistled. "I'd always heard Rognoks were tough buggers. Think this one will give us any trouble?"

"Nothing we won't be able to handle if it comes down to it," Monroe answered.

"I heard this Rognok took out half of Stratum 80 before Alpha Force 5 took him down," chimed in Double-R.

"Heard it took Alpha Force 5 jacking their graviton rifles up to fifty to finally stop him," said Lucky.

"Heard he handed Alpha 5 their butts in their second go-round," drawled Drifter.

"Heard you guys gossip more than a gaggle of teenage females," Fredreek chimed in. "Guess you really can believe everything you hear."

"If that's the case, Lord Goldstone," said Skeptic, "then there's quite a lot to believe about you."

"Is there now?" replied Fredreek, looking amused. "Such as?"

Some of the soldiers chuckled. "I saw a news report that said you're being sued by fifteen women, all claiming to be married to you," said Missionary.

"The Rag Nine gossip site said you were arrested after being found passed out and naked in the Visini Ambassador's pool back on Omnicron," added Skinny.

"I heard you were banned from every casino in Vas Lagas because cleaning up after your parties was more expensive than the money they'd win from you at the *Loquir* tables," said Lucky.

Fredreek gave Wilvelm a wry look. "It would seem my reputation precedes me," he said with a smile before taking another swig from his flask.

"So what's a guy like you doing on prisoner transport duty?" inquired Roadblock.

Fredreek shrugged. "Just Lord Skyborn's way of keeping us busy while his son is off saving his lady love," he replied.

"I've heard Mourdock Skyborn is the real deal," Skeptic said. "Did either of you train at the Conclave?"

"Yep," said Fredreek. "Before we both washed out."

"Couldn't hack it, eh?" commented Roadblock.

"What can I say? Some brains are better left caged," Fredreek replied, tapping at his temple. "It worked out okay, though. Wil and I became friends with Mourdock Skyborn, I went to pilot school, Wil went to military school, and now we're all fighting the good fight together, aren't we?"

"Is that what you guys are doing?" muttered Roadblock. "Fighting?"

"Roadblock…" cautioned Monroe, giving the solider a stern look.

"Just saying, in all the time we've been out here in the Rim, I ain't never seen these two on any battlefield," Roadblock replied.

"We've been in battle before," Wilvelm said, a little defensively. "We're just usually with Mourdock Skyborn when it happens."

"Right," said Roadblock with a skeptical nod. "I can totally see you two on the front lines, going toe-to-toe with the Deathlords. Bet you have them quaking in their boots."

"Hey!" snapped Fred. "Do you have any idea who you're talking to, pal?"

"Forgive me, Lord Goldstone," said Roadblock, not really sounding sorry. "I didn't mean to insult upstanding pillars of the Empire such as yourselves."

"I honestly don't care what you think of me," said Fredreek. "But show Wil a little respect. He comes from a long and storied line of warriors."

"Fred—" Wilvelm started to say.

"No, Wil, he needs to know who he's talking to," Fredreek said before looking back at Roadblock. "You ever hear of Torboron Blackfyre?"

"Why?" asked Roadblock. "Should I have?"

"Torboron Blackfyre was the leader of the Resistance against the Twilight Empire," Monroe said. "He was the only one to ever win battles against Edvard the Undying's Automoton Army, and was instrumental in helping Emperor Hydrion defeat Edvard and recover all the territory the Empire had lost to him. He was also the one who pioneered a lot of our current military tactics, and he was awarded a Legacy in recognition of his service to the Empire."

All eyes turned to Wilvelm, making him feel slightly uncomfortable.

"So without this guy's great, great, great... whatever..." Fredreek said, wagging his thumb toward Wilvelm as he spoke, "none of you would probably be here right now."

"From defeating the Twilight Empire to escorting prisoners from the backend of space," said Roadblock as he gave Wilvelm a mock salute. "The Blackfyre Legacy sure has come a long way, it seems."

Wilvelm glared at Roadblock. If the soldier's intent was to upset Wilvelm, he had succeeded. But Wil kept his cool and didn't respond.

"Alright, that's enough," cautioned Monroe. "Everyone do a suit diagnostic. We're getting close to our destination, and I want us all primed and ready to go when we arrive."

Roadblock chuckled as he disassembled the weapon he'd been tinkering with and attached the pieces to the armor on his thighs. As the members of the Alpha Force squad all began to run the diagnostics on their suits, Fredreek leaned in toward Wilvelm. "Don't let that meathead get to you," Fredreek whispered. "At the end of the day, he's a grunt and you're a Lord. You come out ahead in that comparison."

"Maybe so," replied Wilvelm, quietly. "But in the future, I'd appreciate it if you would stop telling people about my lineage."

Fredreek gave Wilvelm a questioning look. "Why? I wish I had such a storied ancestry. My forebearers were just rich merchants who bribed their way into a Legacy."

"Because it's starting to give me an inferiority complex," replied Wilvelm, testily. "That meathead might be a jerk, but he's not wrong. Compared to what Torboron was able to achieve by my age, nothing I ever do will even be able to come close in comparison."

"Pshhh," said Fred, dismissively. "Let the war heroes have their wars. Ever notice how all their stories usually end in tragedy? Who cares if you're a footnote in the history holos? Civilian life is where all the fun is. Peacetime revelry always takes the cake over wartime heroics. Good booze, good females, and good times is what life is all about, my friend. I'd rather be drunk and happy than fighting Deathlords any day. Speaking of which…"

Fredreek took another swig from his flask and offered some to Wilvelm. Wil thought about refusing it for a half-second before giving in to the notion that he needed a drink to calm his annoyance and accepted the flask from his friend, taking a deep swig of the firebrand whiskey that was inside.

"Sensor contact," came the pilot's voice over the intercom. "Ten minutes to target. Prepare for docking maneuvers."

Wilvelm held onto his harness as he felt the ship maneuver and heard the docking clamps lock. Alpha Force all released themselves from their seats and stood, with Wil and Fred following suit. A hatch in the floor opened, revealing the docking ring leading to the other ship.

"Artificial gravity has been normalized," Monroe stated. "We're good to board the mercenary vessel. After you, my Lords."

Wilvelm and Fredreek exchanged a glance. Fredreek gestured to the docking ring, inviting Wilvelm to lead the way. When Wilvelm finished climbing down the access ladder, he was greeted by the crew of the mercenary vessel. They appeared to be a rather rag-tag assembly of bionically enhanced individuals. All of them had some type of robotic implant, ranging from eyes, to arms and even to legs. There were four of them present, all looking somewhat haggard, as though they hadn't gotten much sleep lately.

As the rest of his team entered the vessel, Wilvelm gave it a quick look around. It wasn't anything close to the military-grade spaceships he was accustomed to. This ship was all metal grates and exposed pipes and machinery. It wasn't pretty to look at, that much was for sure, but Wilvelm guessed that aside from aesthetics, it was a sturdy enough ship to do what a band of mercenary bounty hunters needed it to.

"Who's in charge here?" Wilvelm asked as the last of Alpha Force descended from the docking ring.

One of the mercs stepped forward. He wore a black synthweave vest that showed off his muscles and robotic left arm. Half his head was scarred from what looked like burns, which caused patches of hair to grow haphazardly upon it, and one of his eyes had been replaced with a bionic targeting sensor, which glowed red as it scanned the new arrivals. "That'd be me, I suppose," the man said, his voice gruff. "Name's Copperhyde."

"I am Wilvelm of Legacy Blackfyre. This is Fredreek of Legacy Goldstone. We've come to collect your prisoner."

"Not a moment too soon, neither," muttered Copperhyde. "Please, take him. He's all yours."

"Which way to the brig?" Monroe asked.

"Oh, uh… he's not in the brig," Copperhyde said, sheepishly. "He liked the mess better."

"You're keeping your prisoner in the cafeteria?" Fredreek asked.

"Yeah, well, he just sort of sat down in there and hasn't come back out."

"What type of restraints are you using on him?" Monroe inquired.

"Riiiiight…" said Copperhyde, looking uncomfortable. "He didn't really want to wear any restraints."

All of Alpha Force glanced at each other. "You mean to tell me the Rognok is not restrained at all?" Monroe pressed.

"Well, Wylson went to put an electro-collar on him," Copperhyde replied.

"Finally, someone with some common sense," Monroe said. "Which one of you is Wylson?"

The mercs all looked at one another. "Yeah… Wylson ain't with us no more," Copperhyde said.

"Correct me if I'm wrong, compatriot," Wilvelm said, "but it sounds more like the Rognok has taken all of you prisoner rather than the other way around."

"Look, you want the blasted thing or not?" grumbled Copperhyde.

Wilvelm sighed before looking at Fredreek who shrugged. "By all means," Fredreek said. "Show us to the mess."

Wil, Fred, and Alpha Force all followed behind the mercenaries as they wove their way through the corridors of the ship. Eventually, they arrived at a large door that had been sealed shut. Copperhyde nodded to it. "The big kitten is in there," he grumbled.

"Helmets on," Monroe commanded. Immediately, the domed helmets of the Alpha Force power suits all rotated closed over the soldier's heads. "Graviton rifles. Twenty percent charge. Drifter, ready the gravity shackles."

"Gravity shackles, ready," Drifter replied as all the other soldiers pulled their graviton rifles off their backs and charged them up.

"Alpha Force is prepared to take custody of the prisoner, Lord Blackfyre," Monroe said.

Wil nodded before turning toward Copperhyde. "Open it up," he ordered.

Copperhyde unsealed the door, which swung open to reveal a decent size mess hall with tables and chairs attached to the floor. On a stool at the back of the room, Grohm sat facing the door, his eyes closed. He did not react as Alpha Force entered, fanning out while keeping their rifles trained on him. Wilvelm and Fredreek entered last, looking at Grohm curiously.

"Is he asleep?" Fredreek asked.

"Don't know," Wilvelm replied. "Do Rognok's sleep?"

"Why are you asking me? You're supposed to be the smart one."

"No, I'm the good-looking one," Wil quipped.

"Does that mean I'm supposed to be the smart one?" Fred replied. "Because if that's the case, we are in serious trouble."

Grohm continued to sit stoically, unmoving. Wilvelm glanced around at the squad of Alpha Force soldiers who had taken up positions around the room, their graviton rifles at the ready should the Rognok make a wrong move. Wil took a deep breath and stepped toward the massive alien. "Grohm, my name is Wilvelm Blackfyre, and this is Fredreek Goldstone. We've been charged with taking you into custody for crimes against the Empire. We ask that you surrender yourself to us now and submit to wearing restraints, so we may escort you back to our ship."

Grohm finally opened his eyes. He glanced at Wilvelm and Fredreek in turn, before slowly looking at all the Alpha Force soldiers with their graviton rifles trained on him. Without a word, he stood up, towering over the men before him.

"Easy now," Monroe cautioned as all of Alpha Force prepared to shoot.

Grohm looked at the Lieutenant. "Alpha Force will not fire," the Rognok said. "Put guns away."

"Sure you want to test us, Rognok?" Wilvelm replied. "Alpha Force has laid you out before."

Grohm grunted. He then slowly raised his arm over his head. The members of Alpha Force all took a step back and readied their rifles at him. Wilvelm and Fredreek watched as Grohm's hand hovered a few inches below the ceiling of the mess hall. With a flick of his fingers, the large alien left a golf ball sized dent in the metal.

"Blast it," Monroe muttered. "Lower your weapons."

All of Alpha Force obeyed as Wilvelm and Fredreek looked at them, confused. "Lieutenant, what are you doing?" Wilvelm demanded.

"This ship is made from cheap, non-reinforced metal," the Lieutenant replied. "A stray gravity blast would rip it to shreds. The Rognok knows this. I'm afraid anything we'd do to contain him would end up destroying this ship and killing everyone on it."

Wilvelm and Fredreek frowned as they both looked at Grohm, who slowly lowered his arm once more. "Well, what do you think?" Fredreek whispered to Wilvelm.

"I suppose we could always try asking him nicely?" Wilvelm suggested.

Fredreek sighed. "Would you *please* surrender yourself to us now and put on restraints so we can escort you back to our ship?"

"No," the Rognok replied.

"Okay then," grumbled Wilvelm. "You obviously didn't need to be taken captive in the first place, and you obviously don't want to come with us. So I'll just straight-up ask... what is it you want?"

"Map," Grohm replied.

Wilvelm and Fredreek gave each other a curious glance. "Uh... what?" they both asked.

"Map of Rim," Grohm clarified. "Showing all Deathlord activity."

"And why would you want such a thing?" Wilvelm asked.

"For battle."

"Riiiiiiight…" Fredreek said before turning to Wilvelm. "This beast is crazy," he muttered softly.

"If we give you a map of the system, would you agree to wear gravity shackles and come aboard our ship?" Wilvelm asked. Grohm was quiet for a moment before nodding. "Very well," Wilvelm said as he fished out his datapad from his pocket. "One map of the Rim, coming up."

Wilvelm tapped on his screen a few times before setting his datapad on the table before Grohm. The datapad proceeded to project above it a holographic map of the system, showing red outlines of the areas in which Deathlord raids had occurred. "That's the most up-to-date data we have of the Deathlord incursion," Wilvelm said. "They've been hitting smaller colonies and outposts along the Rim, with a significantly high number in the Maxima system."

Grohm looked at the hologram, his red and black eyes slowly taking it in. He then reached out, touching the image of the Maxima system to expand it, showing details of the system itself. He eyed the map silently for what seemed like a long period of time before touching a small planetoid and enlarging it. "What place is this?" Grohm asked.

Wilvelm looked at the holographic image, curiously. "Um, I believe that's Essox. A planetoid with a mining colony on it."

Grohm's eyes narrowed as he studied the image of the planetoid more closely. "Take Grohm there," he said.

"You want to go to a mining colony?" Wilvelm asked, not sure exactly what the Rognok was thinking.

"Mind if we ask why?" chimed in Fredreek.

"Battle," was all Grohm said in reply.

Wilvelm rubbed his temple in exasperation. "Would you just give us a second?" he said before dragging Fredreek over to Lieutenant Monroe, who lowered his helmet as they approached. "Well, I'll say this for Rognoks," muttered Wil, "they are a chatty bunch who make a ton of sense."

"Think it's a coincidence he wants to go to Essox?" asked Fredreek. "It is the closest settlement to our current location. Maybe he wants to try to escape?"

"Does he look like he needs to escape?" Wilvelm replied.

"I think it's obvious he wants to fight something," Monroe said. "The only question is, what?"

"He wanted to see Deathlord activity on the map," Fredreek said. "Maybe he thinks there are Deathlords on Essox?"

Wilvelm shook his head. "There haven't been any Deathlord attacks anywhere near this area of the system," Wil said. "And if there were, we'd have heard about it. The Skyborn fleet would have been on top of them at the first sign of trouble."

"Well, I know that. And you know that. But does *he* know that?" asked Fredreek.

"Frankly, my Lords, at this point, I think you should simply promise the Rognok whatever it takes to get him onto our ship," Monroe said. "If he wishes to go to Essox, tell him we'll take him there."

"Something tells me he won't appreciate being lied to," muttered Wilvelm.

"What he appreciates is immaterial, my Lord. Once he's on our vessel, we'll be in a better position to subdue him."

Wilvelm harbored some worry as to how the Rognok would react to such deception, but he knew Monroe was right. His job was to get the Rognok onto their ship. Alpha Force could take things from there. Wilvelm turned back to Grohm. "Very well, here's the deal…" Wilvelm said. "You put on these gravity shackles and come aboard our ship. We'll do a fly-by of Essox on our way to rendezvous with the Skyborn fleet. If we see anything suspicious there, we'll have Alpha Force investigate. How's that sound?"

"Like a lie," replied Grohm.

"He's smarter than he looks," grumbled Fredreek, under his breath.

Wilvelm sighed. "If you aren't going to trust us, what's the point of even having this conversation?"

Grohm snorted. "Grohm here to fight Deathlords. Deathlords on Essox. You take Grohm to fight. If not, Grohm stay here."

Wil and Fred both gave the Rognok a curious look. "What are you talking about?" Wilvelm asked. "There are no Deathlords on Essox."

"In fact, the Third Search Fleet just finished a sweep of this sector," Fredreek chimed in. "There are no Deathlords within lightyears of here."

Just then, the ship shook violently as the sound of an explosion rang out. Everyone in the room looked around, alarmed. Grohm gazed up at the ceiling, his lips curling into a snarl.

"Sensor contact!!!" came the voice of the transport ship's pilot over the comms. "It's a Deathlord vessel! It came out of nowhere! We're under fire!"

Fredreek frowned. "Okay, perhaps I spoke too soon," he muttered.

"What the blazes is happening???" demanded Copperhyde.

"We're under attack!" barked Monroe. "Get down to the docking ring and seal it! NOW!"

The ship rocked again as Copperhyde and his men raced back down the corridors toward the docking ring. Monroe followed, along with Wil and Fred. "Alpha Force, we're exposed as long as we're attached to the mercenary ship!" the transport pilot said. "We need to detach!"

"Negative!" replied Monroe as he ran. "Docking ring is not secure! I repeat: docking ring *is not* secure!"

The ship rocked again as more blasts peppered it from the outside. "We can't wait!" replied the pilot. "I'm sorry, we have to detach!"

"NO!" cried Monroe.

Wil saw two of Copperhyde's crew reach the docking ring down the hallway just before the sound of screeching metal rang out. With a loud *POP*, a catastrophic decompression occurred, violently sucking the air from the ship and into space. The two mercenaries who had been trying to shut the hatch screamed as they were pulled through the opening and into the void of space.

Copperhyde had grabbed onto a nearby pipe to keep from being sucked down the corridor, but the sudden decompression had caught Wil off-guard. Monroe quickly shot a grappling cable onto the ground to anchor himself and caught Wil with his free hand, stopping him from being pulled down the corridor. Fred grabbed onto Monroe, as well, and held on for dear life.

Copperhyde reached out for the emergency containment button near the doorway leading to the docking ring's corridor. He hit it, causing the door's hatch to slam shut and sealing the corridor off from the rest of the ship. Once the hatch had been sealed, the pressure in the hallway normalized and Wil and Fred dropped to the floor.

"What the squick was that???" demanded Copperhyde. "Your ship just cost me two of my crew!"

"You can ream me out later," Monroe replied. "Right now, we need to assist the transport if we're going to survive this. Which way to the bridge?"

Copperhyde scowled at Monroe, but he didn't press the argument. "This way," he grumbled.

The group followed Copperhyde to the bridge, where the mercenary slid into the pilot's seat. On the main viewscreen he called up a view of the Deathlord ship. It was a cone-shaped vessel made of black rock. Sharp ridges trailed down from its pointed tip all the way back to its wide base, with jagged outcroppings surrounding the engines like teeth in an open mouth. The Maxima transport was maneuvering away from the vessel, but it was getting hit hard by the plasma blasts from the Deathlords.

"It's a Deathlord Destroyer," hissed Fredreek. "The transport isn't going to last long against that!"

"Not if we don't do something to help it," Monroe said. "This ship have any plasma cannons on it?"

"Two," Copperhyde replied. "But they've both already been damaged. We've got no way of fighting back!"

"Wrong," replied Monroe. "You have Alpha Force. Wait for my signal, then open the rear boarding hatch to the ship." Monroe turned to leave, speaking into his comms. "Alpha Force, meet me in the cargo bay."

"What are you going to do?" asked Wilvelm.

"What we do best," Monroe replied. "Fight some Deathlords."

When Monroe was gone, Copperhyde cursed under his breath. "My ship ain't equipped to handle something like this. We should be running – not fighting!"

"How far you think you'd get before they took out your engines?" asked Fredreek. "Right now, the distraction that military transport is providing is the only reason we're still in one piece. Now power down all nonessential systems, redirect whatever power you can to the shields, and try to maneuver behind that blasted Destroyer before it does any more damage."

"Oy, don't tell me how to fly my own ship!" snapped Copperhyde.

"Any halfway decent pilot would have done all that the moment he took his seat," Fredreek argued.

"Yeah, well, you can thank your Alpha Force friends for that," Copperhyde replied. "Vespran was the ship's pilot, and he just got sucked out into space! So you're stuck with me!"

Fredreek gave Wilvelm a concerned look. As Wil watched the Deathlord Destroyer slowly hammer down the Maxima transport on the screen, he experienced an uncomfortable feeling of dread creeping into his gut and taking hold.

"Lord Blackfyre, do you read me?" came Monroe's voice over Wilvelm's communicator.

"Loud and clear, Lieutenant."

"Alpha Force is in position. Have Copperhyde open the rear boarding hatch."

Wilvelm relayed the command to Copperhyde, who quickly flipped a few switches to seal all the doors to the cargo bay. "I hope those soldiers know what they're doing," he grumbled.

"Yeah," Wilvelm said with a sigh. "Me, too."

The lights in the cargo bay switched to red as the atmosphere was vented, and the rear doors lowered to reveal the emptiness of space. Monroe stood at the head of his squad, which had assembled behind him, ready to deploy.

"Move out," Monroe ordered as he ran to the exit. His squad followed him, leaping at the last leg to clear the artificial gravity of the ship and float into space.

"Grapplers," said Monroe as he turned and fired the grappling claw from his gauntlet, latching onto the exterior of the ship. His squad did as commanded, each one grappling onto the vessel and then reeling themselves toward its fuselage until their boots could magnetically lock onto it.

The moment he was secured to the ship, Monroe reeled in his grappling cable and led his soldiers over the side to the top of the ship. He could feel the ship moving as it maneuvered, and he was careful to make sure his boots magnetically locked with each step before he took a new one. Eventually, he and his squad cleared the side and emerged on top of the vessel. Before them, they

could see the Deathlord Destroyer looming in the distance, dancing with the Maxima transport as they exchanged plasma fire.

The sensor readings from his armor already told Monroe that the transport was in bad shape. Its shields were failing and it had sustained damage to its hull. "Missionary, Drifter," he said through his comms. "Position yourselves to the starboard side of the ship. Lucky, Double-R, you're on the port side. Roadblock, you take forward. Skinny, you're aft. Skeptic, you're with me."

"Roger that," the soldiers said in turn as they moved to their positions.

"Maxima transport vessel, this is Lieutenant Monroe of Alpha Force, do you read?" Monroe said as he opened a channel to the ship.

"We read you Lieutenant," the ship's pilot replied.

"What's your status?"

"We've sustained heavy hull damage. Shields failing. All distress signals have been blocked. We're not going to make it much longer…"

"Bring the bogey toward our position," Monroe said. "We'll see if we can give you some help."

"Roger that."

"Plasma rifles at the ready," Monroe ordered his squad as soon as they were all in position. "Skeptic, you and I will employ graviton rifles. Full charge."

"Acknowledged," Skeptic replied as he unslung his large graviton rifle from his back and began to charge it.

The transport ship maneuvered around the Deathlord Destroyer, peppering it with blasts and drawing it toward Alpha Force. As soon as it was within range, the squad all opened fire. Red streaks shot across the void of space, hitting the broadside of the Deathlord ship, the vessel's shields shimmering with each blow.

The Deathlord ship rotated, firing upon both the transport and the mercenary vessel as it closed its distance. The ship's shield above the squad shimmered with a light blue hue as the blasts from the Deathlord ship met with it, absorbing the blows. Both Monroe and Skeptic hefted their graviton rifles as soon as they were fully charged and fired upon the Deathlord Destroyer as it passed.

The balls of gravity sped toward the Deathlord ship, impacting its sides and taking chunks out of its rocky hull.

The members of Alpha Force continued to fire as they passed, but the mercenary ship failed to keep within range of the vessel.

"Blast it!" muttered Monroe. "Lord Blackfyre! Keep us within range of the enemy!"

The Deathlord Destroyer rotated again, focusing all its firepower on the transport ship. Monroe could do nothing but watch as the ship's shields dissipated and the red streaks of the Deathlord's weapons cut into the hull, tearing it apart.

"Mayday! Mayday! Mayday!" came the panicked voice of the ship's pilot. "Critical hull breach! We're not gonna make it! We're not—"

Suddenly, the transport exploded as the Deathlord vessel continued hitting the ship with its cannons. The flash of fire quickly disappeared as the oxygen from the ship was consumed, and the shattered remains of the spacecraft drifted off into space. The Deathlord ship then adjusted its course and came back around, bearing directly down upon the mercenary ship.

"Brace yourselves," Monroe ordered, his voice grim. "We have incoming."

On the bridge of the mercenary ship, alerts were lighting up Copperhyde's console – none of them telling him anything good. "Shields are almost gone," he grumbled.

"For the last time – cut life support to the rear of the ship! You don't need it!" snapped Fredreek. "Redirect that power to the shields! And for the love of Arcturus, stop flying in a straight line! Blast it, man – are you trying to get us killed?"

"Ya think you can do any better?" snapped Copperhyde.

"I know I can!" replied Fredreek. "I received flight training at the Imperial Space Academy and am a commissioned officer in the Imperial Navy. I know how to fly in a combat situation! If you want to live, give me the controls!"

Copperhyde scowled, hesitating for a moment before pulling a small device from his pocket and giving it a shake.

"What the kitten is that?" asked Fredreek.

"It's my pocket RNGsus," grumbled Copperhyde.

"You can't be serious!" cried both Wilvelm and Fredreek.

"Oy! This decision is too big for me!" snapped Copperhyde. "Times like these require RNGsus ta take the wheel!" Wil and Fred both exchanged a disbelieving look as Copperhyde looked down at the small device and said: "Should I let this moron fly my ship?"

The digitized image of RNGsus on the device was then replaced with that of a ticket, which read: 49873. Copperhyde gave the device a shake, which changed the numbers to: "Do so immediately."

The mercenary cursed underneat his breath before relenting and moving out of the pilot's seat, with Fredreek wasting no time replacing him. Fred quickly redirected all the power he could to the shields, then banked the ship, keeping an eye on the sensor readings.

"What are our chances?" Wil asked.

"Somewhere between 'not good' and 'totally borked'," Fredreek replied. "I've dated women who've moved faster than this tub. That Deathlord Destroyer is quicker than we are, and with all due respect to Alpha Force, it has a lot more firepower, as well. As soon as our shields are gone, we're as good as dead."

"Can we make a run for it?" Wil asked. "Jump to hyperspace?"

"Not while we're inside Maxima's debris field. Any hyperspace window would open right into its gravitational shadow, and flying into that would be like running into a brick wall. Our only hope would be to outpace them, and as I said, this ship isn't fast enough."

Wilvelm frowned. *Dying on a prisoner transfer run*, he thought to himself. *Not exactly the type of death that would do Torboron proud.*

Before Wilvelm could dwell on his impending demise too much, he turned to see Grohm standing in the doorway, the last of Copperhyde's men in front of him. The crewman was a wiry Endolan[34], who looked both scared and confused. "Um... he wanted me to take him to the bridge," the Endolan said. "I didn't know what else to do..."

Grohm looked at the situation playing out on the bridge's viewscreen, his red and black eyes carefully studying what was happening. "Does ship have snare-winch?" he asked.

---

[34] Endolans are dark skinned humanoid aliens with a vestigial third eye.

"What blasted difference does that make?" Copperhyde asked. "Snaring a Deathlord ship would ensure we'd get blown to bits!"

Grohm scowled at the man. "Does ship have snare-winch?" he asked again.

"Just answer him!" Wilvelm demanded.

"Yeah, up top next to what used ta be our docking ring," Copperhyde replied.

Grohm nodded. "Get ship close," he said, before turning to leave.

"Is he serious?" Fredreek asked.

Wilvelm chased after Grohm as the Rognok started to make his way toward the sealed hatch leading to the docking ring. "Wait!" Wilvelm cried. "What are you going to do?"

"Fight," Grohm replied before pushing Wilvelm away and sealing the corridor's hatch. Wilvelm watched through the porthole in the door as Grohm unsealed the hatch leading to the docking ring. He briefly held on while all the atmosphere vented into the open breach, then began to climb to the outside.

"You gotta be kidding me…" Wil muttered to himself before rushing back to the bridge. "Get us as close as you can to the Deathlord ship," he said upon returning.

"Are you crazy???" Copperhyde screeched.

"I'm inclined to agree with cyber-eye, here," Fredreek replied.

"That Rognok just waltzed out into space without a suit or a respirator like he was going for a casual stroll," Wilvelm said. "He's a member of the Earthman's crew. The same crew that took out the entire Planetkiller fleet. If he wants us to get him closer to a single Deathlord ship, I say we do it."

Fredreek met his friend's gaze for a moment before sighing. He took a quick swig from his flask and then tossed it aside. "Everyone buckle up," he said. "Let's hope the Rognok knows what he's doing."

Monroe braced himself as the ship banked once again, doing his best to continue firing upon the Deathlord vessel as it maneuvered to keep pace with the smaller ship. Blasts from the Deathlord plasma cannons streaked by, but only a

few of them impacted the ship's shields. *Whoever's flying this thing got good all of a sudden*, he thought to himself as he charged his graviton rifle once more.

"L.T.!" he heard Skeptic cry over the comms. "To your six!"

Monroe turned to see Grohm climbing out of the docking ring behind him. The Rognok held on to the edge of the opening as the ship maneuvered, pulling himself down as he reached out for a panel on the side of the ship.

"What the blazes…" Monroe muttered.

Grohm ripped the casing of the snare-winch open, revealing the long arm and the spool of cable connected to the magnetic disk at its end. He pulled the arm up and grabbed the end of the cable, unspooling it to create some slack.

"What do you think you're doing???" Monroe barked through his suit's speakers.

Grohm looked at him, the Rognok's mouth contorting into something resembling a smile.

"Lieutenant, is the Rognok up there with you?" came Wilvelm's voice over the comms.

"Yes, he's just opened up the ship's snare-winch," Monroe replied.

"Tell him this is as close as we're going to be able to get," Wilvelm said. "And brace yourselves. Our shields are about to fail."

Monroe frowned. He looked back at Grohm. "Whatever you're going to do," he said, "do it now!"

With that, Grohm turned. He pulled himself along the hull, gaining momentum until he reached the rear where Skinny was stationed. He then used his feet to push himself off the ship, leaping into the void and sailing toward the Deathlord vessel as its plasma blasts streaked by him.

"Are you guys seeing what I'm seeing?" Skinny said over the comms as he watched Grohm hurtle toward the Deathlord Destroyer.

Monroe looked over as the snare-winch's cable spool continued to unravel at high speed. "Cover him!" he ordered, before aiming at the Deathlord ship and firing.

As Grohm got closer, he reeled back his fist. The Deathlord vessel sped toward him and he swung just as the two made impact.

Monroe watched as chunks of the rocky hull of the ship broke off from where Grohm had hit it. Grohm latched the end of the snare winch to the ship and started pounding on the hull until it gave way, and he crawled inside.

"The Rognok has… uh… boarded the enemy ship," Monroe said into his comms, not quite sure how to explain what he'd just witnessed.

"He did what?" Wilvelm replied.

Just then, the Deathlord ship unleashed a volley of plasma fire. The first few blasts ate up the last of the shielding and the rest peppered the fuselage of the mercenary vessel. Skinny cried out as he was hit head-on, the powerful superheated blast cutting through his power armor and sending his remains floating through space. Other blasts streaked across the hull, cutting deep gouges of melted metal into it as they made impact.

"Man down!" Monroe cried. "Return fire!"

Alpha Force fired at the Deathlord ship as the mercenary vessel tried to maneuver, but there was only so much the vessel could do while attached to the enemy with the snare-winch. Monroe heard Double-R cry out as another blast landed, and he saw the remains of his squadmate float away from the side of the ship.

"We're getting torn to shreds out here!" he heard Roadblock cry out over the comms.

"Keep firing!" Monroe said, knowing there was nothing more they could do.

"Cut the line, L.T.!" Roadblock insisted. "Let us get some distance!"

Monroe looked at the snare-winch. Roadblock was right, as long as they were connected to the Deathlord ship, they were easy targets. But he also knew the Rognok had used the snare for a reason. Could he really risk the creature's plan, whatever it might be, just to buy maybe a few more minutes of time?

More plasma blasts landed and one of the ship's engines erupted. The side of the mercenary vessel was almost completely exposed to space, with multiple breeches being torn open by the Deathlord's onslaught.

"L.T., *what are you waiting for???*" Roadblock cried.

Monroe cursed and then aimed his blaster at the snare-winch, firing at it and cutting the cable. Then, as the ship started to bank away, the Deathlords stopped firing.

"Hey, something's happening…" Drifter said.

Just then, an explosion erupted from within the Destroyer and its hull began to break apart.

"Son of a—" Monroe said.

Grohm emerged from the breach he'd made and grabbed onto the end of the snare-winch cable, pushing himself away just as the Deathlord ship exploded. The force of the eruption engulfed Grohm, completely consuming him before the Rognok went spinning off into space.

The snare cable was his escape plan, Monroe thought. *That was how he planned to get away!*

"Drifter! Roadblock!" he barked. "Daisy chain! On me!"

With that, Monroe unlocked his magnetic boots from the hull and used his suit's jump jets to fire himself toward Grohm as Roadblock quickly made his way to Drifter's position. Drifter fired his grappling cable to the hull of the ship before he and Roadblock also fired their jump jets.

Grohm was spinning end-over-end, his skin still smoking from the flames of the explosion, as Monroe closed the distance. Monroe fired his jump jets once more to give him the last bit of acceleration needed to reach the Rognok, grabbing onto him. Grohm's eyes were closed and he appeared to be unconscious.

"L.T.!" he heard Roadblock cry over the comms.

Drifter had reached the limit of his grappler cable and Roadblock had fired his to attach itself to Drifter's breastplate. He, too, was almost at his maximum length. Colliding with Grohm had forced Monroe into a spin, but he fired his jump jets to try to stabilize as he did his best to aim his grappler toward his squadmate. He waited for the right moment and fired. Roadblock reached out just as the grappler missed and grabbed hold of it.

"Got ya, L.T." Roadblock said.

"Reel us in," Monroe ordered. "And hurry. I think the Rognok is hurt."

Back aboard the mercenary ship, the artificial gravity had given way. Alarm lights flashed and there was heavy damage everywhere. Monroe and his squad were protected by their suits, but his sensor readings told him the temperature in the ship had begun to drop.

The squad made their way toward the bridge, pulling the unconscious Grohm along with them. Finally, they made it to the corridor leading onto the bridge and sealed the hatch, allowing what little life support there was to filter back into the room before opening it up. On the bridge, Fredreek was in the pilot's seat while Wilvelm and the two mercs were floating nearby. They'd all put emergency respirators on, but it was obvious they were getting cold.

"Is he alive?" Wilvelm asked as he floated up to the squad.

"He's not breathing," Monroe replied. "But seeing as how he went into the vacuum without a respirator, I'm not entirely certain if he needs to."

"This beast crashed through a Deathlord ship and blew it up from the inside," said Roadblock. "That's the craziest thing I've ever seen. If I had to put money on it, ain't no way someone that tough is gonna let something like a spaceship exploding on top of him kill him."

"Wish we could say the same about us," Wilvelm said. "We were too close when the Destroyer blew up. Our engines sustained heavy damage, comms are down, and we're venting life support. The Rognok may have saved our rears, but we're barely hanging on by a thread here."

"What are our options?" Monroe asked.

"That we make for the closest colony and pray to RNGsus that the ship holds together for that long," Fredreek said.

Wilvelm frowned and looked down at Grohm. "Well, on the bright side of things... looks like we get to keep our promise to take the Rognok to Essox," he said.

"Yeah," muttered Fred. "If we can all survive long enough to make it there."

CHAPTER ✺ 35

The city of Highpoint, the system capital of Maxima, resided on the Hilavan Plateau at the base of the Ivory Mountains. Sometimes known to the locals as "The Third Pole" of the planet, the Hilavan Plateau was Maxima's highest and largest plateau, with its tens of thousands of glaciers serving as the primary water tower of the continent, maintaining flow to its various rivers and streams.

Maxima was an extremely rocky and mountainous planet. Of the settlements on the plateau, Highpoint was the biggest and most modern. This "City of the Sky" was initially created to safeguard the Ancient Temple that had been discovered built into Mount Equinox, one of the tallest mountains in the area. Over time, though, it grew to be the biggest and most important city on the planet – thanks in no small part to a decision by Warland Skyborn, the first of his Legacy, to make it the capital of the entire system.

Judyth Skyborn stood on the terrace of the Legacy offices, gazing at the majestic white mountain of Mount Equinox in the distance, the all-seeing eye of the Ancients chiseled upon its face. Because of the high elevation, the city's air was thin, and the height of the Platinum Tower, location of the offices, made it even more so. But the air was also chill and brisk, a feature Judyth found most refreshing. Many of Maxima's inhabitants always complained that it was never warm on the planet, even in the summer. However, the temperature was fine with Judyth. She liked the cold.

"And now, let us move on to the findings of Patrol Squadron Four," came the voice of General Wessux.

Judyth sighed before stepping back into her office. The system security briefing felt like it had lasted for hours, and she was already weary of General Wessux's voice and the dry delivery of his reports. She took her seat back at her desk and looked at the video display of the General's presentation from his starship.

"Patrol Squadron Four has been searching primarily along the outer edge of quadrant four of the system, which has had the most Deathlord incursions. They've been sweeping the area mainly for some sign of the origin of the Deathlord attacks, but so far they have made no significant discoveries…"

Just like the other Search Squadrons, thought Judyth. *Great Observer, how many different ways does this man know how to say they've found nothing?*

"The next phase of their search will be in hyperspace," General Wessux continued. "In case there are any here in the briefing who may be unaware, the Maxima system is of great strategic importance for hyperspace travel. Because of its location in the spiral arm of the galaxy leading out to the rest of the Rim, the vast majority of space traffic going to and from Rim systems must pass through Maxima. Due to the system's large protoplanetary debris field, this creates a massive gravity shadow inside hyperspace, effectively making the system a roadblock to all hyperspace travel. If a ship wishes to continue on to the core worlds of the Empire from the Rim, it must first exit hyperspace and fly past Maxima, before re-entering hyperspace. This is why Maxima is so key to the Rim, as it is the gatekeeper of all starship trade and traffic into the deeper Rim systems, none of which have portgates. It is also why we believe the Deathlords have focused their efforts here."

He speaks to me as though I'm an idiot who hasn't lived in this system most of my adult life, thought Judyth, bitterly. She knew the General's propensity to over-explain things was his attempt to include her in the briefing as much as possible. Ever since Gebhard informed the General she'd be listening in, Wessux seemed to make it a point to dumb down all his explanations of the state of the system. But truth be told, she probably knew the ins-and-outs of Maxima better than her husband did. She supposed she couldn't fault the General for making his briefing understandable even to a toddler, but it certainly didn't help with the monotony of it.

Judyth was more than ready for the briefing to be over by the time it concluded. She was sure to politely thank the General for his "excellent and thought-provoking analysis" before signing off. She leaned back in her chair and took a moment to massage her temples. *Oh, how I cannot wait for all this to be over,* she thought. *I grow weary of tasks that are so beneath me.*

"My Lady," came the voice of her aide Aimalai over the office's intercom. "Forgive the interruption, but you asked to be notified if your son made contact."

"Mourdock's calling?" inquired Judyth. "Put him through."

"Actually, my Lady, he has sent a recorded message. Forwarding it to your work station now."

On her desk's viewscreen, the image of Mourdock appeared. Judyth smiled when she saw his face. She'd never believed she could love anything so much until he came along. Before Mourdock had been born, she'd seen birthing him as nothing more than her duty. But motherhood had changed her. Now, there was nothing more important than her son.

"Greetings mother," Mourdock began. "I am sorry for not being in touch with you sooner, but I wanted to let you know that I am okay and that I have great news. I found her, mother! I found Anna!"

That made Judyth raise her eyebrows in surprise. *Oh, my sweet child*, she thought after seeing how Mourdock's face lit up upon saying Anna's name. *How I wish I could tell you about your destiny, and how small a role that foolish girl will play in it.*

"Unfortunately, it would seem that the Earthman's claims about her were right," Mourdock continued. "She has indeed been infected by a Deathlord creature. We are at the Conclave now, trying to figure out a way to heal her. I would have alerted you and father about this sooner, but the Order of Peers asked me to refrain from sharing this news until they'd prepared an official statement for the Empire's leadership. And as you know, everything here at the Conclave takes forever to do. I expect Director Casgor will be upset by this news, but I am hoping father can keep him from doing anything foolish before we have a chance to fix Anna. Until such time, I will remain here by her side and attempt to do whatever I can to save her. If you should have need of me, for any reason, you can reach me here. Give my best to father. I love you."

Judyth smiled before turning off the message and getting to her feet. *At least I know where he is and that he's safe*, she thought. *There will be time to message him later. For now, I have other work to do.*

Judyth exited her office and stopped at Aimalai's desk. "I am going to the temple to pray," she informed her aide. "You can reach me there if you should need me for anything."

"Yes, my Lady," Aimalai responded. "I shall call ahead and let the High Pontifex know you are coming."

With that, Judyth made her way to the floor's private teleportation platform and input the coordinates of the Equinox Temple of the Ancients. Instantly, she was teleported to the secure reception room within the temple. The doors to the room opened and High Pontifex Gormon entered, clad in his white robe with golden trim and vestments. The old man smiled at her as she approached. "Lady Skyborn," he said, bowing slightly.

"High Pontifex," Judyth replied, bowing in turn. "There was no need for you to come greet me in person. I've simply come for evening prayers."

"It is no trouble, I can assure you. I would be remiss if I were not to at least escort one of the most devout members of the Church of the Great Observer to her prayer chamber, let alone the Lady of the system and the mother of our future Emperor."

"You are too kind," Judyth said as she took the High Pontifex's arm and allowed him to escort her through the building.

The Equinox Temple was one of the largest known Ancient temples in the galaxy. Though it possessed no relics or technology worthy of scientific study, it had become a location of great importance to the Church of the Great Observer and was one of Maxima's claims to galactic fame long before Mourdock had become the Emperor Ascendant. Faithful members of the Empire's official religion made pilgrimages from all over the galaxy to the Equinox Temple, coming from far and wide to worship the Ancients and all their wondrous creations.

Judyth walked down the sandstone hallway and to the central rotunda of the temple. The floor there was made from veined marble, with the all-seeing eye of the Ancients inlaid within it in gold. The domed ceiling high above contained a painted mural from famed artist Detrivio DaVeeto depicting Emperor Arcturus raising the temple of Regalus Prime. Majestic pillars rose up on all sides of the circular room, and the air was filled with the smell of incense and the somber music of worship.

Nearby, there was a long altar adorned with many lit candles, holo-images of various people and families hovering above it, climbing high along the wall. Bouquets of flowers and personal items were laid before it, and there were a few people weeping quietly as they knelt to pray.

"The memorial seems to grow larger and larger each time I visit," noted Judyth as they passed.

"Unfortunately, yes," agreed Gormon, sadly. "It feels as though no one has gone untouched by the Deathlords' recent raids. So many here on Maxima have friends and relatives in the outer colonies. Their losses are being felt across the planet. Not since the fall of Regalus Prime have I witnessed such widespread grief."

"These are indeed difficult times," Judyth replied, "which is why it is all the more important we have our faith."

"As important as faith is, my Lady, the people are scared. Particularly with the Princess missing. She is the last surviving member of Legacy Prime. Without her, many are wondering what will become of the heritage of the Ancients upon which our church is built. Should Legacy Prime be wiped out, we will have lost our only living link to them."

Judyth nodded. "Allow me to ease your worries, High Pontifex. I have recently heard from my son. He informed me that the Princess has been recovered and that she is safe."

Gormon's eyes grew wide at the news. "My Lady! That is wonderful to hear!"

"Indeed," agreed Judyth. "But I ask that you keep this information to yourself for the time being. The nature of the situation is delicate."

"I shall keep it in the strictest of confidence," Gormon replied as they approached the private prayer chamber reserved for the Skyborns. "Would you like me to pray with you?"

"Thank you for such a kind offer, but if you wouldn't mind, I'd prefer to pray alone today. The time to myself helps me to clear my head and keeps me focused."

"I completely understand, my Lady," Gormon said as he opened the door to the chamber for her. "If you should have need of me, I shall be in the Chamber of Enlightenment, taking confession."

Gormon bowed before leaving her, and Judyth sealed the chamber after he'd gone. The Legacy Prayer Chamber was a modest room. Like the other prayer chambers in the temple, it was circular in shape and made from sandstone bricks. It was lit by small, hovering orbs which mimicked candlelight, situated in sconces around the room. There was an altar across from the entrance, with a holographic rendition of the great, all-seeing eye projected above it.

Tradition dictated prayer be done while kneeling on the floor, but Gebhard had ordered a padded pew installed in the room to make it more comfortable. Not that Gebhard used it much. He was never one for church, which was why Judyth came to the temple so regularly. It was one of the few places she could get away from her oaf of a husband – that, and it was truly the only place she could be alone. No one was allowed to use the chamber but those who were of Legacy Skyborn.

The original prayer chamber dedicated to the Legacy had been closer to the Chamber of Enlightenment, which was where all the services were held. But upon arriving on Maxima after marrying Gebhard, Judyth had requested the official chamber be moved to this particular one. Others thought it was a curious request, since all the chambers were very much identical, but there was one feature this room had that none of the others did. And it was a feature known only to Judyth.

Once she was alone, she reached into her pocket and produced her Imperius device. The rectangular piece of stone was normally meant only for those of Royal Blood to control Ancient technology, but Judyth had had this one in her possession ever since she'd come of age, a gift from her father when he'd told her of her destiny. As she concentrated upon it, symbols began to glow on its surface, and she arranged them to send her to her true destination.

The floor beneath her glowed as the hidden portgate within the room activated. Judyth then reappeared in a darkened chamber. It was not unlike the one she'd just been in. It, too, was round in design, but it was far larger and consisted of coarse black rock instead of sandstone. The portgate which made up the floor glowed briefly before returning to its normal white metal color. The door to the chamber opened, revealing a hooded figure in a black robe.

"My Queen," the robed figure said, bowing toward Judyth. The figure's voice was low and sordid. Truth be told, Judyth would have found it off-putting if she had not grown up hearing it.

"Emissary," Judyth said as she approached the figure. She produced a datapad from her pocket and handed it to the figure, who took it with a boney, white hand. "That contains a recording of the latest system security briefing," she said as she walked down the hallway leading from the chamber. "It details the current position of the fleet and where they'll be headed next. Please forward that on to your master."

"I sssssshall do so, my Queen," the figure replied as it walked alongside her. "How fares the Maxima fleet?"

"Chasing their tails, as expected," Judyth said. "Now that we have access to their positions, it will make our harvests that much easier."

"The Master agreessss with you," the figure responded. "He has already ordered us to sssssstep up our raids."

"Very good. I shall direct you to the most vulnerable outposts. I take it Mellegogg has been pleased with our progress?"

"The Master hasssss been most pleased," replied the figure. "He isssssss confident his work will conclude very soon."

Judyth smiled at that. *Finally, after all these years*, she thought. *I will be able to claim my birthright! Oh, father… if only you'd been able to live to see the glorious day when all our hard work and sacrifice will have paid off!*

Judyth and her companion emerged into a massive circular chamber – a dark reflection of the rotunda from the Equinox Temple. It was cavernously large, with jagged walls of black rock with veins that pulsed with green, red, and purple light. It rose high up into a domed ceiling. The chamber had concentric circles carved into the floor, eventually reaching the center of the room, where a rectangular monolith loomed, jutting up from the floor. The monolith was made of black rock, as well, but it was completely smooth, as reflective as polished obsidian. It contained no veins. It was pure black. Behind it, where the floor ended, was a seemingly bottomless pit, over which a stairway had been erected, leading to a platform that jutted out before two massively tall doors.

"Are the sacrifices ready?" Judyth inquired.

"They were delivered sssssshortly before you arrived, my Queen."

"Bring them out," she commanded.

The figure moved down another corridor which branched off from the circular room as Judyth walked past the monolith and gazed up at the massive doors looming above her. She closed her eyes and breathed deeply, feeling the energy that laid beyond them and reveling in it.

It will have all been worth it, she thought. *When I raise this temple and unleash its power, ascending to my true form, it will have all been worth it! Marrying that fool, pretending to love him, birthing his child… it will all be over and I will be free!*

The sounds of crying and whimpering soon echoed in the chamber, pulling Judyth out of her moment of reflection. She turned to see the robed figure leading a group of captured colonists through the tunnel, herded along by Dark Soldiers. Some of them cried out in fear when they saw the monolith, but the Deathlords pushed them along, hurting them as much as necessary to keep them moving forward.

Finally, the robed figure signaled they'd come far enough, and the Deathlords all forced the colonists to their knees. Judyth approached them. They were all dirty, their hair matted with sweat, their faces stained by tears. Their clothes were ripped, and their hands were bound behind them.

"I present you with your sssssssacrifice, my Queen," the robed figure said, bowing.

Judyth surveilled the offering before her and nodded with approval. The captives were frightened, pathetic, and completely at her mercy – exactly as she liked them. One of the captives, a woman who appeared to possess some rank of authority from whatever colony she'd been taken, looked up at Judyth, her eyes growing wide with recognition.

"L—Lady Skyborn???" she gasped.

Judyth looked down upon the woman and smiled. "Hello, my dear," she replied.

"What's... what's going on?" the woman asked. "Why have we been brought here?"

"To be a part of something... incredible," Judyth said. "I know it may not seem so now, but believe me when I say all of you have a very important role to play in what is to come. All your pain, all your suffering, all your torment... it will not be for nothing."

"I don't understand..." whimpered the woman. "Please! My Lady! You must help us!"

Judyth reached down and caressed the woman's cheek. "Very well," she said. "I will help you. Help you to see..."

Judyth then turned and raised her arms toward the massive doors of the chamber. As if upon her unspoken command, the doors began to lumber open, laboriously moving aside to reveal a swirling tornado of ghostly energy, writhing and wailing in the chamber beyond.

The group of captives all looked in horror at what they saw. There were shapes resembling bodies in the energy, looking as though they were struggling to free themselves. There were faces in there screaming and crying out in torment. There was a palpable feeling of dread pulsating from it, crashing over every captive like a terrible tidal wave.

"Behold!" exclaimed Judyth, looking at the deathly ghost energy as if it were the most beautiful thing she'd ever laid eyes upon. "The beginning of the end! The start of a new and better world! The precursor to the Grand Paradise! And you have all been chosen to be a part of it!"

Some of the captives tried to run, but the Dark Soldiers quickly subdued them. Those who did not try to escape simply wept, feeling the inevitability of their deaths settle upon them.

"WHY???" cried the woman. "Why are you doing this???"

"Because," Judyth said, turning to the woman. "It is my *destiny!*"

"All hail, the Queen of Soulsssss," the robed figure declared.

With that, Judyth reached out her hands toward the captives. They all screamed as their souls were ripped from their bodies. Judyth laughed as their spiritual energy swirled around her, forming into a chaotic circle above her head, which she then walked toward the chamber containing the ghostly pillar of death energy.

"The time is almost upon us!" she cried. "The corruption is almost complete! War and decay have taken root! And with this sacrifice, I hasten the arrival of famine and wrath!"

Judyth stood at the entrance of the next chamber, an insignificant speck before the terror and might of the swirling monstrosity that loomed there. She hurled the souls she'd ripped from the captives toward it, and as the energy joined with the twisting nether, it was as if the voices of those who'd been killed all cried out in despair. She lowered her arms and gazed at the pillar of ghostly energy before her, a look of triumph on her face.

"The Great Death shall soon begin," Judyth Skyborn declared. "And I shall be the mother of it!"

Earthman Jack Will Return In…

EARTHMAN JACK

VS.

THE RING OF FIRE

EPISODE 2 OF THE CONCLAVE TRILOGY

An Important Note From The Author

Dear Reader,

I hope you enjoyed this latest adventure in the Earthman Jack Space Saga. Please know I am working hard to produce the next book in the series. Being an independent author (i.e. a writer with no money) can be quite a fulfilling profession, but it can also be a lot of work.

Since I do not have a big publisher behind me to help get my books into stores and do publicity for my work, I rely on the fans of my book to help spread the word. If you enjoyed this book and would like to support it and the series it belongs to, then you can do the following things to help me out:

1. Write a positive review on Amazon.com. Readers rely on reviews from other readers when deciding whether or not to give a new book a try. This is one of the best things you can do to help promote this book to others. Please take a few moments to do so.
2. Recommend the book to people you know. Word of mouth is a powerful way to help new readers discover books they may like. Be sure to tell your friends and family about the book!
3. Request your local bookstore and library to carry a copy. It can be difficult to get independent books into brick and mortar stores. If enough people request a book, then stores will start carrying them. This can be a great way for new readers to stumble upon these works.
4. Recommend this book on social media. If you're an active user of services like Facebook, Twitter, and the like, be sure to let your friends know about this series by linking to the books in it within your posts.
5. Sign up for my mailing list. This way you can be notified about updates on the series and when new books are released. You can sign up at: www.EarthmanJack.com.

Doing any of these will go a long way in helping to support this series. With the support of fans like you, I hope to expose a whole new generation of readers to Earthman Jack and his exploits.

Thank you very much for your support!

Matthew J. Kadish

Author: Earthman Jack vs. The Intergalactic Manhunt